John Drake lives in Cheshire with his family. His hobbies and interests include muzzle-loaded shooting, history and politics. The Flint and Silver series was inspired by the many unanswered questions left by Robert Louis Stevenson's much-loved classic, *Treasure Island*.

By the same author

Pieces of Eight
Flint and Silver

JOHN DRAKE

Skull and Bones

HarperCollins*Publishers*

Harper
An imprint of HarperCollins*Publishers*
77–85 Fulham Palace Road,
Hammersmith, London W6 8JB

www.harpercollins.co.uk

This paperback edition 2011
1

First published in Great Britain by
HarperCollins*Publishers* 2010

A catalogue record for this book is
available from the British Library

ISBN: 978 0 00 726899 3

Set in Sabon by Palimpsest Book Production Limited,
Falkirk, Stirlingshire
Printed and bound in Great Britain by
Clays Ltd, St Ives plc

Mixed Sources
Product group from well-managed
forests and other controlled sources
www.fsc.org   Cert no. SW-COC-001806
© 1996 Forest Stewardship Council

FSC

FSC is a non-profit international organisation established
to promote the responsible management of the world's forests.
Products carrying the FSC label are independently certified
to assure consumers that they come from forests that are managed
to meet the social, economic and ecological needs
of present and future generations.

Find out more about HarperCollins and the environment at
www.harpercollins.co.uk/green

For *my dear sister LGFF*

Acknowledgements

I am very grateful to those who have given much-valued help and advice in my efforts to write a decent novel. As always I thank my editors Julia Wisdom and Anne O'Brien, for their scholarly reviews, some splendid ideas, and their careful weeding out of my errors. Also I particularly thank my agent, Antony Topping, and my son, who together prevented this novel from turning into a historical documentary on Colonial America, which might have made a nice textbook, but nobody would have bought it for fun.

John Drake

Chapter 1

Three bells of the first dog watch
20th July 1735 (Old Style)
Aboard Isabelle Bligh
The Atlantic

The six-pound shot came aboard with a scream and a hiss, smashing one of the mainmast deadeyes, punching holes through the longboat secured over the waist, taking off the arm and shoulder of a seaman, as neat as a surgeon's knife . . . and throwing the limb shivering at his feet, as if still alive. The man screamed, and sat down flat with his back to the windward bulwark.

In the horror of the moment, Olivia Rose, sixteen years old and at sea for the first time in her life, turned from her father and clung to the heavy bulk of the lad who'd been doing his best to stand between her and the flying shot.

"Get below!" cried Josiah Burstein, her father. "And get away from *him!*" He snatched her away, blinking nervously at the boy, for Burstein was a small man while the boy, also only sixteen, was broad and heavy with thick limbs, big fists and a dark, ugly face. But the boy stood back, nodding.

"Get below, Livvy," he said. "Your pa's right."

Seizing the moment, Burstein hustled his daughter down a hatchway, out of the way of shot. He cursed the day he'd set

1

out from Philadelphia to make his fortune in London with his skills as a mathematical instrument maker, for nothing good had come thus far: only Livvy Rose keeping company with that lumpish oaf of a ship's boy.

Boom! A distant gun fired, and on deck, the crew ducked as another shot came howling down and smashed into the hull. The boy looked astern as his captain yelled from the quarterdeck.

"There, sir!" cried Captain Nehemia Higgs, seizing hold of the man beside him, the ship's owner Mr Samuel Banbury, and shaking him angrily. "Now where's your *peaceful way?*"

Banbury said nothing, but pulled free and, wrenching off his coat and shirt, ran forward to jam the crumpled linen deep into the fallen seaman's hideous injury in an effort to stem the flow of blood.

"Aaaaaaaah!" screeched the wounded man.

"And may I now – in God's name – turn to my guns?" yelled Captain Higgs.

"Aye!" roared the crew, nearly two dozen of them, angrily waiting for the order. Their captain might be a Quaker, but at least he was one of the *right* sort – unlike Mr Banbury, who was clearly one of the *wrong* sort. The crew, on the other hand, weren't no sort of Quakers at all – not them, by God and the Devil! And they weren't about to give up their wages at the mere sight of a black flag!

Ignoring them, Banbury tugged off his belt and managed to strap it round the wounded seaman's chest to hold the dripping red bundle in place. Looking around him for help, he spotted the boy.

"You!" cried Banbury. "Give me your shirt!"

So two shirts were clapped on the wound, with the boy close enough to be sprayed by the victim's spittle and drenched in his blood. But he could see it weren't no use. Soon the screaming stopped and the man's eyes closed. Tommy

Trimstone was his name; from Ilfracombe in Devon, and now dead.

The boy stood up from the corpse, wiping his hands on his breeches. He'd never seen death and didn't know what to make of it. He looked to his captain again, cussing and blinding as no Quaker should, and then finally raising a telescope to check on their pursuers, before calling to the boy.

"Come here, you young sod!" he cried. "Take this bastard glass and get into the bastard top, and keep watch on *that* bugger –" he pointed to the oncoming ship –."and be quick about it, or I'll skin the bleeding arse off you!" With all hands on deck, standing by to man his guns, Higgs needed a lookout.

The boy went up the shrouds at the run, and got himself nice and tight into the maintop. He levelled the glass . . .

"What d'you see?" yelled Captain Higgs.

The boy saw a sharp-keeled, rake-masted brig of some two hundred tons: deeply sparred, and with ports for twenty guns. The wind was weak so she was under all sail, and coming on only slowly, but her decks were black with armed men, which was not surprising for a vessel that flew the skull and bones.

Boom! Up went another cloud of white from the enemy's bow, followed swiftly by the deadly howl of shot heading their way. It shrieked high over the masts as the boy called down to the quarterdeck, telling what he'd seen.

"You heard that," said Higgs to Banbury. "We must defend ourselves!"

"Can we not outrun them?" said Banbury. "You have *three* masts to their *two*!"

Higgs sneered from the depth of his seaman's soul at this ludicrous dollop of landlubber's shite. *Isabelle Bligh* was a Bristol-built West Indiaman: well found, and fit in all respects for sea. But she was designed for *cargo,* not swiftness. In her favour, however, was the fact that she bore sixteen guns and was heavily timbered, so if it came to cannonading, she might well drive off a lighter vessel that was built purely for speed. Higgs yelled this thought at Banbury, but dared not act without his word.

Up in the top, the boy looked down, puzzled. Banbury and Higgs were Quakers that weren't supposed to fight. But the ship had guns, like other Quaker ships, so why not use them? The boy shook his head. He didn't know. He only knew that Banbury was a very special Quaker, come out from England to staunch the slave trade among the Pennsylvania Quakers, and now going home. Clearly Cap'n Higgs was afraid of Banbury. Perhaps it was like the Catholics with their pope?

Boom! Another shot from the pirate's bow-chaser. They were close enough now that the boy could see the men working the gun. Again the shot went wide, and he watched them haul in, sponge out and re-load. And then he had a nasty thought. For the first time it occurred to him – in his youth and innocence – that the pirates . . . *might actually capture the ship!* He groaned in fear of what they would do to Olivia Rose.

Plump and luscious with shining skin and titian hair, Livvy was the only female aboard. He blushed for the things the hands said about her, behind her back. What chance would she stand if such men as them – but worse – got hold of her?

Then another flag went up on the pirate brig: a plain, red flag. The boy didn't know what it meant, but his mates did, down below.

"Bugger me," said one, "it's the Jolly Roger!"

"Gawd 'elp us," said another.

"Higgs," demanded Banbury, "what's that red flag?"

"The *Jolie Rouge*," said Higgs. "The 'Pretty Red One' of the French Buccaneers."

"What does it mean?"

"It means no quarter to those that fight," he said. "It's death to all aboard."

"But only if we fight?"

4

"Aye." Higgs scowled, for he knew this gave the game to Banbury.

Banbury heaved a sigh of relief as if a tremendous burden had just fallen away, relieving him of the agonising balancing act between principle and expediency. For he was a merchant as well as a Quaker, and wasn't quite so firm against fighting as he'd said. The truth was that he had his reputation to consider, having risen high within the Society of Friends, for he was clerk to The Meeting for Sufferings of the London Quakers, which was as near to a governing body as their prayerful egalitarianism permitted, and thus his actions would be closely examined upon his return by rivals ever-eager to take his place.

"Strike your colours, Captain," he said, "and pray for deliverance!"

The boy saw everything. *Isabelle Bligh* lowered her ensign and backed her topsail in surrender. The pirates cheered and came alongside in a squealing of blocks and a rumble of canvas, taking in sail and heaving grapnels over the side to bind the ships together. Then they were swarming aboard, fifty strong and heavily armed, as the two vessels rolled under the rumble of boots on timber.

The boy didn't understand their speech, which seemed to be French. But they yelled merrily and a man with a feathered hat and a bandolier of many pistols embraced Captain Higgs and kissed him on both cheeks for a good fellow, while his men herded the crew for'ard. Then the boy gulped as Sam Collis, biggest man aboard, took exception and started shouting . . . *and they shot him dead!* It was ruthless, merciless and hideous. Bang! Bang! Two puffs of smoke, and a decent seaman went down and was kicked aside like a piece of rubbish.

Isabelle Bligh's people groaned in horror, but they were pushed to the fo'c'sle with the pirate captain – he of the feathered hat – yelling at them in English: "Your lives are yours, messieurs! Be good and make no fight, and you shall have your ship when we are done with her!"

"Aye!" cried Mr 'Meeting for Sufferings' Banbury. "It is loot they seek, not blood!" And he joined in, shoving Captain Higgs and the rest for'ard as if he were one of the pirate's own band, and agreeing with every word the villain spoke. The boy frowned heavily.

"Bleedin' traitor!" he muttered.

And then the pirates got down to the serious business of smashing open everything that was locked, and breaking into the cargo, and up-ending every bottle in the ship with the most tremendous noise, but all in good temper. Most of them vanished below for this vital work, leaving a dozen men, well armed with firelocks, to guard the crew.

And none of them took the trouble to look up into the maintop where the boy was hiding. And since nobody saw him, he watched as the smashing and cheering went on and on, and men staggered about the decks in the captain's best clothes and Mr Banbury's hat, gorging on pork and pickles and wine and brandy.

Later still, the boy shuddered in horror as a girl's shriek came from below, and men emerged through the quarter-deck hatchway, grinning and leering, with Olivia Rose and her father dragged behind them. The father was bloodied and staggering, and was kicked into a semi-conscious heap by the mizzenmast. But there was a roar from the pirates on sight of the girl, and greedy hands reached out to paw and grab and grope. Her long hair was loose, her gown was ripped, pale flesh gleamed and she screamed and screamed.

But the pirate leader – he of the feathered hat – kicked his way through the press, seized Olivia Rose by the arm, and merrily fired a pistol in the air for attention.

"*Après moi, mes enfants!*" he cried, grinning at his men.

"*Je serai le premier!*" And they cheered and laughed, and fired off a thundering fusillade in salute.

Up in the maintop the boy shook with rage.

Rage doesn't just conquer fear. Rage annihilates it. Rage brings boiling fury such that no grain of self-preservation remains, nor any consideration of danger, nor threat of weapons. Hence the Viking berserker transported into blood-spattering frenzy . . . and the ship's boy that leapt bare-chested into open air from the maintop to slide down one of the backstays and launch himself – twenty feet from the deck – as a human projectile, landing feet first on the feathered head of the pirate captain – who went down with his neck snapped on a jutting boot, and his face burst open like rotten fruit as the impetus of the boy's fall drove him smashing into the pine of the quarterdeck planking.

Then . . . uproar and confusion. The pirates bellowed and roared, surprised for an instant, shocked and disbelieving, then snapping pistols at the boy, forgetting they were empty. Taking their example, he snatched the pistols from the dead pirate's bandolier – there were seven of them, ready loaded – and let fly, left and right. Men shrieked and fell as the bullets struck, and the rest hung back while the pistols lasted, then charged, and the boy was blocking slashing blades with the heavy barrel of a hot, smoking pistol, which soon got lost. Bodies heaved and bundled and swayed, and more men piled in, and the fight rolled and staggered, with the boy in the middle, armed only with his own two fists and his unhinged, manic fury. And then he got hold of a cutlass, which he couldn't swing in the dense press, so he used it two-handed as a spear, shoving it into an open mouth and out the back of a head, then wrenching it free and punching out another man's teeth with the iron hand-guard, and on and on . . .

But with nearly twenty pirates on the quarterdeck and more coming up from below, there could be only one end to the fight . . . except that the pirates were remarkably clumsy and got in each other's way, and they'd fired off their pistols and muskets . . . and on the fo'c'sle, seeing their guards with backs turned, gaping at the fight on the quarterdeck, Captain Higgs had his own moment of rage.

"Sod *you*, you bugger!" he said to the hand-wringing Banbury. "Come on, lads!" he cried, pulling a belaying pin from the pinrail, swinging it down with a *crunch* on to the blue-kerchiefed head of a mulatto pirate and snatching up the carbine that he dropped. The guards hadn't fired off their arms, so Higgs blasted lead and flame at three-feet range into the chest of another pirate even as he turned back to face the sudden danger.

After that, it was hellfire and damnation aboard the good ship *Isabelle Bligh* and Quakerism went over the side with the dead. For *Isabelle Bligh*'s crew were seething that they'd not manned their guns in the first place, and were out for vengeance for their murdered shipmate. So even though they were outnumbered more than two-to-one, they recaptured their ship, fighting at first with belaying pins and sailor's knives, and then taking up the weapons of their foes . . . and with the considerable advantage that many of the pirates were blind staggering drunk.

When Captain Higgs finally called an end to the slaughter, less than a quarter of those who'd come aboard as bold dogs and roaring boys were left alive to be clapped like slaves under hatches, and the pirate ship was sailing under a prize crew, behind the triumphant *Isabelle Bligh*, such that even Samuel Banbury's conscience was eased by the money he'd make in selling her.

As for the boy who'd saved the day: he was ship's hero! Without his plunge from the maintop there would have been no fight, and no triumph. So there were glorious weeks of a merry voyage when even Olivia Rose's father did not try to keep her and the boy apart, and the two fell as deeply in love as ever it is possible for a pair of sixteen-year-olds to do: he loving her for her beauty and sweet kindness, and she loving him for those things that she saw that others did not, especially his limitless capacity to love. She saw that he would never be happy without a cause to follow and a loved one to serve. In her eyes this transformed Caliban the ugly into Ariel the shining one.

It was a wonderful, golden, glorious romance that approached . . . reached . . . and *transcended* Heaven on Earth, for the two young lovers.

"You are my *beau chevalier sans peur et sans reproche*," she said to him once.

"What's that?" he said.

"It means . . . my fair knight, fearless and pure."

He blushed.

And so they sat together, and talked together, she telling him stories and playing that ancient game with seashells – at which she was adept – whereby swift movement of the shells deceives the onlooker who cannot tell which hides the pea. He loved the game, and the curious West Indian shells she played it with, and of which she had a collection. And he loved the country love songs that she sang to him of an evening, with the crew sitting quietly and joining in the chorus.

But voyages end. This one ended in London, and there the two were parted by duty: hers to her father, and his to his trade. There were bitter tears and mighty promises of faithfulness when finally, in the Thames below London Bridge, she was about to go into the boat that would take her and her father ashore to their new life. In that tragic moment, he gave her the traditional seaman's love-token of a staybusk that he'd carved from whalebone with his own hand. In return, she gave him a lock of her hair, and half a dozen of the West Indian shells that he loved.

"I'll be back for you, Livvy Rose," he said, "when I've made me pile!"

"Be a good boy," she said. "And remember me."

And indeed he did. He remembered her to the dying second of his dying day, and he really did try to come back to claim her. But he never quite made *his pile*, and day by day other duties intervened, until finally it was too late, because – in the meanwhile – he had become something very other than a *good boy*.

For he was led astray. He was led bad astray was Billy Bones.

Chapter 2

Chk-chk-chk! Groggy the monkey chattered and reached his little hands for the horn mug. At first, when they saw his love for strong drink, the crew had called him "Old Grog". But they turned this into a pet name when the monkey became ship's favourite and ran from mess to mess at dinner time, and they fed him drink till he staggered and lost his nimble footing and couldn't even lie on the deck without hanging on, and they laughed and laughed at his merry antics.

But they didn't laugh today. Not with most of them too sick for their dinners and busting with headache besides. That made for a quiet dinner time in the close wooden cave of the lower deck, even with twenty mess-tables and near two hundred men trying – and mostly failing – to shovel down their dinners. They managed the drink though, except what they gave to Groggy.

"Here y'are, matey," said one of the tars, holding out his mug for Groggy to take a sip and marvelling at the near-human way the monkey took it. The tar stroked the furry head and smiled, for Groggy was a handsome creature: big

11

for a monkey, almost an ape, with thick brown fur, a creamy-white face and chest, bright, intelligent eyes and a long tail that served as an extra hand when he went aloft and leapt through the rigging as if in his jungle home.

He was the pet of all the squadron, for his reputation had spread and he'd been aboard the sloops *Bounder* and *Jumper* to be shown off, and all hands had crowded round to see him. But it was the flagship that owned him, for rank has its privileges as all the world knows.

"Take a drop o' mine," said another tar, offering his mug, but:

"*No!*" cried a voice from the quarterdeck, and Groggy flinched and looked up, as they all did.

Captain Baggot, commander of the squadron, was bellowing loud enough to be heard from keelson to main-truck. "*No!*" he cried. "I will not be deterred!" Then the voice sank to an incoherent rumbling, and the men at the mess-tables looked at one another in silence. As in most ships, there were no secrets aboard *Oraclaesus,* whatever delusions her officers might have in the matter, and the entire crew knew what was under discussion by their masters. They knew it, and it made them uneasy.

Above, Baggot stood with his hands clasped behind his back in the brilliant tropical sunshine and stamped his foot in rage, for he was confronted on his own quarterdeck by the only man in the entire squadron whom he could not dismiss, disrate or discipline: Dr Robert Stanley, the ship's chaplain.

Fizzing with anger, Baggot turned his back on Stanley, and tried to ignore the fact that he was under the gaze of numerous spectators: lieutenants, master's mates and midshipmen, together with all those of the ship's lesser people who were on duty and not at their victuals down below. Baggot avoided their eyes and stared fixedly ahead, past mainmast, foremast, bowsprit and rigging, over the deep blue waters of the anchorage, to stare at Flint's blasted island with its blasted jungles and its blasted sandy beaches and its blasted hills, not ten minutes by ship's boat from where he was standing . . . and which island – God knows blasted where but *somewhere* – hid a most colossal fortune in gold, silver and stones: a treasure estimated at the incredible amount of *eight hundred thousand blasted pounds*, which he – Captain John Baggot – was determined to find, dig up, bring aboard, and take home in triumph to England where a fat slice of the treasure would be his, as prize money, and with it a promotion and, in all probability, a seat in the House of Lords!

But . . . staring into the back of his head, even this blasted instant, and wearing his blasted clerical wig, was Dr Robert Stanley, who in the first place was appointed by the Chaplain General and not by the Royal Navy, and who in the second place had a brain like a whetted razor, and in the third place – which place out-ranked all other places – had tremendous and powerful patrons.

"Captain," said Dr Stanley, "a moment's reflection will show you that I speak for the good of the squadron and all those embarked aboard." He spoke quietly and politely, but Baggot only shook his head.

"Be damned if I'll be told by you, sir!" he said. "Be damned if I will!" And he stamped his foot like a petulant child sent on an errand who refuses to go but knows he must obey in the end.

"Ah!" said Dr Stanley, for he saw that he was winning, then he nodded briefly at two young officers standing on the downwind side of the quarterdeck with the rest. These were Lieutenant Hastings and Mr Midshipman Povey: old enemies of the pirate Flint. They'd suffered in the blood-drenched mutiny he'd engineered on this very island, and had then been set adrift by him with the few loyal hands, saving the lives of all by their seamanship. And now they were most important young gentlemen – especially Lieutenant Hastings, since

13

his mother was the society beauty Lady Constance Hastings, sister-in-law to Mr Pelham the Prime Minister. Lady Constance – outraged at Flint's mutinous ill-treatment of her son – had badgered Pelham into equipping and sending out the crack squadron – comprised of *Oraclaesus* and her consorts – that had caught Flint . . . and now had him in irons down below!

Thus the Prime Minister himself stood behind the expedition and he had taken an active interest in many of the posts within it . . . including that of Dr Stanley, who now turned to another of the spectators, Mr Lemming the ship's surgeon. Lemming had been summoned to the deck by Stanley in readiness for this moment, and was now wrenching his hat into rags in trepidation at the role he must play.

"Captain," said Dr Stanley, "Mr Lemming will vouch for the truth of what I say . . ." He turned to Lemming.

"Um . . . er . . ." said Lemming, in terror of his captain's wrath.

"Come, sir!" said Stanley to Lemming. "A good three-quarters of this ship's people and those of *Bounder* and *Jumper* are struck down with fever and headache, are they not?"

"Yes, sir," said Lemming, for it was unchallengeable fact.

"And it is the invariable characteristic of West India fevers," said Stanley, "that they strike worst upon ships anchored close inshore, and especially those in enclosed anchorages such as this –" He waved a hand at the great crescent sweep of the shore, over three miles from end to end, that curved in foetid embrace around the anchorage, with festering swamps and steaming, livid-green jungles crowding down upon the white sands of the beach. It was a bad enough fever-trap by itself, made worse by the small island that lay close off it, preventing the sea breeze from sweeping away the miasma.

"Yes," said Lemming, finding courage in truth. "Damn place stinks of fever. I said so as we came in." Which latter statement was only partly true, for he'd said it to himself and hadn't had the courage to voice it aloud, not when all hands were wild eager for a treasure hunt.

"There, sir!" said Stanley, to Captain Baggot's back. "There you have it from our surgeon. If we stay anchored here – for whatever reason – we shall see this fever grow among the crew, perhaps taking the lives of all aboard."

"Aye, Cap'n," said Lemming, at last. "The yellow jack and the ague can kill seven in ten of those that ain't seasoned. And we don't even know what this fever *is*, for I've never seen the like before."

But Captain Baggot wasn't quite ready to give in. Not yet. Not even when he was unwell himself, having brought up his last meal like a seasick landman, with the pain throbbing behind his eyes and getting worse with each passing hour.

"Flint!" he spat. "It's all down to blasted Flint. He knows this blasted island and all its blasted tricks. Damn me if I'll not go below and question him again." He turned to face Stanley. "And you, Mr Chaplain, shall come with me!"

"Gentlemen," said Flint, smooth face glowing in the lantern light, "I really do not know how I can be of service to you." Graceful and elegant, he was an intensely handsome and charismatic man, with Mediterranean, olive skin, fine teeth, and a steady gaze that made lesser men nervous – most men being *lesser* in that respect.

"But I must protest again," said Flint, "against the monstrous injustice that has been done to Mr Bones, here, who is a loyal heart and true."

"Aye!" said Billy Bones. "And ready to do my duty now, as ever I was before!"

Bones was the perfect opposite of Flint: a huge, broken-nosed, lumpish clod with massive fists, broad shoulders and a strong whiff of the lower deck about him – for all that he'd been a master's mate in the king's service, accustomed to walk the quarterdeck and take his noon observation.

Flint and Billy Bones had spent the last week secured down below, deep in the damp, evil-smelling, hold where it was always dark and the rats cavorted and played. Both men wore irons on their legs and a chain passed between them, secured to a massive ringbolt driven into the thickness of the hull.

"You're a bloody rogue and a pirate, Flint," said Baggot. "The only reason I don't hang you now is that I'm ordered to take you home for the Court of Admiralty to string up at Wapping!"

Stanley sighed. The interview was going the way of several others that had preceded it. Baggot could not control his lust for gold and his hatred of a mutineer, and the sight of the urbane Flint, smiling and smiling and talking of innocence, provoked him beyond endurance. But where others were concerned, Flint was devilish persuasive. Stanley looked at the two marines who'd accompanied them, bearing muskets and ball cartridge as a precaution. They were hanging on every word Flint uttered, and Stanley knew that rumours were circulating on the lower deck that Flint wasn't a pirate and mutineer at all, just a victim of circumstance, while Mr Bones was innocent of all charges whatsoever. That was Flint's work, day by day talking to the hands sent down to deliver food and water and take away the slops.

"Mr Flint," said Stanley, "cannot we set these matters aside? We are faced with an unknown fever, and we seek your advice. So I beseech you to behave . . ." Stanley paused for effect ". . . to behave as a man should . . . who must soon face *divine* judgement." The chaplain peered closely at Flint, trying to gauge the impact of his words. "So, what is this pestilence, sir? Speak if you know, for your mortal soul is at risk."

Flint contemplated Dr Stanley.

Clever, he thought. *Very clever*. Then he turned to Baggot, a man for whom he had nothing but contempt. If he, Joe Flint, had been granted power over a man with hidden treasure, that man would have been put to merciless torture

16

until he revealed its whereabouts. So he sneered at Baggot; for any man who denied himself these obvious means deserved to stay poor! Stanley, however, was clearly a different proposition; subtle means would be required with him.

"Dr Stanley," said Flint, and lowered his eyes, "it is true that I myself am beyond hope . . ." He raised a weary hand, as if against life's iniquitous burdens. "Evidence is contrived against me and, corrupt and mendacious as it is, nevertheless it proves too strong for truth to prevail!"

"Oh, shut up, you posturing hypocrite!" said Baggot. "Lying toad that you are!"

"Sir!" protested Stanley. "I beg that you allow me to conduct this interview."

"Damned if I will!" said Baggot and turned to go.

"Gentlemen!" cried Flint. "I beg that you listen. I am a lost man, so take these words as dying declaration, and accord them the special credence that is their due . . ."

There was silence. Such was the power of Flint's address that no man moved or spoke, not even Captain Baggot, while the two marines were goggling and even Dr Stanley was impressed.

"I offer *truth for truth!*" said Flint. "I shall tell you the source of this island fever. I shall give it to you freely. But in exchange I ask that you accept this blameless man –" he looked at Billy Bones – "as the innocent that he is."

Stanley looked at Baggot. Baggot looked at Stanley. The two marines looked on. Baggot frowned.

"What about the treasure?" he said.

"Sir," said Flint, "I swear on my soul, and in the name of that Almighty Being before whose throne I must soon present myself . . . that I know nothing of any treasure."

"Oh bugger," said Baggot, but quietly.

"And the pestilence?" said Stanley.

"It is caused by the island's monkeys, sir," said Flint.

"*WHAT?*" Baggot, Stanley and the marines spoke as one.

"The monkeys. Because of them, you dare not land on the island."

"But we've got one aboard!" said Baggot. "Little Groggy."

"Then kill him!" cried Flint. "And get to sea. You are in peril of your lives!"

"Oh Christ!" said Baggot.

"*Sir!*" protested Stanley.

"Sorry, Mr Chaplain . . . but, oh Christ!"

There was a pounding of feet as four men raced for the ladders and companionways that led to the light. Then there was a great shouting, and drums beating, and calling up of all hands, and the rattling, clattering, rumbling, squeaking of a great ship getting ready for sea, with capstans clanking, blocks humming, yards hauling aloft and the anchor cables coming aboard, dripping wet and shaking off their weed, to the stamping and chanting of the crew.

Down below, forgotten for the moment, Joe Flint and Billy Bones sat with one dim lantern between them, listening to the sounds that had defined their lives as long as they could remember.

"Why did you tell 'em about the monkey?" said Billy Bones. "You brought him aboard on purpose, for to spread the fever!"

Flint smiled. "Indeed, Mr Bones. But now his work is done. He's been aboard all three ships."

"How d'you know that?"

Flint sighed. "Don't you ever listen, Billy, to the men who come to feed us?"

"Oh." Bones frowned. "But you didn't tell 'em it was *smallpox* the monkeys bring. And a special smallpox besides, that's fearful worse than usual."

"No. They'll find that out soon enough . . . when it kills nine out of ten of them."

"But some'll be unharmed?"

"Yes. Those who've had it before and survived."

"And you and me, Cap'n."

"Yes. For you've had it, and I'm protected."

"And will I be freed, now, for what you told that Parson?"

"I think so. The learned doctor believed me."

"And then what'll I do?"

Flint told him: in detail. Billy Bones pondered, asked a few more questions to be sure, and then the two sat quiet as the massive wooden hull began to move.

"Cap'n," said Billy Bones, finally.

"What?"

"The *goods*, Cap'n. The gold . . ."

"Well?"

"They took all your papers and such, didn't they?"

Flint smiled. "Did they?"

"So how'll we . . . how'll *you* . . . find the goods again, without charts and notes?"

"Billy, my Billy! Billy-my-little-chicken! You really must leave all such matters to me. Do you understand?"

Billy Bones gulped. The tone of Flint's voice had barely changed but Billy Bones knew that this subject must not be raised again. He was immune to smallpox, but not to fear of Flint.

"You just do as you've been bid, Mr Bones. When the time comes."

"Aye-aye, Cap'n," said Billy Bones, for Livvy Rose had measured him with the precision of her father's mathematical instruments, recognising that the faithful Billy was born to follow. And now he would follow Flint – even stripped of rank and bound in chains – and keep on following him to the ends of the earth. For Flint was Billy Bones's chosen master.

Chapter 3

Dinner time, 12th March 1753
Aboard Walrus
The Atlantic

*A*ll aboard who weren't on watch gobbled down their
dinners with knives, fingers and spoons, lounging among
the guns on the maindeck in the sunshine, while *Walrus*
bowled along under all plain sail. They cheered and raised
their mugs, spluttering grog and food in all directions as they
bawled out their song, to the tune of a fiddler and a piper.

> *Here's to Bonnie Prince Charlie,*
> *That does our king remain,*
> *And save him from his exile,*
> *To bring him home again!*

Two men looked on in silence. They were not gobbling their
dinners because they were on watch, and they weren't singing
because they weren't Jacobites. They were Long John Silver,
elected captain of the ship, and his master gunner, Israel Hands.
Both wore the long coats and tricorne hats that proclaimed
their rank, and they stood by the helmsman at the ten-foot
tiller on the quarterdeck, braced against the ship's canted deck
with practised ease, even Long John with his timber limb.

Israel Hands smiled to see Long John recovering at last, after wounds that had struck him down in the fight with the navy over Flint's Island, which *Walrus* barely escaped, leaving Flint in the navy's hands, and his Treasure still hidden ashore.

Now Tom Allardyce the bosun was on his feet and giving the second verse. He was a tall, yellow-haired Scot who'd fought at Culloden seven years earlier, when the English army's modern musketry butchered a medieval mob of Highland swordsmen: the Protestant House of Hanover defeating the Catholic House of Stuart.

> *Here's to the devil to take fat George,*
> *And fetch him down to Hell,*
> *To trim his Hanoverian ears,*
> *And roast his arse full well!*

Allardyce was a Jacobite to the soul and hated King George with a passion. As he sang, he went among the crew slapping shoulders while they cheered him on. Some cheered because they supported his cause, while others had no loyalty to a king who was chasing them with a noose.

"Merry buggers, ain't they?" said Israel Hands, looking at the crew. Then he glanced anxiously up at Long John's big, square face.

"Will they do, John? And have you chosen your course?"

Silver reached up to pet the big green parrot that sat with its claws clamped into the material of his coat.

"What do *you* think, Cap'n Flint?" he said, tickling the bird's chest. She squawked and shifted her feet and nuzzled his ear.

"*Merry Buggers!*" she said, for she had a perfect gift of mimicry, and used words to purpose, and with meaning.

Long John sighed, for he had much on his mind.

"Well, the *ship* won't do," he said, looking *Walrus* over. She was a New England schooner: two hundred tons burden, a hundred feet from bow to stern, sharp-hulled and with a broad spread of canvas on two raked masts. She mounted fourteen six-pounder guns and had once been a swift, handy ship, but she'd suffered a battering in recent actions, and hadn't been careened for months, which meant – in these tropical waters – that the underwater hull must be a seething tangle of weeds and growth.

"A Thames barge would out-sail her as she is!" said Silver.

"Does that mean we'll be chasing one?" said Israel Hands.

"We've just thirty-two hands," said Silver, ignoring the remark.

"Gentlemen o' fortune every one!" said Israel Hands.

"Mostly . . . but *them two* ain't! Useless bloody lubbers!"

Silver nodded at a pair of men who were sitting miserably apart from the crew. They wore long coats and were the ship's navigating officers – such as they were – for neither Silver nor anyone else aboard had that skill. The pair of them had been taken out of the merchant service under Silver's promise to be freed at Upper Barbados – *Walrus*'s destination – for they were honest men. *Honest*, but found wanting. They might be able to feel their way up a coastline, but they were at a loss on the deep waters, and growing more nervous each day.

"Them swabs has only got this far by dead reckoning and fair weather!" said Silver. "One good blow, and we'll be off their charts. Then God help us all!"

"Never mind them," said Israel Hands. "We'll hire afresh and take on others, too." He looked sideways at Long John and decided to broach the great question: "What worries me, John, is that thirty-three hands is plenty for a merchantman, but not for such business as ours."

Silver, however, wouldn't be drawn. He shook his head and fell deep into his own thoughts. He'd never wanted to be a pirate – a "gentleman o' fortune" – but had become one because it was that or certain death. And thus by easy stages to robbery and murder, and putting a pistol ball into a child – which, of all the things he'd done, came back most often to flog him with guilt, though he'd done it of necessity, to stop the spread of island smallpox. Even now he could feel the jump of his pistol firing and see the open-mouthed disbelief on the face of Ratty Richards, ship's boy, as he dropped down dead; slaughtered by the captain he worshipped.

And now he had a wife whom he loved fiercely, and who'd made clear that she'd not live with him unless he became an honest man. Or so she said . . . But did she mean it? She loved him; he knew that much. Or so he thought.

So . . . there was what the *crew* wanted, which was prizes, gold, tarts and rum. There was what *she* wanted, which was an honest life for Mr and Mrs Silver. And then there was what *he* wanted . . . which he didn't know, and couldn't decide because he couldn't live *without* her and maybe couldn't live *with* her. The bitter internal conflict was turning him sour and angry.

"John," said Israel Hands and nudged him, "it's *her* . . ."

Silver turned. She'd come up from below decks without him even seeing. Now she stood with her hands on her hips facing him. She was a small, slim, black girl, not yet eighteen years old, extremely lovely in face and figure, with a dainty elegance of movement, and of speech and manners too. She stood in a cotton gown and a straw hat, looking up at Silver and defying him.

"Well?" she said, but he avoided her eyes and said nothing. "*Huh!*" she said, investing the simple sound with eloquence.

All hands were watching. They shifted and muttered and a few got up for a better look. These arguments had gone on for days, and now Silver roused himself and tried to speak gentle. He tried to explain. So did she, for a while, but soon they were shouting and screeching, with fists clenched and words spat viciously, as tempers burst and fury rose in the passionate rage of a man and woman for whom no one else in the whole wide world mattered quite so much as the other.

As for the spectators, they shrugged their shoulders and scratched their armpits and turned away, no longer entertained by a piece of theatre that had been played out flat. They thought Silver should put the rod across her plump little arse till she saw reason. But that was his business and they'd chosen him as their leader, so there weren't no more to be said in the matter. Selena was his wife and that was that.

But later, the ship's surgeon, Mr Cowdray, was forced to join the quarrel. The only gentleman in the ship, he'd practised in London till learned rivals drove him out for his ludicrous insistence on boiling his instruments before surgery, which *he* said prevented sepsis, and which *they* couldn't abide because it did. Selena liked Cowdray and valued his opinion, and thus she'd asked him to meet her on the forecastle after dark.

"What do you want, girl? Bringing me here?" he looked back down the dark length of the ship, past masts and bulging sails, and hung on to the rail against the ship's motion, flinching as spray came over the plunging bow.

"It's wide open here," she said, "so nobody can say you're meeting me in secret."

"And why should I do that?" he said.

She shrugged. She'd seen how he looked at her. He might be a surgeon, but he was a man, even if he was middle-aged.

"You can always say you were going to use the heads," she said.

"Huh!" said Cowdray, looking at the "seats of ease" on either side of the bowsprit: a pair of squat boxes with holes cut in them for seamen to relieve themselves. "So what is it?" he said.

"Why won't he give up being a pirate?"

"He's not a pirate, he's a gentleman of fortune."

"It's the same thing."

"No! We sign the Book of Articles and every man votes. It is the *democracy* of the Greeks."

"*Articles!* He talks about them all the time, and he –"

"Selena, listen to me."

"But he does."

"Please, please, listen. I can't be *him*. I can't speak for him."

"So who do you speak for?"

"For the crew! It's a good life for them. Equal shares and light work. Merchant owners save money with small crews that must rupture themselves to work the ship, while we have many hands to ease the load. And we sail in soft waters: the Caribbean, the Gold Coast, the Indian Ocean . . . You should try the whale fisheries, my girl, up beyond Newfoundland! The ice hangs from the rigging and the lookouts are found frozen dead when the watch changes. And with us, there's no flogging the last man up the mast nor the last to trice his hammock as the navy does, and there's music and drink when you want it, and the chance to get rich –"

"By thieving and killing!"

"In which regard we're no worse than the king's ships, that kill men and take prizes!"

"But that's war."

"*Dulce bellum inexpertis*: war is sweet to those who don't know it!"

"Bah!" she said, striding off and leaving him in the dark. Him and his annoying habit of spouting Latin.

So the matter was not resolved, and Silver and Selena lived apart in the ship and couldn't meet without a quarrel. And Silver became bad tempered, and not the man he had been. And that was bad . . . but worse was to come.

25

Chapter 4

Half an hour before sunset
12th March 1753
Aboard Oraclaesus's *longboat*
The southern anchorage
Flint's Island

*B*oom! A signal gun blew white powder smoke from *Oraclaesus*'s quarterdeck, and echoed across the still waters. It was the signal for boats to give up for the day and return to their ships.

"Thank God!" said Mr Midshipman Povey to himself, and "*Hold water!*" he bellowed at the boat's crew. At least he tried to bellow, but his throat was sore and his head ached, and he hadn't the strength.

Twenty sweat-soaked men collapsed over their oars, shafts stabbing raggedly in all directions, crossing and clattering in a disgraceful fashion that should have earned a blistering rebuke from the coxswain. But he was preoccupied with scratching the blotches on his face and barely hanging on to the tiller, he was so dizzy.

"Bloody shambles," mumbled Povey. He looked across the anchorage in the dimming light, taking in the idly swirling boats and ships, and the voices everywhere raised in bickering argument. There was no wind in the anchorage, so the squadron was kedging out: each ship launching its best boat, a light anchor slung beneath, waiting until the smaller vessel had pulled ahead and dropped anchor before manning the capstan to haul on the anchor cable, thereby laboriously drawing the ship forward. Then up anchor and do it again! Then again and again till the sails should feel the wind of the open sea.

The drill was simple. It was heavy work needing no unusual talent. The squadron should have been out of the anchorage and under way in a few hours. But they weren't. Everything had gone wrong: cables fouled, oar stroke lost, tempers gone and men falling exhausted at their duties who couldn't be roused, not even with a rope's end.

It was the island fever. The enemy that they were trying to escape was already among them! Povey grinned stupidly, thick-headedly. It was just like those dreams where you were desperate to run but couldn't because your legs were made of lead. The fever was doing its utmost to keep them on the island.

"Cast off hawser!" said Povey, and the hands made clumsy shift to loose the heavy rope by which the anchor was suspended beneath the boat. The boat wallowed heavily as the great load was shed, and the anchor went down to the bottom; they'd find it easily enough tomorrow by following the cable. "Back larboard, pull starboard!" said Povey, and the longboat turned in the water. "Give way!" he commanded, and they began pulling for their food and their grog, and a few hours' sleep. That should have cheered them up, but it didn't. Povey looked down the banks of oarsmen, most of whom were sweating heavily even though it was cool evening. Some – like the coxswain – were coming out in a rash.

Bounder and *Jumper* were likewise recovering their boats and dropping their main anchors to moor for the night, as was the flagship. Povey sighed at the thought of all the heavy labour of weighing that would have to be performed again in the morning. But by this time they were bumping against the high oaken side of *Oraclaesus* and he was ordering "Toss Oars!" – the hands making a dog's breakfast of this simple command – and himself about to go first out of the boat and up the ship's side . . . when the officer of the watch leaned over the rail and called down to him.

"Mr Povey!"

"Aye-aye, sir?"

"I'd be obliged if you'd take the longboat and bring aboard the person who is calling from the shore."

"Sir? What person, sir?"

The officer of the watch frowned. He was feeling unwell and in no mood for explanations. "Obey your bloody orders and be damned, Mr Povey – and don't answer back!"

"Aye-aye, sir!"

Povey sank down into the longboat, almost in tears. He'd not realised how tired he was and how much he wanted to be out of the boat and into his bed. The crew obviously felt the same. They were moaning and snivelling.

"Oh, bloody-well-bugger the lot of you," said Povey. "And pull for the bloody shore."

Once they came round the ship, which happened to be between the longboat and the beach, Povey could make out the dark little dot of a figure outlined against the white sands of the beach, and he could hear a wailing cry coming over the still water. He'd not noticed it before, not with so many others shouting and the sick nausea rising in his belly again.

"*Uuurgh!*" Povey retched over the side, bringing up nothing and wrenching the muscles of his stomach. He dipped a hand in the water and splashed it over his face. The crew stared as they swayed to their oars. Some of them felt as bad as Povey.

"What are you bloody sods looking at?" he snarled. "Bend your bloody backs!"

The forlorn figure on the beach grew and took shape in

the twilight. It was a man kneeling right on the water's edge, with hands raised over his head. He moaned and wept and offered up prayers as, finally, the big boat ground ashore and Povey jumped out – and was astonished to be recognised.

"Mr Povey, sir! God bless and save you, sir, for it *is* Mr Povey, ain't it now?"

"Damn my blasted eyes," said Povey. "It's Ben Gunn!"

Memories flooded in. Bad memories of HMS *Elizabeth* – the vessel which had first brought Povey to this poisonous island – and Flint's mutiny, which had resulted in the death of her captain and loyal officers.

"Ben Gunn," said Povey in amazement, peering at the bedraggled figure with its straw-like hair, deep-lined, deep-tanned face, barefoot raggedness – and the wide, staring eyes of a madman. A madman who grovelled and pleaded before Povey, crouching to kiss his feet, and grasping for his hands to kiss them too. Povey pulled away, embarrassed.

"Back oars, you swab!" he said, and frowned heavily. "You were one of the mutineers, you blasted lubber! One of those that followed Flint! You were aboard the ship *Betsy* that Flint made on the island. You were aboard her, with Flint, when I was cast adrift!"

"No! No!" groaned Benn Gunn, shaking his matted head in an agony of self-pity, betraying himself comprehensively by protesting too much. "Not poor Ben Gunn," he moaned, "what-never-was-a-mutineer-nor-followed-Flint-on-the-island-nor-later-aboard-*Betsy*-nor-later-yet-aboard-*Walrus*-and-always-was-a-loyal-heart-and-true-God-bless-King-George-and-God-bless-England-and-bless-the-navy-too . . ."

It rattled out non-stop, ending only when Ben Gunn ran out of breath.

"Says you, Ben Gunn!" said Povey. "But you must come aboard and go before Captain Baggot to be examined."

"Yes! Yes!" said Ben Gunn. "Aboard ship and not marooned. Not left lonely with only the goats for company.

For there's only them now . . . what with the *others* being gone."

"What others?" said Povey.

But a cunning look came over Ben Gunn, and he fell silent, as if realising he'd said too much.

Within a sand-glass fifteen minutes, Ben Gunn found himself standing in the bright lights of Captain Baggot's cabin with the blue coats and gold lace of officers seated in front of him, and red marines behind him, and Ben Gunn goggling at the astonishing fact that among the officers, though not in the king's uniform, was Mr Billy Bones – Flint's most loyal follower. Ben Gunn pondered over that, and perhaps he wasn't so looney as he seemed, for he spotted two other things. First, most of those around the table looked like seasick landmen on their first cruise: pale and sweating heavily. And second, Ben Gunn could see that Mr Povey was as astonished as himself to find Billy Bones among the company. Alongside Bones was a clerical-looking gentleman who proved to be Dr Stanley, the chaplain, and he was treating Mr Bones with favour, almost apologetically.

Povey caught Lieutenant Hastings's eye where he sat with the other officers, and looked questioningly at Billy Bones. Hastings nodded at Dr Stanley. He risked mouthing the words:

"It's his doing!"

For his part, Billy Bones stared fixedly at Ben Gunn, who had not featured in the instructions he'd received from Flint. Thus Billy Bones was forced to extemporise, which he did to such creditable effect as would have amazed the master down below, who believed him incapable of initiative. Though perhaps Billy Bones shone more lustrously by comparison with Captain Baggot, who was not himself, being now quite ill.

Baggot did little more than extract a repetition of Ben Gunn's whining innocence, attempting only half-heartedly to examine such interesting matters as just what the Hell had been happening on the island while Flint was there? Especially to the north where John Silver had escaped aboard *Walrus*? All such matters Ben Gunn refused to discuss, fearing self-incrimination. Finally, bleary-eyed, swaying in his chair, and with red blotches now livid on his face, Baggot turned to Billy Bones.

"Will you have a word with him, Mr Bones? Were you not shipmates once?"

"Aye, Cap'n. Aboard *Elizabeth,* at the beginning of all these troubles."

"What troubles, Mr Bones?"

"Cap'n Flint's troubles, sir . . . and the wicked conspiracy against him."

"Rubbish!" said Povey, who knew exactly what had gone on aboard *Elizabeth*.

"Poppycock!" said Lieutenant Hastings who'd served alongside him.

"Be silent, there!" cried Baggot irritably. "Do not interrupt your betters!"

"Indeed not!" said Dr Stanley, and the other officers nodded.

Hastings and Povey gaped. They couldn't believe that they weren't believed, for all England knew they'd been Flint's shipmates. Had they been fit and well, they'd have fought for truth. But, like most others present, they were not fit and well. They were sick with headache and a nausea that was getting steadily worse as the day ended and the night came on. They hadn't the strength for so fearful a task as opposing their superiors.

Billy Bones, however, being immune to the peril that was bearing down on his shipmates, pressed on clear-headed and determined.

"Now then, Mr Gunn!" he said, sending Ben Gunn quivering in fright.

"I don't know nothing," came the response.

"Yes, you do. For you was helmsman aboard of *Elizabeth*, wasn't you?"

"Aye, but it weren't my fault she run aground."

"So whose fault was it?"

"Cap'n Springer's!"

"That's Springer as was cap'n of *Elizabeth*," said Billy Bones for the benefit of his audience, before turning back to Ben Gunn. "So it were Springer as done it, not Flint?"

"Not him!" said Ben Gunn. "It were that swab Springer, damn him!"

"And who flogged you for it, Mr Gunn – you that was helmsman?"

"Springer! He flogged me, though I was steering to his own orders."

"That he did, Mr Gunn. You that was innocent, as all hands knew!"

"Aye!"

"And when we was run aground, who was it as couldn't get us off?"

"Springer!"

"And who was it got drunk day after day?"

"Springer!"

"But who was it built the *Betsy* out of *Elizabeth*'s timbers, to escape the island?"

"Flint!"

"So I akses you, Mr Gunn . . . who was the true seaman – Springer or Flint?"

"Cap'n Flint, God-bless-him-and-keep-him!"

And there Billy Bones stopped, being enormously wise to do so, for it was all truth thus far. It was plain truth, every word of it, and cast a most radiant light upon Joseph Flint, lately a lieutenant in His Majesty's sea service, and now accused of mutiny and piracy. Billy Bones was doing wonderfully well.

"The rest is lies and spite," he said, inspired with the genius of simplicity.

"Well?" said Baggot to Ben Gunn.

"Couldn't say, Cap'n. For I weren't there, and took no part."

"Mr Hastings? Mr Povey?" said Baggot, turning at last to these vital witnesses.

But by this time Mr Povey's bowels were squirting hot fluid down the leg of his breeches, and he was staggering, grey-faced, out of the cabin, trying not to foul the neat-patterned oilcloth floor, while Mr Hastings was slumped glassy-eyed in his chair, under the impression that the ship was rolling in a hurricane. Neither was in a position to contribute much to the discussion of Flint's guilt or innocence.

Billy Bones smiled. He'd been lucky. He'd won a flying start to his campaign. One more heave and the irons would be struck off Flint's legs as surely as they'd been struck off his own. It only awaited the next developments, as forecast by Flint.

And looking round the cabin, Billy Bones could see those developments already going forward very nicely.

Chapter 5

*W*ith *Walrus*'s keel sprouting too much weed for swift
sailing, she was brought alongside of *Venture's Fortune*
only by cunning: *Walrus* having hoisted British colours upside-
down – a sign of distress – and left her sails hanging in a
slovenly manner as if some disaster had befallen her people.

"Steady, boys," said John Silver to the armed men hiding
behind the bulwarks, and anywhere else where they couldn't
be seen from the approaching ship.

"Steady boys," croaked the parrot on his shoulder and the
hands laughed.

"Stow that!" hissed Silver, and clapped a hand on the bird's
beak.

It would be a tragic waste to spoil things now. The sun
was high in the blue heavens, the sea was calm with a fresh
wind, and there were even gulls above, ventured out from
the land just under the horizon, while a fine, fat three-masted
ship came offering itself up, all bright and spanking new, with
fresh white sails and bright-coloured flags that hadn't seen a
drop of weathering, and jolly tars aboard who couldn't

34

imagine what a mistake they were making in coming to give aid.

"John," said Selena, standing next to him by the tiller, "I give you one last chance not to do this. It's shameful deceit. How can you do this to others who use the sea?"

"Belay that!" he said. "We can't take a prize no other way – we're too slow. It's this or nothing! D'you think I'd not rather bear down with colours flying?" He cursed and beat the deck with his crutch, and he looked at her and sneered: "An' if you're so moral and mighty, what're you doing on deck in your gown so they sees a woman and ain't afraid?"

"Huh!" she said. "You know why! If they're taken by surprise there'll be less fighting, that's why!" But she blinked and looked away, for that wasn't entirely the truth. She wasn't so sure of anything now, having considered what Dr Cowdray had said . . . and . . . and . . . a soft word now, from John Silver, a friendly smiling word, might have closed the gulf between them. But Silver was too angry. Too many harsh words had been spoken.

"Well, there you are then!" he said with extreme bad grace. "So stand fast, and clap a hitch on your jawing tackle – or go below with them two swabs of navigators as I've locked in my cabin to save their precious innocence!" And there followed even more temper and more shouting, which ended in her being *ordered* below – at which she screamed defiance – and then being *dragged* below . . . causing consternation aboard *Venture's Fortune*, the big West Indiaman, coming on under close-reefed topsails, for her quarterdeck people were studying the wallowing, helpless *Walrus* through telescopes.

"There, sir!" cried Mr Philip Norton, a big, young, muscular man, well dressed and handsome, with the confidence that comes with power. "Did I not say it was madness to approach her? Look at the number of gun-ports! And now there's fighting aboard her."

"Bollocks!" cried Captain Fitch, a veteran seaman and a

master of his craft, but cursed with the short stature which turns a man to bloody-mindedness when the tall look down on him and tell him what to do. And that went double when the tall one represented something that all decent men despise: the government. He glared defiance at Norton. "I shall render assistance to a mariner in distress, according to the ancient traditions of the sea," he said. "And as for the risk that terrifies *you*, Mr Norton, you well know that I have a *Protection* in case of that!" And clapping his eye to his glass again, Fitch told himself there was nothing to worry about in the sight of two men manhandling a shrieking woman down a hatchway while a one-legged man with a green bird on his shoulder looked on, shouting and pointing, and apart from which there wasn't another soul visible on deck other than the helmsman . . .

"Jesus wept!" said Norton. "D'you think a piece of paper will save you from pirates? Do you not understand what I have under hatches?" And then, as Fitch steadily ignored him, Norton suddenly displayed a remarkable degree of seamanship: "Mr Mate," he cried to the first officer, "shake out the topsails! Put up the helm and bring this ship about!" He pointed at *Walrus*: "And steer me clear o' that 'un!"

His voice rang with command. It was the dominant bark of a man used to being obeyed, and the mate instinctively touched his hat in salute and started to bellow at the hands. But Fitch spat fire.

"Avast!" he cried, and stamped a foot at Norton and glared up into his eyes. "Slam your trap, you bloody bugger! I don't care what you was before, but don't you by-God-and-all-his-bloody-angels give commands aboard my ship, for I'm cap'n here, and there ain't none other!"

Thus Fitch and Norton were still arguing when *Walrus* came within spitting distance and her crew leapt up at Long John's command, gave a cheer, and commenced hurling grapnels to bind the two ships together. Led by Long John himself, they came roaring over the side, taking command of *Venture's Fortune* in a matter of seconds.

It was incredibly easy. Not a blow was struck or a grain of powder burned other than that which went into the air to terrify the West Indiaman's crew, of which there were only twenty foremast hands, who'd not been stood to arms and were thus empty-handed in the face of John Silver's thirty-two, who between them bore enough pistols, cutlasses, muskets and pikes to equip a small army, and who moved with practised speed: some to guard the prisoners while others – led by Allardyce and Israel Hands – went below to search the ship.

It was a sweet, clean capture, and the only injury to any man on either side – to the hilarity of Silver's men – was a broken leg suffered by one Dusty Miller, a notoriously clumsy seaman who'd fallen badly as he swung aboard the prize on a line from the mainyard.

"Who's cap'n?" cried Silver, stumping across the quarter-deck to where his men had herded the ship's officers. He reached up to his shoulder to pet the big parrot that had fluttered back with wide-beating wings, after flying aloft as she always did when there was fighting. Silver was grinning in triumph, which turned to instant amazement as a small, thick-bodied man among the prisoners started yelling and waving his hands in fury.

"I, sir!" he cried, trying to push aside the firelocks aimed at him by Silver's men.

"Huh!" said Silver. "Let the bugger through" and Captain Fitch stamped forward to stand looking up at Long John Silver, who towered over most men let alone one only five feet tall. The sight was greeted with laughter from the crew, which was deeply unfair to Fitch, who despite being unarmed, and facing death for all he knew, was fearlessly brave, and told Silver off something ferocious.

"I'm Fitch," he cried. "Cap'n of *Venture's Fortune* with

cargo and supercargo bound for London. And I may not be touched, God damn-your-eyes, sir! You may not lay a finger on me! For I sail with *protection*, sir! Protection from Sir Wyndham Godfrey, Governor of Upper Barbados, and which Protection . . ."

"Clap a hitch, you bloody dwarf!" cried Long John, but Fitch persisted, stabbing a finger up at him and shouting until finally Silver drew a pistol, cocked it, and shoved it into Fitch's belly.

"See here, mister," he said, "either you pipe down or I give fire. I don't mind which, so please your soddin' self!"

"Bah!" said Fitch, but he shut up.

"Good," said Silver. "Now what's this about blasted protection? What're you talking about?"

"A Certificate of Protection of Free Passage from Sir Wyndham Godfrey!" said Fitch. Then he lowered his voice: "Protection from gentlemen such as yourself, sir!"

"What gentlemen?" said Silver.

"Gentlemen o' fortune, sir."

"Oh?" Silver's eyebrows raised.

Fitch nodded knowingly. "Aye, sir! For isn't Upper Barbados the only port where you may safely call?"

Silver frowned. The old days were gone when there were a dozen safe havens for pirates on the Spanish Main. There was still Savannah, of course, and maybe one or two others, but none that boasted a dockyard like those of Williamstown, Upper Barbados, where gold talked all languages and the law looked the other way. Fitch read Silver's face.

"So," he said, "spurn Sir Wyndham's Protection, and he'll turn the guns of his fort on you."

"Where is it? This 'Protection'?"

"Below, in my cabin. I'll show you . . ."

"Back your topsail," said Long John. "Time for that later." And he looked around.

For the moment, all was well. The weather was fine, the

prize taken, the prisoners under guard. And that included five passengers – now trembling in each other's arms on the main-deck, wealth written all over them – who had cabins for the passage to England. These were Fitch's "supercargo". Two were women: one middle-aged but handsome, and clearly a lady of fashion, wearing a Leghorn straw hat to save her complexion from the sun and a fine linen gown, cut prac-tical for the ocean journey but underpinned with a full rig of hooped panniers. The other was her elderly maid. No blushing virgin, either of 'em, but they'd need watching for fear the hands – bless their hearts – forgot what they'd signed under articles, concerning the punishment for rape.

But greater matters presented themselves . . .

"Long John! Long John!" cried Allardyce, coming up from the maindeck hatchway and leading a tall man with chains dangling from his wrists and ankles. "Look!" said Allardyce, with reverence. "It's *Himself!* It's the McLonarch! Him that led the charge of Clan McLonarch, between Clan Chester and Clan Atholl, and me behind him – my mother being a McLonarch – right to the British bayonets where he killed *five* with his own hand!"

"What's this, Tom Allardyce?" said Silver, stepping forward. He looked at the creature Allardyce was referring to and detected the authentic look of a holy lunatic. The man was as tall as Silver, round-eyed, gaunt and woolly-haired, with a straggling beard, a great beak of a nose and high, slender cheek-bones. His clothes were unkempt but clean, for though he was in chains, he'd not been ill-treated and there was no stink of the dungeon about him. He had decent shoes and stockings besides, and silver buckles, so he'd not been pillaged neither.

"Who are you, my lad?" said Silver.

"*My lord!*" corrected Allardyce. "He is the McLonarch of McLonarch!"

"Very likely," said Silver. "But I'll hear it from *him*, not *you!*"

The tall man stirred, fastened his eyes on Silver, drew himself upright and spoke with the soft, Irish-sounding accent of the Scottish Highlands.

"I am Andrew Charles Louis Laurent McLonarch-Flaubert – ninth Earl of McLonarch, and First Minister of His Most Catholic Majesty King Charles III, who is known to men as *Bonnie Prince Charlie*." He was bedraggled and in chains, and spouting utter nonsense. But nobody laughed. Nobody laughed at the McLonarch.

"Are you now?" said Silver. "And what does King George say to that?"

"George of Hanover is a pretender and a heretic," said McLonarch calmly. "He faces the block in this world and damnation in the next."

"I see," said Silver. "So what're you doing in chains? What with you being *prime minister*, an' all?"

McLonarch looked around until he spotted the group huddled against the lee rail, menaced by pistols. He pointed at Norton.

"Ask him," said McLonarch, and nodded grimly. "He is one whom I have marked for future attention, for he is deep in the service of the Hanoverians."

Everyone looked at Norton, who shrugged his shoulders.

"I serve my king!" he said, afraid to say more.

"And what might that mean?" said Long John.

Norton thought before he spoke. He was a brave man but he was nervous, and with good reason. He couldn't guess whose side these pirates might take, and he knew McLonarch's power with words.

"McLonarch is a leader of Jacobites," he said. "He would raise rebellion – civil war – to soak England in blood. He is under arrest by the Lord Chancellor's warrant, and I am charged with escorting him home for trial." Norton looked round to see how this was received.

"Bah!" sneered McLonarch. "The man is a catchpole, a

40

thief-taker, an agent sent to return me to England for judicial murder. He used bribery and deceit to capture me, and to steal the treasure lawfully gathered by my master the king."

"Treasure?" said Silver, just when the politics was getting dull.

"*Treasure?*" said a dozen voices.

"A war chest of three thousand pounds in Spanish gold, which –"

"THREE THOUSAND POUNDS?" they cried.

"Which I was delivering to my master's loyal followers in London."

"Where is it?" said Silver.

"*WHERE IS IT?*" roared his crew.

"In the hold, in strong boxes," said McLonarch, and pointed again at Norton: "He has the keys. He stole them from me."

There followed half an hour of the most delightful and congenial work. Having been told exactly what would happen to him if he *didn't* co-operate, Norton swiftly produced a heavy ring of keys from his cabin. Meanwhile the main hatchway was broken open, a heavy block rigged to the main-stay, with lifting tackles, and the crew of Venture's Fortune set to the heavy labour of burrowing through the cargo – rum, sugar and molasses – to get to the heavy strongboxes which were on the ground tier down below.

Then the captured crew were made to haul up the boxes, one at a time, for opening on the quarterdeck at Silver's feet, to thundering cheers, the fiddler playing, hornpipes being danced, and joy unbounded as rivers of Spanish coin poured out all over the decks, such that it was a tribute to Long John's leadership that all hands did not get roaring drunk and lose the ship.

The only thing that puzzled Silver in that merry moment was why McLonarch had given up his treasure so easily. Silver pondered on that. Of course, the gelt was lost to McLonarch as soon as his ship was taken . . . but why speak up *quite* so helpful: saying how much there *was*, and who'd got the *keys*, an' all? It wasn't right. No man behaved like that. So what was going on?

He got his answer later, when Tom Allardyce brought McLonarch down to the stern cabin, where Silver was sitting at Captain Fitch's desk, going through the ship's papers for anything that might be useful.

"Cap'n!" said Allardyce. Silver looked up. Allardyce stood with his hat in his hands, bent double in respect for the man beside him, and whom he kept glancing at, in awestruck respect. McLonarch, free of chains and even more imposing than he'd been before, stood beside Allardyce with his nose in the air, and gazing down upon Silver as if he were a lackey with a chamber pot. Silver frowned.

"Who took his irons off, Mr Bosun?"

"Er . . . me, Cap'n."

"On whose orders?"

"Seemed the right thing, Cap'n," said Allardyce, torn between two loyalties.

"*The right thing*, you say? Now see here, my lad, I'll not –"

"Captain Silver!" said McLonarch. "That is your name, is it not?"

Silver stared at McLonarch, whom he did not like – not one little bit – having taken against him on sight, for McLonarch was a man who expected doors to open in front of him and close behind him, and who sat down without looking . . . such was his confidence that a minion would be ready with a chair! Silver forgave him that, for it was the way of all aristocrats. What made him uneasy was McLonarch's belief that he was the right hand of Almighty God, and his uncanny gift of convincing others of it: which gift now bore down upon John Silver.

"Aye, milord! Silver's my name," said Long John. "Cap'n Silver, at your service."

42

Silver couldn't believe he'd just said that. He disowned the words on the instant. But he'd said them all right, and worse still, he felt an overpowering urge to stand up and take off his hat! A lesser man would have been up like a shot, and even Silver was half out of his seat before he realised what was happening and slumped back, scowling fiercely. But McLonarch nodded in satisfaction, and waved a gracious hand.

"Captain," he said, "I welcome you into my service. There is much work for you to do, and you will begin by locking His Majesty's monies into their strongboxes once again and replacing the boxes in the hold."

Chapter 6

One bell of the afternoon watch
18th March 1753
Aboard Oraclaesus
The Atlantic

*F*lint's leg-irons were secured by the curled-over end of an iron bar. Billy Bones got the bar nicely on to the small anvil he'd brought below for purposes of liberation, took up the four-pound hammer, frowned mightily for precision . . . and struck a great blow.

Clang! said the irons.

"Another," said Flint.

"Aye-aye, Cap'n!"

Clang!

"Ahhh!" said Flint, and pulled the straightened bar through the holes in the loops that had encircled his ankles before hurling the irons with passionate hatred into the dark depths of the hold, where they rattled and clattered and terrified the ship's rats as they went about their honest business.

"Dear me," said Flint, not unkindly, "I do apologise, Lieutenant!" For the hurtling iron had knocked off the hat, and nearly smashed in the brow, of the goggle-eyed young officer of marines – he looked to be about seventeen – who knelt holding a lantern beside Billy Bones.

"You *do* give your parole?" said the lieutenant. "Your parole not to escape?"

"Of course," said Flint, ignoring the nonsensical implication that there might be some place to escape *to*, aboard a ship at sea. He sighed, and stood, and stretched his limbs, then turned to the lad as if puzzled: "But has not Mr Bones already made clear," he said, "that Captain Baggot was about to order my release?"

"Was he?" said the lieutenant, weighed down by responsibility and peering at Billy Bones as they got to their feet. Billy, for his part, was bathed in the warm smile of a man entirely free of responsibility, since all future decisions were now in the hands of his master.

In fact, Billy Bones was so happy that he was quite taken by surprise: "About to release Cap'n Flint?" he said doubtfully. But a glimpse of Flint frowning nastily was sufficient to restore his memory. "*Ah!*" said Billy Bones. "'*Course* he was, Mr Lennox!" And recalling his manners, he jabbed a thumb at the red-coated officer. "This here's Mr Lennox, Cap'n, sir . . . the senior officer surviving."

"Senior officer . . . *surviving?*" said Flint, relishing the concept, before correcting Billy Bones. "You will address Mr Lennox as *'sir'*, for he bears His Majesty's commission."

"Oh!" said Bones, peering at the skinny youngster. Flint was right: he was out-ranked! Billy had never risen higher than master's mate, a rank far below a marine lieutenant. This lapse of protocol embarrassed him, for contrary forces were now at work within Billy Bones. He was still Flint's man, but – being aboard a king's ship once more – he was starting to think in the old ways: the *navy* ways he'd followed before Flint.

"Beg pardon, sir, I do declare," he said, saluting Lieutenant Lennox.

"Granted, Mr Bones," said Lennox.

"Aye-aye, sir," said Billy Bones, and attempting reparation

in words, added: "At least you're one o' them what's immune!"

"Am I?" said Lennox, and looked at Flint, sweating in anxiety.

"Oh, yes," said Flint, placing a comforting hand on Lennox's shoulder. "If you have not yet succumbed, then you are safe." He nodded gravely. "For reasons known only to God, some ten men in every hundred are safe."

Lennox closed his eyes and trembled in relief. "What about the rest?" he asked. "Will they die?"

"Yes," said Flint, "most of them. I am very sorry."

Lennox bowed his head and shed tears for his comrades. But so wonderful was the prospect of escaping the hangman that Flint had to pinch himself to affect solemnity and crush the urge to laugh! Merriment would not do: not now. It would undoubtedly upset Mr Lennox, who must be kept sweet until such time as Flint's freedom was assured – and that time was some way off as yet.

"Come, Mr Lennox," said Flint, with every appearance of kindness, "let us go on deck. I must know the worst, if I am to be of any help."

Soon, Flint did know the worst, and it was a very dreadful worst. It was so bad that even he was shaken.

The ship stank worse than a slaver, and it echoed with a dreadful, communal moan, like a long discord of bass violins, which was the constant, unceasing groan of the dying: one voice starting up as another paused to draw breath, and dozens more in the background, over and over in a hideous choir of grief and pain.

The lower deck was a fetid dormitory of helpless men, swinging side by side, in massed, packed hammocks slung fore-and-aft from the deckhead beams, some with just eighteen inches of width per man. Such closeness was normally prevented at sea by the traditional watch system, which had half the hands on deck while the others slept, giving a comfortable thirty-six inches per man. But now, with most of the crew too sick to move or even to go to the heads, the lower deck was crammed – stinking, roiling, foul – with slimy hammocks that dripped a vile liquid mixture of urine, vomit and excrement.

That was bad enough, but the mutilating horror of the disease itself, on the faces and arms of the victims shivering in their blankets – cold in the steaming heat of the lower deck – was atrocious to behold. Some were in the full-flowering pustular rash of the disease, others were shedding skin in sheets, leaving raw, bleeding wounds. Still others were already – and very obviously – dead, with the tropical climate working upon them and rendering their bodies swollen and black.

Flint, Lennox and Bones, having come up from the hold, stood by the main hatchway plumb in the middle of the swaying hammocks and festering bodies. They crouched under the low deckhead and flinched from contact with the horrors around them and their stomachs heaved, for the stench was hideous beyond belief.

"God save us!" said Flint. "Can nothing be done with the stink?"

"No, sir," said Lennox. "The fit hands won't go below to clean and swab."

"Won't they, though?" said Flint. "We'll see about that!" He affected grim resolve, but bells of joy rang inside his mind. Lennox – senior officer surviving – had just called him *sir*! Unlike Billy Bones, Flint had been a sea-service lieutenant, outranking the marine equivalent. Perhaps Lennox knew that? More likely he was desperate for someone to take over. It didn't matter. Not so long as he said *sir*.

"Come!" said Flint. "We must go on deck."

The three climbed the ladder up to the maindeck, with its lines of broadside guns, which was open to the skies at the waist, apart from the ship's boats lashed to the skidbeams that spanned the gap. So the air was fresher, but conditions were as bad as the lower deck, with a dozen or more dying men wallowing in their own filth. One was sitting with his back against the mainmast, moaning and cursing in the ghastly act of peeling the skin from his hands so that it came off whole, like a pair of gloves.

Flint heaved at the sight: sudden, violent and helpless. He threw up over his shoes and shirt and coat-front, and staggered to one of the guns and sat on the fat barrel and glared at Billy Bones.

"Water!" he said. "Get water!" Lennox stood dithering while Billy Bones dashed off, and Flint stared up and down the ship. All the precision and cleanliness of a man-o'-war was gone. The deck was in vile disorder, with tackles and gear left muddled and un-secured. And the awful stench of the lower deck rolled up from below. Flint blinked. He who was so fastidious was be-smeared with his own vomit. He was ashamed. Ashamed he'd disgraced himself and . . . possibly . . . just possibly . . . he was ashamed of what he'd done in bringing the smallpox aboard.

But then Billy Bones was back, labouring with a full bucket of fresh water, and Flint was kneeling over it and ducking his head in it, and scrubbing himself clean.

"Ohhhh!" said Flint and shuddered, and shivered and shook. But then he mastered himself. He buttoned up his coat. He made himself as tidy as he could. He put on his hat. "Quarterdeck!" he said. "Come on!" And briskly he led the way up a ladder to the larboard gangway, and then aft past the barricade, to the quarterdeck, the capstan, the binnacle and the ship's wheel, where a group of men were huddled with gaunt, frightened faces. They were mostly lower-deck hands, barefoot and pigtailed.

By sheer, ingrained habit of discipline, the appearance of Lennox in his officer's coat and gorget had the hands saluting and standing to attention, each making an effort to hold up his head. They looked mainly to Lennox, but glanced at Flint and ignored Billy Bones completely.

Careful now, thought Flint, for he needed these men. "Who's officer of the watch?" he said to Lennox.

"Me, sir!" said an elderly man with a long coat and a tricorne hat.

"Who's he?" said Flint to Lennox.

"Baxter, sir. Ship's carpenter, sir," said Lennox.

"The carpenter? Are there no navigating officers?"

"All sick, sir. He's the best we've got."

"What of the captain and the lieutenants?"

"Bad sick, sir."

"Sick but *alive*?"

"Yes, sir, thank God, sir."

"Hmm . . . then how many fit men do we have aboard?"

"Don't know, sir," said Lennox, but Baxter stepped forward and saluted politely.

"Us here, sir. Us, an' them there," he said, and pointed.

Flint looked and saw a man in the foretop, and five hands standing by to trim the rigging if need be, although the ship was snugged right down under minimum possible sail: just close-reefed fore and main topsails.

"What course are you steering?" said Flint, and so it went on. The more questions Flint asked, the more Lennox deferred to him, and the more the hands took note, and spoke direct to Flint, and he to them, and Lennox gratefully stood back. Thus – cautiously at first – Flint took over. He straightened his back, he clasped his hands behind him . . . and . . . after a break of some four years devoted to other pursuits . . . he resumed his career as a British naval officer: *pretended* to, at any rate.

"So!" he said. "I have seen the disgraceful condition of this ship and am resolved to put it right in the name of King George, God-bless-him!"

"God bless him," murmured the hands miserably.

49

"*God bless him!*" roared Flint. "And damn him as don't!"

"God bless him!" they cried, for Flint had them in his eye now, and so did Billy Bones, who instinctively stood beside Flint, with scowling brow and fists clenched in the old way that had never failed him . . . and Mr Lennox looked on, like a three-legged horse at a steeplechase.

"I'm Flint," said Flint. "You don't know me yet, but soon you shall, and I'll start by sending a team below with mops and buckets to clean away the filth. For I tell you two things: first, that you're all safe from the pestilence, and second, that no man ever born shall suffer as any of *you* shall suffer who disobeys my orders!"

Lennox gaped, for there wasn't even a token resistance from the men. But he looked at Flint and Bones again and understood. They were the very incarnation of the officer caste that the lower deck was bred up to obey. Meanwhile, Flint was still speaking . . .

"Mr Lennox himself shall lead you to your duties!" he said.

"Aye-aye, sir!" they said.

"Oh?" said Lennox, and "Aye-aye, sir!"

Soon, the bucket brigade was below, while the carpenter and two hands kept the ship on course, enabling Flint to have a private word with Billy Bones, aft at the taffrail.

"Where's Ben Gunn, Mr Bones? You said he came aboard! He survived the smallpox as a child, so he should be among the living."

"Oh, him!" said Bones contemptuously.

"What of him?"

"Went over the side, Cap'n, when we was putting to sea."

"Did he now?"

"Aye, Cap'n: the minute he heard you was aboard."

Flint laughed. "The old rogue! Did he drown?"

"No, Cap'n! Last seen swimming for shore. Going strong."

"Pity. His was a mouth to be closed. Still –" Flint shrugged and turned to other matters "we have begun well, Mr Bones," he said, "but the problem is *hands!*"

"Hands to work her, sir?"

"Aye, Mr Bones." Flint looked at the ship with her towering masts and broad yards. She was the biggest vessel he'd been aboard for years, and a seaman's delight. Over eight hundred tons burden, and mounting twenty-eight twelve-pounders, she was a superb modern frigate: lavishly equipped and even boasting copper plating on her hull – a recent innovation which gave greater speed than a normal hull and complete freedom from the ship-worm, that menace of tropical seas that burrowed into timber hulls and ruined them.

"*Oraclaesus*," said Flint, savouring the name. "She came to the island with two hundred and fifty-one men aboard, including a commodore, a captain, three sea-service lieutenants, a sailing master, a lieutenant of marines – our Mr Lennox – and six midshipmen . . ." He smiled. "After misfortunes ashore, she came away with one hundred and eighty-five men, having lost her commodore, a lieutenant, three mids and a miscellany of foremast hands and marines."

Billy Bones shook his head in wonderment.

"How d'you know all that, Cap'n?"

Flint sighed. "Have I not told you, Mr Bones, that I listened to those who came to feed us during our captivity?"

"Oh!" said Billy Bones. "I see."

"Good. And do you also see that, once the smallpox has done its good work . . ." But here Flint swallowed and faltered, having seen the awful reality of the death he'd inflicted upon this splendid ship.

He looked away.

He hadn't always been a villain.

There had been a time when he was proud to serve his king.

He felt the pull of being a king's officer once more.

Even though it was *supposed* to be a pretence and a sham.

For he'd served aboard ships like this one, had Joe Flint. And aboard this particular ship the crew were England's finest: mostly lads in their teens and twenties. They were hand-picked volunteers, to a man.

And Joe Flint trembled on the brink of remorse.

He trembled a long, hard moment . . .. then:

"Urrrrgh!" he growled like an animal. Ordinary men *wrestled* with conscience, but Flint – who was neither ordinary, nor normal, nor even entirely sane – turned upon *his* in selfish fury. Why should he feel sorry? He who'd been robbed of a vast treasure? He who'd been brutally rejected by the only woman he'd ever loved? *No!* He spat upon conscience, he spurned it and reviled it, he seized it by the throat . . . and strangled it.

"Huh!" he said, and grinned, and pulled Billy Bones's nose.

"Ow!" said Bones.

"So," said Flint, "our situation is this: the smallpox should have killed nine out of ten, but we were lucky – I counted nineteen men on deck, plus the lieutenant. But that is still dangerously few for so great a ship as this."

"Aye!" said Billy Bones. "I'd want fifty at least, just to sail her, and a hundred or more to man the guns."

"Indeed, Mr Bones." Flint looked out to sea. "Ah!" he said. "See those ships?"

"Aye, sir. Thems are *Bounder* and *Jumper*, the sloops in company with us."

"Each having some fit men still aboard."

"The which we can employ, Cap'n?"

"Yes. But we must avoid gentlemen with long coats."

"Officers, Cap'n?"

"Indeed, for they might think it their duty to remind the hands of what I am."

"What about *them below*? Cap'n Baggot and the rest?"

Flint smiled. "Those unfortunate officers who are '*bad sick but still alive*'?"

"Aye, Cap'n."

"Why, Mr Bones, you and I shall visit them . . . to *ease* their suffering."

Billy Bones bit his lip and looked at his boots.

"Especially," said Flint, "we must visit Lieutenant Hastings and Mr Midshipman Povey, those old shipmates of ours who were witnesses to our past actions, and thereby have the power to put a rope around my neck." He nodded: "And yours, too, Mr Bones. We must see to Hastings and Povey first of all, for our lives depend upon it!" He smiled. "What a blessing it is that we have them safe aboard this ship, laid in their hammocks and awaiting our visit!" He even laughed.

"Oh!" said Billy Bones, suddenly remembering something.

"What?" Flint frowned. Billy Bones radiated guilt.

"Well, Cap'n . . . I meant to say . . ."

"Say what?"

"Well, Cap'n, it were a great struggle, a-gettin' of the squadron to sea . . ."

"Yes?"

"What with so many sick aboard all three ships . . ."

"So?"

"So *Bounder*, there –" Billy Bones looked at the distant sloop "– well, she had no navigating officer, and what with Mr Povey being so clever a young gentleman, and all others laid on their backs . . ."

"So?"

"So Mr Povey was given command of *Bounder* and is aboard her now."

Chapter 7

Afternoon (there being no watches kept nor bells struck)
18th March 1753
Aboard Venture's Fortune
In the latitude of Upper Barbados

*S*ilver glared at McLonarch and reached up to pet his squawking bird.

"See here, mister," he said, "I'm in my own bloody service. Mine and these hands aboard, and no other man's, be he *lord*, *king* or *pretender*!"

"But, Cap'n," said Allardyce, "all's changed. There's a new way! All we have to do —"

"Stow it, you lubber!" said Silver. "Did you not hear what he said?" He jabbed a finger at McLonarch: "'Put the dollars back in the hold' – Huh!" he sneered, "Shave mine arse with a rusty razor!"

"Captain Silver," said McLonarch, "may I sit?" And with that he placed himself in one of Captain Fitch's cabin chairs, and drew it up to face Silver.

Fast losing his temper, Silver slammed a broad hand on the desk in front of him and yelled at Allardyce: "Get up on deck and send down some good lads to drag *this* bugger —" he pointed at McLonarch – "out of my sight. And stick the irons back on him, too, for I've had enough of his long, ugly face!"

54

But Allardyce turned nasty. "No!" he cried, scowling at his captain. "Not a step will I take, till you hear what he's offering!"

"Hear what? He ain't got bloody nothing that I want, and that's gospel!"

"Not even a pardon," said McLonarch, "and the chance to be an honest man?"

Silver stopped dead. He looked at McLonarch, who sat calmly in his chair in the well-furnished stern cabin that even had carpets, pictures in frames, and candlesticks. It had books too, and musical instruments: all fixed to the bulkheads in shelves with wire-mesh doors so the ship's motion shouldn't unseat them, for Captain Fitch lived in style. So it was a fine, heavy chair with carved arms that McLonarch had chosen, and which he occupied like a throne, while gazing down his nose at John Silver.

"Pah!" said Silver.

But McLonarch, the consummate politician, having pumped Allardyce beforehand for knowledge of Silver, smiled at him.

"Captain," he said, "I hear that you were a decent man before you were forced into piracy."

"Maybe," said Silver, frowning.

"And even now," continued McLonarch, "you are renowned as a man of honour, and a beloved leader whom men trust. And one who permits no cruelty to prisoners . . ." He paused and had the satisfaction of seeing Silver blush. Nodding in emphasis, he continued: "Thus you are still – even now – a decent man."

"Huh!" said Silver, but such was the power of McLonarch's personality, and the aura of aristocracy that hung about him, that Silver had the feeling that he'd just heard the definitive, official pronouncement upon himself, as if a judge in court had spoken.

"Captain Silver," said McLonarch, "what I offer you is my master's royal pardon, together with such pension as shall enable you to become again the honest mariner that you once were, washed clean of all past offences, of whatsoever kind or description."

There was silence. The words were magical, mystical. They were a dream. Silver thought of Selena. He thought of the normal life she wanted, and he was drawn into McLonarch's web, and dared to believe. But then he frowned.

"What about my lads?" he said. "Them what chose me, under articles."

McLonarch beamed.

"God bless you, John Silver!" he said. "Had I entertained the least doubt, it would now be gone. Only such a man as I believed you to be would think first of the men he leads, and it is my pleasure to assure you that the same free pardon shall extend to them."

"See, Cap'n?" said Allardyce. "Didn't I tell you?"

"There could even be more . . ." said McLonarch.

"Oh?" said Silver.

"Are you a Catholic?"

Silver shrugged. "I was raised that way, my father being a Portugee."

McLonarch nodded.

"Then know that I am empowered by the Holy Father to reward those who assist my sacred mission." He paused as one does who makes a mighty offer. "I am empowered to grant the rank and dignity of the Order of the Golden Spur!"

"A papal knighthood?" said Silver, and twisted under deep emotions. But he looked McLonarch in the eye. "See here," he said, "Bonnie Prince Charlie's shut up in Italy. He had his chance at Culloden, and got beat!" He shook his head. "Give up, milord. Your cause is lost!"

"Lost?" said McLonarch. "Give up? Did Charles II give up when exiled to Holland with the world saying Cromwell had won? *No!* He kept faith for eleven years in exile . . . yet returned in triumph, with the cathedral bells pealing, the great guns sounding, and the people rejoicing in the streets!"

It was true. Silver was impressed. But he was cautious too, because maybe this wasn't the only bargain in the market?

"Pretty words, milord," he said. "But just for the moment I'm sending you back among the others. I'll spare you the irons, but I'm done talking."

"Well enough, Captain," said McLonarch, satisfied for the moment.

The prisoner went off with Allardyce bowing and scraping behind him, leaving Silver alone with his thoughts, but it wasn't long before Allardyce came clumping back with men behind him. They burst in without knocking. They were looking for trouble.

"What's this?" said Silver. Allardyce looked behind him for support.

"Go on!" they growled.

"Cap'n!" said Allardyce. "We must take *Himself* safe aboard *Walrus*!"

"Oh? And is it *yourself* giving orders now, Mr Allardyce?"

"Tell him!" said the rest.

"We must save him," cried Allardyce, "for he's the McLonarch!"

"Oh, stow it!" said Silver. "D'you think I'm not taking him anyway?"

"Oh . . ." they said.

"Aye!" said Silver. "Now get about your blasted duties!"

"Oh," they said, and, "Aye-aye, Capn'." And with that they trooped out, looking sheepish.

Alone once more, Silver sighed. What he hadn't told them was that McLonarch was too big a prize to let go. Maybe King George would make an offer for him? Even if he did, Silver knew that he was pressed into a corner and he'd need to be very careful of the Jacobites among his own crew from hereon. Wearily he went up on deck, and found Israel Hands by the mizzenmast, gleefully making notes of the prize's cargo.

"Where's that swab that had hold of McLonarch?" said Silver.

"Norton?" said Hands. "He's forrard, with the rest."

"Bring him here!"

"Aye-aye, Cap'n!"

Norton came at the double, with two men behind him bearing cutlasses. Silver watched his approach, noting the way he darted nimbly across the crowded deck, leaping up the ladder from the waist to the quarterdeck, as if it were second nature to him. And when he was brought up before Silver, who stood looming over him, parrot on shoulder, Norton never flinched. He was a hard case, all right.

"You sent for me, Cap'n," he said, and touched his hat like a seaman.

Cheeky bugger, thought Silver, looking him over. He wore a smart suit of clothes in biscuit-coloured calico and a straw tricorne. By the sound of his voice, he was almost a gentleman, but not quite.

"Just what are you, mister?" said Silver, and saw him blink and think before making a very bold admission.

"I'm a Bow Street man," he said, "a runner. Sent out to arrest Lord McLonarch on a royal warrant."

Silver whistled. "A thief taker? A gallows-feeder?"

"Some call me that."

"And there's gentlemen o' fortune as would hang you for it!"

Norton blinked again, this time in fright.

"Oh, stow it," said Silver, waving away the threat. "Just look at him there!" He pointed down the length of the ship to where McLonarch stood head and shoulders above all the prisoners. "Tell me what that man is, and why you was sent to get him."

"He's the '45 all over again."

"How's that?"

"What d'you know about Jacobites?"

"Plenty!" said Silver.

"And there's plenty of 'em left. Even in the colonies."

"Is there?"

"Yes. *They* raised the dollars."

"Why'd he want the money? For himself?"

"No! He already had the men, but not the funds."

"And now he's got the money he needs . . .?"

"He's well on the way to getting it. And have you spoken to him? *Listened* to him?"

"Aye! Never heard the like!"

Norton nodded. "And he knows all the old families, and the colonels of all the regiments."

"Are you saying he could do it? Raise rebellion?"

"We don't know. But we fear that he might."

"Who's *we*?"

"The Lord Chancellor, the cabinet, and me."

"Bugger me!" said Silver. "Precious high company you keep." Then a thought struck him: "Hold hard, my jolly boy . . ." He frowned. "If McLonarch is so bleedin' dangerous, why was just yourself sent out to nab him?"

"A naval expedition couldn't be sent for fear of someone warning McLonarch."

"Jacobites in the navy?"

"Perhaps. So I was sent quietly, with five good men."

"Only five?"

"*Them* . . . and papers for me to command local forces."

"So where are they? Your men?"

Norton sighed. "Dead or wounded, as are several dozen colonial militiamen."

"And what about the Jacobites? How many of them are dead?"

"I lost count."

Silver laughed. He liked Norton. But there was more. Silver put his head on one side and looked at the tough, self-assured man who stood so sure on a rolling deck.

"Are you a seaman, Mr Norton?" he said.

Norton shrugged. "I can hand, reef and steer."

"Aye! But I'll warrant you ain't no foremast hand."

"Not I!" said Norton with pride. "I was first mate aboard a Bristol slaver."

"Ah!" said Silver. "The blackbird trade? That breeds good seamen!"

"Them as it don't kill!" said Norton and saw the respect in Silver's eyes. But then he wished he'd kept his trap shut.

"Right then, my cocker," said Silver, grinning. "Whatever else I take out of this ship . . ." he looked the prize up and down ". . . I'm having *you!*"

"What?"

"Aye! 'Cos I've two cock-fumbling bodgers for navigators what can't find their own arseholes with a quadrant, and I want at least one bugger aboard what can!"

On *Walrus*'s quarterdeck, Selena smiled at Mr Joe, the young black who'd once been a plantation slave and was now gunner's mate. He was a slim, handsome man, with a rakish patch covering a lost eye, and was further distinguished by the heavy Jamaican cane-cutlass that he wore in his belt instead of the customary sea-service weapon.

"Thank you, Mr Joe," she said.

"That ain't no matter, ma'am," said Joe. "I'll have your box brought up, an' if you wants to leave the ship, ma'am, why so you shall!" And Mr Joe stepped forward to send a man for the box –

"Stand clear there!" cried Dr Cowdray, ship's surgeon. "Stand clear!" Cowdray was hurrying aft from the waist, followed by four men bearing the broken-legged Dusty Miller on an improvised stretcher.

Miller was whining pitifully and shedding tears. "Ow! Ow!" he cried. "Rum, for the love o' fucking Jesus!"

"Later, sir!" cried Cowdray. "You shall have rum to ease the reduction of your limb. Indeed: *fiat haustus*! Let the draught be prepared!"

"Ugh!" said Selena, catching sight of Miller's injury.

"Oh mother!" said Mr Joe, for the leg was crooked into a right-angle between ankle and knee, and a bloodied end of bone stuck out through the flesh of the shin.

"Here!" cried Miller, seeing their reactions, and grabbing at Cowdray's arm. "You ain't gonna cut orf my fucking leg, now . . . are you?"

"*Stultum est timere quod vitare non potes*!" said Cowdray. "Do not fear that which you cannot prevent!"

"Ahhhhh!" screamed Miller. "You bastard! You ain't cutting orf my sodding leg, you mother-fucking sawbones!"

"No, sir," cried Cowdray, "you misunderstand. We shall *save* it!"

The surgeon was frowning as if in utmost concern, but inwardly he was rejoicing. As ever when *Walrus* went into action he was ready for the wounded in a fresh-boiled linen apron, sleeves rolled up, spectacles on his nose. And now, here was a wonderful case of compound fracture to test his skills, since – unlike most surgeons – he believed amputation to be unnecessary. With cleanliness and care, the limb could be saved – and he was itching to prove it.

"Let 'em through," said Mr Joe, and he stood back as Cowdray, still spouting Latin, manoeuvred his patient down a hatchway, addressing the filthy-tongued Miller with the same courteous politeness he'd used towards honest patients years ago.

When they'd gone, Selena looked to *Venture's Fortune*, heaving up and down on the ocean swell alongside of *Walrus*, the lines that bound them together creaking and stretching under the strain. "She's home-bound to England, isn't she, Joe?"

"Aye, ma'am. Bound for Polmouth with rum and sugar under hatches."

"And will Long John let her go?"

"Once we've plucked her. That's Long John's way."

"Good. Then I'll go aboard . . . and leave with her."

"But –"

"*Don't!*" she said. "I won't live this life. I've told Long John."

Mr Joe tried, nonetheless. He told her that she'd never even *seen* England, and had no friends there, and that – should she be recognised – the crimes she'd committed in the colonies would hang her just as dead in the mother country. And he reminded her of Silver: fine man that he was, and how the hands would follow him "down the cannon's mouth" when it came to action: a bad choice of words in the circumstances, but the best Mr Joe could think of.

Wasted words, all of them. When he'd done, Selena – in her print gown and straw hat – attempted to clamber over two ships' scraping, bumping rails that weren't even hard alongside but divided by a gap of a yard or more that opened and closed like a crocodile's jaws, with the white water frothing far below. Finally Mr Joe lifted her up and heaved her over bodily, into the arms of the men aboard *Isabelle Bligh*, who surged forward on sight of her, gaping and wondering, stretching their arms to catch her, and nervously glancing back at Long John, for every man aboard knew about their quarrels.

Then her sea chest came after her with a bump and a thump, with her few goods and the money she'd saved, and the men stood back, touched their brows and doubled to their duties again with Israel Hands and Tom Allardyce yelling at them.

Selena's heart was beating, she had no idea what to do, she hadn't even thought about how she might be received aboard this ship. Long John (who had his back to her) was deep in conversation with a hard-faced man in a calico suit. He didn't see her, or hear, so she was left to look at the ship, which was well found, spanking new, and bursting with activity as *Walrus*'s men hoisted up a series of heavy chests from the waist and swung them back aboard their own ship.

She looked forrard and saw the men, and some women, crammed into the fo'c'sle under guard. Instinctively she made her way down the ship towards them, *Walrus*'s men stepping aside to let her past, all of them giving the same uneasy glance towards Long John, who was still engrossed with the hard-faced man.

"What's this, ma'am? What're you a-doing of?" said Israel Hands, looking up from the notebook where he'd been making a record of the cargo. He frowned and, as the others had done, glanced in Long John's direction, then seemed about to speak, but up above a chest slid out of its lashings, and fell, and men jumped aside as it smashed open and showered silver dollars on the deck.

"You slovenly buggers!" cried Hands. "You idle swabs! You . . ."

Selena walked on, squeezing past the toiling seamen, stumbling now and again at the ship's sickening, rolling motion, and made her way to the fo'c'sle and past the guards and blinked at the prisoners. There was a crowd of seamen, a few officers, and some landmen – presumably passengers – and two women. They stared at Selena, not knowing what to make of her, though the men looked her over as all men did at first sight.

"Ah-hem!" said a little man: squat, short, and heavy, in a big hat and a long shiny-buttoned coat. He touched his hat and smiled, and was about to speak, when one of the two women pushed past him and threw out her arms to Selena.

"My dear!" she cried. "My poor creature! I see that, like ourselves, you were made prisoner by these wicked pirates!"

"Oh!" said the short man. "*Ahhh!*"

"Ahhhh!" said the rest, nodding wisely to one another.

"Yes!" said Selena, seizing upon this excellent explanation, which was so obvious that it was amazing she'd not thought of it herself.

The woman advancing upon Selena was in her mid-fifties with twinkling eyes, a tiny nose and delicate bones in a neat-little, sweet-little, dear-little face. She was expensively dressed, and had the speech and manners of a noblewoman, with artfully contrived gestures. She smiled radiantly at the world, and she simpered and flirted at men. She did it so well that it had never failed to control them, not once in forty years. Nonetheless, she was utter contrast to Selena, for while the lady – despite her years – was quite glitteringly *pretty*, she was not *beautiful*. She did not have that spiritual quality that Selena had, which takes the breath away and makes mortals stare, and stare, and worship. She was merely pretty, like a china fairy.

"My dear!" said the lady, "I am Mrs Katherine Cooper: Mrs Cooper of Drury Lane." She laughed, a sound like a tinkling bell, and added: "I have some reputation as a thespian."

"Aye!" said the rest, nodding among themselves, for Mrs Cooper's reputation had been spread assiduously by Mrs Cooper, and they were very well aware of it.

"*Thespian*?" said Selena, for this was not a word in everyday use aboard ship.

"Actress, my dear," said Mrs Cooper, embracing Selena. "But you must call me *Katty*, for it is my pet name among my friends."

"Ahhhh!" sighed the audience as Selena closed her eyes and rested her head on Katty Cooper's shoulder, inexpressibly relieved to be amongst perfumed femininity and not rum-soaked, sweat-soaked, sailormen.

But her moment of contentment was brief. Behind her she heard the distinctive thump, thump, thump . . . of John Silver's timber leg advancing up the deck.

64

Chapter 8

*T*he storm was not a great one, but it nearly did for
Oraclaesus. It came roaring out of the night, with streaks
of black cloud chasing the moon and the white spray steaming
off the wave-tops.

Soaked from stem to stern, the big frigate heeled far over
under the steady blow, the splendid curves of her hull enabling
her to ride the glossy rollers, but she dipped at every down-
ward plunge, and heaved up again with green water pouring
from her head rails and figurehead.

Oraclaesus was doing her utmost best, and was a credit
to the men of Woolwich naval dockyard who built her.
Nonetheless, she was riding out the storm only because of
the seamanship and foresight of her new commander, Joe
Flint. For Captain Baggot had long since been heaved over
the side, sewn up in a hammock with a roundshot at his feet:
him and all his sea-service officers, together with Mr Lemming,
the surgeon, who never did recognise the disease that killed
him. These great ones were gone, together with over a hundred
of the ship's lesser people, who received ever-more perfunc-

tory funeral rites as Flint grew tired of reading the service and the surviving hands, exhausted and over-worked, despaired of the whole dreadful process.

So the ship was surviving – and only just – because, with too few men to work her in a blow, and foul weather only to be expected in these latitudes at this time of year, Flint had long since sent down t'gallant masts and yards, taken in the fore and main courses, and set only close-reefed topsails and storm staysails: a task the hands could manage in easy weather. This left the ship with bare steerage way, but saved her when the storm struck, for otherwise she'd have lost her masts, rolled on her beam ends, and drowned every soul aboard of her.

Now Flint and Billy Bones stood braced on the soaking, sloping planks, hanging on by the aid of the storm-lines rigged across the deck, and draped in the tarred blouses and breeches they'd taken from dead men's stores. They huddled together to yell into each other's ears against the howling wind and the dense salt spray that came up over the bow at every plunge of the ship, drenching as far back as the quarterdeck. But however hard they shouted, the wind blew away the sound such that no other could hear: not even ten feet away at the ship's wheel where the helmsmen were fighting to hold the ship on course.

"It's no good," said Flint.

"It ain't neither, Cap'n!" said Billy Bones.

"We must have more men. We'll not survive another like this!"

"And we ain't steering no course. Just running afore the wind."

"When this blows over, I shall signal *Bounder* and *Jumper* to come alongside."

"What about Mr Povey? He's aboard *Bounder* and he'll blab to all hands!"

"Yes, but –"

66

Flint was about to argue that, without more men, they'd die anyway. But the storm spoke more persuasively, with a roar and a crackling from above, like the volley of a thousand muskets, as the wind got its claws fairly into the fore topsail and ripped it from its reefs and flogged it and shredded it and blew it out into streaming rags that stretched ahead of the ship and threw off bits of themselves to vanish instantly into the howling night.

"Bugger me!" said Billy Bones.

"Helmsman!" cried Flint, stepping close to the wheel.

"Aye-aye, sir!" said the senior man.

"Can you hold her?"

"Aye-aye, Cap'n!"

Flint came back to Billy Bones, hauling himself hand over hand by a storm-line, and leaning his head close to Bones's.

"She'll run like a stallion in this. She'd run under bare poles –" he looked at the men at the wheel "– so long as they don't tire."

"Shall I send up fresh hands?"

"No! Can't risk it. They'd take time to get the feel of the helm, and we could be broached-to and rolled over while they do."

Billy Bones nodded. The wheel was a double, with spokes radiating out from either end of the drum round which the steering tackles were rove. That meant two big wheels, one ahead of the other, such that four men – one to each side of each wheel – could steer as a team in heavy weather. It was a task best left to those who'd got the knack of it, working with *these* particular shipmates, under *these* particular conditions.

"Aye-aye, Cap'n," said Billy Bones.

"So," said Flint, "there's something *else* we can do in the meanwhile, for we're no help to these excellent men at the helm."

Billy Bones couldn't actually see the leer on Flint's face. It

67

was too dark for that, but he knew it would be there, and he trembled in a fright that had nothing to do with the storm.

For a storm was nothing to Billy Bones. Standing on a wet wooden slope with the wind shrieking in his ears was nothing to him. Likewise, the cold seawater that got under his collar and ran down his neck. And neither did he fear the tremendous power of the elements that could take a ship, and break it and sink it and drown him. All that was meat and drink to Billy Bones. He'd faced it all his life, and if ever he pondered on so philosophical a matter as his own death – why, Billy Bones would naturally *expect* it to come at sea, in a storm, and a fitting seaman's death it would be an' all! So he wasn't afraid of the weather . . . only Joe Flint, the infinitely charismatic Flint, whom he feared and worshipped all at once, as if by evil enchantment.

Meanwhile Flint was speaking:

"Stand to your duty!" he yelled to the helmsmen.

"Aye-aye, sir!"

"Mr Bones and I am going below."

"Aye-aye!"

"We shall soon return."

"Aye-aye!"

Beckoning Billy Bones to follow, Flint made his way through the dark night and the screeching wind, with the rain and spray lashing his face so hard he could barely breathe, and the ship heaving up and down, twenty feet at a time, beneath his feet. Sight was nearly useless and he went by feel, storm-lines, and seaman's instinct.

There was no hatchway on the quarterdeck, so he descended the larboard gangway ladder to the maindeck, and groped his way aft beneath the quarterdeck, where there was shelter at least from the wind and wet. Around them the great guns strained and heaved in their lashings, ever seeking the opportunity to snap a rotten tackle and break loose for a playful plunge about the deck, grinding and smashing and killing . . .

Except that there was nobody to kill, only Flint and Billy Bones; the few others aboard were either up above or down below. The main deck, the *gun* deck which was the raison d'être of a man o' war was unnaturally empty of men.

In the darkness, Flint went just aft of the capstan and forrard of the bulkhead that divided off the captain's quarters and slipped carefully down the ladderway to the lower deck. And there he paused, with his back against a cabin door, until Billy Bones came rumbling after him.

There was no weather at all down here, and the mighty voice of the wind was shut out by solid oak that admitted only a dull, demonic wailing. But all the wooden music of ship's noises was playing: the creaks, squeaks and grumblings of eight hundred tons of carpentry, fighting to stay together while the wind and the sea tried to pull it apart.

Flint tingled with sudden excitement. He blinked in the black darkness, relieved only by a few feeble lanterns. Pulling off his tarred frock, he dumped it under one of the lanterns so it could easily be found; tarred clothes rustled and made a noise, and were awkward. Billy Bones did likewise. Flint sniffed. It still smelled vile down here, but better than it had done. There were only a few sufferers still alive in their hammocks, and the hands had got ahead with their swabbing. Flint peered in the darkness and made out the shape of a few hammocks up forrard. He grinned. They were of no concern. His interests lay aft.

Just astern was the bulkhead, and the door that led to the gun-room: province of the ship's gentlemen, where Lieutenant Hastings and the Reverend Doctor Stanley were laid in their cots, deciding whether to live or to die of the smallpox.

Flint sniggered. This hadn't been possible before. Even with only twenty men in the ship, there had always been someone to see and to notice, some servile clown bringing food or drink for *the poor gentlemen*. Flint laughed. Billy Bones jumped. Flint pulled his nose.

"Nobody here but you and me, Mr Bones," he said. "It will be so easy!" And he crept aft, opened the door to the gun-room and passed inside . . . soundless, purposeful and malevolent as a vampire. Clump! Clump! Billy Bones followed, and Flint frowned at the spoiling of the moment.

"Shhh!" he said.

"Sorry, Cap'n."

Flint looked round. There was one lantern only. The gun-room had no natural light. It was mainly occupied by a great table running fore and aft, with a little passageway on either beam and rows of doors leading into the tiny cabins that lined up against the ship's sides. The place was crowded with the traps and tackles of the ship's officers: quadrants, swords, books, old newspapers, gun-cases and silver mugs hanging on hooks. It smelled of snuff and claret – not surprising, considering the quantities of these stimulants that had been consumed in this small space.

"Cap'n," said Billy Bones, "I wants to say summat."

"Shhh!" said Flint.

"But, Cap'n –"

"Shut up!" Flint was listening . . . for breathing . . . coughing . . . anything.

"I wants to say –"

"Ah!" Flint darted forward and pulled open a door. It was canvas stretched on a wooden frame. The cabins themselves were made only of thin pine boards. "Fetch the lantern, Billy-my-chicken," said Flint, entering the dark space. Just seven feet long by six feet wide, it was barely enough to hold a few sticks of furniture and a bed where a man lay stretched out, his mouth open, the sweat glistening on his face. He was unconscious but alive, and sleeping soundly.

"Cap'n, you're a fine seaman, as all hands agree, and –"

"Oh, shut up, Billy! D'you know – I do believe this one would survive!"

"– and you know as how I'd follow you wherever you lead –"

"Bring the lantern. See! The skin's not peeling off any more."

Billy Bones brought the light and he and Flint looked down on Dr Stanley. The chaplain didn't look the same without his clerical wig, but it was him all right, and he was definitely not dying.

"Cap'n!" said Billy Bones. "I akses you . . . *not to.*"

Flint frowned. "Not to *what*, Mr Bones?"

"Not to do it, Cap'n."

"Shut up, Billy! Just you hold his arms."

"Don't, Cap'n. *Please.*"

Flint turned to look at Billy Bones as he stood with the lantern raised and his dark, ugly face gleaming in the amber light. Bones was shaking with fear, but he looked his master in the eye and begged:

"Don't do it, Cap'n. Let's be better men than that!"

"What's wrong with you?" said Flint. "Brace up!"

Billy Bones shook his head. "No, Cap'n. I ain't gonna do it."

And there, alone in the heaving, groaning dark of the lower deck, Billy Bones faced the Devil coming out of Hell as Flint turned the full force of his personality upon him: the maniac personality, hidden by a handsome face, which was Flint's fearful strength. It was his strength even above the fact that he moved so swift and deadly in a fight that he was terrifying in a merely physical sense. But it wasn't *that* which frightened men who looked into Flint's eyes. It was something else, something uncanny and deep, and which now burst forth in its fury: scourging and burning . . . and shrivelling Billy Bones's honest little attempt at humanity into futile, smoking ashes.

Billy Bones could never recall what it was that Flint said to him – for it was all done with words, and never a finger raised – but those few minutes in Dr Stanley's cabin became the evil dread of nightmares that woke Billy Bones, sweat-soaked and howling, from his sleep for the rest of his life.

After that – having been disciplined – he was made to hold Stanley's arms while Flint smothered the good doctor with his own pillow for the crime of being too clever by half. Next, Flint found the cabin where Lieutenant Hastings lay: just eighteen years old and already dying. Billy Bones was made to hold *his* arms too. Billy wept as he did it, but could not resist.

"And now only Mr Povey is left . . ." said Flint, and smiled.

Chapter 9

Early morning, 23rd March 1753
Upper Barbados
The Caribbean

The four forts that guarded Williamstown bay mounted between them nigh-on fifty twenty-four-pounder guns, and they were excellently placed, high above the sea, with a clear field of fire into the channel whereby ships entered the bay.

They were capable of resisting anything less than a major battlefleet, and even one of those couldn't be sure of forcing an entry: not with one pair of forts at the mouth of the bay, where it narrowed to less than a quarter of a mile's width, and the second pair placed to sweep the approaches just north of Williamstown's harbour. Thus, the last time the attempt had been made – British intruders vs Spanish defenders – the fleet was driven off trailing blood and wreckage, and the town was taken only by landing five thousand redcoats at Porta Colomba, ten miles to the south east, and marching them overland with a siege train.

"Huh!" said Israel Hands, as *Walrus* came through the jaws of the bay, right under the guns of the outermost forts. "Wouldn't believe this was safe haven for the likes of us!"

Long John frowned, irritably.

"And why not?" he said. "Ain't we flying British colours

73

like them?" He pointed up at the forts. "And haven't we just saluted King George with all our guns?"

"Aye," said Israel Hands. And forcing a grin, he waved a hand at the smoke still hanging about the ship. "But you know what I mean, Cap'n. It's all down to Sir Wyndham, God bless him!"

Sir Wyndham Godfrey, governor of Upper Barbados, was a figure of fun among sailormen. He'd been a scourge of piracy until the bribes grew too great to refuse, and now he closed his eyes and opened his hand, such that men chuckled at the thought of him, and Israel Hands was hoping to cheer up Long John by the mention of his name. But Silver merely sniffed and turned away, stroking the parrot and staring at nothing.

Hands sighed. He'd been like that, had Long John, ever since Selena went off aboard *Venture's Fortune* to make her fortune in London. It weren't right for a seaman to take it so hard when he lost his doxy. There was always more of *them*. You soon forgot. Especially when you dropped anchor in a new port.

"Bah!" he said, and stopped fretting over John Silver, and looked instead at all the busy activity aboard *Walrus*: anchors were off the bows and hung by ring-stoppers at the catheads, bent to the cables flaked out on deck ready for letting go. The ship was scrubbed clean from bow to stern and under easy sail as she came up the dredged channel.

All hands, with the exception of Long John, were delighted at the prospect of going ashore. This was especially true of the two redundant navigators, who stood grinning at approaching freedom. But the shore party would not include the McLonarch, who was locked up below, or Mr Norton, who had been allowed above decks to check the course to Upper Barbados, only to be locked up again as soon as it was sighted. He was now the most miserable creature aboard.

Putting his glass to his eye, Israel Hands focused on the

town, less than a mile away, with its whitewashed buildings – tiers and layers of them, rising up the flanks of the bayside mountain still known by its Spanish name of Sangre de Cristo – blood of Christ – for the rosy colour it took in the sunset, as did the white houses themselves. He shifted the glass to the excellent dockyards, which included dry docks capable of receiving anything up to a ship of the line.

And he looked at the offshore anchorage, which was full of every imaginable kind of vessel, with countless masts and yards, and busy boats pulling to and fro. There was one ship ahead of *Walrus* in the channel, coming into the wind to anchor, while yet another was astern of her, coming through the jaws of the bay.

It was a wonderful sight. After so many weeks at sea, alone on the empty ocean, it made *any* man cheerful to see such life. Overhead the gulls wheeled and called, the sun shone bright and hot, the sky was blue, the wind was fresh . . . and Long John was eating his heart out in despair.

Bugger! thought Israel Hands.

Later, with *Walrus* moored, Israel Hands took his place in the launch with six oarsmen done out in their best rig, and Long John, Allardyce and Dr Cowdray in the stern. These chosen ones would make first contact with the shore authorities – just to be sure, just to be careful – for there was much to be done and arranged before any of the rest of the crew would be allowed to partake of the whoring and boozing and fighting that was any seaman's honest amusement, fresh ashore . . . especially gentlemen o' fortune.

"Give way!" cried Allardyce, and the boat began pulling for the harbour. All aboard looked back at the strange sight of the ship which had been their home, now seen in its entirety, bobbing at anchor among the innocent merchantmen . . . not that all of them were *quite* that innocent. *Walrus* wasn't the only ship with a black flag in her locker. Not in Williamstown Bay.

"Look!" said Allardyce. "She's down by the head. You'll have to haul some guns astern, Israel."

"Not I!" said Hands merrily. "Shift the sodding cargo aft!"

Allardyce grinned.

"What cargo?" he said. "Only cargo we've got is dollars!"

"Clap a hitch!" cried Silver nastily. "Who knows what bugger's listening!"

They looked round the harbour. There wasn't a human being within earshot. They made faces behind Silver's back and fell silent.

Ashore, Silver, Allardyce and Israel Hands went to the harbour master's office, while the six hands – chosen for their ability to stay sober – were let off the leash, bar one unfortunate who was left to guard the boat.

Dr Cowdray set off into town by himself in search of medical stores, and replacements for some of his worn-out instruments. Having found what he wanted, he then spent a pleasant couple of hours in the cool, shady streets, shaking off hawkers and beggars, enjoying the sight of women and children after so long in the company of men, and looking into the shops, especially bookshops. Then he searched for a tavern – a respectable one – for a drink and a meal, for the rendezvous was hours away yet.

He knew he had found just the place when he clapped eyes on the Copper Kettle. Situated on the shady side of King William Square, it looked bright and clean, with a long awning and tables in the fresh air. The clientele was entirely respectable, with waiters in long white aprons attending, while the vulgar populace was kept back by a fence of neat white posts with chains slung between. Cowdray stepped forward with purpose, but:

"Oh!" he said, and stopped with his bundle of books and his brown paper parcel of medical gear. He dithered and stuck his load under one arm so he could wipe the sweat from his brow with his handkerchief. In amongst the respectable patrons of the Copper Kettle, seated at a table, his parrot on his shoulder, was Long John Silver. In his current foul mood, the captain made the worst imaginable company.

Cowdray stood in the hot, scented air of a tropical spice-island. It would soon be noon, and the sun was fierce. The streets were emptying as people headed indoors ... and Cowdray was thirsty ... then ... *Ah!* Debate was irrelevant. Silver had seen him.

"Captain!" said Cowdray, advancing across the square, through the gate in the fence, to take the seat beside Silver. The latter nodded miserably. Cowdray unloaded his goods, and took off his hat in the welcome shade.

"Pffffff!" he said, and fanned himself with his hat.

"*Salve, Medicus!*" said the parrot, greeting Cowdray in Latin as she always did. At least the bird was pleased to see him.

"*Salve, avis sapiens!*" said Cowdray. "Hallo, clever bird!"

"Ain't she, though?" said Silver, stroking the green feathers. "And you love Long John, don't you?"

"Love Long John!" she said, and bobbed and nodded and rubbed her head against his with every sign of affection. Silver smiled, a real smile, and he turned to Cowdray to make apology.

"Sorry, Doctor," he said, "I ain't no use at present, not to man nor beast."

"Not you, Captain!" said Cowdray stoutly. Another sigh was Silver's only response.

Then a waiter came, and they ordered food and drink, and sat silent for a bit, and the victuals were served, and Silver went heavy on the drink, and at last the two fell into conversation. Perhaps it was the rum. Perhaps it was because Cowdray wasn't properly a gentleman o' fortune, and he certainly wasn't a seaman, and he *was* a surgeon – the one who'd saved Long John's life by taking off his shattered leg – but Long John's misery and trouble began to tumble out bit by bit.

"What am I to do, Doctor?"

"In what respect?"

"Taking prizes? Winning dollars? Choosing allies?" Silver shook his head. "All of it, Doctor. Living my bleedin' life! *What* soddin' life? What am I? Who am I?"

"Oh!" said Cowdray. He was a surgeon, but like any medical man he knew that men can be wounded in the mind as badly as in the body, and that such wounds could be severe. He glanced at Silver. To Cowdray, Silver was still young: thirty-two? Thirty-three? Cowdray could almost have been his father; moreover he liked Silver and wanted to help. He thought of something to say, to get Silver talking . . . to explore the wound.

"You let the prize go," he said, "*Venture's Fortune*. Why did you do that?"

"Had to," said Silver morosely, "or we'd not be refitting in that dockyard yonder."

"Is that arranged?"

Silver nodded. "It was just a matter of money," he said. "And plenty of it."

"Why didn't you keep the prize?"

Silver shrugged. "We'd get away with that once or twice, but *he*'d find out in the end."

"Sir Wyndham Godfrey?"

"Aye. He issues these *Protections*. I saw one in Cap'n Higgs's desk." Silver shook his head irritably. "You see," he said, "if we . . . *I* . . . am to follow this life, we need a port."

"Like this one?"

"This is the *only* bloody one, damn near! So we can't upset him what owns it."

"King George, you mean?"

Silver laughed and the parrot squawked loudly.

"And that's another thing," said Silver. "I've got to choose between them two under hatches aboard ship: Lord *fancy-drawers-McBollock*, and Mr *Bow Street* Norton, both of 'em reckoning they've a king behind 'em. So which do we favour?"

"You took Norton as a navigator . . ."

"Aye, but he might be useful as a go-between with the law."

"I see," said Cowdray. "And in the meantime you stole Bonnie Prince Charlie's dollars . . ."

"And how long would I've been cap'n if I hadn't?"

"Hmm," said Cowdray. "Of course, Allardyce is for McLonarch."

"Him and others! They worship the paper he wipes his arse on."

"What do *you* think?" said Cowdray.

Silver sighed heavily. "See here, Doctor, there could be pardons in this for all hands. McLonarch has offered one, but *only* if Prince Charlie comes home . . . while maybe we could get one out of King George for handing McLonarch over – if Allardyce would let us." Silver shook his head, and took another hefty pull from his tankard. "And there's civil war brewing if McLonarch gets home, and no way of knowing which side might win . . . or even if we should try to *stop* it, for the bloodshed it would mean for all England."

"I see," said Cowdray. "But why need there be a decision now? We could take both men to England, ask questions when we get there, and decide *then* what to do with them." He bowed his head in thought. "The great prize would be a pardon. That would be precious beyond riches." He looked up, the evidence weighed, a decision reached: "We should go to England! Then, at worst, if the matter proves too complex, we could set Norton and McLonarch ashore in two different places – thus keeping Allardyce happy and ourselves still holding the dollars."

"Bugger me blind!" said Silver, tipping back his hat and gazing at Cowdray in admiration. "Where have you been all these months, Doctor? You never speak at our councils and yet here you are, the sharpest man aboard!"

"I never thought the hands would listen to a sawbones," said Cowdray.

"Well, I'm damned," said Silver. "You almost persuaded me."

"Oh? Will you not go to England?"

"I don't know. The risk is so great. We might be found out. We might be taken . . ." He looked around King William Square. "*This* place might be up for bribes, but the Port of London won't be. And the seas'd be thick with navy."

"Well," said Cowdray, looking sideways at Silver, "England is where your wife has gone . . ."

Silver groaned and rubbed his face with his hands, for *that* was the heart of his troubles, not the choice between McLonarch and Norton. It was the unspoken pain that not even Cowdray had dared mention until now.

"Did you hear what she said to me?" said Silver. "Aboard the prize?"

"No. I was down below, reducing Mr Miller's fracture of the tibio-fibula."

"Oh. How's he doing?"

"Nicely, Captain. I am pleased to say that he will walk again on two legs!"

"Huh!" said Silver.

"Oh!" said Cowdray, mortified. "I do apologise. How thoughtless. I am so sorry."

Silver sighed again.

"I tried to stop her," he said. "Told her what *I* thought. Then she told me what *she* thought, which was 'no more gentleman o' fortune' . . . and so we fell to hammer and tongs again, and then that pretty-faced cow stepped up and took her part, and said she'd carry my girl off to England and make a great actress out of her. And she believed it, and so she went."

"What pretty-faced cow?"

"The actress. She's supposed to be famous in England."

"Who told you that?"

"Cap'n Fitch and the rest, aboard *Venture's Fortune*."

80

"What was her name?"

"Cooper. Mrs Katherine Cooper of Drury Lane. Said my Selena was so beautiful – which she is – that she *must* succeed upon the stage." He smiled sadly. "I hope she does."

Cowdray shot bolt upright in his chair.

"Captain," he said, "was this a small, very pretty woman in her fifties?"

"Aye. That'd be her."

"And her name was Katherine Cooper?"

"Aye."

"*Katty* Cooper?"

"I did hear that was her name . . . among friends."

"Friends?" said Cowdray. "Friends be damned! Katty's her *professional* name. She's no actress! She's *Cat-House* Cooper, the procuress! She ran the biggest brothel in the Caribbean, and made a speciality of importing fresh young black girls from the plantations. God help us . . . we've sent Selena to London to be made a whore!"

Chapter 10

An hour after dawn (there being no watches kept nor bells struck)
2nd April 1753
Aboard Oraclaesus
The Atlantic

*B*illy Bones ran from end to end of the lower deck. He'd already checked the hold.

"Ahoy!" he roared. "Shake out and show a leg!" And he beat a drum roll on the ship's timbers with a belaying pin, brought down for the purpose. Finally he stopped to listen: there was silence except for the ship's own creaking and sighing, almost as if she knew what was coming. "With me!" he said, and ran up to the main deck with two men in his wake, and roared out the same challenge.

He bellowed and yelled from end to end of the ship, past the silent guns, staggering under the sickening motion of the rolling, hove-to vessel that clattered its blocks and rattled its rigging and complained and moaned.

"Ahoy there! Show out, you lubbers!" cried Billy Bones. But nobody answered. The ship was empty except for him and his two men. Finally they checked the quarterdeck, the fo'c'sle and the tops . . . all of which they already knew to be empty. But Billy Bones checked them anyway. Only then did he give the order, and one of his men opened the lantern kept secured on the quarterdeck and took a light from the candle within, and lit the three torches: long timber treenails with greasy rags bound about their tips. Taking the torches, Billy and his accomplices doubled to the three carefully prepared fire points in the hold.

In each place a pile of inflammables had been assembled: crumpled paper, leading to scraps of small timber, leading to casks of paint, and linseed oil ready broached, and finally to stacked heaps of canvas and small spars: a vile mixture aboard a wooden ship, and one which made Billy Bones's flesh crawl, for the time he'd done the same aboard Long John's ship, *Lion*, for which action he was deeply ashamed. Old Nick would surely claim him for that deed when the time came.

But this was different. They were burning a plague ship under Captain Flint's orders, to save poor mariners from certain death should any come upon her afloat and the miasma of the sickness still aboard – which, from the stink of her, it certainly was. Bones and his men had already set *Jumper* aflame for the same reason, and now it was the frigate's turn.

Billy's face glowed in the firelight as he waited a minute to see that the fire was really under way. Then, with the crackling flames eating hot upon his cheeks, he cried: "All hands to the boat!" And he leapt to his feet and got himself smartly up on deck. Not running, for that might unsettle the hands, but moving at a brisk pace to get away from the flames now roaring down below. And he was right not to run, for the two men were waiting on deck with round eyes and mouths open in superstitious dread of what they'd done.

Billy Bones took one last look – fore, aft, aloft – at the great and beauteous work of man that they were destroying: the soaring masts, the wide yards, the sweet-curving coppered hull and the mighty guns; the cables, anchors, boats and spars; the stores of beef, beer and biscuit, of oil, pitch and tar, of candles, tallow, rope and twine. God knows what she'd cost the king and the nation!

More than that, a ship was a community afloat, bearing the cooper's adze, the tailor's shears and the chaplain's bible, together with all the small and beloved goods of her people: their books, letters and locks of true-love's hair.

By Flint's orders, all possible goods and stores had been taken off, including the squadron's war chest of two thousand pounds in gold. All else had been left behind – including the personal wealth of her officers: their purses, pistols, jewels, watches and wines – for even when it came to such precious items as these, there was a limit to what could be crammed into a sloop one quarter the size of the big frigate. And in any case, so far as Billy Bones was concerned – now increasingly believing that he served the king once more – it was grave-robbing and an unclean deed to pillage the sea-chests of brother officers.

So all these wonders were put to the flames, including the contents of the ship's two magazines: which – even leaving aside the ready-made, flannel cartridges – contained two hundred ninety-pound, copper-bound kegs holding a total of eight tons of powder.

"Go on!" said Billy, and the two hands were over the side at the main chains and scrambling down into the boat that was bumping and rolling alongside. It was a launch, chosen for speed, and six nervous men were waiting at the oars. Billy Bones's two men made eight: enough to make the launch fly. He sighed, and followed at the dignified pace of the senior man. "Give way!" he cried at last, and the oarsmen threw their weight – heart, soul, mind and strength – upon the oars in their eagerness to escape the doomed ship and her brim-full magazines.

It was woven into Billy Bones's nature to tell *any* crew of oarsmen to put their backs into it; to spur them on, just as a matter of principle . . . but even he could see that it wasn't needed on this occasion. The hands were terrified and pulling like lunatics. For one thing, they could see what was happening astern. They could see the red flames pouring out of *Leaper*'s hatches, and the smoke curling up from *Oraclaesus*. But Billy Bones thought it beneath his dignity to look back, and he steered for the distant *Bounder* where Flint awaited with the new crew, and the new future.

They were nearly alongside of her when the first explosion came, and the oarsmen lost stroke as they gaped at the ghastly sight. Now even Billy Bones couldn't resist looking, and he turned in time to see *Oraclaesus* break her back: stern and bow drooping, and midships blown clear out of the water by the enormous violence of an explosion that threw flame and smoke and fragments of smashed gear tumbling high into the air, including – hideous to see – the entire, massive, one-hundred-and-eighty-foot mainmast – topmast, t'gallant and all – hurled its own length and more, straight up, with the great yards snapping like cannon-fire and trailing a tangle of rigging and sailcloth . . . only to hang . . . and curve . . . and fall smashing and rumbling down into the blazing wreckage of the ship, throwing up sparks and flame and ash.

Billy Bones sobbed. He was a seaman born and bred, an embodiment of the sea life, and he couldn't bear to see a ship – especially so fine a ship – come to such an end. As for the oarsmen, they'd served aboard *Oraclaesus* and she'd been their home and their pride: they threw their faces into their hands and wept . . . and the launch lost way and rolled horribly, with her oars to all points of the compass.

Soon after, *Jumper* exploded, the flames for some unfathomable reason taking that bit longer to find her powder. But there were no more tears, only dull misery, for Billy Bones had his men pulling again, and running alongside *Bounder*, where he went up the side and was received by tars saluting. Having lifted his hat to the quarterdeck, he made his way aft to report.

Flint – who didn't share Mr Bones's views on grave-robbing – was immaculate in a cocked hat and the gold-laced uniform coat of a lieutenant, with a fine sword at his side. He was standing at the windward side of the quarterdeck with his officers clustered in his lee as tradition demanded. These were Lieutenant Comstock, a lad of twenty, lately in command of *Leaper* and now rated first lieutenant; the red-coated Lieutenant Lennox, who was even younger; and finally Mr Baxter, ship's carpenter, but rated a watch-keeping officer by Flint. There was also the equivocal Mr Braddock, who was no seaman at all. He'd been Captain Baggot's band-master aboard *Oraclaesus*, and being in the captain's personal service was excused fighting and flogging, and considered himself a gentleman.

Billy Bones looked at Braddock and sniffed. The lubber was full of himself and needed taking down. Then Billy glanced at the hands in the waist, and nodded in approval. Having combined the surviving crews of three ships, Flint now had a total of thirty-three men aboard *Bounder*, including twenty-five able seamen, one sergeant of marines, and two marine privates: a full and satisfactory number to work a two-hundred-ton, two-masted sloop and sail her anywhere in the wide world, especially as she was now provisioned to bursting point. Nonetheless, thirty-three was only a small complement should ever it be necessary to man her twelve six-pounders.

"I'm come aboard, Cap'n!" said Billy Bones formally, giving a smart salute.

"Well done, Mr Bones!" said Flint. "It is a sad task, that with which you were charged, but a needful one, and you have acquitted yourself well."

Billy Bones bathed in the warmth of his master's approval, and also in pride at his master's splendour and all that he had recently achieved. Flint had saved all aboard *Oraclaesus*, and made the hard decision to abandon the frigate and concentrate all hands aboard *Bounder,* and to fire the other ships. He'd persuaded the men to follow him, and had acted in so fine and officer-like a manner as to prove that he was indeed the matchless leader that Billy Bones knew him to be . . . enabling Billy Bones – despite hideous and recent experience – to hope that his beloved master had changed for the better and become – once again – the man who'd won his undying allegiance all those years ago.

The dog-like expression on Billy Bones's face was bad enough, but when Flint turned to his officers he nearly ruined his entire performance . . . for the two young lieutenants and the elderly carpenter stood to attention and touched their hats the instant his eye fell upon them. And as for the hands in the waist, standing with their hats in their hands, awaiting his orders: Flint didn't dare *look* at them.

What *dupes* they all were! What credulous morons! He'd won them round in a few days, with a bit of seamanship, an absolute denial of guilt, and a firm protestation that all the tales against him were *spite and lies* – which phrase he'd lifted bodily from Billy Bones without bothering to say thank you: not for *that* nor for the superb job Billy Bones had done in extracting innocent praise for Captain Flint out of Ben Gunn, thus commencing Flint's redemption.

So Flint fought hard not to give way, he really did, for here he was, in front of them all, posing as a loyal sea-service officer with two lieutenants calling him *sir,* and Billy Bones in raptures of joy, and the lower deck ready to eat out of his hand if he filled it with nuts. And so, and so . . . Flint frowned magnificently, and dug the nails of his right hand into the palm of his left, where they were clasped behind him, so that the pain should kill his sole and *only* admitted fault: the unfortunate reaction that his inferiors drew from him on moments like this: a desire to laugh hysterically in their faces.

But . . . *hmmm,* thought Flint, that fine gentleman Mr Braddock – that blower of horns, that performer upon the sackbut and dulcimer, and in all probability the Jew's harp as well – *he* had a frown upon his face. Flint recalled that Mr Braddock had been the most reluctant of all to set aside Captain Flint's past activities. Indeed, he'd been most decidedly insolent, and had made reference to a store of "wanted" posters – now thankfully incinerated aboard *Oraclaesus* – that the squadron had brought out to the Colonies to be pasted on every wall between New York and Savannah, denouncing *former lieutenant Flint* as a pirate and mutineer!

Yes, Flint nodded to himself, it would soon become necessary for Mr Braddock to suffer a *tragic-and-ever-to-be-regretted accident* such as – sadly – was all too common in the dangerous confines of a small ship upon the mighty ocean.

Meanwhile:

"Gentlemen!" said Flint.

"Aye-aye, sir!" they cried, and Flint suffered agonies in choking the mirth.

"Our course is to England, and Portsmouth!"

"Aye-aye, sir!"

"Mr Comstock!"

"Sir!"

"You are officer of the watch."

"Aye-aye, Cap'n!"

That nearly did it. So nearly that Flint had to pretend to cough and to splutter before recovering himself. The fool had actually called him *Captain*.

"A-hem!" said Flint. "You have the watch, Mr Comstock, to be relieved by Mr Baxter and he by others according to the standing orders I have drawn up."

"Aye-aye, sir!"

Then Flint drew upon his memories of another captain whom even Flint recognised to be a true leader of men: a man who had once been his dear friend and whom – in the dark depths of his mind – he still admired. Flint asked himself how John Silver would have behaved at that moment, and the answer came back bright and clear.

"Now then, my boys!" he cried, stepping towards the lower-deck hands. "We've come through bad times. We've come through fire and pestilence and we've seen good comrades die . . ." He paused to let the dreadful memories drag them down, then judged his moment and lifted them up: "But now," he cried, "we've forged a new crew. We've a good ship beneath us, and home lies ahead! So here's to new times and new luck aboard the good ship *Bounder*. For the ship, lads: for her and all aboard of her: hip-hip-hip –"

"Huzzah!" they roared, three times over.

"And three cheers for Cap'n Flint!" cried Billy Bones. "Hip-hip-hip –"

And they cheered, for there was indeed a damn fine officer inside of Joe Flint, along with all the rest, and Flint realised that as long as he had mastery of *Bounder* he must behave – of sheer necessity – as the very paragon of a naval officer, with no torment and exotic punishments, such as had been his way before. No! These pleasures must be set aside, and such true leadership displayed as John Silver would have done in his place, for Flint's own precious life might depend on the account of himself given by *Bounder*'s crew should ever, and *if* ever, his case come to court.

Later, with the ship plunging gallantly along, sails trimmed and lines coiled down, and all hands content, if not actually merry, Flint had a quiet word with Billy Bones, down in *Bounder*'s tiny, box-like stern cabin.

"I am optimistic, Mr Bones," said Flint.

"Are you, Cap'n? But we're sailing for England and a court martial."

"As we must! The ship's people would accept no other action. It is a vital part of our protestation of innocence. Any other course would betray us as seeking merely to escape."

Billy Bones licked his lips in fear. "Shall we go before a court then, then? One as could hang us?"

"Not if I can avoid it, Mr Bones! Much can happen on a long voyage . . ." And here Flint's talents turned to poetry:

> *Storm and adventure, heat and cold,*
> *Schooners, islands and maroons,*
> *Buccaneers and buried gold!*

Flint laughed: "Thus some men can be lost overboard, and the loyalties of others changed . . ." He turned and looked thoughtfully at Billy Bones. He looked him up and down, and this way and that . . . and smiled. "And we must get you a new coat! I have just the thing, saved from *Oraclaesus*."

"A new coat, Cap'n?" Billy Bones fingered the cuff of his old ragged coat. It was the same one he'd worn on the island. It never had fitted very well, and was now weather-stained and dirty.

"Indeed, Mr Bones," said Flint. "For it is in my mind to rate you as *acting second lieutenant*!"

Billy Bones gasped in the joy of this wonderful promotion.

"God bless you, Cap'n. But . . . can you do that?"

Flint smiled.

"Of course! Such promotions are common enough in emergencies."

"Aye," said Billy Bones, nodding wisely, for it was true.

"Of course," said Flint, "their lordships of the Admiralty, would need to confirm the promotion with a commission."

"Of course," said Billy Bones, squinting furiously and working his jaw as if chewing, the better to measure his chances with their lordships. Flint smiled again, for he saw that Billy Bones was now entirely converted into the ludicrous condition of mind that accepted the present voyage as being in the king's service and Flint as captain under the Articles of War. But Billy Bones should not be blamed for that, since there were only two men in the ship who thought differently . . .

"Lieutenant Bones," said Flint.

"Aye-aye, Cap'n!" said Billy Bones, sitting bolt upright.

"There are two problems aboard of this ship."

"Problems, Cap'n?"

"Yes. A small one and a large one."

"Cap'n?"

"There is Mr Braddock, who has no status, no evidence, and no likelihood of influencing a court martial."

"Oh . . ." said Billy Bones, brought horribly back to the present.

"Mr Braddock," said Flint, "is the *small* problem."

"Is he?"

"Oh yes, Mr Bones." Flint smiled. "But it is my feeling that, were he to . . . *disappear* –" Billy Bones gulped, for he knew what that meant, and who was likely to be responsible for the disappearance "– few tears would be shed." Flint waved a hand. "Braddock is a landman, with ideas above his station; he is not loved by the lower deck."

"Is he not, Cap'n?" said Billy Bones, in awe of his master's insight.

"He is not, Lieutenant Bones."

"Oh."

"But now we turn to the real problem . . ." Flint sighed.

"What's that, Cap'n?"

"Mr Midshipman Povey. He is one of those who was not immune to the smallpox, and who caught it, and yet survived!" Flint shook his head. "What a remarkable young gentleman he is! Despite all his cramps and pains, he kept on his feet, commanding *Bounder,* and never gave in until I arrived to take up his burden." Flint smiled. "He is now confined to his cot, in his cabin, where he is still weak but recovering."

"Aye, Cap'n," mumbled Billy Bones in despair, for he knew what was coming.

"Unlike Mr Braddock, Mr Povey is in the sea service. His word is evidence. And, most important of all, he will have the backing of the powerful Hastings family, whose son – now so tragically dead – was his close comrade." Flint looked straight into Billy Bones's eyes. "All this, upon his full recovery, gives Mr Povey as much power aboard *Bounder* as it would in a court martial, and this is a small ship, filled with sentimental tars who will watch over their brave young gentleman while he lays a-bed." Flint smiled. "So we shall have to move very carefully."

Then he laughed and looked at Billy Bones, who, so amusingly and so late, was developing a set of moral principles. They were little green shoots, tender and sweet . . . and awaiting the grinding heel.

"So there is much to do, Lieutenant . . ." Flint paused. "Assuming, of course, that you wish to keep your new rank? And your neck . . . unstretched? And your share of eight hundred thousand pounds?"

Billy Bones thought this over and hung his head in shame, for he found that he wanted to keep all these things.

"Good!" said Flint. "Now pay attention to me . . ."

Chapter 11

One minute before two bells of the forenoon watch
2nd April 1753
Aboard Venture's Fortune *on course for Polmouth*
The Atlantic

Dinner time aboard *Venture's Fortune* was an hour after noon, to allow Captain Fitch to take his observation, make his calculations and be ready at the head of the table to receive his passengers, which now included Miss Selena Henderson, the ship's darling, the delight and despair of every man aboard. It was her presence that demanded Fitch spend much more time in his cabin, before dinner, powdering his wig, washing his face, and peering into the mirror at his grimacing teeth to convince himself that they weren't too bad, and that he himself – while not the tallest of men – was a fine enough fellow for his age, and a master mariner besides.

Clang-Clang! said the ship's bell, and Fitch gave a tug at his wig, straightened his neck-cloth, took a final glance at the mirror, left his quarters and stepped the short distance to the great cabin. Aboard a big ship like *Venture's Fortune*, the cabin was spacious and elegant, and presently set for dinner with a service of fine china and real silver on the table, and a white cloth spread, and servants – foremast tars with white cotton gloves over their ever-black nails – standing by each chair, to hold everything secure against the ship's motion, which was now heavy, for they were getting the back end of a storm.

"Oof!" said Fitch, as the ship took a deep plunge. "And up she rises!" he said as the deck heaved up beneath him, and he grabbed one of the brass hand-rails that lined the cabin. They were intended for the succour of no-seaman super-cargoes, but were damned useful even to himself on days like this.

"Gentlemen!" he said as Mr O'Riley and his son entered, looking green. They were father and son, the elder being a rich planter, a man in his fifties, who'd sold up and was on his way to England to become a country gentleman. They staggered and gripped the hand-rails, gazing fearfully at the big wet waves that rolled up and down on the other side of the windows that spanned the entire stern of the cabin.

"Urgh!" said the elder O'Riley as he caught the scent of food – fish soup – in the big tureen balanced in the hands of the cook's mate. Then "*Urrrgh!*" he said, and turned on his heel, and fought his way out of the cabin, past his son and past Mr Roslind, a middle-aged planter like himself and likewise on his way to the country life, but blessedly immune to the ship's motion. Roslind grinned as O'Riley went past, and nodded to Fitch.

"Captain!" he said.

"Captain!" said the younger O'Riley.

"Be seated, gentlemen," said Fitch. "We await the ladies."

So servants bowed, chairs scraped and the gentlemen – powdered and dressed in their best – waited and made conversation for the ten minutes that Mrs Cooper always allowed to be certain of arriving last. Or at least Fitch and Roslind spoke. Young Patrick O'Riley was devoting all his strength to not being nauseous, so that he should appear a man in the eyes of the glorious Miss Henderson. Soon after, Fitch's first mate joined them: a thin, mournful man named Gladstone with an old-fashioned pigtail and no powder on his hair. He was pure tarpaulin and didn't care who knew it.

Then female laugher was heard outside, and a servant was opening the hatchway.

"Ah!" said Fitch.

"Ah!" said Roslind.

"Ohhh . . ." said O'Riley.

Chairs scraped again as the gentlemen stood and Mrs Katherine Cooper entered with her protégée close astern. The gentlemen gaped at Miss Henderson, barely noticing the elder woman. But Katty Cooper smiled. She didn't mind that. Not at all.

Then the whole ship shuddered as she buried her bow and shipped it green over the fo'c'sle.

"Whoa!" cried Fitch.

"Huh!" cried Gladstone.

"Ohhh," said O'Riley.

"Oh dear!" cried Mrs Cooper and raised a dainty hand to her brow, for although her stomach was granite, she affected the *mal de mer* for femininity's sake.

"Poor Katty!" said Miss Henderson, and put an arm protectively round her patroness, for Miss Henderson moved easily aboard a ship underway. Indeed – as everyone had remarked – she was wonderfully expert in all matters appertaining to seafaring.

Then the company sat down, and they laughed, except for Mr O'Riley, and made a good dinner, except for Mr O'Riley. They laughed as the crockery slid up and down the heaving table. They laughed as the cook's mate spilled much of the fish soup, through mis-timing his lurch to set it down. They laughed as a bottle leapt off the table and bounced merrily across the deck, slopping wine, and they laughed as the cook's mate – attempting to retrieve it – skidded over and sat down in a pool of claret.

And all the while, every man in the cabin continued to

gaze adoringly at Miss Henderson. By now, they'd profoundly forgotten their first reaction to her: which was that, however lovely she might be, she was undoubtedly *black*, and therefore ranked somewhere between the raggedy-arsed ship's boys and the livestock carried aboard for fresh meat. But that was before Mrs Katty Cooper had taken the girl in hand and dressed her in some of the many gowns she had in her numerous sea-chests, and before even Katty Cooper herself realised that Selena had no need of training in drawing-room etiquette, for she knew it already.

"Ahhhh!" Katty Cooper had said, when Selena revealed that she had been raised as a slave, but a slave who had been the childhood favourite of her master's daughter, living in the Big House, and receiving – side by side with the white girl – the same privileged education, which even included mastering fluent French. It was no surprise therefore that Selena held a table knife or a teacup with the same daintiness as her every movement, for even setting aside her training, the girl had the most magical, graceful elegance. And she was quite young . . . only seventeen . . .

Katty Cooper saw a great future for her. Oh yes indeed she did.

"So shall you make an actress of our Miss Henderson?" said Fitch, turning the conversation to the London theatre, which he loved and which he visited every time he was in port. To him it was a surreal world of wonders, with its miraculous stage machinery and its special effects that caused dragons to appear, water to cascade, and girls to dance upon pillars that rose up out of the stage.

Katty Cooper smiled and patted Selena's hand.

"What do you think, my dear?" she said.

Selena shrugged.

"Perhaps," she said.

"We could make an Ophelia of you, or a Portia?"

"Bah!" said Fitch. "None o' that Shakespeare claptrap,

ma'am! That's for mincing macaronis. What Miss Henderson wants is a thundering melodrama. She must be the heroine chased by a villain with big hairy hands, trying to strangle her! *That's* what brings in the public!"

"Aye!" said the gentlemen, nodding furiously – even Mr O'Riley – for they were not men of exquisite taste, and they licked their lips at the thought of stranglers' hands, slender necks, and luscious flesh bouncing as it was chased across the stage.

"Buckets of blood and gore!" said Fitch. "Murder and pirates!" He laughed . . . then plunged into guilt as Miss Henderson looked away in tears. "Oh! Oh!" he said. "I do apologise, my dear miss. I should never . . . I'm so sorry. I do declare such matters must be beyond your experience . . . That is, *no* . . . I mean . . ."

"Captain, I do wish you would be a little more solicitous of a lady's feelings," said Mrs Cooper primly, and the rest of the meal passed in silence, for the gentlemen saw a long voyage ahead and wanted the pleasure of Miss Henderson's smile, and couldn't bear to upset her, while Miss Henderson herself didn't know what she wanted, or where she should go, or what she should do.

Chapter 12

Early morning, 7th April 1753
Dry Dock 1, Williamstown Harbour
Upper Barbados

*I*t would be pointless to describe *Walrus* as being in a bugger's muddle, since – in her present state – that was a condition to which she could only aspire.

Her foremast was out, much of her rigging was gone, her crew was ashore and her decks were spattered with pitch and wood chips, timber and tools, and stank of bilge water and tar, sawdust and beer, and steak-and-onions frying over charcoal braziers. Caulkers sat on their boxes battering merrily, while women hawkers yelled their wares of bread, fish and fruit. Bosuns' pipes shrieked as teams of men hove powder and shot aboard, small boys dashed everywhere on errands, and the crowded voices of a dozen trades bellowed and yelled and squabbled.

Long John stamped through this pandemonium with Israel Hands in tow, haggard exhaustion etched on his face. He'd not slept for two days, nor slept soundly since Dr Cowdray had told him where Selena was gone.

"Ah!" said Silver. "There he is!" And he shoved through the press, clambering over an empty gun-carriage, a spar, two pitch buckets and a caulker's mallet, to get at a grey-wigged gentleman in a long coat who was standing by the quarterdeck rail with a couple of shirt-sleeved, waistcoated minions in attendance.

"Mr Pollock!" cried Silver, coming alongside of this gentleman and forcing himself to touch his hat.

"Ah, Captain Silver!" said Pollock, touching his own hat. "I suppose it is the usual question?" He smirked and his followers sniggered.

Silver ground his teeth.

"It *is*, Mr Pollock," he said. "So, when might my ship be floated out?" Silver resented the careful politeness required to get these blood-sucking bastards of dockyard clerks to do their duty. Even normal, decent bribes weren't much good: not when there was an endless queue of ships waiting, and a huge sum already gone into Sir Wyndham's pocket just to get *Walrus* into the dockyard at all.

"*When*, sir? *When*?" Pollock pursed his lips. "Oooooo," he smiled, winking at his sycophants. "Why, sir, she will be floated out, sir ... *the instant she is ready, sir!*" And he laughed, and his men laughed, and none of them knew how close they came to butchering bloody slaughter on the spot.

"John!" said Hands, seizing Silver's arm. "Come away! Leave 'em to it!"

Silver was white with anger, but he let himself be led off for he knew that one more spark of wit from Mr Pollock would see his hands around that gentleman's neck like a Spanish garrotte.

So Israel Hands and Silver went aft.

"See here, Cap'n," said Israel Hands, looking over the ship, "we ain't done so bad as all that. We could've been here months! She was heavily hit and she was thick with weed." He took in the busy activity on board. "She looks a mess, but I'd say the job's nearly done and she'll be afloat in a couple of days."

"D'you think so?"

"I do."

"But they may be in England now . . . her and that cow."

"John, there ain't nothing more we can do."

"Ain't there, by thunder? 'Cos by Jesus and Mary I'll find a way if there is one! *Any* damned way. I'll piss on God and kiss the Devil's arse, if that's what it takes to save that girl!"

Silver's face contorted as horrible images burst into his mind: images of men slobbering over the woman he loved, while she smiled and opened her legs and let them do it.

"Hellfire!" he said. "Bloody hellfire!"

"I know, John."

Fortunately Israel Hands was right. *Walrus* floated out of the dry dock two days later, and with some furious work by a sheer hulk's crew to re-step the foremast, and all hands to set up rigging, she was under way and outbound from Upper Barbados on the morning tide of 17th April, in all respects fit for sea, and a dozen extra hands aboard: each one carefully chosen.

In addition, the two reluctant navigating officers were gone, and in their place stood Mr Warrington, rated as first mate: a vital necessity in case Mr Norton might not be willing to take up duties again. Warrington was a stout, greying man, who came with his own charts, instruments and tables. But unlike the foremast hands, he'd *not* been carefully chosen.

"Dirty bugger, ain't he?" said Israel Hands to Long John, as Mr Warrington came up on deck for his noon observation, doffing his hat towards his captain. His coat was soiled, his fingernails were filthy and a broken feather drooped from his hat.

"Aye," said Silver, as Warrington went to the rail with his quadrant for a view of the sun. "But he's all we could get! There's a shortage of first mates in Upper Barbados . . . or at least there is for our trade!"

"He stinks, too," said Israel Hands. "Let's hope Mr Joe ain't made the wrong choice." Silver grinned and looked at

100

Mr Joe. He'd started out as gunner's mate under Israel Hands, who'd taught the lad his letters and his numbers, only to find that he liked them so much that he wanted to be a navigator and not a gunner! This left Israel Hands jealous but Silver delighted that so intelligent a member of his crew was showing interest in one skill that he himself could never master.

Now Mr Joe was standing beside Warrington, receiving instruction in the use of the quadrant – and an odd pair they made: the slim, serious young black with his handsome face and his eye-patch, and the sweating, greasy Warrington with his loud voice and his coarse, leering jokes.

Later, it grew worse. Warrington got roaring drunk at dinner time, and bellowed verses at the top of his voice until a bucket of water was thrown over him. Then he staggered on deck, still grinning and sniggering, and played the dirty-minded trick of creeping up behind another man and grabbing his arse with a middle finger upraised between the cheeks: not the wisest of tricks to play upon a gentleman o' fortune. Warrington got badly beaten, suffering broken ribs, a dislocated thumb, severe bruising about the face, and a split forehead for Dr Cowdray to sew up.

"How is he?" said Silver, peering in through the door of the first mate's cabin as Warrington was heaved into his cot by Cowdray and his mate, Jobo. Seeing the bandages and Warrington's closed eyes, Silver knew the answer before Cowdray spoke.

"Unfit for duty, Captain. He's half-conscious and he can't see."

"Bugger!" said Silver.

"Uhhh . . ." said Warrington, and stirred. "Now is the winter of our discontent . . ."

"What?" said Silver, as Warrington mumbled on.

"Made glorious summer by this son of York . . ."

"What's he blathering about?"

"And all the clouds that lowered on our house . . ."

"It's Shakespeare," said Cowdray. "*Richard III.*"

"Then shut his bloody trap! Give him some rum."

"He's had *quite* enough of that!" said Cowdray.

"No! No!" growled Warrington, in his slurred voice. "Dost thou think because thou art virtuous, there shall be no more cakes and ale?"

Silver cursed and damned and got himself up on deck, and sent for Norton, who was duly escorted up into the light, blinking and sniffing the fresh air. After a brief time on the quarterdeck, making sure *Walrus* found Upper Barbados, he'd spent the last few weeks below decks, as had McLonarch, and he was not best pleased. That displeasure was evident now, as he stood in the waist, facing Silver and his officers at the quarterdeck rail while the hands looked on.

"Now then, mister," said Silver, "how'd you like to be first mate again? Or shall you go back to the hold as live lumber?"

"Depends," said Norton truculently. "What's your course? What's your trade? And what else will I have to do?"

"You'll have to swim back to Williamstown if you ain't careful, my cocker!"

"Aye!" said the crew.

"Cap'n!" said Allardyce, glaring angrily at Norton, the principal enemy of his beloved McLonarch. "We got to hold council according to articles." He looked to the crew: "These good lads have sailed on trust, ain't you, lads?"

"Aye!" they cried.

"We've slung our hook, and we've come out on the tide . . . trusting Long John to take us on a cruise . . ." He paused. "But no bugger's said *where* we's going, nor *why*."

"Aye!" they said.

"We held no council ashore," said Allardyce. "But now's the time." Emboldened by the sight of the crew nodding agreement, he concluded: "So . . . Long John . . . I akses you to bring up the McLonarch, God save him! Bring him up that his voice might be heard alongside of this sod of a Bow Street Runner!"

"Aye!" cried Long John. "Let there be a full council! I'd have said it myself if nobody else had." Then he added: "And bring up *Mister* McLonarch an' all."

There was cheering and furious activity as men vanished below to put on their best clothes and collect their arms, and to bring up a chair and table, and to spread the table with the black flag, and to lay open the Book of Articles upon the flag, with pen and ink, and a sand-caster. Soon, only the look-outs and the helmsmen were at their duties, and all hands paraded in silks and plumes, jewellery and buckles, and bearing whatever combination of firelock, sword, knife and hatchet that each man desired in this ultimate, armed democracy where every man was every other's equal. Even Sammy Hayden, ship's boy, had a pair of sea-service pistols stuck in his belt, primed and loaded with ball.

Among the crowd, McLonarch stood out by his height and by the total confidence of his bearing. Norton was constantly glancing his way, wondering and calculating, while McLonarch looked at his enemy just once . . . and smiled . . . and looked away as if from some small matter of no importance.

McLonarch watched quietly as these barbarians went through their ceremony, seating Captain Silver at the single chair, raised up on a platform like a throne, and then all hats were doffed but his. McLonarch sneered in contempt . . . which turned to incredulity at the equality of the proceedings, such that each man was given the chance to speak and be listened to, or to be howled down in derision, if that's what the company desired. And some who were strange and ugly, like Blind Pew the sailmaker, were listened to with rapt attention for their skill as speakers.

The debate concerned the vital matter of where the ship should be heading and to what purpose. McLonarch was amazed that there were no secrets among these people. His offer of a pardon was common knowledge, and the ship's surgeon was asked by Silver to explain his plan – shared by Silver, for his own reasons – to sail to London and there decide what to do with himself and Norton. At this, Norton pushed forward, bellicose and muscular.

"The law must have him!" he cried, pointing at McLonarch. "He's bloody murder! He's anarchy and civil war!" He appealed to their patriotism: "You may be outlaws, but you're still Englishmen! Surely you care for your own land? Surely you don't want –"

But they howled him down. They hated him for what he was, and besides they weren't all Englishmen, and he had no gift of speech.

McLonarch saw that his time was come. He caught Tom Allardyce's eye and nodded. Allardyce nodded back, and began to yell and shout that McLonarch should be heard. Allardyce was consumed with passion for the cause that pulsed in his blood, and his fervent, near-religious conviction was the drum roll and fanfare for what was to come. Thus McLonarch stepped forward, tall and ascetic. Though he faced the mass of heavily armed men alone and unarmed, he remained serene in his dignity and charisma.

His eyes swept over them in such a way that every man present felt that he personally was being addressed. He raised his hands above his shoulders, and a silence fell that was so complete every creak of the ship could be heard, and every chuckle of water under her bow. He stood tall, he took a breath . . .

He hadn't spoken a word and already they were gaping.

His voice, when it came, was majestic.

It rang with beauty and resonance.

It was poetic and solemn.

It was magnificent.

If he'd read them a cockle boat's bill of lading they'd have been entranced. But he offered infinitely more than that. He spoke of riches in this life, and salvation in the next. He made them laugh, he made them cry, he led them dancing down the flowery path towards . . .

THE TRUTH OF THE HOLY STUART CAUSE.

Even the Protestants were welcome. Even *they* might be saved, if only they followed him. By the time he'd finished they were hoisting a noose to the yard-arm for Norton, screaming defiance in Long John's face . . . and threatening to hang him too.

Chapter 13

Three bells of the middle watch
6th April 1753
Aboard Bounder
The Atlantic

*I*n the dark, heaving night, Mr Braddock the musician – he who knew Flint for what he was – found it hard to see who was waiting for him on the fo'c'sle. *Bounder* was well named, for while she was extremely fast, no man would have called her comfortable. So Braddock hung on to the pinrails when he could, and staggered from one handhold to another when he couldn't, and tried not to notice the enormous gleaming waves that rose and sank on either side of the rushing ship.

"Ah!" he thought, seeing a wet, glistening figure crouched by the foremast. He glanced behind and around himself. There must be lookouts in the tops, and men at the helm, but he couldn't see any of them: only the sodden decks and whatever tackles and gear he'd got his hands on at any given moment.

"Wheeeeeep!" A soft whistle came from the dark figure. Braddock waved his arm. The figure waved back. He got closer . . . and closer . . . with the ship working under his feet, and himself trembling all the while, for he'd never become much of a seaman, and tonight he was afraid of perils worse than the sea.

"Mr Braddock!" said the figure.

"Welles?" said the musician.

"Aye, sir!"

Reassured, he got himself right next to Welles, who was one of the marines, a straight and decent fellow who detested Flint as much as Braddock did, and who had promised to share information that would bring the villain to justice: information to be imparted at this secret meeting. Braddock looked at Welles's face. The marine appeared nervous and kept glancing about, which was hardly surprising.

"Did anyone see you come forrard?" asked Welles.

"No," said Braddock, and the marine looked over his shoulder and groaned. Braddock had a sudden moment of fright. Why wouldn't Welles look him in the eye? What if . . . "*Uuuuch!*" said Braddock. "*Uch! Uch! Uch!*" And his eyes popped and his face darkened and his tongue stuck out, and he kicked and fought with the superhuman strength that nature gives to a man who is being strangled.

But it did him no good. The silent figure that had risen behind him had thrown a two-foot length of log-line over Braddock's head, hands crossed to form a loop of it, and a neat wooden toggle made fast to each end of the line. With the toggles gripped firmly in two strong hands, Braddock's efforts to free himself served only to throttle him all the quicker, the thin line crushing his larynx and trachea, and biting deep into flesh to nip the great pumping vessels that fed the brain.

"Ah!" said Flint softly, as Braddock suddenly went limp and hung heavily in the embrace of the cord. It looked as if a sorely troubled heart had given up the struggle and stopped beating. But Flint hung on, just to be sure, just to be safe and only let Braddock fall when his arms could take the strain no more.

Flint looked up. He saw Welles's face and almost laughed. Mr Welles had proved susceptible to an offer of gold, but now he'd seen actual murder, he was clearly regretting it.

"Quick!" said Flint. "Over the side with him!"

"Over the side?"

"Yes! Or perhaps we should take him home to his mother? What do you think?"

Welles groaned again, but set to, and with Flint's help heaved Braddock over the side. The dark body went in without a splash.

"Now, follow me," commanded Flint. "You must be paid!"

"Aye-aye, sir," said Welles, cheering up at the prospect, and the two men groped forward to the bowsprit that stood out over the white water as it gushed and foamed and threw up a constant heavy wetting. In the dim starlight, their slick-wet, tar-coated garments gleamed like sea-lions, and they hung on hard, for the ship's motion was especially severe right up at the bow.

"Come closer," said Flint. "I don't want to shout!"

"Aye-aye, sir."

"No – *closer!*"

Welles came right next to Flint so that their heads were almost touching. Then: "Back off a little," said Flint. "Give us room."

"*Us*, Cap'n?"

"Us!" said Flint as Billy Bones's cord flickered over Welles's head, and that *straight and decent fellow* began his choking. He sprayed spittle in all directions and – being a man with horny fingernails – he clawed blood all round the line that bit into his flesh as he shook with mighty convulsions. But like Mr Braddock he soon fell silent, and Billy Bones dropped him over the bow to be pounded, scraped and over-ridden by the speeding ship.

After their exertions, Flint and Bones crouched silent by the bowsprit for a while. Then Flint threw his strangling-line into the sea and motioned for Bones to do the same.

"Come!" said Flint, when he'd got his breath back, for even *he* didn't strangle a man entirely without disturbance to his inner peace. As for Billy Bones, he was drowning in a whirlpool of horror and guilt, and his hands shook like a drunkard's.

The two men groped their way back to the small quarterdeck, where the watch was on duty, having seen nothing and heard nothing, for the night was dark and the sea was loud. The watch saluted Flint, and he acknowledged them. Then Captain Flint and Lieutenant Bones straightened their backs – as British officers should – and went to stand beside the weather rail.

"Well, Lieutenant," said Flint, "that removes the lesser threat. And I have taken measures to ensure that the greater one stays nicely asleep."

"How's that, Cap'n?"

"I'm dosing Mr Povey with laudanum . . . to ease his pain."

"Ah!"

"But I think we must now face the truth."

"Truth, Cap'n?"

"We are bound for England, Billy-boy; I can enter *two* men as 'lost over the side' in the ship's books, but not many more. We must keep up the pretence of being in the king's service, or we'll find ourselves back in irons again." He shook his head regretfully. "Alas, not all aboard are completely stupid!"

"So we're bound for England, Cap'n?"

"Bound for England – and God knows what we shall find there!"

Two bells of the second dog watch
6th April 1753
Aboard Venture's Fortune
The Atlantic

Given the blessing of easy seas and good weather, Miss Cooper and Miss Henderson stood wrapped in their cloaks on the quarterdeck in the soft evening. It was nearly dark, and the light gleamed from the binnacle into the faces of the men at the wheel, with more light shining up from the skylights of the cabins below. The ladies were talking about the usual subject, for Miss Cooper was endlessly persistent.

"Cannot you see how advantageous it would be, my dear?" she said.

"To become an actress?" said Miss Henderson.

"Yes! You were born for it, believe me."

"But I've never *seen* a play, or been to a theatre."

"Then trust me – I know every theatre in London and all the managers."

"But how can I remember all those words?"

"Bah! The audience will want to *look* at you, not listen! Half the actresses in London fake their lines." Katty laughed. "Well, the beauties do, anyway!"

Selena sighed. The truth was that she didn't know what she wanted, nor whether she'd done the right thing in leaving John Silver. She knew only that she thought about him every day, and every night. As for the theatre: the idea of standing up in front of thousands of people and pretending . . . *acting* . . . It sounded terrifying, and she shuddered and shook her head.

"Oh dear," said Katty Cooper, with trembling lower lip. "I do hope you shall not disappoint me. For I am quite alone in the world . . ."

Selena looked at her. Katty, utterly feminine as always, had adopted her pleading look: a tragic expression of innocence wounded. On those rare occasions when people refused to do her bidding, she invariably resorted not to anger but tears, and her helpless, pretty, tear-stained little face became an iron lever that she pulled without mercy, to crush the will of others and force them to her bidding. For Katty was a woman who saw her own point of view with such blinding clarity that she was unaware, even, that others had feelings.

"Hmm," thought Selena, for she was beginning to understand Katty Cooper. But . . . on the other hand . . . Katty had been extremely helpful in enabling Selena to be accepted aboard this ship. It was thanks to Katty that nobody now paid any mind to the fact that Selena had come aboard with no story to explain what she'd been doing among pirates. Katty had taken Selena's vague mumblings in response to questions about her past and enlarged upon them with remarkable skill, such that Selena now had a surname and a family – not her real family, who had been left behind on the Delacroix plantation – but a pretend family invented by Katty Cooper, and a sad tale of how she lost them when pirates stormed a merchant ship, slaying all aboard but herself. Even Captain Fitch had shed a tear when Katty told that one.

Selena sighed. What *did* she want? Even being an actress couldn't be as bad as some of the things that had happened to her aboard Flint's ship . . . and Long John's . . .

"*Ah!*" thought Katty Cooper, reading the signs. She turned off the mask of tragedy and took Selena's face in her hands.

"Listen to me, my beautiful creature," she said, looking Selena in the eye. "If you follow me I will promise you wealth beyond your dreams. You shall never want! You shall never be afraid! The world shall court you and adore you. You shall make towers of guineas and roll . . . you shall *roll* . . . in strings of diamonds."

Katty Cooper managed – just – not to say "roll *naked* in strings of diamonds", something which gentlemen never failed to appreciate.

"Shall I?" said Selena.

"Oh yes!"

Selena shrugged. In the absence of a better offer, that didn't seem too bad. And there were no better offers available. In fact, there were no other offers. Not one. So she smiled. Perhaps she might be an actress after all.

And Katty Cooper smiled, too, pleased that *the theatre* was such useful bait, and a subject of which she knew so much, since she had indeed been an actress herself . . . until superior opportunities presented. Her tales of the London stage would do to keep Selena happy for now, and in time she would learn as Katty Cooper had learned.

"So let us be happy, my dear," she said. "We are bound for England!"

Yes, thought Selena. *Bound for England and the stage. And who knows where that might lead?*

Nightfall (there being no watches kept nor bells struck owing to the mutiny in progress)
12th April 1753
Aboard Walrus
The Atlantic

So determined were the hands to hang Norton that, when Silver spoke up for him, Tom Allardyce – white-faced in rage – drew steel and rushed at Silver from behind and swung a blow aimed at splitting his head to the chin.

Which gave Norton his chance. As the two men holding his arms flinched at Allardyce's charge, Norton wrenched himself free, struck left and right with his elbows, smashed a fist into the nose of one who still hung on, then sprang forward to grapple Allardyce from the side in full run, throwing him skidding over, with Norton biting flesh to the bone of the wrist that held the cutlass, and punching with a hard right hand into the soft meat between Allardyce's thighs.

"*Aaaaargh!*" shrieked Allardyce, then "*Ugh! Ugh! Ugh!*" as Norton spat out his wrist, took his head by the ears, and slammed it three times into the deck, before leaping up, kicking away the cutlass, and slamming a boot repeatedly and with mighty force into Allardyce's kidneys until he was dragged off by his victim's mates.

"Bastard!" they screamed.

"Gut him!"

"Chop him!"

There was a rush for the quarterdeck companionways, but:

Bang! Bang! Silver let off a pair of pistols into the air, while Israel Hands, Mr Joe and Black Dog instantly lined up alongside him and drew weapons and levelled them at the mob.

"'Ware the buggers!" cried the crew, and two or three dozen firelocks were made ready and aimed. Anger was rampant: it scorched the decks, it addled their brains until mass, mutual slaughter was a second away.

"Hold hard there!" cried Long John, yelling above all others. "And blind the bastard with red-hot irons who fires on his own shipmates!"

"Arrrrrrrgh!" they growled, but they stopped.

"Captain!" cried McLonarch, stepping forward. "May I say . . ."

"NO, YOU MAY NOT!" roared Silver in uttermost rage. "By God and all his bleedin' angels you've had your whack, my son, and now it's my turn!" He appealed to the hands: "Ain't that fair, brothers?"

"Aye!" roared Israel Hands, Mr Joe and Black Dog.

"Aye," said others, but with bad grace.

"So!" cried Silver, pointing to Norton. "You're set to hang him, are you?"

"Aye!" they screamed and shook their fists in the air.

"Shiver my timbers," said Silver, "if that don't beat all for piss-brain-pleased-with-shit-head-stupid!"

"What?" they said.

"D'you not see?" he cried. "Norton's the only bugger aboard what's fit to plot a course! We're all fo'c'sle hands as can *steer* a course, but who's to *set* one? Who's to labour with quadrant and dividers?"

"Oh!" they said, even McLonarch, who'd not thought of that.

"Ah!" cried Silver, seeing the change. "Or maybe I'm

113

wrong? Maybe you swabs is happy with miscalculations and endin' up lost in the ocean on a spoonful of water a day?"

They were not. The anger ran out and the guilt ran in.

"So," said Silver, "make safe them barkers! Stick 'em where they'll do the most good . . . and then listen to me!"

There followed a shame-faced clicking of guns being set to half-cock. Then all hands – and the McLonarch – looked up at Silver.

"Here's my word in the matter," he said. "It's Dr Cowdray's plan for me! So him there –" he pointed at Norton "– is rated first mate. And him there –" he pointed at McLonarch "– is rated *ship's guest*, and neither to bear arms nor strike the other, nor any man to take their part . . . until we reach England, and there a full council of brothers will decide what we shall do with 'em!"

There was silence. Silver looked at Israel Hands.

"All show for Brother Silver!" cried Israel Hands, and he, Mr Joe, Black Dog, Dr Cowdray, Blind Pew and others instantly voted for Silver. Then, slowly . . . first one hand went up . . . then another . . . and another . . . until a good majority showed.

"All against?" said Israel Hands.

No hand was raised.

And that was it. The ship returned to normal and arms were put away. Silver wiped the sweat from his brow, Israel Hands and Mr Joe clapped him on the back and smiled, and Cap'n Flint the parrot rubbed her head lovingly against his cheek. She was a great comfort at such times.

"You're the boy, John!" said Israel Hands admiringly. "Ain't none like you!"

"Aye!" said all who heard.

But later, Silver spoke privately both with Norton, whom he liked, and the McLonarch, whom he detested. He told each that he would take his part when they reached England. For Silver was desperate to save his lady and didn't know

114

who he might need on his side, so he played both ends against the middle. And that wasn't the old John Silver. That wasn't *him* any more. That was something new.

In his cabin, alone with a bottle of rum and Cap'n Flint, he sighed and tickled the parrot's beautiful green plumes.

"We're bound for England, my girl," he said. "And God knows what we'll find there!"

Chapter 14

Dusk, 10th June 1753
Shooter's Hill
In the ancient borough of Greenwich
Southeast London

The Berlin was a magnificent example of the coach-builder's art. It was light and strong, with big dished wheels, and the body hung on leather braces. It thundered onward at cracking speed, sending dust and clods flying in all directions, driven from the box by a liveried, plume-hatted coachman who thrashed mightily on the backs of the four horses, them being mere post-cattle, put on at the last change five miles back, and himself resolved to go up this famous hill in style and not like a fat-arsed yokel on a farm wagon.

"*Go* on! *Go* on!" he yelled.

Crack! Crack! Crack! went the whip and the wretched beasts leapt onward.

Under its layer of road dust, the coach body gleamed splendidly: the result of many dozen coats of olive green paint, and the arms of the Second Earl of Maidstone applied to its doors. But it swayed and rocked, since, for all its sophistication of design, it was rumbling over the rutted, potholed, cart-track that these modern times called "*a highroad*" and which a Roman engineer would have laughed at.

In the velvet comfort of the coach, with its luminous glass windows and rich upholstery, two gentlemen sat side by side, hanging on to hand-straps against the motion. They were Lieutenant Flint and Lieutenant Lennox, now dressed in fashionable civilian attire, complete with wigs. Flint beamed for the hundredth time upon young Lennox, who'd turned out to be most wonderfully well connected: his uncle being Admiral Sir Toby Lennox, in command of the Channel Fleet at Portsmouth, and his father Lord Anthony Lennox, Second Earl of Maidstone from whose great house the Berlin had started on its journey to London that morning.

Flint chuckled.

"What is it, Joseph?" said Lennox, smiling, for he idol-worshipped Flint and was delighted to see his hero happy.

"Nothing, dear fellow," said Flint and smiled back. He was reflecting on the happy accident that the house of Hastings – which stood for Mr Midshipman Povey and against Joe Flint – was Whig, while the house of Lennox . . . was Tory. Thus they'd gobbled up every word of young Lennox's outburst of admiration for Flint on arrival aboard his uncle's flagship at Spithead: telling how Flint had fought the pestilence, put hope into the crew, excelled in leadership, shone in seamanship, overcome perils at sea, etc, etc, etc . . . and brought all hands safe home!

Likewise they'd swallowed Lennox's vehement protestation – modestly supported by Flint – that Flint was not only innocent of all charges against him, but was a hero, a true-born Briton, and undoubtedly the victim of some foul and deep-laid plot!

Meanwhile, the representatives of Clan Hastings had carried away poor Mr Povey, still swimming deep between life and death, and unable to bring his vital evidence to bear on the case . . . which was not surprising, considering the amount of laudanum that had been poured down him over the preceding weeks. Indeed, it was his exasperating refusal to *die* under the treatment which had caused amazement in some quarters.

Since Clan Lennox's power was rooted in the navy, and it was the navy that had hold of Flint, great levers were pulled in the Admiralty such that Flint emerged a free man . . . pending Mr Povey's recovery, and a search for any others whose evidence Clan Lennox considered relevant. Meanwhile Flint was taken to Maidstone House in Kent to meet Lord Maidstone, and was entertained, and shown off to rural society, until – desperate in every way to escape – he suggested a journey to the culture and sophistication of London, which he claimed never to have seen.

Such was the Berlin's capacity for speed, and so frequent the changes of horses, a mere five hours on the road had brought them some fifty miles to Shooter's Hill, where Lennox insisted that Flint must not miss the inspirational first sight of London from this famous vantage point, and neither should the faithful Mr Billy Bones, for whom there was not room in the two-seater coach body, leaving him perched in the servants' seat behind, which at least had its own little hood in case the weather turned nasty.

"Whoooooooa!" cried the coachman as they reached the top of the hill. He hauled on his reins, stopped the coach, set the brake, then clambered down, rigged the passengers' step, and threw open the door, doffing his hat and bowing low, with his whip held respectfully across his chest.

"Shooter's Hill, Mr Lennox!" he said, and backed away, still bowing, as the gentlemen got out, stretching their cramped limbs, and Mr Bones's heavy body swayed down from the rear seat, making the carriage rock and tremble and causing the horses to whinny.

"Thank God!" said Lennox, and grinned. "I have to . . . er . . ." And he darted off to some trees that stood dark and shadowy in the gloom.

Billy Bones took station beside Flint and they gazed at the

118

view, which was indeed spectacular. They were on open ground, with a copse of thick woodland behind them, the new building of the Bull Inn to the west, near the summit of the hill, and a vast expanse of England stretched out on the plain before them, with the road winding ahead and down.

Northward, the flat, shining curves of the River Thames could be seen, from Woolwich in the east to the pool of London in the west and beyond, where lay the vast and glooming mass of the world's biggest city, with its twinkling lights, its forest of spires, its pealing bells and the smoke of hearth fires so numerous as to be beyond counting. It was a noble and splendid sight.

It was a sight that profoundly impressed Billy Bones, for London was so vast, so complex, and so *different* to anything in his life thus far, that it stirred tremendous emotions within him. He thought of Livvy Rose, for this was where he'd left her, and where she might still be living. Thus aroused, all the old passions burned as if new. And being full of love for Livvy Rose, there was – for the moment – no room in his heart for any other love. So Billy Bones glanced at Flint, then glanced again at London . . . and his mind trembled, and shivered, and grasped at the possibility of a life *without* Flint . . .

But then Billy Bones sniffed the air.

"Hoss-shite and chimbley-smoke!" he said.

"Your sense of smell is exquisite," said Flint. "Likewise, your gift for poetry."

They gazed a while at the view, each in his own thoughts.

"Cap'n," said Billy Bones, "what we doin' here? In London?"

"Trying to disappear, Mr Bones."

"What? In a city full o' people?"

"Oh, Billy," said Flint, "where better?" He pointed at the gleaming river. "It is also a great seaport, offering the chance of clean and entire escape."

"But we *have* escaped."

Flint sighed, despairing.

"Imagine, Billy, a man hanged off a great tower. He falls with a long rope round his neck. While he falls, he lives . . . and enjoys false hope. But when he reaches the end of the rope, he dies. Yes?"

"Yes, Cap'n."

"I am that man. And so are you."

"Oh."

"Ah," said Lennox, coming back still buttoning the falls of his breeches, "that's better! Fine view, is it not?"

Later, when the horses had rested and the moon was shining and night fallen, they were just about to get into the carriage again when the thudding of hoofbeats sounded and four horsemen emerged from the wood behind them, faces masked and black.

"Oh, buggery and 'ellfire!" said the coachman. "Get aboard, gents!"

"Damnation!" said Lennox. "Highwaymen!"

"Pistols, Billy!" said Flint, leaping for the coach.

But it was too late, the horsemen came in at a thundering gallop, two getting between their victims and the coach with ready firelocks, and two swinging round into the lead horses of the coach, which whinnied in fright only to drop in their tracks as –

Bang! Bang! gunshots sounded, bright flashes seared the shining horseflesh, and the two leaders were dead in their harness, the remaining pair shrieking and kicking and the coach going nowhere.

"Stand and deliver!" roared one of the horsemen, and his horse reared in the night as his three mates got themselves around Flint, Billy Bones, Lennox and the coachman, as smoothly and efficiently as drilled dragoons. Between them they had several brace of pistols, a double coaching carbine, and a blunderbuss.

"On your knees, you sods! Get down, or I'll have the eyes and bollocks off you!"

"Down!" said Flint, and dropped, and Billy Bones followed him.

"Down, I said!" And another pistol boomed. Lennox and the coachman promptly knelt. "That's better! Now, behave your bleedin' selves and I'll leave you alive, but one cough and you're croaked! For I'm Captain Lightning, knight of the road, and I'll have your watches, your rings, your gelt, and anything else that might stop me pulling a trigger!"

A throaty snort came from Flint, whose shoulders shook and shook, and he bent his head forward that his face might not be seen. Then he took hold. He looked up and lifted his arms in supplication.

"Oh, sir," he begged, "take pity on a poor man afflicted with the stone such that he can barely breathe, and who suffers more than can be borne, being crouched as I am!"

Lennox and Billy Bones gaped in astonishment at this cowardly snivelling, for they knew Flint. The coachman was merely surprised.

"Fuck you! Fuck your fucking stone!" said Captain Lightning. "Stay on your fucking knees!" But Flint risked all and got unsteadily to his feet.

"Oh, sir! Oh, sir!" said Flint, staggering towards the high-wayman, pulling coins from his pockets and holding them out. "Take! Take all! But do not condemn me to my knees and the tortures of the damned, I beg you." The moonlight showed the tears that streamed down his face and on to his trembling lips.

"Nyaaaah!" said Captain Lightning in contempt as Flint fell against him, clutching his knee, weeping and moaning, and wouldn't be shaken off. Clutching the reins in his left hand, Lightning swung his carbine with the right, and clouted Flint with the butt. But Flint just moaned and hung on, whining and slobbering. "Solly!" cried Lightning. "Come here and get rid o' this cove. I ain't got a free hand. Stick him if you have to, but get him off!"

One of his men holstered his pistol, drew a long knife and rode forward. He got between Flint and the rest so they couldn't see . . . and then there was a scuffle and a jump, and a yell from Captain Lightning, and both horses were rearing and plunging and three men were struggling on the ground under the hooves . . . then the horses bolted, and Flint leapt up with a carbine – which was a double – and fired twice.

"Uh!" said one of the surviving horsemen, and fell from the saddle, with an ounce ball gone in at his right eye and out through the back of his head.

His companion did better, for Flint's shot whistled past his ear and he managed to let rip with his blunderbuss, drilling many holes in empty air, before going over the head of his horse, which was bucking and kicking in a frenzy. He landed heavily, face down, with Flint darting forward to sit squarely on his shoulders, where he settled himself, leaned forward, took his man by the chin, pulled upwards to expose the dirty grey throat, and slit it nice and deep with the dagger-point, razor-edge knife that lived in his left sleeve, and which had already seen off Captain Lightning and his friend Solly.

Later that night the Berlin pulled up, behind two horses at the home of Sir Frederick Lennox.

"God-damn-me, God-damn-me!" he cried, as servants dashed to and fro, and passers-by looked on, and luggage was whisked from the Berlin's trunk and into the house. "All four of 'em? And Captain Lightning too?"

"Yes! Yes!" cried little brother. "*By himself alone!*"

Thus Flint's reputation in London was assured. Flint smiled, Billy Bones put aside all earlier thoughts of desertion and swelled with pride, and Sir Frederick slapped his thigh and damned himself deeper as he shook Flint's hand. A red-faced man in his forties, running to fat and dressed in the extreme height of fashion, with magnificently embroidered clothes, a coat with elaborate skirts and multiple pleating. Sir Frederick was by far the elder brother, the son of a previous marriage and heir to the family fortune. He took to Flint something wonderful.

"D'you know what the reward is for Captain Lightning?" he said.

"Reward?" said Flint.

"Yes, from the Meteoric Diligence Company – five hundred in gold!"

"So much?"

"Aye, m'boy. And all yours!"

Hmm, thought Flint, for there would be a need for ready money.

"I'll take you round the town tomorrow," said Sir Frederick, "bold dog that you are! By God, the ladies'll love you!"

Slapping Flint on the back, he led them all into the brilliant, candle-lit interior of a house stuffed to the ceilings with objets d'art, and paintings, porcelain and gilt.

"This way!" he cried. "To the library!"

It was a long night and vast quantities of port were consumed as Sir Frederick explained that his house – which was on the corner of Russell Street and the Covent Garden Piazza – though not in the most fashionable part of London, was well placed to take in all the life of the city, with its theatres, print-shops, taverns and restaurants . . .

"And the finest whores in town!" he cried.

It was late in the small hours by this time; many confidences had been shared, and Frederick's secret store of erotic prints had been brought out to be ogled . . . at least by Sir Frederick, for little brother and Billy Bones were merely embarrassed, while Flint had special needs in this matter, though he smiled and pretended enthusiasm.

"Look, sir!" cried Sir Frederick, and staggered up under a load of drink to wave from a window. Even at that hour two well-dressed ladies in the piazza below waved back at him.

"Look! Look!" he cried. "A fine pair: all plump and bouncy!" Then he laughed and laughed, and sat down again and reached for the decanter. "I've got a bloody wife somewhere in the country, but she don't trouble me here." He winked at Flint. "So if you're in need of a good, hard poke – which you must be, being a sailor . . ." He laughed some more, spluttering port. ". . . then I'll take you to the best house in London, where it ain't cheap, mind, but you can take your pick: fourteen to forty, black, white or piebald, and never a fear o' the clap!"

"*Black?*" said Flint quietly.

"Oh yes!" said Sir Frederick, and a thought struck him: "Better still . . . tell you what I'll do . . . Tomorrow . . . I'll take you to meet Flash Jack the Fly Cove and he'll fit you out with anything you please: any colour, any shape, front or back entry, all fresh and juicy!"

"And who might this gentleman be?" said Flint.

"'Gentleman' be damned: he's the biggest rogue un-hung! Pays off the law, may'n't be touched, and can get any *man*, any *thing* he pleases."

"*Anything?*" said Flint.

"Anything from an elephant to a line-o'-battle ship! And tarts, of course."

"A ship?" said Flint, and looked at Billy Bones, who was half asleep, but stirred under his master's gaze.

"Oh, by God yes!" said Sir Frederick, waving his hand dismissively, and taking another deep glass. "Get you one o' them with *no* trouble."

"Then I should like to meet this gentleman," said Flint. "Tomorrow."

Chapter 15

10th June 1753
Abbey's Amphitheatre
King Street, Polmouth

A pair of white horses charged at dizzy speed around the sandy-floored circular enclosure, with a dancing girl leaping from one to another, turning cartwheels in the air, while a bizarre clown in red-and-white stripes and conical white cap chased after them on an ostrich, blowing a trumpet to the accompaniment of a full, costumed chorus singing on the stage behind. All this against a dazzling backdrop of brilliantly painted scenery panels which shifted in a rainbow of colour, while a band of two dozen musicians blared furiously in the orchestra pit between.

Selena stared in wonderment. She'd never seen any kind of theatrical performance, let alone a spectacle like this. It assaulted the senses in colour, music, voices and skills. She clapped her hands and cheered, as did Katty Cooper, for it had been a long time since even she had seen the like.

But theirs was the only applause. They were the entire audience on this Sunday rehearsal, for no plays nor entertainments might be performed on the Lord's day.

And then the scene was over, and the performers – even the horses and the ostrich – were bowing to an empty house, and the clown clapping his hands, and giving all present his review of their performance, praising some, cursing others, before sending them off to their dressing rooms and stables.

Soon, nothing was left but the hoofmarks and footsteps in the sand, and a strong smell of horseflesh and greasepaint.

"Mrs Cooper!" said the clown, stepping forward to where his audience of two were seated. "My dear, my very dear!" And he waddled forward, less than five feet tall in his blouse and pantaloons, and his white stockings and his flat-white makeup with red lips and painted black eyebrows.

He bowed and took Katty Cooper's hand, then, with astonishing grace for so grotesque a creature, he knelt to plant a gentle kiss in the centre of her pink palm.

"Oh, my dear Mr Abbey!" she said, and for once a genuine smile shone from her pretty little face, for even Katty Cooper had been a girl once, and had memories of innocence. He bowed again, this time towards Selena.

"And is this the sable nymph? *La belle fille noire*?"

"May I present Miss Henderson, my protégée," said Katty.

"Ah!" said Abbey. "Let us say *Mrs* Henderson, for this is not London."

Abbey stepped back, and gave yet another bow, this time of such extravagant and comical elaboration that it was a work of art, and Selena couldn't help but laugh. The clown clapped his hands and smiled.

"And may I present . . . the amphitheatre, of which I am owner and manager!" he said. "Empty today, but all the better for you to see it. Come forward! See!"

Selena stared. It was wonderful. The sandy circle in which they were standing was enclosed by a bright-painted barrier some four feet high. To one side was a pit for musicians, then a great proscenium arch and stage, and on the other side were three tiers of seats running in a semi-circle, with many more seats packed in at ground level around the circle.

"A full house holds nearly seven hundred persons," said

Abbey. "It is admirably adapted for spectacles – especially equestrian – and the scenery, machinery and decorations are executed by the finest artists in the country." He pointed upwards: "Illuminated by one of the biggest glass chandeliers in England, supporting over two hundred fine wax candles!"

"One of the finest auditoriums . . . in the provinces," said Katty Cooper.

Abbey winced.

"You seek to wound!" he cried, raising his arms in self-protection. "We are mere peasants to the daughter of Drury Lane!" They both laughed.

"So!" said Abbey to Katty Cooper, and looked at Selena. "What can she do?"

Katty Cooper had been thinking about that all the way to England, and now they were safe arrived in Polmouth, and lodged in its best hotel, and favours had been asked of her old friend . . .

"Let us first see her in costume!" Katty smiled. "As requested in my letter."

"As in your letter!" said Abbey. "Will you follow me, ladies?"

He took them to a private dressing room, laid out a costume, bowed and left them to it.

Ten minutes later, Katty Cooper led Selena back, taking her to the middle of the stage and propelling her forward for Abbey to see.

"*Ah!*" said Abbey. One syllable, short and sharp, for the "costume" could have been stored in a thimble, being engineered from one silk handkerchief and a handful of glittering stars. "Thank you, Mrs Henderson," said Abbey. "Would you be so kind as to excuse Mrs Cooper and me while we hold a brief, professional discussion?"

They left the stage, walked to the far side of the circular enclosure and stood, looking back at Selena, left standing in mid-stage with her arms folded, tapping one foot and staring suspiciously towards them. Abbey smiled and waved. Katty smiled and waved.

"Where *did* you find her?" whispered Abbey. "She is quite, quite, *spectacularly* beautiful. I have never seen the like. She is very lovely indeed, and I am lost for words!" He looked at Katty Cooper. "Is she in your trade, dear heart?"

"Not yet. She's got to be shown off."

"On the stage?"

"Yes. Enough public performances to make her name . . ."

"Followed by some select *private* performances?"

"Then we'll be open to offers," said Katty.

Abbey sighed. "And I suppose these performances must be in London?"

"Of course!"

"And the provinces are but stepping stones?"

"Yes. An unknown girl doesn't walk straight into Drury Lane."

"Huh!" said Abbey. "So, I ask again, what can she do?"

"No," said Katty, stooping to kiss his white cheek. "You tell me . . ."

Back on the stage, Abbey produced a small violin, which he played with tremendous skill. The sound was so merry that it was a wonder the seats didn't get up to dance.

"Follow me, Mrs Henderson," said Abbey. "Do as I do." And he danced around the stage with Selena following and attempting to mimic his moves, which started simple and grew complex, till she strained and ached. At last Abbey put down the fiddle and clapped time, rather than playing, and danced step after step after step.

"And *this!* And *this!* And *this!*" he cried, and seemed never to tire.

Then he gave her a brief rest and a glass of water before taking up the violin again, this time for a simple country song.

"Follow the tune, my dear," he said. "La-la-la if you don't know the words."

Which progressed to more difficult works and finally to Selena singing a song of her own choosing. And then:

"I shall speak some lines from a play. I want you to repeat them to me, as clearly as you can, and with as much passion as you can . . ."

An hour later, Selena was sent back to the dressing room, where a jug, bowl and towels had been set out for her to wash the sweat off herself before she put on her own clothes again.

"Well?" said Katty Cooper.

"She'll never make an actress. She sings passing well. She dances with moderate grace . . . and every man in England will fall in love with her! She enchants the eye, she ravishes the senses."

"So?"

"She'll do! Songs and dances can be arranged to suit her limitations, and she should appear in melodramas and spectacles . . . wearing as few clothes as decency will allow!"

"Good," said Katty. "Then you'll book her?"

"Of course." He shrugged. "And I suppose you'll tour the provinces?"

"Getting letters of recommendation from such as yourself."

"And will descend upon London in triumph . . ."

"Yes," said Katty. "It will take some months, but I'll do it."

Abbey looked miserable. "And you'll show her off on stage," he said, "then sell her to the highest bidder?"

Katty Cooper smiled with exquisite prettiness, and sighed in peaceful contentment. She nodded.

"Oh yes," she said, "as many times as I may."

Chapter 16

Three bells of the afternoon watch
11th June 1753
Aboard Walrus
The Thames, England

Captain Warrington stood proud at the helm as *Walrus* came up the two-mile stretch of water from Rotherhithe towards London Bridge, where the slow, brown river – swept by two tides a day – ran to mud-flats on either hand with ancient embankments shored up by massive timber piles that had been driven home when Queen Bess was a girl. To *Walrus*'s people, the docks and the city they served seemed enormous beyond belief; veteran seamen though they were, they'd spent their lives out of England, and had never seen the like of London town. So all hands lined the rail and gaped as they passed row upon row of quays, wharves, warehouses and cranes, and ships whose number was beyond counting, and whose masts and spars arose like virgin forest.

Thus all aboard were merry except McLonarch and Norton, who were down below in irons: Norton bitterly resentful at his fall from first mate's rank, while McLonarch pretended calm understanding. And all the while, "Captain" Warrington strutted the quarterdeck, and the crew jumped to his orders and raised their hats . . . for Warrington had redeemed himself halfway across the Atlantic.

He did it during a heavy blow, when Norton was standing alongside Long John in the cramped master's cabin under *Walrus's* quarterdeck, testing Mr Joe's growing competence at navigation.

Norton had just nudged Silver and nodded at the back of Mr Joe's curly-haired head, as the lad leaned over the table, stepping his dividers across the chart and making neat pencil notes on a piece of paper, calculating his latitude and the previous day's run.

"See?" whispered Norton. "I told you!" Silver shook his head in wonderment. "He's natural born for it," breathed Norton. "Coming on at the gallop."

"Buggered if I could do it!" said Silver, and Mr Joe never even heard, so intense was his concentration.

"A-hem," said another voice, from the hatchway. Silver and Norton turned. It was Warrington, up from his sickbed at last, and washed into some semblance of cleanliness – even his fingernails were dark grey rather than black – though he bore a livid scar across his brow as a souvenir of the fracas that had landed him in trouble.

"Shhh!" said Norton, frowning and pointing at Mr Joe.

"Oh!" said Warrington, then mouthing the word "Captain?" he stabbed a grubby finger hopefully upwards a couple of times, towards the quarterdeck.

"Pah!" said Silver. He patted Norton on the shoulder and clumped out as quietly as he could. Since there was too much wet and wind above for talking, he led the way back to the stern cabin. "Well?" said Silver, getting himself into a chair and pointing at one for Warrington, who licked his lips, blushed a bit, and sat facing Silver.

"Captain," he said, "I have made a complete arse of myself."

"Aye," said Silver, "nicely put, Mr Mate, for indeed you have."

"Yes," said Warrington, "and I wish to apologise."

Silver shrugged. Warrington had the look of a man who would be apologising as long as he lived.

"Please yourself!" said Silver. "I got two men now as can do your work."

"Aye," said Warrington, and sniffed, "but I have something to say."

"Do you now?"

"Yes. That fellow who nursed me when I was . . . a-hem . . . *ill.*"

"Jobo? Dr Cowdray's loblolly boy?"

"Yes. He said we are bound for London and told me of your plans."

"Did he!"

"He did, Captain." Warrington shook his head severely. "And it won't do!"

Silver frowned mightily and Warrington wriggled under his gaze and nervously picked his nose, and wiped his finger on a cuff that was already shiny with the fruits of previous pickings.

"And why not?" said Silver.

Warrington took a breath. "In the first place, sir, you must assume that *Venture's Fortune* has preceded us to England and spread word of a pirate ship led by yourself . . ." He paused and pointed at Cap'n Flint, perched on Silver's shoulder. "And you, sir, are a man easy to describe and to recognise!"

"Maybe," said Silver. "What if I am?"

"Then you must establish a new identity, sir, for yourself and this ship. A history, a purpose – and all of it backed with papers. You cannot sail into the greatest port in the world like bollocky-Bill the pirate and expect to be received with open arms."

"No?"

"No, sir you cannot! There must be letters, receipts, and a contract from your owner establishing your authority."

"What bloody owner?"

"There, sir! D'you not see?"

"See what?"

"See that you will have to deal with officials and persons of all kinds: Customs, Trinity House, port authorities, tradesmen, guildsmen, perhaps even officers of the law. You cannot behave as you might in Upper Barbados or Savannah."

"Can I not?" said Silver, already realising that he couldn't. He frowned and looked Warrington in the eye. "And who are you, then, what knows so much about bloody London?"

"I was born there, sir! Born and raised, and . . . a-hem . . . after *other* endeavours, I eventually went to sea out of the Port of London, where I am . . . to a degree . . . known and trusted."

"To a degree?" Silver laughed.

"Bah!" said Warrington. "I am no saint, sir, and I acknowledge the bottle as my invincible foe. But I know which palms to grease in London's port, and how much grease to apply . . . *and I'll bet my soul that you don't!*"

Silver fell silent. He was listening to wise counsel, and he knew it. He reached for the parrot and tickled its warm feathers. She squawked.

"*Bet my soul!*" she said.

Silver sighed. He took a breath and let out a great shout. "Sammy Hayden!" he roared. "Pass the word for Sammy Hayden!"

Soon, Sammy Hayden, ship's boy, came running into the cabin, touching his brow and stamping his foot in salute.

"Sammy-my-lad," said Silver, "my compliments to Mr Hands, Mr Joe, Dr Cowdray and Black Dog, and beg them to repair aft to this cabin at their earliest convenience! At the double, now . . . Oh, and Blind Pew besides, for he's got a head on his shoulders."

The meeting that followed had shaped a new life for *Walrus* and all aboard, including John Silver.

"A cook!" he cried, aghast. "A sodding *COOK?*"

The rest howled with laughter.

"Aye!" said Blind Pew, whose idea this was. As he explained in his Welsh lilt: "It's na-tural in the king's service, see? The cook is always such as has lost a pre-cious limb."

"We ain't *in* the king's bleedin' service!"

"But it'll *look* right, see? For you can't be cap'n when others is aboard: pilots, revenue and such. And you'll only need to pre-tend to be a cook."

"Good! 'Cos I soddin'-well ain't soddin' cooking!"

"Not you, Cap'n!" they said. "Not 'less we needs poisoning!" And they laughed.

"But you'll be our Cap'n, as ever," said Pew, "when none's aboard than us."

Warrington proved even more useful when it came to documents. He had a fine literary style, was a fluent draughtsman, and made best possible shift with such papers as were in the ship: the original bill of sale for *Walrus* from her builders in Sag Harbour, the Colony of New York, joined Sir Wyndham Godfrey's letter of introduction and his Protection for *Venture's Fortune* – now duly altered to show *Walrus's* name, for Warrington was an accomplished forger. Drawing upon his imagination and knowledge of London, he made sure that all papers as might prove necessary were at their disposal.

Finally, seeing how fluently he conducted these arcane matters, it was decided by council of all hands that he should be captain for all purposes of negotiation with shore authorities. The meeting ended with Warrington chaired shoulder-high and blind drunk round the ship to celebrate his captaincy.

Thus *Walrus* sailed into the Pool of London, which enormous port only Warrington knew well – him and the Trinity House man piloting them up-river, and Captain Warrington stood tall in the clean coat, decent linen and proper hat he'd been given, and declaimed in a booming voice, pointing out the sights while the pilot conned the ship.

The hands sniggered at this, and Israel Hands, Dr Cowdray and Mr Joe smiled. But they all listened, because what he said was interesting. He spoke about trade and money and riches.

"Greatest port in all the world," he said, sweeping an arm towards the packed warehouses, "receiving some thirteen thousand ships per year, carrying a trade worth over one hundred million pounds. The revenue on the West India ships alone runs to over a million pounds, and that of the East India Fleet is . . ."

Long John alone was not listening. He was looking upriver, past the barrier of London Bridge through which no ship could pass for its line of close-packed piers, and the taverns, shops and businesses above: a village in itself. Beyond lay the smoke and spires of the metropolis, where lived – according to Warrington – over three-quarters of a million people, and growing day by day. He sighed in despair. Choosing between Norton and McBollock would be nothing compared with finding Selena in this monster! Where would he start? How would he start? Which question was all the worse for the ghastly answer that in all probability he should look for his beloved darling . . . in the brothels.

So that night, with the pilot gone, and the ship moored in mid-river, Long John took Warrington aside to test his knowledge of London, especially its tart shops. They stood by the taffrail, aft, the ship and the river silent, the night dark and only an anchor watch on deck.

"Oh," said Warrington, when clumsily, awkwardly and with great reluctance, Silver explained the nature of his quest. Despite his own failings, Warrington had suffered a rush of blood to the brain on being allowed to pose as captain, and was about to be censorious in the matter of whoring, when – "Listen!" he said, seizing Silver's arm. There was a soft rumble from the bow, then the sound of a muffled blow, and a man falling. Standing where they were, in the dark, the mainmast and foremast hid Silver and Warrington from the bow . . . and *it* from them.

"Shh!" said Silver, moving quietly to the mainmast with Warrington in his wake. Peering round it, he could make out the anchor watch – two men, one of them Tom Allardyce, captain of the watch – lying unconscious on the deck, while six dark figures moved about running bars into the head of the capstan and muffling the pauls of its ratchet with rags. More men were appearing over the side from the fore chains, and – all in deathly silence – they began to lean on the bars and to bring the cable in.

"The sods!" said Silver. "What the buggery-an'-damnation are they doing?"

"They're *mudlarks,* Captain," said Warrington, softly.

"What the bastard Hell are they?"

"River pirates – and they're stealing your cable and anchor."

"*What?* With all hands aboard, in the bloody Thames, in bloody England?"

"Oh yes! They bribe the authorities and –"

"Shh!" said Silver. He beckoned Warrington and the pair slipped below to rouse all hands, silently and stealthily.

The men rolling out of their hammocks grinned and shook their heads at the thought of what was going on above.

"Cheeky bastards!" said Israel Hands.

"Aye!" said the rest, but in a whisper.

Above, on *Walrus*'s quiet maindeck, an exceptionally skilful team of men continued about their work under a thin moon, a few stars, with masts and furled sails above, and the deck gently rolling beneath their feet. *Walrus* was moored to two anchors by two cables, one of which had been slipped that the other might be hauled in and brought aboard . . . except that it wasn't coming aboard, but being passed over the side from the capstan and into a big boat made fast alongside the ship.

All was well. All was peaceful. All was the contentment of a good job being well done . . . when:

"AAAAAARGH!" roared the men who poured out through the aft hatchways.

"AAAAAARGH!" roared the men who poured out forrard.

And there followed five or six lively minutes of another good job being well done, as half *Walrus*'s crew leapt on the busy gang at the capstan, and the other half leapt into the boat receiving the cable, and both lots set about delivering the most comprehensive battering the mudlarks would ever receive.

By Silver's command, it was all done with pistol-butts. But it was thoroughly done and lovingly done by men enjoying the finest sport they'd had since leaving the Caribbean.

Afterwards, those of the intruders who could stand were lined up in the waist, with *Walrus*'s men grinning and laughing all around them, for it was indeed comical. There were ten of them, well caught and well battered.

"Who are you then, you swabs?" said Silver, stamping up and down the line.

The mudlarks stayed silent: snivelling, spitting teeth and dripping blood.

"Right!" said Silver, and grabbed one by the collar and dragged him to the side, yelling to his crew over one shoulder, "Fetch me a rope, and a dozen of roundshot in a sack!"

"Wassat for?" cried the mudlark.

"For you, my cocker. You're going for a swim!"

"You can't do that. We're King Jimmy's men! He'll have you, you –"

Smack! Silver let fly with a heavy fist.

"Ow!"

"Shut up! And who's King Jimmy?"

"King o' the fuckin' river, that's who, and he'll be asking after us, you wait!"

"A-hem, Captain . . .?" Warrington stepped forward.

"What?"

"These people have a certain influence . . ."

"See?" said the mudlark.

"Shut up!" Silver cuffed him backhanded and looked at Warrington. "Well?"

"'King of the river' is a sort of honorific for the biggest rogue among these people." He gestured at the men huddled on the shadowy maindeck.

"Is it now?" said Silver.

"They make so much money as to be able to bribe any officers of police as are sent after them, thus the forces of law pay no heed to their depredations in the night. Not even to the clash of arms! Not even to gunfire!"

"See? 'S'what I told yer!" said the mudlark.

"Aye!" said his mates.

"So you bleedin' let us go or it'll be the worse for you!"

"Aye!" said his mates, and Silver shook his head in amazement. Far from acting guilty or ashamed – or even fearful – the mudlarks were angry and resentful, as if some foul trick had been played upon them, and rules broken that decent men respected. Now they growled and muttered and glared at their captors.

"Shiver my timbers!" said Silver. "Well, I never did have hopes of putting the law on you, but here's two of my men beat unconscious, and you swabs trying to steal our cable. So I'll have a word with these good brothers, here –" he pointed to his crew "– to decide what's to be done with you."

After a swift debate, a motion proposed by Brother Pew was adopted, and soon after the mudlarks were sitting miserably in their boat: stark naked, shaven bald, with ship's tar coating their marriage tackle, while all aboard *Walrus* who could muster the necessary stood on the bulwarks pissing on their shiny white heads, and laughing fit to bust. All being finished, and shaken free of last drops, the mudlarks were allowed to cast off and pull away into the night.

It was a huge joke, enjoyed by all hands. But a few hours later, it didn't seem so funny.

Chapter 17

Early afternoon, 11th June 1753
Jackson's Coffee House
Off the Covent Garden Piazza
London

Mr Peter Jackson dazzled the eye and assaulted the senses. He was not merely dressed in the height of fashion: he defined it – or so he thought. His long, collarless coat was gold-laced blue silk, pierced with three dozen buttonholes; the yellow waistcoat beneath came down to the knees and was unbuttoned at the top to reveal the exquisite lace of his shirt-front, below the white stock around his neck.

An exotic waft of perfume complemented the ensemble, together with a white-powdered wig worked into elaborate side-curls and caught in a blue silk bow at the back. Combined with an elegance of speech and manners, the result was something so close to a gentleman that many onlookers couldn't tell the difference.

But it was there, if a man looked hard enough. It was written on Mr Jackson's face – fair and pleasing though it was, with long-lashed eyes, smooth chin, and easy smile – because any real man had only to look into Mr Jackson's eyes to see him for the sly, cunning, treacherous viper that he really was. It was for this reason he had become known

139

far and wide as Flash Jack the Fly Cove: Flash Jack for short, or simply Jack to his friends, of whom there seemed to be a great number, given that he was proprietor of the renowned Jackson's Coffee House – renowned less for its coffee than the various other goods and services on offer. So when Flash Jack walked down the aisle between the tables at Jackson's, smiling to all sides, he could expect to be cheerfully acknowledged.

Jackson's occupied the finest site in London: hemmed in by the main theatres and the bustling Covent Garden Piazza, it catered to a clientele of actors, musicians, artists, writers, publishers, and all those gentlemen who wished to be thought civilised. It opened early, closed late and was always busy.

Being on a corner, Jackson's had the advantage of two rows of windows, and the big main room was immaculately clean, its two long lines of tables equipped with high-backed benches that formed dozens of private booths for convivial talk, while still affording a good view of the life and fashion of the house and the city outside. Like most coffee houses, it was as much a club as anything else, and the *wrong* sort of persons were told – to their faces, by the waiters – that there was "No room! No room!" when plainly there was. And while *ladies* were charmingly received into a side room, the girls of Covent Garden were absolutely prohibited: even those who charged a guinea.

Today, Flash Jack was in excellent spirits. There were no less than four noblemen in the house, and the sun was shining brightly through his sparkling clean windows. All the world looked good; the table talk was of sport and racing, and not sombre fears of the great war that all the newspapers said was imminent. But as he was chatting deferentially to a clod-faced baronet and his party – fresh up from Devon with dung on their boots – lightning struck.

"Jack!" cried a voice. Flash Jack bowed to the baronet,

making careful note of the dullard's name so that he should be greeted by it ever after, and looked down the aisle towards the door. He looked . . . and he looked . . . and his jaw went towards his boots.

Sir Frederick Lennox was advancing with a friend at his side. Sir Frederick was familiar, having a house not five minutes away. But his friend was something marvellously, wonderfully new. With the sun shining into the dark interior, the new gentleman was bathed in golden light; indeed, he appeared golden in every way. He was the most beautiful creature that Flash Jack had ever seen. A perfect Mediterranean man, such as the sculptors of the Greeks had recorded in marble: handsome, athletic, graceful . . . and dangerous.

Flash Jack shuddered in delight, for his taste was very, *very* much for dangerous young men, and he carried the scars beneath his clothes to prove it. But now he saw that all previous incarnations had been mere bruisers. The man walking towards him was seriously, deadly dangerous. Flash Jack blinked, and gulped and gasped.

"Jack!" said Sir Frederick, coming alongside. "I should like you to meet Lieutenant Flint."

"Flint?" said Flash Jack, who kept abreast of all the news. "Flint the mutineer?"

The choice of word was unfortunate. Flint turned his gaze upon Flash Jack, and poor Jacky nearly died with pleasure at the cobra's stare that pierced normal men with fright.

"Mutineer be damned!" Sir Frederick frowned. "All that is lies put out by the Hastings clique."

"Indeed, sir," said Flint, taking Flash Jack's hand, "there has been a foul conspiracy."

Flash Jack never entirely remembered the next few minutes, except in a rapture of wonder, but eventually his sharply focused mind took hold of itself and he came to seated at one of his tables together with Lieutenant Flint, who sat oppo-

141

site, talking to him, with Sir Frederick got rid of, seated at a table with other friends at the far end of the room.

". . . or so I am told," said Flint with a smile.

"Beg pardon, my dear sir?" said Flash Jack.

"I am told that you can supply anything. Absolutely anything."

"Ah!" Jack smiled, for he was on sure ground. "That would depend upon price."

Flint paused. A distant expression came into his eyes and Flash Jack could see that he was thinking furiously. Then Flint fixed him with his hypnotic gaze.

"How much money can you imagine? How much can you desire?"

"What do you mean?" Flash Jack frowned slightly. He was no fool.

"Have you heard of Captain Lightning, the highwayman?"

"Who hasn't?"

"I killed him last night. Him and his crew."

"*Killed him?*" Flash Jack shuddered in ecstasy.

"Yes. And I'm due five hundred as reward."

"Five hundred?"

"And that's only the beginning."

There was a pause like that of swordsmen who have clashed blades, exchanged strokes, and leapt back to recover.

"So what is it you want?" said Flash Jack.

"I want a ship, with a crew and provisions for the West Indies."

"Then go down to the Pool of London and hire one."

"Ahhhh . . . there are circumstances."

"What circumstances?"

"I am freed by the navy under restrictions. I may not leave England."

"No?"

"Nor would it be advisable for me to seek a ship."

"Yet you come to me?"

142

Flint smiled and leaned close, and every hair on Flash Jack's body tingled in delight.

"I do so because I trust you," said Flint.

"Flint! Flint!" cried Sir Frederick, stumping up the aisle waving a booklet.

"Later," said Flint to Flash Jack.

"Look –" said Sir Frederick "– I've got a copy of this rogue's book!"

Lennox leered at Flash Jack, and Flint tapped his foot under the table.

"What book?" he said.

"The one I told you about: *Jackson's List*. His guide to the whores of London!"

"Oh," said Flint, who was tired of Sir Frederick constantly turning every conversation to the subject of whores. Flint was a singular man in this regard. It wasn't that he was incapable with women: those shameful days were gone. But he could play the man's role only in highly restrictive circumstances, and it galled him that a creature like Sir Frederick could so easily manage what he could scarce achieve.

"Look!" said Sir Frederick, laughing, and he squeezed himself in beside Flint and opened the book he'd just bought. He pointed a pudgy finger at Flash Jack: "*He* writes this, you know. Jackson's his real name!" Flash Jack smiled modestly. "It's the most capital book: a guide to all the tarts of the town – their looks, prices, services offered. And damned funny, too, because he knows who's poking whom, and he puts it all in – in code – and you have to work it out! Fellows go through it pissing themselves laughing when a new edition comes out at Christmas, which it does every year. Now let me see . . ." He looked down and flicked through the book, searching for something.

"Ah! Here it is! Here you are, Flint," said Sir Frederick merrily, nudging Flint. "I saw your face last night when

I mentioned black girls. Here's just the little beauty for you . . ."

Billy Bones stood and looked at London's great arena of pleasures, amazed that so vast an open space could exist within the dense mass of churches, domes and chimneys that was the capital.

He'd been sent away on his own by Flint, who was off to a coffee house with Sir Frederick for a private talk. Billy Bones didn't mind that, because if he'd had to spend a moment longer in Sir Frederick's company it would have ended in trouble. The pompous ass had made a big show, in front of everyone, giving Billy a handful of coins to spend, as if he was rewarding some bloody servant! He'd been all set to teach the bugger a lesson when a glance from Flint warned him off, so instead he mumbled, "Aye-aye, Sir Frederick!" and pocketed the money with a touch of his hat in salute.

He'd left the house fuming about it, but the moment he entered Covent Garden Piazza all thoughts of Sir Frederick vanished as he stood and marvelled at the great canyons of brick. He was surrounded on all sides by rows of buildings running to four and five stories high, with windows ranked like guardsmen on parade, and some with stone colonnades and shops within, and some with carriages pulling up outside, and the grey mass of St Paul's church to one side, with its four columns and its pediment above, and the golden-capped Sundial Column rearing up over all, and what seemed like thousands upon thousands of people, rich and poor, young and old, tradesmen and beggars, soldiers and cripples milling about the place.

He started by walking along the line of fruit and vegetable

stalls running the length of one side of the square, and he treated himself to some splendid oranges – for Billy Bones loved oranges – and one by one he peeled them with his clasp knife and ate them, then sat down on the steps of St Paul's to lick the juice from his fingers. Afterwards he wandered into the square, past the heavy white-timbered fence that marked out the inner heart of the Piazza. There was such noise and bustle as could hardly be believed, with street musicians, tumblers, hawkers, jugglers, fire-breathers and men on stilts. Billy Bones looked on, amazed, and some of the misery of his recent life lifted off his shoulders.

More than that, there were tides flowing within Billy Bones's mind. He knew he'd done bad things. He'd done *very* bad things . . . *atrocious* things. And he knew who'd led him to it! He sighed. He groaned. And yet, aboard *Bounder* – for a precious while – he'd been a king's officer again. He'd worn uniform. He'd wallowed gloriously in all the practices and traditions of the sea service: the service that he'd joined as a lad and grown to love. He looked around the seething, heaving Piazza and again felt the urge that, in this different place, he could be a different man, and a better one. But first he had to find . . .

"'Ere!" said a lively girl in a bright-coloured costume: all lozenges and stars and a big red hat. She nudged Billy Bones with an elbow, breaking his thoughts. "Yore a likely wunanmall, aintchernow?" She poked him in the ribs, and laughed, causing her tits to wobble in her low-cut dress. Billy Bones grinned. He could hardly understand these Londoners with their nasal, ugly speech, but he liked the look of the girl. He was just wondering what she was at when a drum rolled and a trumpet blew . . . and two more girls appeared, dressed identically: one a drummer, one a trumpeter. When he turned back to the first girl, she was gone – off to find more men, from the look of it.

Then a large, fat man in good clothes mounted wooden steps to a platform that raised him up above the mob.

"Gentlemen of England," he roared, "and all those beef-and-beer-men who relish the noble art of fisticuffs!" He paused to draw breath and the drum and trumpet sounded again. "Stand forward now to show the ladies the strength of your arm –" he raised a hand and spoke to one side of it, as if in confidence "– *if* you has the pluck!"

Hmmm, thought Billy Bones as the fat man blathered on. So, the fellow was a prizefighter's barker. Beside the little platform on which he stood, Billy now saw a ring marked out with rope and stakes, and a tent behind, and a number of big, broken-nosed men, stripped to the waist, pumps on their feet, all waiting in a row with their arms folded over their chests, and the public gathering thick around them, already taking bets.

"Thass Pat Cobbler, that is!" said a Londoner beside Billy Bones.

"I'll avva dollar onnim!" said another, as Billy Bones strained to understand.

"Yeah! Eezevvywate chaampyun, ee is. Anniss ten-pun to the cove wot noksim dahn."

Ahhh! thought Billy, and he pushed his way through the growing crowd.

He stood and watched the first couple of fights, which – astonishingly – were carried out strictly according to rules, with no biting of ears or gouging of eyes, and rounds timed by the sand-glass, and bully boys standing by to beat intruders out of the ring with cudgels. They even matched the fighters by weight, which was a great novelty to Billy Bones, as was the amazing fact that when one man was thrown down by a cross-buttock, and his opponent – to Billy Bones's loud approval – began to kick him about the head, the beaters dashed in and drove off the standing man . . . until the other got up!

Billy Bones shook his head at this namby-pamby business and wondered what England was coming to. But when the fight was over, and Pat Cobbler the heavyweight was standing in the ring with no takers stepping forward and all eyes searching for one, the same girl Billy Bones had seen earlier appeared at his side and linked her arm in his.

"'Ere-za-bulldog-boy!" she cried, winking at Billy. "'Ere-za-cockerthewalk!" And she pulled him towards the ring. "Cummon tiger!" she cried, and a great cheer went up from the crowd as they caught sight of Billy Bones and measured him up against the champion.

Well, thought Billy Bones, *why not?* He hoisted the girl clear off her feet, planted a smacking kiss on her lips, put her down, and threw his hat into the ring.

And when they took off his shirt, and the crowd saw the breadth of Billy Bones's chest and arms, and the way he took up his stance and milled the air with heavy fists – why, the cheers shook the windows of the Piazza, and a great rush from all sides swelled the crowd . . . to the delight of the fat barker, for it was sixpence each into his bully boys' collecting boxes from those who wanted to stand and watch, and sixpences were falling like rain!

It was a hard fight for Billy Bones, for they insisted on stopping him from doing perfectly reasonable things: stamping Cobbler's feet, hacking his shins and slamming him round the ear with the side of the head. Moreover, Pat Cobbler hadn't come by his reputation for nothing. He was a fighting Irishman and a crafty boxer who used his fists with skill and economy of effort. And this told against Billy Bones, whose method of fighting was neither artful nor clever nor skilful.

But Pat Cobbler hadn't lived Billy Bones's life. He'd never fought to kill. He'd always fought by rules, and was used to fighting clumsy, drunken yokels, or other professionals like himself, who likewise fought by rules, and only for money. Certainly he used dirty tricks, as they all did, but he'd never seen decks slopping in blood, and men's limbs torn off, or heard the shrieks of the wounded and the groans of the dying.

And he didn't fight like Billy Bones: head down, shoulders forward, never retreating, and hammer hammer hammer with both fists, up to and beyond exhaustion, and ignoring the pain, and never, *ever*, admitting defeat. This ferocious, simple-minded discipline, born of a ferocious, simple-minded life, and matched with the powerful body God had given Billy Bones, put Pat Cobbler over on his back after five long, punishing rounds, such that not even repeated buckets of cold water could get him up.

So Billy Bones got his ten pounds, and was chaired by the mob, shoulder high round the Piazza. Then he picked one of the tarts who'd ogled him, took a private room at an inn and rogered her till she squealed, and was so heartened by his victory that courage rose within him: courage to do the thing that he had been dreaming of since first he came to London, and that otherwise he'd not have dared to do.

Chapter 18

Three bells of the morning watch
12th June 1753
Aboard Walrus
The Pool of London

The night was alive with flaming torches. *Walrus* was enclosed within boatloads of angry men, and the shining, black river reflected the flames rising over the little fleet. There were twenty boats in all, with more than three hundred men aboard . . . and drawn steel and firelocks gleaming in the torchlight.

One boat pulled forward, and a man stood up in the stern. He was thick-bodied, stubble-chinned, and grim-faced. He wore cross-belts loaded with arms, and a hat stuck with three huge white ostrich plumes. Cupping his hands round his mouth, he let forth a shout:

"Ahoy, you bastards! I'm Jimmy Ogilvy, king o' the river, and I'm come for what I'm owed!"

"AYE!" roared his men, and there was a great waving of torches and shaking of arms.

"Stand forward, him who's in command, say I!" cried King Jimmy. "Stand forth or be boarded, plundered, and burned!"

"AYYYYYE!"

"What the buggery is this?" said Long John to Warrington,

149

as all hands stood to action stations, looking out on a force that outnumbered them nearly five to one, and had crept up so quiet, and with torches unlit, that they were all around the ship before the watch had even seen them.

"It's King Jimmy," said Warrington, legs trembling in fear.

"I can see that, you swab!" said Long John. "But what's he want?"

"Revenge, Captain. For the shaming of his men!"

"God damn it, this is bloody London. What bloody law runs here?"

"His!" said Warrington, looking at King Jimmy. "So long as it's dark, and there's nobody to come to our aid."

"STAND FORTH!" cried King Jimmy. "LAST WARNING!"

"Oh, Mary and bleedin' Jesus!" said Silver.

"What we going to do, John?" said Israel Hands.

Silver sighed. He tipped his hat back, stroked the parrot, and thought. Too late to run out the guns and sweep the buggers with grape. They'd be aboard as soon as they heard the gun-trucks squeak. Too late to rig boarding nettings, even if *Walrus* had any – which she didn't – and it couldn't come to a hand-to-hand fight, not against so many. So what to do?

"Can they be paid off?" said Silver to Warrington, who trembled and shook.

"I don't know. They may want blood for blood!"

Silver cursed horribly.

"Then we'll just have to find out!" he said, and called his people together. "This is what we'll do . . . And you, Mr Mate –" Silver poked Warrington in the chest "– you pay close heed to me . . ."

"WITH ME, BOYS!" cried King Jimmy. "GIVE WAYYYY!"

A great roar went up from the boats, followed by a clunking of oars, as the mudlarks pulled to grapple and board.

"Wait! Wait!" Warrington, having clambered up on the bulwark by the main shrouds, was hanging on with one arm, a sheer drop into the Thames looming in front of him. He

150

was plainly terrified, puffing and wheezing and glancing nervously back at the man behind him holding his legs so he shouldn't fall off. "We've ten thousand Spanish dollars aboard," he cried, "and willing to pay reasonable reparation!"

"What?" cried King Jimmy, and turned to his men. "Hold hard, my lovely boys!"

"What?" they said, and laid on their oars.

"Who are you, you fat sod?" cried King Jimmy to Warrington.

"Master of this ship!"

"What's this about dollars?"

"We are willing to pay reparation, for the insult done to your people."

"A-ha!" cried King Jimmy, and stood up and twirled his ostrich plumes and looked round at his men. "See, boys?" he cried. "Ain't I king o' the river and no mistake? See what I can get you?"

"AYE!" cried some, but not those with shaven heads and the tar still clinging to their balls. They wanted the red meat of revenge, not the gruel of money.

"I want his teeth for a blasted necklace!" cried one of the shaven, pointing at Warrington. "And twelve dozen of the cat for all hands, and . . . and . . ."

"Yes, yes!" said King Jimmy, "time for that later – let's get the dollars first!"

"AYE!"

"Then please to come alongside," said Warrington, and he reached down to those behind him and was handed something, which he hurled towards King Jimmy's boat . . . and there was a twinkling and glittering and chinking of metal as the little missiles landed aboard.

"Dollars!" cried King Jimmy's oarsmen. "Dollars, lads!"

"Huzzah!"

"We are *not* the valiant who taste of death but once!" said Warrington.

"Bollocks!" cried a voice from the boats.

"Friends, Englishmen, countrymen, lend me your ears! We seek mercy!"

"Pig-shite!"

"For the quality of mercy is not strained!"

"Fuck off!"

"It droppeth as the gentle rain from Heaven."

As he spoke, Warrington threw more dollars and the boats crowded in beneath him, King Jimmy's in the lead, and all aboard sneering and laughing at the miserable figure spouting above, who was giving in so easily and without a fight . . . And thus the mudlarks came alongside of *Walrus*, slow and easy, and threw no grappling hooks and made no attempt to board but sat looking upward in expectation, until . . .

CRRRRASH! A tremendous, rolling volley of small-arms fire roared out from *Walrus* and night turned to day in livid daggers of muzzle-flash as Silver's men fired every pistol, musket, blunderbuss and carbine in the ship into the writhing mass of men in the boats alongside, only spitting distance away. Over a hundred rounds of well-aimed lead came sizzling down into flesh, timber, blood, bone and some of it into Father Thames. Ears were deafened by the roar, and eyes temporarily blinded by the flash.

A horrible moan arose from the mudlark boats even as a picked team of men, all good swimmers and led by Mr Joe, dropped over the side from *Walrus* – splash-splash-splash – while a reserve of five of the ship's best marksmen, armed with muskets, kept up a steady fire into King Jimmy's boat so that none aboard should hinder Mr Joe's team as they hauled themselves into the launch. Some went down, nonetheless, under cutlass strokes and pistol fire, but most clambered aboard and set about seizing the oars. And all the while *Walrus*'s people were loading and ramming with fresh cartridges and ready for another united volley . . . which they gave with a flash and a roar, at Long John's word, as the other mudlark boats saw what was happening to King Jimmy and tried to go to his aid, only to find themselves on the receiving end of another withering storm of lead that smashed and pierced and tore, until one boat began to fill and to settle as holes were knocked squarely through its bottom.

"Ahhhhh! Ahhhh! Ahhhh!" cried the mudlarks.

"Fire at will, boys!" cried Long John as the smoke swirled over *Walrus*'s decks, "but bring Mr Joe safe aboard: him and all his lads – and that swab of a King Jimmy – and then run out the guns and load with grape!"

"Huzzah!" roared the crew, and soon the dazed, bedraggled king o' the river was dragged over *Walrus*'s rail with three of his men, while the long black snouts of her main battery rumbled clear of the ship's sides, proclaiming death and disembowelment to any fool who chose to approach unasked aboard of a boat, which none did, for they saw they were beat and hung back.

The butcher's bill for Silver's men was three dead or drowned, and Tom Allardyce still so deep unconscious that Dr Cowdray feared for his life. But the mudlarks suffered worse, with bodies face down in the water and cries and moans, and one boat sunk, and blood in the bilge water, and oars smashed and their captain taken . . . who nonetheless would not give up.

"You'll pay for this, you . . ." he shrieked into Silver's face, and let loose such a string of filth as left even *Walrus*'s men impressed. "You can't touch me!" he cried. "I got a lord mayor's badge! I got magistrates! I can buy every damn glutman, lumper and revenue-man on the river. I can –"

Thump! Silver clouted him with a heavy fist, and King Jimmy staggered and suddenly fell over as his left leg twisted . . . came apart below the knee, and a wooden peg-leg rattled and bumped and rolled across the deck. King Jimmy fought to get up: growling, cursing and helpless . . . and a great pity fell upon Silver, and guilt for what he'd done to a man like himself: a poor ruined cripple. For deep inside of John Silver, the pain had never gone away: the awful grieving over the cruelty of his own mutilation, and the loss of his manly swagger. It hadn't gone, nor ever would it, and in the present moment it swelled into agony.

"Ugh!" cried Silver, and wiped away the self-pitying tears with the back of his cuff. "Here, shipmate!" he said, reaching down to haul King Jimmy up . . . where he stood hopping and balancing, and hanging on to Silver's hand for support.

"You long streak o' fuckin' piss," said King Jimmy. "Why don't you gimme a loan o' your'n?" And he pointed at Silver's crutch.

Silver laughed uneasily, staring at King Jimmy. "Huh!" he said finally. "Fetch him his timber limb, lads!" And a couple of hands found it and helped King Jimmy strap it in place, so he could stand up like a man again, even if a far smaller one than Long John, who towered over him.

"What am I going to do with you?" said Silver.

"Hang him! Gut him! Skin him!" cried the crew.

"Belay all that, you swabs," said Silver, "for I'm taking this bugger below, for questioning."

And so John Silver found a new friend in a strange place, for as he sat in his cabin with a couple of men outside, in case King Jimmy turned nasty, he was amazed how much he had in common with his prisoner.

"Cart horse, it were," said King Jimmy. "Us kids was playing knock-belly, running in line under horses and slapping them, and I was last, and I got kicked, and it festered." He looked down at his wooden leg. "Local carpenter took it off with his saw. We hadn't no gelt for a surgeon. Did a rough job, and it still bleeds sometimes, for it ain't never healed quite right."

Silver shook his head in sympathy.

"Him as ampytated *me* was a master surgeon," he said. "Latin by the bucket! He's aboard this ship now. D'you want him to look at your leg?"

154

King Jimmy shuddered.

"Not for a pension!" he said. "I still remember the saw grinding the bones."

"Aye!" said Silver, and he got out the rum, and they raised glasses.

"Here's to that old actor you put up there!" said Jimmy. "Fooled me!"

"What actor?"

"Charles Warrington. Cap'n, indeed! I only recognised him when I came aboard."

"*Warrington?* Was he an actor?"

Jimmy nodded. "I saw him in that play where a moll gets done in by a blackamoor, and me and the lads went with cobbles to pelt the bleeder . . ." He grinned. "Warrington was playing the blackie, but he came on three sheets to the wind and fell into the orchestra pit."

Silver laughed, and as they talked he found King Jimmy – though completely illiterate – to be quick and clever, and facing the same problems as himself in leading men and keeping them sweet. Thus they talked, for all captains are lonely, and there are things said easier to a stranger than a friend. So they told their stories, and even found common cause.

"How did I become a gentleman o' fortune?" said Silver. "Why, my own ship was took, and I did for a few of them as took it, and they made me make up the loss."

"Oh?" said King Jimmy. "Chopped a few, did you? How many?"

"A few," said Silver.

King Jimmy winked.

"Garn! You can tell me. How many?"

Silver shrugged. "Six," he said.

"Gor blimey!" King Jimmy raised a glass in salute.

"Well," said Silver, as if in explanation, "I had ten toes in them days."

"Huh!" said King Jimmy. "And now I'm a few men short, because of you!"

"Serves you bleedin-well right!"

They laughed, and the talk turned to the future and what Silver was going to do with the two prisoners he'd brought to London.

"Start with Norton," said Jimmy. "I know him – pick o' the Bow Street men. He needs to be in the river with his throat cut."

"No, no, no," said Silver, "I can't do that!"

King Jimmy shook his head.

"You're a funny bugger for a pirate, John."

"Gentlemen o' fortune! Not a pirate."

"No? Ain't you never done nothing bad?"

Silver closed his eyes . . . and saw Ratty Richards's face. He sighed.

"There you are then," said Jimmy. "But never mind, for others is worse: like members of parliament! You can't do *their* job without telling lies and getting men killed! And them bastards wants another war! How many thousands will *that* kill, beside the few that you and I pop off, John Silver?"

Telling lies, thought Silver, for that stood out from all the rest, and it sank his heart like lead.

"John, John," said Jimmy, and leaned forward and put a thick, gnarled hand on Silver's arm. His face was battered and ugly, he was grey and stubble-chinned. He was twenty years older than Silver, and he wanted to help. "What is it, lad?"

"I don't know what to do," said Silver. "I've come here to save my wife, if she's to be saved. But I've told all hands another tale, and they've trusted me."

"Well then," said King Jimmy, "we must help one another, you and I. So set me free –"

"I'd do that anyway!"

"Set me free . . . *with a sack of dollars*, so I can go back with me head high and me feathers in me hat, and I'll be your eyes and ears in London. I knows every receiver in town, all the watchmen, the night coves, pickpockets and burglars, and the Jew-boy money-lenders too: and *their* fingers go up every hole and crack!" King Jimmy nodded. "Oh yes! I'll find out about your Jacobites . . . and . . . I'll send out word for a new black girl in the knocking shops."

Silver groaned and put his head in his hands.

King Jimmy patted his shoulder. "You got to face it, lad. If she's in that trade, then that's where you'll find her."

Then a thought struck him.

"Wait a bit," he said, "your girl's something special, ain't she? A real bang-up prancer: a great beauty? And young?"

"Aye," said Silver miserably.

"So, listen here, John Silver," said King Jimmy, "and I'll tell you what to do with your crew and your ship and your wife . . ." Then he paused and frowned. "The kiddie you want, for top-of-the-trade such as your Selena would be, is one as wouldn't let me through his door. But he might talk to *you,* if you was dressed up proper."

"And who's that?"

"Flash Jack the Fly Cove!"

Chapter 19

*M*iss Jenkins tottered across the room towards Flint wearing white stockings tied over the knee with red ribbons, and small red shoes with neat little heels. She wore that and nothing else, for that's what Flint liked and what he needed.

Flint gazed at her shining black skin and all the wonders between waist and chin that bounced and swayed and quivered. Miss Jenkins offered him the tea-cup that she'd just re-filled on the neat and pretty little table by the window, where a neat and pretty little tea service was moored, and none of it as neat and pretty as Miss Jenkins's posture as she'd worked the tea-pot: straight back, straight legs, knees together, and delectable round bottom aimed at the client as she bent over the table to pour.

Flint sighed and wondered if he could manage another bout? But he'd fired three rounds already that morning. He smiled and his eyes wandered to the tousled bed, on the other side of the lavishly furnished room, for Miss Jenkins did not work cheap, and her gentlemen demanded the best.

She smiled at Flint, curtsied delightfully, and handed him the teacup, saying:

"Ee-yah Capting!" Flint took the cup, set it aside, and kissed her neatly on the point of each breast. "Ooo!" she said, "Wannabit more do ya?" And she folded her arms round his neck, and wriggled her behind.

Flint smiled. The voice was wonderfully coarse. It so thoroughly completed the necessary mixture, for Flint's capabilities were limited to those who followed Miss Jenkins's profession, while to all other females he was null and void: true to the ferocious prohibition driven into him by his long-departed religious maniac of a father, who doubtless sizzled in Hell this very instant, nodding in grim satisfaction over his son's impediment.

Why else – the Reverend Flint would ask – should the Almighty permit the existence of fallen ones, except for the detestable expression of vile and contemptible lust? It was a question impossible for a child to understand, let alone answer, but it had been screamed at little Joseph Flint so many times, and with such venom, that the sense of it had penetrated, if not the entire meaning. Thus Flint could perform only with whores.

He was also limited to black girls. But the reason for that was painful beyond contemplation.

Meanwhile, Flint kissed a few more choice parts of Miss Jenkins, got himself up, got fully dressed, paid a generous tip, was rewarded with a smile, and was shown out. The only thing that had marred a delightful encounter, he mused as he made his way down the stairs to the street, was the inevitable, unavoidable, un-crushable thought that Miss Jenkins – pretty as she was – could not compare with . . . with . . .

Flint's face twisted. It contorted. He stopped in his tracks in the busy street, closed his eyes and clenched his fists, gritted his teeth and groaned, for there were a thousand ways in which Joe Flint was not as other men were.

And then the spasm was gone. Flint opened his eyes, stared down those passers-by who were looking at him strangely, and walked briskly to Sir Frederick's house, to keep an appointment to see one of the great ones of the town, someone of whom Sir Frederick stood in awe and was delighted to have obtained an invitation to meet.

Flint was intrigued that Sir Frederick was showing signs of interests outside his usual range, and was happy to be taken to a splendid house in Bramhall Square, where that renowned leader of fashion, Lady Faith Carlisle, kept a salon.

Carriages lined the pavement outside the house, coachmen and footmen stood politely awaiting their masters, and a small crowd of the common herd was hanging about by the entrance, gawping at the famous and the splendid as they made their way up the flight of five broad steps to the main door.

Flint and Sir Frederick were admitted with deep bows, and led upstairs to the salon: a splendid room on the first-floor front, complete with Chinese wallpaper, pier glasses, huge windows, and opulent soft furnishings. They were announced by a butler, received by Lady Faith, and led down the centre of the room towards a knot of gentlemen centred on an enormous man in grey, scholarly wig. He was untidy and of bizarre appearance, being afflicted with twitches and odd gestures. But nonetheless he was holding forth, to the delight, respect and admiration of all present: and these were the cream of London society.

"Look," said Sir Frederick proudly, "it's Johnson!"

"Who?" said Flint, and Lady Faith winced.

"*Johnson!*" said Sir Frederick.

"Who's he?" said Flint, and Lady Faith all but fainted.

"Johnson! *Dictionary* Johnson. The lexicographer!"

"Sir Frederick," said Flint, perceiving that he was the only man in the room who didn't know the name, "I've lived a strange life, mostly out of England, beyond Christian civilisation –" he smiled with gleaming teeth "– you must instruct me."

Sir Frederick had that uneasy feeling again. The feeling

160

that came when Flint looked him in the eyes. He didn't want to admit that the feeling was fear – stabbing, unholy fear – but it was.

"Ah . . . er . . ." said Smith, and found words: "Johnson is the foremost man of letters in England," he said. "He has published a magnificent dictionary, which he has written alone in a matter of years. A tremendous achievement! In France, the entire Academy Française laboured for a generation to produce a lesser work."

Sir Frederick turned to gaze at Johnson, in the midst of his admirers, bellowing loudly and slapping a huge hand on the table to emphasise his point.

"He is a genius," gushed Lennox, "and the entire fashionable world is educated by his pronouncements."

Flint and Sir Frederick found seats close to Johnson, and were served tea – making Flint smirk, recalling the last cup he'd drunk. But when he settled down to listen, even Flint was fascinated by the power of Johnson's conversation, his cunning wit, his vast learning, and his tremendous vigour, along with a gift for superbly crafted phrases that delighted the ear, tickled the mind, and took root in the memory.

Thus all was smiles and respect – until a sudden disaster occurred. Coming to the end of a story, Johnson rocked on his seat, in his odd fashion, loudly cried "Huh!" . . . *and passed a rolling thunder of wind*: loud, strong and tremendous, as only a big man can who has a large dinner digesting inside of him.

At once there was a united attempt to pretend that nothing had happened. All around, ladies and gentlemen studied the floor, the ceiling and the pictures hanging on the walls, and there was a great clearing of throats and coughing, as if these innocent sounds would embrace Johnson's as one of their own.

But none could avoid sniffing . . . and knowing . . . and blushing.

"Urrrrgh!" growled Johnson, and his heavy face twitched, and reddened, and the mighty brows darkened. A profound silence descended on the room. Not even the mice beneath the floorboards dared breathe. But the Devil spurred Flint to speak:

"My poor sir!" he said, leaning forward in impertinent familiarity and daring to place a hand on one of Johnson's. "I do sympathise."

"*Uhhhhhhhhhh!*" gasped the company: trembling, horrified, and fearing an explosion.

"Sympathise?" cried the giant. "What d'ye mean, sir? Explain yourself!"

"Sir," said Flint with eyes of utmost innocence, "I *sympathise* with you in your struggle to contain these formidable pressures!"

"WHAT?"

"Indeed, sir, I know from experience the burden of your struggle."

Johnson was now on a hair trigger, and risen half out of his seat. He was a vastly big man with hands like oak roots and limbs like Corinthian columns. His face was purple, his lips were working and it was the spin of a coin whether he would anathematise Flint with soul-shrivelling castigation – to damn him as the butt of all the town – or attack him physically with the aid of the heavy walking stick that he'd seized in his right hand. The company reacted as one, forming a sea of gaping mouths, staring eyes and paralysed horror.

"*WHAT?*" roared Johnson.

Flint, adopting an air of utmost innocence, spread his hands in explanation: "My own father, sir," he said, "was a being of such exquisite sensibilities that disdaining all vulgarity in himself, he employed others to break wind on his behalf: a common fellow on weekdays and a superior person – a gentleman – to fart for him in church on Sundays."

162

"*Ohhhhhhh!*" groaned the company. But Flint sat so solemn, and stared at Johnson with such an air of seeking to be of assistance . . . that Johnson perceived . . . and snorted . . . and broke into booming, convulsive laughter. He laughed over and over, for the best part of five minutes, till the tears flowed, his body shook, the rafters trembled, and the room was merriment from end to end as the courtiers followed the king's example. Folk even looked up in the street to see what the laughter was all about.

"You rogue, sir!" cried Johnson, when he regained control. "You jolly dog! You saucy fellow!" And he beamed at Flint. "Who are you, sir? *What* are you?"

Flint told his story with customary skill, so nearly telling the truth that it was wonderful how innocent of all blame he turned out to be. Thus Johnson and the company nodded wisely and smiled.

"A sailor and an adventurer!" said Johnson, as if lost in admiration. "Every man thinks the less of himself for not having been a soldier, and not having gone to sea," he said. "And I see, Mr Flint, that you are, in both senses, a paragon!"

"Ah!" said the company.

"You are a Ulysses, sir," said Johnson. "Such a man as makes England triumphant at sea, and the terror and despair of her enemies!"

All present cooed their agreement, especially the Brownlough brothers, two large and lumpish sons of a London banker, who sat together in a corner. Had Flint been able to read the future, he would have fallen at their knees. But he couldn't and he didn't. Nevertheless he returned to Sir Frederick's house in the highest of good humour.

Sir Frederick having business in his study, Flint adjourned to the library, generously allowed to himself and Billy Bones as a day room. He entered just as Billy Bones was going out. Flint was full of himself, laughing and chuckling, casually

163

flinging hat, coat and wig aside for the servant to deal with, before he threw himself into an armchair.

"Billy-my-chicken!" he cried.

"What?"

"What, *sir*. Will you never learn?"

Billy Bones scowled.

"Them ways is shipboard ways," he said.

"Indeed?" said Flint. "Are they indeed?" And he laughed. He was too merry to take offence. "In that case, Mr Bones, would you do me the honour to bring me a bottle and a glass from the sideboard?"

"Huh!" said Billy Bones, and did as he was bid.

"So where are you going, Mr Bones? I see you have your hat and coat on, and your walking stick at your side. Are you off on another voyage of exploration?"

Billy Bones blushed. He actually blushed, unwilling to reveal the nature of his mission.

Oh? thought Flint, instantly spotting Mr Bones's mood. *What's this?*

So Billy Bones was put to the question: which, with Flint probing, soon drew out the truth. It came out like a nail prised up by a crow-bar: squealing and protesting, but drawn inexorably by the leverage of Flint's intellect.

"It's a woman, Cap'n. That's to say, *she* is."

"Is she indeed?"

"Aye. One as I knew long ago . . . and which was . . . *special* to me."

"God save our precious souls! Mr Bones, are you saying you have a wife?"

"No, Cap'n. None such as that."

"A-hah! A mistress, then? A sweetheart?"

Billy Bones blushed scarlet, and blushed deeper still when – stumbling and halting – the tale of Olivia Rose was dragged out into the open for Flint to mock and taunt.

"So," said Flint, when the game was done, "you don't

know where she lives, you don't know if she's dead or alive, and you don't even know if her father stayed in London! Is that the course you're steering?"

"Aye, Cap'n. For I went to sea again soon after, and never came home for years."

"And now you would tramp the streets of London, hoping to meet her by chance?"

"Aye, Cap'n. That's about the length of it."

"Billy, my Billy!" Flint shook his head. "Has it not occurred to you that her father is in trade, and that the name *Burstein* is uncommon, and that there are directories published in this city listing alphabetically, by name, all the tradesmen of the town and the addresses of their premises? You have only to go to the nearest bookshop – and there is one on the corner of the Piazza over there –" he pointed through the window "– where you may purchase such a directory. With God's grace and a fair wind, you will have the father's address within ten minutes, and the father will likely lead you to the daughter."

Flint laughed, for an eloquence of amazement was displayed in the dumbstruck face of Billy Bones.

"Bugger me!" he said, "Fuck, pluck and draw me!" And he was off through the door and thundering down the stairs with mighty boots, and Flint's laughter behind him.

The directory cost half-a-crown, a sum that made the eyes water, but Billy Bones had most of his fisticuffs money left, and he paid up and elbowed his way through the wigs, brocades and feathered hats and out into the noisy street with its grinding, iron-tyred traffic and clumping hooves and bellowing hawkers. He opened the book, thumbed through the pages . . . missed his way a few times . . . and then . . . heart thumping, fingers shaking, legs trembling . . . THERE IT WAS! Under *Mathematical Instrument Makers . . .*

BURSTEIN, JOSIAH: 14 CRIPPLE LANE, ST PAUL'S CHURCHYARD.

Billy Bones stood gaping and gasping. Not only had he found the address but he'd be guided to it by the biggest landmark in the entire city! He set off at once, and as with the book, he got lost a few times, but asked the way and was soon gazing up at the soot-blacked pillars, the mighty dome, the arches, pediments and cornices of Christopher Wren's masterwork. Finding Cripple Lane was easy after that . . . but then . . . he who'd never flinched in all his life . . . he who'd stood shot and shell and plunged into the fight slashing left and right . . . he – Billy Bones, the terror of the lower deck – stood backing and filling, unable to go ahead nor astern, nor larboard nor starboard, nor yet to drop anchor and do nothing.

Over twenty years had passed since he'd seen her, and then she'd been a child. So what would he do if he *did* find her? What would he say? What could he offer?

And while he stood dithering, alone in a crowd of busy Londoners, Mr Josiah Burstein himself walked past and into Cripple Lane, and entered a large, double-fronted shop with huge glass windows and a glazed door.

Billy drew closer. The window display featured a gleaming range of instruments for sale: brass and glass, steel and boxwood, ivory and ebony. There were quadrants, octants, dividers and compasses, and mysterious others that Billy Bones had neither seen nor heard of.

But that was nothing compared with proof that this was indeed Josiah Burstein – Olivia Rose's father! His hair was grey, his face was lined and he walked with a limp from a damaged knee . . . but he was beyond a doubt the man Billy remembered from the *Isabelle Bligh*. Clearly he had grown tremendously prosperous during the intervening years: he was excellently dressed, and he went about with his nose in the air, for all that he dragged one foot.

And thus doubt struck again. Billy Bones didn't dare enter the shop. He hadn't the courage. He didn't know what they'd do or what they'd say. So finally he went away. He went back to Sir Frederick's house. He bowed his head and bore the mockery and cynicism of Flint . . . And returned next day to Cripple Lane, and paced up and down around St Paul's, orbiting the cathedral and returning to Cripple Lane every few minutes.

He did that all day, for four consecutive days.

And on the fifth day *he saw her!* It was a hammer-blow. She was coming out of the shop. Her father was kissing her cheek. She was so lovely. So very, very lovely. The beautiful child was now a voluptuous woman . . . And all the tender feelings of Billy Bones's youth rose up from the deep of his soul as if no time had passed and he was a lad once more.

But he dared not go near her, so he ran away and hid. And then he followed at a distance. He followed her the brief, five-minute walk to a smart, respectable street where he saw her go into her smart, respectable house.

It wasn't far, and all the way he struggled to find something to say to her – but couldn't; or something to do – but couldn't. As before, in the end he gave up and returned to Sir Frederick's. This time, not even the utmost persuasion from Flint could draw the truth from Billy Bones, who growled at his master like a mad old dog that will stand the whip no more.

He went back the next day, and watched her house. He saw a man emerge, whom she embraced, and who must be her husband. He looked a decent fellow. And he saw the children that stood beside her and held up their hands to Daddy.

Billy Bones found that he wasn't jealous, and wondered why. He was much puzzled until, finally, it dawned on him that there was nothing here for him: only ghosts and dreams. And so he very nearly escaped unscathed.

But he waited too long, for he was still watching the house as she came out into the street a few minutes later with two of her youngest children. Billy Bones tried to step into a doorway, but it was no good. At a range of twenty yards she saw him . . . their eyes met . . . and Billy's heart stopped to see how she would receive him: the love of *his* childhood and *hers* . . . a faith kept and a promise cherished for over twenty years . . .

A brief second followed . . . then she shuddered in disgust, gathered her little ones in her arms, and walked past Billy Bones on the other side of the street.

She didn't know him. He was just a huge, rough man with a seaman's walk, a tarred pigtail and a mahogany face. If he wasn't exactly a monster, he was something precious close.

It pierced him to the heart and extinguished all hope of escape from Flint.

So he wept many tears.

He found a tavern and got drunk.

He thought of hanging himself.

And the only thing that stopped him was the sure and certain fear of Hell.

But others too faced agonies . . .

Chapter 20

1 a.m., 24th June 1753
Lavery's Wharf, Bermondsey
London

Even this late it wasn't quite dark. Not in late June. There was a glow in the sky, and *Walrus*'s launch was clearly visible as she came quietly to rest among the rows of dark boats moored alongside the wooden pier. But nobody noticed her, and even if they had, they'd have not seen the two men carried as prisoners, blindfolded and bound and under orders to keep quiet else they'd be heaved over the side.

With Allardyce recovering but still unable to stand or speak, for the moment, the Jacobite interest aboard ship had lost its leader, and much of its passion. Spotting this change in the wind, like the good seaman he was, Silver had called a council of all hands, and persuaded them that it would be best to take McLonarch and Norton ashore to set them free – so he told them – and he made sure that he chose the right men for the job: men loyal to himself.

Thus the launch's crew shipped oars, and made all neat and tidy, and one man stayed aboard, while the rest got their awkward cargo up the stairs to the planking twenty feet above. The only sound was the steady, bump, bump, bump

169

that a one-legged man must make as he climbs a set of wooden stairs with the aid of a wooden crutch.

"Long John!" said a figure looming out of the half-light from the little watchman's hut at the end of the pier.

"King Jimmy?" said Silver.

"Aye!" Jimmy looked at the bound, blind figures. "You brung 'em then."

"I did," said Silver.

"Good. Follow me."

King Jimmy led the way along the pier, past bollards, cranes and old casks, above the slopping, greasy water below, and the stinking squalor of old bottles, rotting food, dead cats, bog-paper and worse that lapped into quiet corners of the river. For the Thames was not only London's highway and water supply but its sewer and rubbish tip.

"In here," said King Jimmy, and light showed as a big warehouse door swung open and lanterns burned within.

"At the double!" said Silver, and eight men dashed forward, four to each prisoner, and brought them inside. The door swung shut, the newcomers blinked in the light, and Silver saw that he and his men were once again outnumbered by King Jimmy's. There were at least thirty mudlarks in the high-packed warehouse, and they were standing in groups, giving Silver the hard eye and looking to King Jimmy. They were all armed, though not so heavily as gentlemen o' fortune: cudgels and cutlasses aplenty, but few firelocks.

"Huh!" said Silver, wondering who'd win if it came down to it.

"Hmmm," said his men, and felt for their pistols.

"John! John!" said King Jimmy. "We're all pals together, here."

"Aye," said Silver.

"Come along o' me," said King Jimmy. Then, turning to his men: "See these kiddies?" He pointed to Silver's crew. "Give 'em a drop o' drink and some shrimps, and see if you can manage not to murder one another 'til I get back – and Gawd help the bugger what starts anything!"

"Yeah," said his men.

"Same goes for you!" said Silver, to his men.

"Aye-aye!" they said.

"Come on, John," said King Jimmy, and he took a lantern and led the way into a big office that ran down the side of the warehouse. "Here we are, old chum!" he said, lighting some candles and dragging two chairs to a table. Then he fished out some mugs and a couple of pots of shrimps. "Here you are, John," he said, and smiled.

But Silver was busy heaving a heavy load out from under his coat, where it had been slung on a strap across his shoulder. It was a canvas bag that clinked and clunked as it landed on the table.

"That's another lot on account – as agreed," he said, and King Jimmy's eyes gleamed. "And five times that, if you find her," said Silver.

King Jimmy laughed and felt the bag, and filled the mugs from the tap of a barrel. Then he shook his head.

"Which ain't yet," he said. "Sorry, John."

Silver sighed. He waved a hand as if he could brush pain away. He paused, gathered strength, and moved on.

"What about McLonarch?" he said.

"Ah!" said King Jimmy, taking a swig. "McLonarch, you say!" He whistled softly and shook his head. "That's the kiddy! That's the bouncing boy!" He nodded and looked at Silver. "He might do it, John. He really might. There's mad buggers like him all over England, keeping quiet since the Scotch got thrashed at Culloden, but who'd follow him given the chance."

"Would they?" said Silver.

"Aye! And especially in the old families, the Catholic families. I could take you to a dozen coves that make no secret of it. And that's not the worst of it!"

171

"No?"

"No. Here – have a drop."

"Not I," said Silver. "What is it?" He raised his mug, sniffing suspiciously.

"Beer."

"Ain't you got no rum?"

"No."

"Never mind, go on . . ."

"Well. McLonarch's been talking to the army."

"What?"

"Aye. He knows lots of colonels and such."

"And?"

"They're listening . . ."

Silver rocked back in his chair and reached for the parrot that wasn't there, because she was fastened to her perch in his cabin. She didn't like boats, and tonight's work was dangerous. He sniffed.

"So," he said, "he could start a war. But could he win it?"

"Dunno about that . . ."

"And what's he worth to King George?"

"If you hand him over?"

"Aye."

King Jimmy thought long and hard. He helped himself to a handful of shrimps and peeled them and chewed them and swallowed. Finally he shook his head.

"Dunno, my son, but I'll tell you this: King George'll want everything done quiet. Deep and quiet, so's no cove hears a word, and none gets upset, especially in the army. They won't chop him – McLonarch – 'cos he don't do murder, don't King George, but they daren't put him on trial, so they'll shut him up nice and tight . . ." Then he pointed at Silver: "– and *you* with him! You and all your men. You might come out smelling of roses in the end, my son, but they'll take their time deciding."

Silver sighed. He knew most of this already, for he wasn't

relying just on King Jimmy. Not for something so important. Israel Hands, Dr Cowdray and even Warrington had been ashore and asked their questions, and all had come back with the same answer: McLonarch and the Jacobites were the twin horrors of which King George and his government stood in dread. Last time the Jacobites were up in arms – only eight years ago in 1745 – their army came down from Scotland as far south as Derby, and all the London militias were raised in panic to defend the capital. And so . . . and so John Silver bowed his head. Then he looked up.

"What about Norton?" he said. "Have you done what I asked?"

"Easier my way," said King Jimmy, and grinned. "And cheaper!"

"But have you done it?"

"Aye."

"Then let's get up on our wooden spars and go and see him."

They had four of Silver's men bring the two prisoners to a quiet corner of the warehouse where nobody else could see. Vast bales of cotton were piled high, and deadened all sound. The rest of Silver's men, now boozing merrily with King Jimmy's, couldn't even be heard.

"Back to your shipmates now," said Silver, to his four men.

"Aye-aye, Cap'n!" they said and vanished. Silver looked round.

"Where are they?" King Jimmy raised a lantern.

"Wait!" he said, and found a small side door, and opened it and waved the lantern.

Cool air blew in . . . then came a patter of feet and two seafaring men in dark clothes slipped in through the door. They greeted King Jimmy, spoke in whispers, and looked at Long John and the two blindfolded men.

"This here's the one," said King Jimmy, pointing to the smaller man.

173

"He'll need to see where he's goin'," said one of the seamen. "I ain't leadin' the sod!"

"Aye!" said his mate. "And where's the rhino?"

Silver produced another heavy bag from under his coat.

"Ah!" they said, and took it.

"Let's see the light of your eyes, then," said Silver, untying Norton's blindfold.

Norton looked around him, white-faced and wide-eyed, certain that he was about to die.

"You bastard!" he said to Silver. "And I took you for a decent cove!"

"Stand easy!" said Silver. "You ain't goin' in the river. You're goin' with these matelots here –" he jabbed a thumb at the two seamen – "back into your old trade. I shouldn't wonder if you won't get your old rating afore long!"

"What?" said Norton.

"You're out-bound for the slave coast, and then to Cuba, where these gennelmen'll let you off . . . some time next year, when you get there."

"Oh . . ." said Norton.

"Oh?" said Silver. "Is that all?"

"What d'you want: *thanks*?" said Norton. "You bloody pirate!"

"Ah, get rid of him!" said Silver, and turned his back.

"And what about McLonarch?" said Norton, but he was dragged off into the dark, with two or three others waiting outside with cudgels in case he tried to fight.

King Jimmy closed the door. Silver's heart was beating heavily.

"Now then," said Silver, and took the wrappings off McLonarch's eyes. Gaunt, staring and with his hair all askew, McLonarch looked more than ever like an Old Testament prophet.

Silver's heart thumped and bounded. The thick blood beat in his brow. He drew a pistol from his belt and cocked it.

"Why don't you go for some shrimps and beer, Jimmy?" he said.

"What?" said King Jimmy.

"Go on, like a messmate and a pal."

"Why?"

"Just sod off, Jimmy . . . *sod off!*"

King Jimmy walked away. The McLonarch of McLonarch looked at Silver. His mind ran differently to other men's but he was masterly clever at knowing their thoughts and he knew John Silver's at once.

"Shall you stoop to murder, Captain?" said McLonarch in his deep, beautiful voice. Long John cringed in shame, the pistol hung limp in his hand, and the blood thundered in his head. He was sick and dizzy and his head ached. McLonarch was a bloody mad maniac that couldn't be let free. He'd be the death of thousands, perhaps tens of thousands. So . . .

He could be sent to sea like Norton. But he'd talk to the crew till they kissed his arse.

He could be kept in irons aboard *Walrus*. But Allardyce wouldn't stay silent forever.

He could be given to King George to lock up. But King George'd lock up Long John too.

And *then* what of Selena? If she was fallen into whoring she must be got out of it quick! Silver shuddered at the thought of men using her, for the longer she was at it, the more ruined she'd be. Then he raised the pistol and thrust it into the centre of McLonarch's breast.

"You're a Christian, ain't you?" said Silver.

"Yes, I am."

"Then make your peace with God."

McLonarch smiled.

"Captain," he said, with infinite calmness, "you are too good a man for this."

"Am I?" said Silver, nearly blind with pain and nausea.

He thought of Selena . . . and groaned and wiped tears from

his eyes, knowing that before all else – even at cost of his soul – he could not fail her . . . not her! Not his little darling! He could not see her corrupted, desecrated and soiled.

So he shot McLonarch through the heart.

Chapter 21

Mr Abbey stood on tiptoes to put the blindfold round Selena's eyes. Then he led her to the table. She was wearing her new costume: the one with the riding boots – her own suggestion, having been used to wearing boots aboard ship and feeling comfortable in them – but the gleam of skin *above* the boots was the genius of Mr Abbey's costumiers. He looked at her and sighed. What was it that made her quite so lovely? Sometimes he thought it was the tiny waist over curving hips, sometimes it was the lovely eyes, sometimes the slender, round limbs. He shook his head.

Whatsoever, he thought. *Who cares, so long as she's playing to packed houses!* Aloud, he said, "There, madame, all is prepared. Let us see you do it!"

He stepped back and went to stand with Katty Cooper and his entire company, together again for Sunday rehearsal. They whispered and whistled at Selena's latest outfit, even those of the men who stepped lightly; perhaps them especially, for they truly appreciated costume, and marvelled that so much could be contrived out of so little.

"Go on, Selena!" they cried.

177

"Selena!"

"Go on, girl!"

And there was a cheer as Selena stamped her foot, slapped her thigh and stood forth bold and heroic: legs apart, hands on hips, tossing her head.

"Aha!" she cried. "Now, sir, take your guard!"

Another cheer and applause, for Abbey had discovered that the way to get the best out of Selena was to send her strutting boldly round the stage on her long legs, since that was guaranteed to raise a stand within every pair of britches in the house.

As he'd said to Katty Cooper: "When she comes on, dear heart, don't worry if there is profound silence from the men ... for that is *not* a bad sign." And indeed it wasn't. And now, not just audiences, but the entire city of Polmouth – the biggest town in the West Country – were falling in love with Selena. Yet there was still further development to come, from a chance remark Selena had made.

"Now then," cried Mr Abbey, clapping his hands. "Let's see you do it!"

Selena stretched out her hands, and found the pistol and paper cartridge on the table in front of her. She felt for the flint, to make sure it was in place, set the lock to half-cock, bit off the end of the cartridge, primed the lock with powder, snapped down the steel, poured the rest of the charge down the up-ended barrel, and rammed ball and paper down the barrel with the ramrod, which she neatly replaced before cocking the lock, levelling and giving fire with a flash and a bang ... and a loud *CLANG* from the great sheet of iron plate hung on a ropes ten paces to her front.

Cheers filled the amphitheatre as Selena pulled off her blindfold, threw it away, put down the smoking pistol, and stamped forward again, smiling and bowing with easy grace to left and right, and blowing kisses to all the house ... as she'd been taught.

Mr Abbey, Katty Cooper and the company surged forward, ears ringing from the shot and the clang, and laughed and surrounded Selena.

"Where did you learn that?" said Mr Abbey. "Do you hunt?"

"No," said Selena.

"Then what do you shoot?" said Abbey, for he affected gentlemanly pursuits, including shooting, and went out after game of all kinds, and it was his own conversation on this favourite topic which had led to Selena's boast that she could load a gun blindfolded. "So what have you shot?" he repeated. "Do tell us!"

"Nothing . . ." she said, in a small voice ". . . only men."

Everyone thought this a wonderful joke. They laughed enormously, even Katty Cooper, who knew less about Selena than she thought. And as they laughed, inspiration crept up on Mr Abbey. He noticed that some of the dancing girls were clustered around Selena in their gowns and pumps, which made them seem smaller than Selena with her boots and her pistol . . .

"Stap me!" he said, growing excited. "Do you know, dear heart, I think I might cast Mrs Henderson as the principal *boy* player in one of my pantomimes!"

Katty Cooper frowned.

"But she's a woman."

"That's the whole point!"

"What is?"

"Well, if we present her – with legs and tits – stamping around the stage pretending to be a man, firing off pistols, *and taking the heroine in her arms . . .*"

"Ahhhh!" said Katty Cooper, beginning to understand, for many gentlemen of her professional acquaintance were *exceedingly* partial to such displays between women.

"We'll have something the men will adore," said Abbey, "while the ladies and children will think it mere innocent nonsense . . ."

"Which will offend nobody."

"Not at all, not even clergymen," said Abbey, and laughed . . . and gasped and all but staggered, as he received the second wave of inspiration. He spun Katty Cooper around by the arms, and looked up into her pretty little face. "D'you know what I'm going to do?"

"No?"

"I'm coming with you!"

"You are?" Katty frowned.

"Yes! In fact, I'm taking you. We shall tour together: York, Edinburgh, Exeter, Chester – all of them, at my expense!" Katty's frown darkened, but Abbey failed to notice. "I shall form a travelling company. I shall write a piece!" He waved a hand. "Songs, dances, scenery – everything. We shall tour!" His eyes gleamed. "And then we shall descend upon Drury Lane in triumph!" Katty Cooper growled. "And the lynch-pin and keystone shall be Mrs Henderson," he said. "And I shall make *her* fortune, *mine* – and *yours*, dear heart!"

"Mine?" said Katty Cooper with a twinkling smile, for until that instant she'd seen herself written out.

"Yes!" said Abbey. "And you must not even think of entering her into your profession –" He blinked. "I mean . . . I mean . . . your *old* profession, dear heart."

"*Must I not?*" she said nastily, for the dear little face could display tremendous spite when it chose to do so.

"God stap me, no! You'll make ten times the money this way!"

"Ahhhhh!" Katty smiled again. That was different.

"Then you agree?"

"Oh yes," said Katty Cooper, and delivered yet another pretty smile.

She smiled and smiled . . . but Katty Cooper hated Mr Abbey from that moment on, because although she could never say *no* to money, she was so corrosively – so viciously

– selfish that she could abide no plan than her own, nor any hand than hers upon the tiller.

Worse still, Katty Cooper now hated Selena, too, for being better than her mentor and not needing her.

And so, Katty Cooper began to think of ways to punish Selena.

Chapter 22

"*N*o room, sir!" said the head waiter, shaking his head. "No room at all!" And he planted himself defiantly in front of John Silver and Dr Cowdray as they came through Mr Jackson's neatly glazed door.

The waiter had been appalled the moment he spotted them through the glass. They were clearly *the wrong sort* – seafarers, no less! None such were admitted, save officers in His Majesty's sea service, or nabob captains of East Indiamen, and then only if properly dressed. The two men in front of him wore plain old clothes and not a wig between them. And if that weren't bad enough, the tall man was ruined by the loss of a leg and leaned grotesquely upon a crutch, which Mr Jackson would never allow, for he permitted no disfigurement within the house.

"No room?" said Silver, his big, square-chinned face looming down over the waiter as he fixed him with his eye. The waiter swallowed and trembled but stood fast, for his job was at risk. "So what's them empty benches, my lad?" said Silver, pointing into the room.

"Reserved, sir! Reserved for a large party."

"Ah!" said Silver, and nodded, and smiled kindly down on the wretched waiter in his long white apron. "Now see here," he said, "you're a bright lad: smart as paint! I see'd it the instant I clapped eyes on you." The waiter blinked. Silver patted him on the shoulder, and brought out a clunking fistful of big silver coins. "D'you know what these are?" he said.

"Spanish dollars," said the waiter.

"That they are, my lad! And could you tell a poor sailorman, fresh arrived in port, what they might be worth, in King George-God-bless-him's own money?"

"Four to the pound, sir."

"And how many pounds might a lad like you earn in a year? Ten? A dozen?" The waiter nodded. "Well, lad," said Silver, "there's four dollars here what's telling me there's room for me and my matey, over in the corner yonder."

"Ah . . . hmm" said the waiter. "Perhaps you may be correct, sir. If you'd just follow me . . ."

"Aye, lad," said Silver. "And I've another four that says, so soon as Mr Jackson's in the house, why, he'd like to lay alongside o' me, for to parlay."

The waiter went chalk white. He knew Flash Jack very well, and all his likes and dislikes. Silver saw his expression, and smiled a wide smile and winked, and prodded the waiter in the ribs and leaned very close.

"Could be more than four dollars," he whispered. "Very much more. Heaps and piles of 'em. Ready cash money. You just tell Mr Jackson that, and send him to me!"

And so they were duly seated, and served, and they drank their coffee and ate their cakes, and ignored the sneers of the other occupants of the room.

"You've grown cunning, John," said Cowdray, smiling. "The man I knew three years ago would have knocked down that waiter as soon as look at him!"

"Well, I ain't that man," said Silver with a scowl. "Not no more."

"Hmm," said Cowdray, and shrugged. "If you're offering money about, how much is left of McLonarch's three thousand?"

"Some," said Silver.

"But how much?" said Cowdray.

"Pah!" said Silver. "Let me worry about that."

"What about Allardyce? He was strong for McLonarch –"

"Who's *dead!*" said Silver, interrupting.

Cowdray looked him in the eye. "How did Norton do it? How did he *really* do it?"

Silver scowled.

"I told you. He broke free, got a knife from his boot . . . and did him!"

"And King Billy's men shot Norton?"

"Aye!" said Silver. "Nice drink, this *coffee*, ain't it? Right tasty."

Cowdray shut up and looked away. He kept quiet after that, and took refuge in the London newspapers that were lying about the table. Silver ignored him and glowered out of the window, and looked at the bustling heart of London, and ignored that too, and thought his own thoughts.

Then Cowdray sat bolt upright.

"Good God Almighty!" he said. "Flint's in London!"

"What?" said Silver. "How d'you know?"

"Look!" said Cowdray, showing him a copy of the *General Advertiser*.

"Where?" said Silver.

"Here . . . under 'Reported Explosion of the Lexicographer'."

"What?" said Silver. "Is that a ship blown up?"

"No! It's Flint, being clever, at a salon in Bramhall Square, last week."

"Are you sure it's him?"

"Read it!"

Silver peered at the article and read aloud from it: "'Such subtlety of expression as won the approval of Johnson himself, for Lieutenant Joseph Flint, whom we had previously been led to believe was a mutineer and a rogue' . . . It's him all right!" said Silver. "Him as knows where the goods lies. Well, bugger me!"

"If you insist, sir!" said a laughing voice, and a waft of perfume rolled across the table. Cowdray and Silver looked up at the eye-blinding sight of a creature as different from themselves as it was possible to be and yet still remain a human being. Silver recognised him instantly from King Billy's description.

"Mr Jackson?" he said. "Flash Jack the Fly Cove?"

"The very same, sir! At your service, sir," said Flash Jack, and smiled beautifully and delivered the quintessence of a bow.

Huh! thought Silver. *At least he flies his colours from the mainmast. No mistaking what he is.*

"And would you be the seafaring gentlemen who wished to speak with me?"

"Aye," said Silver. "I'm Cap'n . . . Hands . . . and this is Dr Cowdray."

"Gentlemen!" said Flash Jack, and sat down.

They spoke for an hour, but achieved little. Flash Jack knew of no such girl as Silver wanted, and he knew every new arrival in town. The best he could do – for the promise of a hundred in dollars – was to alert Captain Hands aboard the good ship *Walrus* anchored off Wapping Stairs at such time as his young lady should appear.

The one-legged captain and his friend, who had remained silent for the most part, were getting up to leave when the latter spoke:

"Mr Jackson?"

"Yes, Dr Cowdray?"

"What do you know of Flint – Lieutenant Joseph Flint? I believe he is in town . . ."

"Flint?" said Flash Jack, and his shutters closed with a slam. "Who would that be? Flint the bookseller? Flint the juggler? I know several gentlemen of that name."

"He is a seaman," said Cowdray. "An old shipmate."

"Back your topsail, matey," said Silver, and laid a hand on Cowdray's arm. "We shan't go bothering Mr Jackson with old tales o' the sea." He smiled. Flash Jack smiled. Cowdray shrugged his shoulders . . . Then Silver tipped his hat to Flash Jack and led the way up the aisle, hopping his leg and bumping his crutch, and out through the front door with Cowdray astern of him.

Well, gentlemen, thought Flash Jack, and looked at the long-case clock that stood by the serving counter, and which showed that it was nearly noon, *if only you'd stayed a little longer!* And a short time after, Flash Jack's heart fluttered as the door opened and Lieutenant Flint himself came in, and smiled his wonderful smile and came to sit with Flash Jack, whose every nerve tingled and whose eyes shone like stars.

"Jackie, my boy!" said Flint. "Have you found me a ship?" Flash Jack smiled.

"For you . . . it can be done," he said. Flint looked into Flash Jack's eyes, and Flash Jack nearly swooned. He was so transported with delight that he missed Flint's next few words, and only recovered when Flint shook his arm.

". . . how much?" Flint was saying. "What's it going to cost?"

"Ah!" said Flash Jack, and named an enormous sum. He might be in love, but business was business. Flint laughed and Flash Jack nearly swooned again. Then Flint thought fast and made a series of promises about great monies hidden in strange places.

"Hmm," said Flash Jack, when this discussion of finance ran quite entirely aground. "Someone was asking after you this morning. A sailor with one leg."

186

"*WHAT?*" said Flint, and Flash Jack was astonished at the strength of his reaction, and was forcibly pumped dry of all memory of his conversation with a man who Flint assured him was called John Silver. The inquisition was utterly thrilling to Flash Jack, and he loved every moment of it, for it felt as if Flint was physically laying hands on him. When Flint was finally done with him he was so exhausted that he had to lie down with his dreams.

Flint frowned all the way back to Sir Frederick's house. His mind was galloping. Freedom would be his *only* if he could find ready money: the fatuous, ludicrous, ridiculous Flash Jack wouldn't move without it! Meanwhile, what did Silver want? Damn, damn, *damn* Silver! Thus Flint was so occupied that he failed to notice there were people waiting for him at Sir Frederick's. Perhaps it was because the Piazza was especially crammed that day. So he failed to observe the four blue-jacketed, canvas-trousered tars who were following him with pistols and cutlasses in their belts. And more of the same were waiting round the corner, just out of sight – his sight but not theirs – by Sir Frederick's house. And a good many more persons were waiting inside.

Flint, blissfully unaware of this, leapt up the stairs, hammered on the knocker, and only knew anything was wrong when the door swung open to reveal Mr Midshipman Povey with a pair of sea-service barkers in his hand, and the barkers levelled at Flint, and a couple of gold-laced grim-faced lieutenants behind him, and a lobby-ful of marines and Bow Street men behind them, and a scraping and ringing of steel behind Flint, and a dozen tars at the foot of the stairs with blades leaping out of scabbards and points twinkling in his face.

Flint could fight any man who ever lived, and the wise chose not to face him. He was unnaturally quick and uncannily accurate in every blow he struck. But even he had his limits. He couldn't fight thirty armed men with nothing in his hands.

Someone had taken careful measure of Flint, and come with sufficient force and more.

Povey stepped forward. He looked like death. His face was spotted with little scars. His eyes were sunken. He was thin and ill, and his hands were like birds' claws. But he gripped his pistols hard and glared at Flint with sizzling hatred.

"Flint!" he said. "Got you, you bastard!"

Chapter 23

The evening performance
Saturday, 17th November 1753
Croxley's Odeon Theatre
Drury Lane
London

The applause hit Selena like the blast of a siege gun. It bellowed and echoed from the pit and the four tiers of galleries of the biggest theatre in London, which supposedly held an audience of six thousand, but on a night like this, when the bodies were crammed, jammed and rammed into the groaning boxes and on to the endless rows of benches, there were far more – dangerously more – bodies in the house.

They clapped and roared and cried *encore*, and the smiling company pushed Selena forward in her boots and spurs, and she strutted and slapped her thigh and stamped her feet, and the cheering rose to yet more deafening heights. Then she took up position, front and centre stage, and raised a hand for silence . . . which came . . . and she nodded to the orchestra and the conductor waved his baton . . . and the jolly, jaunty music started up again . . .

And so, for the fourth time, she sang "The Pollywhacket Song" the clever little ditty that Mr Abbey had composed for her, and which she'd taken from one end of England to the other, with its nonsensical chorus:

Pollywhacket! Pollywhacket!
Pollywhacket! Pollywhacket!
Pollywhacket diddle-diddle eye-dee-oh!

Which didn't sound half so nonsensical when thundered out by an enraptured audience of eight thousand, ranging from London's finest, in jewels and powder in their boxes, to London's lowest, in rags and lice, up near the ceiling, close to God.

Being tired, she sang just one verse and the chorus, and was grateful when the audience let her off with only two more encores. Then at last the curtain came down, and the company could sigh, and smile and hug one another at a wonderful house and a darling audience, and Mr Croxley himself – a vastly fat man whose belly protruded like the ram of an Athenian galley – came bustling forward with Mr Abbey, Katty Cooper and a tail of privileged favourites. Croxley clapped shoulders, pinched cheeks, and beamed in the sublime relief of an impresario who has backed the right horse and sees money coming in on the tide.

"Mrs Henderson!" cried Croxley, advancing through the press of gaudy, half-clad artistes, who bowed and made way and smiled, as he spread wide his arms and smiled in joy. "Mrs Henderson, my own darling girl! Come and give me a kiss!" and . . .

"Ahhhhhh!" they all cooed as she stepped forward, dainty and lovely, and kissed the fat cheek, and accepted the bear-hug, and the slopping return kiss, and was swept off her feet and swung around and around, and planted down again, and introduced to such a choice selection of the Town's finest gentlemen as transported Mr Croxley into further raptures at the joy of having them within his walls. Meanwhile a pair of maids pressed forward with Mrs Henderson's dressing gown, which they struggled to wrap round her, while the gentlemen bowed and ogled her luscious limbs and fine breasts, seen almost in a state of nature, and for the first time at close range.

Croxley boomed and laughed and chattered, left lesser beings in his wake, and led his little star to a private room, where a meal had been prepared for his special guests, and where later – after much drink and food had gone down, and Mr Croxley was leading the singing of the Pollywhacket song ... one of the gentlemen – a lumbering, ugly fifty-year-old by the name of Blackstone – managed to take Selena aside.

He was excellently dressed. He was excellent company. He was excellently attentive, and he made no excuses for his plain, rough self. For he was Sir Matthew Blackstone the brewer: member of parliament, fellow of the Royal Society, and celebrated patron of the arts. He was highly amusing, with choice tales of the other gentlemen now sinking rum punch alongside Mr Croxley, and getting drunk.

He made Mrs Henderson laugh. He put her at ease. He was kind and patient, and only when Selena was entirely charmed did he make his gentle, civilised approach.

"I've got a stallion worth a fortune which I bought for his beauty," he said.

"Have you?" she said.

"And I've got a house in Berkshire, which is the most beautiful in the county."

"Oh?"

"And paintings, and statues, and porcelain ... all beautiful."

"Oh?"

"All that ... and an ugly wife."

Silence.

"She had land, you see. And family. And my pa insisted."

Silence.

"I love beauty, Mrs Henderson, and you are – without doubt – the most beautiful creature, the most perfect piece of loveliness, the most glorious work of God, that I have ever seen in all my life."

Warrington gasped and groaned. He'd run all the way from Drury Lane, which was a very long way indeed and he was near dead with exhaustion and sweating under his greatcoat even on this freezing night.

"Come on! Come on!" cried Sammy Hayden, well in the lead and yelling for Warrington to keep up. "Boat! Boat!" he cried, and waved a hand in the air, shoving his way down towards the river where boatmen waited for fares. But it was a busy night and plenty of others were after a ride.

"Ger-cher! You little bugger!" cried a dark figure as Sammy bumped him. "Who you bleedin' shoving?"

"Sorry-sir-indeed-I-beg-pardon!" gasped Warrington, coming along behind, biting his lip and taking care to be polite, for London was dangerous at night. A man could get knifed in a lamp-lit theatre queue, let alone in the shadowy stairs that led down to the Thames.

"Fuck off!" said the wounded party, and Warrington stepped back and was patient, and ground his teeth and Sammy Hayden danced on the spot, until at last they were clambering into the stern sheets of a boat.

"Where to, Cap'n?" said the boatman.

"There! The schooner *Walrus!*"

"Right y'are, Cap'n!" said the boatman and shoved off. "What name, sir?"

"Warrington, first mate."

"Aye-aye, sir!"

Five minutes later they were under *Walrus's* quarter, where a ladder was rigged and the boatman calling out

192

Warrington's name, and Warrington giving him a coin and going aboard.

"Where's the cap'n?" he said to Mr Joe, who was officer of the watch.

"Below. In his cabin . . . what is it?"

But Warrington and Sammy Hayden were tumbling and rumbling down companionways and dashing to the stern cabin and hammering on the door, and bursting in, and there was Silver's parrot squawking and cursing, and Long John getting up from the long padded bench under the stern lights that he used as a bed.

"Shiver me timbers!" said Silver. "What is it, you swabs, waking me up at . . ."

"*Tell him! Tell him!*" cried Warrington to Sammy.

"*It's her, Cap'n! We found her! It's her!*"

Silver gaped, Silver gasped, he launched himself one-legged and hopping, leaning on the cabin table, and leaping at Sammy Hayden, and hanging on to him, and looking down into the boy's delighted face.

"Where is she?" cried Silver. "*How* is she? Is she . . . is she . . . is she in one o' them . . . in a . . ." But words dried up in fear and shame.

"No, no, *no!*" said Warrington, seizing Long John's arms. "She's well, John! She's wonderful! She's on the bloody stage! She's Mrs Henderson, the *famous* Mrs Henderson that's appearing at Croxley's Odeon! I was there tonight. I took the lad. He wanted to see a theatre. And just as well, for I'd not have known who it was, never having set eyes on her. BUT HE DID!" He smiled joyfully. "It's her! It's her! She's not . . . she's not *fallen*, John . . . she's full, plump and happy. She must be making a bloody fortune!"

Long John blinked and felt dizzy. The relief rolled over him and his head swam and emotion soared, and the cabin swirled and whirled and turned.

Ten minutes later, he was laid out on the bench with Israel

Hands, Mr Joe, Black Dog and Warrington leaning over him.

"Take a pull, Cap'n," said Israel Hands, holding out a glass of rum. Silver struggled up, got his back against the cushions, his one leg on the floor and the parrot on his shoulder.

"Long John," she said, and stroked his cheek with her head.

He took the glass and gulped it down.

"All this time," he said, shaking his head, "looking in the wrong place."

Israel Hands grinned. "Never mind, Cap'n," he said, "at least she's safe!"

"Aye!" they all said.

He looked at their cheerful faces and sighed. And he had another drink for good fellowship, then sent them all away – all but Israel Hands, for he needed to think, and talk a bit in quiet.

"Why so glum, John?" said Hands.

Silver shook his head. There were things he couldn't say. Not even to Israel Hands. He closed his eyes, and there stood McLonarch, beside Ratty Richards, now and forever. It was bad enough doing a dreadful thing for a rightful reason . . . but what if there weren't no rightful reason? So Silver spoke of something else: something equally tormenting.

"All the tart shops we been in an' out of these past months!" he said, shaking his head. "We been wasting our time."

"And Mr Joe, wearing himself out!" said Israel Hands.

"And you too, Israel," said Silver, and he sighed. "The thing is, I'd always imagined seizing her away: at pistol point if need be! Coming to the rescue, like."

"Aye," said Hands.

"And herself grateful, and the two of us happy together."

"Aye."

"But now . . . If she's rich and famous, what'd she want with a cripple like me?"

"*Cripple?* Not you, John! You're Long John Silver, gentleman o' fortune!"

"Aye! That's the trouble, Mr Hands."

Israel Hands shook his head.

"She's your wife, John. She knows that."

"Does she? D'you think she even thinks about me?"

"'Course she does!"

But Silver simply groaned and looked away. Searching for something to cheer up his friend, Israel Hands grinned merrily:

"Well, at least we can look forward to seeing Flint do the hornpipe! He gets his dish of *hearty-choke and caper sauce* one week next Monday."

"Bah!" said Silver. "Where's the fun in that? If the bastard dies, then the greatest treasure in all the world is lost. For none can find it but him!"

11 a.m., Sunday, 18th November 1753
The Chapel
Newgate Gaol
London

Flint, Flash Jack and Billy Bones sat among the public in the viewing gallery that looked down upon one of the most famous sights of London: a fenced-off enclosure some fifteen feet by twenty, containing a table and a pair of benches, where a dozen wretches – in the extreme of religious devotion – wrung their hands, beat their brows, sang hymns mightily along with the congregation, and screwed up their eyes in passionate invocation. For these were the chosen ones . . . who would be hanged tomorrow. And in case they'd forgotten it, a nice big coffin was laid open on the table before them as a handy reminder.

And all around, the curious, the morbid and the seekers-after-sensation who'd paid to come in for the fun, goggled and gaped, laughed and chattered, and comprehensively ignored the sermon preached by the bewigged and white-robed

Ordinary – the prison chaplain – as he discharged his impossible task of redeeming the unredeemable, while comforting himself with the thought that he was well paid and a good Sunday dinner awaited him.

Flint leaned close to Flash Jack, and pointed out the celebrities among those lost in prayer.

"From the corner, clockwise, we have: Uriah Kemp, utterer of base coin; Mrs Tetty Hammond, the Dover Square abortionist; Mrs Alice Whitebread, poisoner of three husbands; Will Stuart, the butcher who divided his wife with a cleaver; Mrs Sal Porter, who drowned unwanted infants, farmed out by the Parish of Bednal Green . . ." he smiled "and sundry others who are merely common thieves."

Flash Jack blinked, awestruck by the close proximity of Flint, whose shoulder was actually rubbing against his own.

"You seem . . ." he searched for words ". . . *comfortable*, here, Joe."

"Oh yes," said Flint, "I have a pleasant room, good food, good clothes. And as you can see," he said, smiling at the worshippers below, "the company is splendid!" Then he shrugged and looked down. "Of course, there are these –" he clanked the manacles that joined his wrists and were fastened by chain to the irons about his feet "– and them," he said, casting a glance at the pair of gaolers waiting by the door: heavy men in black hats, with keys and cudgels hanging from their belts. He nodded at them, and they touched their hats respectfully.

"Cap'n!" said their lips.

"Money," said Flint, "buys everything here . . . *almost*."

"And you have money . . . from Sir Frederick?"

Flint nodded. "He advanced me five hundred against my reward money."

"Is the Lennox family still behind you?"

"Only Sir Frederick. The rest were thrashed in court and went away bleeding."

Flash Jack shuddered at the recollection of Flint's trial. It had been poor, nasty, brutish and short: deeply disappointing as a spectacle. The Hastings clan had easily found others beside Mr Povey who'd seen Flint's mutiny: common seamen of no consequence, but whose sincerity was obvious, and whose testimony – beside the stellar performance of the midshipman himself – had assured Flint's doom. The only point of interest was a legal squabble over rights and place of execution, what with Flint being – all in one man – a mutineer, a pirate and a felon, falling under three jurisdictions: the sea service, the Lord High Admiral, and the civil judiciary.

The result – in the opinion of Flash Jack – was a true British Compromise, whereby the civil authorities would hang him at Tyburn, but preceded by the Silver Oar of the Lord High Admiral, and with a bosun's mate actually putting the halter round Flint's neck and making all secure: in which matter the sea service's special proficiency with knots was acknowledged by all parties – except the public executioner, who thereby lost his fee. But this was immaterial since he had no great or powerful friends, and his misery was lost in the joyful expectation of a massive turnout for one of the most notable hangings of modern times.

"Joe," said Flash Jack, "what are we going to do?" He looked at the condemned down below. "Shall you be among them . . . next Sunday?"

Flint laughed in contempt, and Flash Jack was overwhelmed at his masculinity and his wonderful beauty. "Never!" cried Flint. "I'll face the devil alone when my time comes!" He saw how Flash Jack looked at him. "Listen," he said in a low voice, and Flash Jack tingled, "what about my ship?"

Flash Jack dithered as the worship of money fought a mighty alliance of true love allied with lust.

"Perhaps . . ." he said.

"I haven't the sum you need," said Flint. "Not here in England."

"I know."

"What else will you take . . . instead of money?"

Flash Jack fluttered his long eyelashes, bit his lip, took a firm grip of his courage, and with madly beating heart, leaned close to Flint and whispered in his ear. Flint listened. He said nothing. Finally he nodded and squeezed Flash Jack's hand, who once again nearly died of pleasure, and trembled to the roots of his toenails. "But first I must remain un-hanged," said Flint.

"I can't get you out of here," said Flash Jack, falling from Heaven to Earth in one bump. "Money won't do that."

"I know," said Flint. "So this is what you must do." He pointed at Billy Bones, gawping miserably at the condemned. "You and *him* – if there's enough of him left for the task! Now listen closely: you must seek out John Silver, whom I believe you already know . . ."

11 a.m., Sunday, 18th November 1753
12 Bramhall Square
London

"The first Whig was the Devil!" cried Johnson, massively filling a flamboyant chair by Foliot of Paris, which supported his weight only by the triumph of French genius over British beef, while the company applauded, being Tories through and through. "And it is Devil's work that has been performed upon Lieutenant Flint!" he added with a roar.

"Bravo!" they cried: the three dozen privileged favourites attending Lady Faith's salon this day, and Lady Faith and her sisters clapping white hands in a fury of agreement.

"I tell you all," said Johnson, "that this entire business is much rooted in the political hatred of the Whiggish House of Hastings for the Tory House of Lennox!" He smiled graciously at Lady Faith, who was a Lennox by marriage.

"Bravo!" they cried . . . except for the Brownlough brothers, Reginald and Horace, who leaned forward in their chairs, nodded grimly at one another, and waited for whatever Johnson should say next.

"But there is more!" said Johnson. "Those who know the Caribbean say that so great is the fear in which the Spanish and French hold Captain Flint that his mere presence at sea is enough to offset the rivalry to England's trade which otherwise they would inflict upon us!"

"But is he not a pirate?" protested a small voice at the back.

"Who said that?" cried Johnson, looking round.

"He did!" said the Brownlough brothers, pointing out the villain.

"Who are you, sir?" said Johnson, rising up from his chair like a python discovering a piglet. A mumble came in reply, as the speaker withered and wished himself safe at home in bed, and thought it wise to keep quiet about Flint's attacks on English shipping. "*PAH!*" cried Johnson, sitting down. "And was not Drake a pirate? And Hawkins and Frobisher and Raleigh?"

"No!" they cried, and "Yes!" depending upon their perception of the subtleties of double negative.

"My point is this," said Johnson: "far away, across the Atlantic, lies a vast continent which I believe to be the future of all mankind! It holds fabulous wealth in its far horizons, its lofty mountains and its limitless resources of every kind: animal, vegetable and mineral!"

There was utter silence as all present contemplated the thirteen British colonies in America, which were so dreadfully threatened by the American colonies of France and Spain. Johnson nodded.

"As all the *old* world knows," he said, "this *new* world shall soon be the cause of a world-wide war, whereby the great powers will compete for control of America." He

199

thumped his knee with a huge fist and stabbed a finger at the company. "And I tell you – I tell you all – that Flint and those like him are *at worst* merely premature, and *at best* exemplars of the manner in which a mighty empire shall be won for England! We should not be hanging the man. No! We should be sending him forth in command of a ship of war!"

The company cheered. Johnson nodded wisely, and sought another cup of tea, which Lady Faith poured, in happy satisfaction that all this would be reported in the press tomorrow – writers being present among the company for that very purpose – thereby exulting the prestige of her salon over those of her rivals.

Meanwhile the Brownlough brothers put their heads together and made plans: fierce plans, for they worshipped Johnson, they took his word as law, and they were bold, young, patriotic . . . and stupid.

Chapter 24

Dawn, Monday, 26th November 1753
The Press Yard
Newgate Gaol
London

The winter sun rose in splendour over the elegant squares, coppered domes, soaring spires, two great bridges, and the filthy, stinking tenements of London. The day was crisp, and all was merry brightness, showing that the Almighty smiled upon the vast crowd – the greatest in living memory – that was assembling for the hanging of Joseph Flint.

So thought Flint as he stepped out into the Press Yard surrounded by lesser beings, for Flint shimmered in the gold-laced, black velvet suit of clothes which had been purchased at vast expense for the occasion. Likewise the shining, soft-leathered boots, the black-feathered hat, and the diamond-hilted sword that hung from a golden baldric across his shoulder. They'd snapped off the sword blade, of course, but the weapon looked just as good in its scabbard and perfectly suited the dignity of the principal performer in the tremendous act of theatre that would soon take place.

Flint looked around and smiled. His had never been a normal mind, and to him it was hilarious that the Press Yard was so called because it was here that felons who refused to plead guilty or not guilty – thereby saving their loot for their families – were spread-eagled upon the ground to be pressed under weights until either they entered a plea or died. Flint laughed, for the same law that called *him* a villain, permitted this cruel torture.

Clang! Clang! Clang! The prison blacksmith struck off Flint's irons upon his anvil, and there was a brief, unseemly scuffle as the prison's yeoman of the halter attempted to tie Flint's hands in front of him and drape him with a noose, for this was his prerogative. But a sea-service bosun, immaculate in shore-going dress, elbowed him aside.

"Urrumph!" said the sheriff.

"A-hum!" said the prison chaplain.

"Huh!" said a sea-service captain.

And the yeoman blinked, and stood back, remembering what had been agreed for this special occasion.

"Oh," he said, "beg pardon, I'm sure."

"Cap'n!" said the bosun to Flint, producing a cord and halter of his own, all neatly worked in Turk's heads and seizings.

"Ah!" said Flint. "I can see that you have served before the mast!"

"Aye-aye, sir!" said the bosun, and sought to tie Flint's wrists.

"A moment!" said Flint, raising a hand in admonition.

"Cap'n?"

"I have a duty to perform," said Flint, and snapped his fingers towards the fellow who'd been his servant these past weeks – one Edwards, a failed writer who'd battered a publisher in despair at rejection. This sorry creature crept forward with a tray bearing a number of doe-skin purses.

"Ahhh!" said all present.

"Gentlemen," said Flint, and presented a purse to each of the big gaolers who'd followed his every step.

"Gor bless you, Cap'n!" they said, and sniffed and snivelled.

202

"Weren't no wish of our'n, Cap'n!" said one.

"No finer gennelman ever lived!" said the other.

"Reverend, sir," said Flint, turning to the chaplain, "for those in want . . ."

"Oh, sir!" said the chaplain, deeply affected, taking the purse.

"Mr Bosun!" said Flint, handing out the last purse.

"Aye-aye, sir!" said the bosun, and saluted as if to an admiral.

"Proceed, Mr Bosun!" said Flint, and he offered his hands.

So Flint was tied and the noose draped round his neck and the slack bound round his body, and he was led through doors, gates and passages, and outside the prison . . . where an enormous cry went up from the mob already assembled. Even so early as this, they were ready and waiting: tinkers, tailors, chair-men, lumpers, washerwomen, gentlewomen, gentlemen, and dogs, hogs, chickens and beggars. Them and all the cocky young apprentices of the town, who – by kindly tradition – had been given the day off for the hanging.

Seeing this, Flint doffed his hat, and bowed left and right, to cheers and applause, and climbed up into the big, black-bodied mourning coach – hired by himself at still further expense – with a coachman on the box, and footmen on their steps at the rear, all liveried in sombre black, and stood to utmost attention, and four splendid horses in harness, with black plumes nodding from their heads.

Even more splendid were the uniformed, mounted javelin-men, two troops of them, formed up to front and rear of the coach. They were there to keep back the mob and guard the prisoner, but with their big, ceremonial lances, tasselled below the steel points, they resembled a royal escort.

"Ahhhhhh!" gasped the crowd, pressing forward as Flint caused the folding roof to be lowered such that he could see – and be seen – all the better.

The only thing that let down the magnificent display was

the clumsy, two-wheeled farm wagon rumbling along behind the rearmost javelin-men, drawn by two plodding nags. This was the vehicle upon which the *common* condemned rode to the gallows, sitting on the coffin in which they would later ride away from it. Today there were no common condemned for it to carry, but no amount of money could dispense with the coffin.

"Three cheers for the cap'n!" cried a voice, and the mob huzzahed to shake the windows and rattle the tiles, as the sheriff, the chaplain, and the sea-service captain crammed in beside Flint and the astonished bosun, who'd never been so close to so much rank in all his life.

"Forward!" cried the sheriff, and the procession moved off to the mournful beat of four drummers, dressed in black, who marched behind the Lord High Admiral's Silver Oar bearer, and were yet another expense down to Joe Flint. But what did that matter? He wasn't going to spend his reward money on anything else: not now.

And so, the long, slow two miles to Tyburn, which a galloping horse would cover in minutes, but which took over three hours when the Town was turned out, lining the streets in swaying, heaving, grinning multitudes that came armed with the traditional missiles: rotten fruit, turds in paper, and the ever-popular dead cats – some not entirely dead – which, when swung by the tail and thrown, were the supreme expression of the mob's displeasure.

But none of these were thrown at Joe Flint: not him! For he stood gallantly in the carriage, and blew kisses to the ladies, saluted the gentlemen, and struck the boldest figure that London had ever seen . . . and so he was received with roaring acclamation . . . the same acclamation as proceeded from the sheriff, the chaplain, the sea-service captain and – most especially – the bosun, who grinned in red-faced merriment, for Flint had provisioned the carriage with spirits, and the bottles were soon uncorked and going down.

204

Custom prescribed two stops along the way, at favoured public houses, which paid vast bribes for the privilege of being chosen, since this meant being drunk dry of drink, and eaten bare of food, by the colossal and merry increase in business on a hanging day.

Thus, first to the Stump and Magpie, St Giles's, where roaring trade was capped by Joe Flint's singing of a song – new to London – which became the choice of the mob, long after.

Fifteen men on the dead man's chest . . .

He sang beautifully, stood up on a table with the rope round his neck and his bound hands, and soon the cram-packed sweating company learned to roar out the response, and all those in the streets outside bellowed along with them.

Yo, ho, ho – and a bottle of rum!

"Listen," said Billy Bones, "that's his song!"

"Aye, Mr Mate," said Black Dog.

Billy Bones scowled.

"*Lieutenant!*" he said.

"If you says so . . . Lieutenant," said Black Dog, grinning.

"What song?" said Mr Joe.

"Before your time, my son," said Black Dog.

"Ah!" said Billy Bones, listening to the song and cheering up for the first time in months. "That's my Cap'n!" he said, swelling with pride. "That's my boy! Hark to the manner of him. And him on his way to be hanged!"

"Aye!" they all said, all of them: twenty of Long John's men, and another twenty of King Jimmy's who were following the coach on foot, glad of the long coats they wore for the cold, and which hid what they'd got underneath.

It was the same at the Green Man in Oxford Street, except that knowledge of the song had swept ahead of the lumbering coach, and when the big vehicle pulled to a stop and the javelin-men used the butt ends of their spears to force a way into the inn yard, the mob surged in behind, roaring the song out to Heaven, even as Flint, the sheriff, the chaplain, and the bosun were stood in line, relieving themselves in the privy. But not the sea-service captain. He was snoring peacefully in the coach.

However, all good things come to an end and eventually, seated in his splendid carriage beside his foolishly grinning companions and surrounded with a Roman Triumph of screeching faces, Flint caught his first sight of the Tyburn tree where it reared up, right in the middle of a great crossroads to the west of London, in open ground where Oxford Street became Tyburn Road, before branching into the Uxbridge Road and the ancient Roman Watling Street.

It stood like a squat timber cathedral, high over all else. Its three massive legs supported a great triangle from which as many as twenty-four sufferers could be turned off at one time with the utmost convenience. But now it was occupied only by a hangman's mate, who lazed on its topmost height with the smoke of his pipe drifting up into the cold air.

Even Joe Flint gulped at that, and even he staggered under the enormous noise of the crowd assembled at this most favourite spot, for London's most favourite day out: an entertainment offering not only tremendous spectacle, but moral instruction besides, and therefore suitable for the entire family, from doting grandmas to precious children. Flint shook his head. He thought he'd seen a multitude in the streets . . . but it was nothing compared to this! The number was beyond counting.

There were timber grandstands, built by entrepreneurs to give a fine view of the gallows at two shillings a head. There were coaches of the gentry, whipping inward for better places, their splendid occupants leaning out and yelling and quarrelling. There were men stuck in muddy potholes, struggling clear. There were pick-pockets, whores, and pox doctors.

There were fights with cudgels, fists and clawing fingernails, while cripple-beggars worked the crowd with rattling tins, infants got dropped and trampled, little boys piddled in corners, and pie-men, gin vendors, hawkers and broadsheet sellers bellowed their trade – especially the latter:

"Last true confession of Flint the pirate!" they cried, promising Flint's own words, giving all his crimes in blood-curdling detail.

The Brownlough brothers stood in the middle of their own private mob, turned out for the price of a guinea a man and a bottle of gin, and wearing white bands in their hats so they shouldn't smash one another's brains in by mistake. They stood to one side of the main mob that bawled and roared around the *three-legged mare*.

"So! Shall we see him hang?" cried Reginald Brownlough, the elder.

"*Noooooo!*" they roared, their voices lost in the general din.

"So who's with me, for the honour of old England?"

"Me!" they cried, even the Scots and Irish among them.

"Then will you follow me?"

"Aye!"

He'd been preaching the same sermon for days, had Reginald Brownlough, to stevedores, chair-men, and butcher's boys, down in the gin shops and ale houses of East London. He was intoxicated with it now: even more than they were on his gin. But . . . by virtue of much money and a certain gift for words, he'd got them worked up for a fight.

After all, these kiddies didn't need much excuse for that; and there were nearly three hundred of them.

The javelin-men forced a way through the mob, which genially bellowed and shrieked, and gave way, and pressed, laughing and gawping, against the coach as their stink rolled over Flint,

207

and dirty hands pawed, and children were held up to see him, and the gallows came close, and the enormous mob roared out his own precious song, in a bad-breath, gin-sodden, mountain of sound . . .

> *Fifteen men on the dead man's chest,*
> *Yo ho ho, and a bottle of rum!*

And here Flint changed. As he looked around to all sides, even the tight-shut compartments of his singular mind – which had kept him jolly thus far – could not keep out the plain threat of destruction of the self. As far as he could see, all had failed and death was certain. And so, the devil-may-care actor who'd put on such a show for the crowd . . . became simply the devil.

His face darkened. Expression vanished. His muscles tensed . . . and he began to blink furiously . . .

Silver shouted in King Jimmy's ear. The mob's roar was like a storm at sea. It was deafening. King Jimmy and Flash Jack leaned closer to hear, the three of them standing up in the chaise which swayed beneath them, for it was built for speed, with two huge, light wheels and a pair of blood horses harnessed in tandem, stamping their hooves in fright, with Israel Hands holding their heads and trying to calm them, while two dozen men in long coats forced their way through the crowd, elbowing all others aside and forming up in a body around the vehicle.

One of them looked miserably at Long John, and couldn't meet his eye, for they parted bad on Flint's island.

"Huh!" said Silver. "Here's Billy Bones and our lads. So where's the others?"

"They're here already," said King Jimmy. "Look!" and he pointed.

"Ah!" said Silver. "The buggers with white in their hats?"

"Aye!" said King Jimmy. "The Brownlough boys. We all

know *them* down Wapping way! Them shit-heads ain't even made a secret of it."

"Can we trust them?" said Flash Jack, who trusted nobody, and was unrecognisable as his exquisite self, being dressed in plain dull clothes, and no wig but a big hat pulled low over the bald head which he shaved for cleanliness. Nobody would have known him who'd seen him shimmering down the aisle at Jackson's.

"Can we trust *you*?" said King Jimmy. "It's only *you* as says Flint knows how to find the treasure!"

Flash Jack sneered.

"Who else can find Flint's treasure, but Flint?" he said.

"Aye," said Silver, and looked at Flint, waving to the mob in his carriage. "By thunder!" he said. "I know the bugger, burn and beach me if I don't." He nodded grimly. "He'll know where it lies, cunning bastard that he is, by God, for there ain't none like him! And trust me, Jimmy, no bugger could get it off him. Not if they stripped him bare-arsed. But *he'll know* and he'll have it secret somewhere . . . and there ain't no finding of it without him!"

"An' it's *eight hundred thousand*?" said King Jimmy, relishing the colossal sum.

"Aye," said Silver, "why else d'you think we're here?"

Flint went mad as they got him out of the mourning coach and up on to the tail of the farm cart with its open coffin, where the bosun threw the slack of his noose up to the hangman's mate so it could be made fast to an overhead beam, and the chaplain produced his prayer book and began to rant.

The javelin-men were well clear now, to give the public a good view, but there were plenty of men around Flint, nonetheless: the bosun, the public hangman – present even if he wasn't being paid – the sea-service captain, the sheriff, a couple of muscular assistant hangmen, and of course the chaplain, for all the good he could do.

And then came an incredible, unique and totally unprecedented sight which prompted a truly stupendous roar from the mob: the condemned man was making a last fight beneath the gallows!

Flint, having bitten through the bonds around his wrists in manic, shrieking fury, drew his sword – that still had a three-inch stump of sharp steel and a knuckle guard and a pommel – and used it to kill the bosun and the sea-service captain, quick as thought, stabbing into their throats. He killed the terrified sheriff, smashing in the back of his head with the pommel as he turned to run. He went for the chaplain, who screamed like a girl and saved his life by taking the sword stump into the thickness of his prayer book. Frustrated, Flint kicked the chaplain's legs out from under him and was stamping a heel into his face when the hangman and his two assistants dived in with fists and boots, white-faced, wide-eyed and spitting fury.

"Now, boys!" cried the Brownlough brothers, and a united howl arose from their three hundred.

"Flint! Flint! Flint!" they roared and surged forward, cudgels raised, trampling all before them as they charged the gallows.

"Forward, lads!" cried Silver. "But let them Brownloughs take the first fire!"

"*Giddyup*!" cried King Jimmy, whipping the horses.

"Aye!" cried Silver's men.

"Aye!" cried King Billy's.

And they threw off their coats to reveal pistols and cutlasses, and drew steel with a scrape and a ring, and the chaise drove through the crowd hedged in blades, bowling along behind the wave of the Brownlough mob, with Silver's and King Jimmy's men alongside, all cheering madly, even as the javelin-men wheeled about to face the Brownloughs.

Beneath the gallows, Flint bit and stabbed and kicked and butted. He pummelled and spat and shrieked, he fought beyond strength, beyond reason, beyond endurance . . . and could even now have prevailed, even with three men hanging on to him, of which two at least were marked for life and losing strength, had not the captain of the javelin-men sent four reinforcements to help the hangman, even as he was wheeling his troop into line to face the mob.

"Chaaaaaaarge!" cried the captain.

"Arrrrrrgh!" cried his men, dipping their spears and spurring their horses.

"Flint! Flint!" cried the Brownloughs, hurling cobbles, bricks and bottles.

"Steady, lads," cried Silver, holding back his men. "Let the buggers fight!"

"Grab his bastard hands!" cried the hangman, as fresh men dashed in.

"*Ahhhhhhhhhh!*" shrieked Flint. He tore an ear with his teeth, gouged an eye with his thumb, sliced a scrotum with his sword . . . but:

"Gotcher!" cried the hangman, and he pulled the noose tight under Flint's chin, and steadied himself on the blood-soaked planks of the farm cart, and then – with the satisfaction of a craftsman showing soddin' amateurs how a job should be done . . .

he pushed Flint off the back of the cart, with three men still hanging on to him . . .

. . . men who flailed and swung their arms, and two dropped swiftly to the ground, and one had to beat Flint to make him let go, and he dropped too, and the vast mob shrieked tremendously again, and all those in the grandstands leapt to their feet and roared as Flint swung . . . and choked . . . and throttled . . .. and his hands clawed the crushing rope . . . and his eyes bulged . . . and the blood thundered in his ears . . . and his legs danced . . . and his body dangled . . . five feet clear of the ground.

Chapter 25

Noon, Monday, 26th November 1753
The Rotunda
Ranelagh Gardens
London

*S*ir Matthew Blackstone was in love with Selena. She could see it in his adoring expression. And he might be over fifty and ugly, but he was one of the richest men in England.

She knew what was coming. She'd guessed. Her entire life was hers to change with a single word. That's why she'd been brought here. But for the moment, she gasped, for the Rotunda was exotic beyond belief, even to her, though she was no longer an innocent in such matters, having grown as familiar with the gilded luxury of salons as with the spectacular cunning of theatrical effects.

The huge dome was the pride of Ranelagh, the most civilised of the London pleasure gardens. It was all fresh painted in pale cream, with an oriental profusion of elegant pillars and relief-work in red, and two great tiers of private boxes running round the walls, where patrons could take tea while looking out on the crowd sauntering around the vastly complex and gloriously decorated central column, which was itself a feat of architecture and which supported the ceiling. Several dozen huge chandeliers hung by scarlet cords, while one of the finest orchestras in London played in a huge canopied box to one side, and the admission price was set high enough to ensure that only the most proper and fashionable persons might gain entry.

"Well," he said, "do you like it?"

"It's beautiful," she said. "I'm glad we came."

"Good," he said, "'cos it ain't normally open this time o'year." He shrugged. "But a little word in the right ear ..."

"Oh!" she said. "Did you cause it to be open: *for me?*" She fluttered her eyelashes and laid a hand on his arm, and gazed at him with pouting lips and round eyes ... and laughed. And he laughed too and shivered at the beauty of her in the yellow silk which was her favourite colour, and was thrilled at the pleasure of simply being with her, and her acting a silly part as she did on the stage, and doing it just for him!

"Well, *did* you?" she said.

"Yes. I did."

"Then thank you!" But she frowned, puzzled. "Then who are all these people?" She looked at the ladies and gentlemen strolling around, greeting friends, nodding to acquaintances.

"Well," he said, "if it was going to be open, I wanted it looking alive and not dead, so I put the word around ... and of course that lot –" he pointed to Katty Cooper, standing twenty paces off with Mr Abbey and others of his company – "they're our chaperones, my lass, for the benefit of them as knows me and knows Lady Blackstone, too: the old trout back home in Berkshire."

"Oh!" she said.

"Oh, indeed!" Sir Matthew sniffed and looked round. "Most of 'em know me, here." And he caught the eye of the conductor of the orchestra, and raised his hat and gave a nod, whereupon the conductor bowed in acknowledgement ... tap-tapped his baton ... stopped the orchestra in full flood ...

213

"One, two!" he said, and the orchestra broke into "The Pollywhacket Song", to general delight and applause towards Selena, while she – now very much the artiste – made her curtsey to all points of the compass. Having sung the wretched song hundreds of times, she now detested it, but the public didn't, and Sir Matthew didn't, and he was seeking to please, for he was kind and thoughtful and generous.

"Well," said Sir Matthew, when she turned to him with a smile that sent shivers down his backbone, "it's better than Captain Flint's hanging, which is where most of London is gone this day, and where I'd have gone myself if not for you . . ." But he saw her reaction and knew he'd said something wrong.

"God love you, my little dear," he said, and put an arm around her. "What is it?" But she groaned for painful memories, and *he* groaned to see it. "Tell me, my lovely. Tell old Matty," he soothed, for he was a decent man and couldn't bear to see her unhappy.

"Could we sit down?" said Selena.

"Of course," he said, and led her to one of the private boxes and sat her down at a table, and took a seat beside her and ordered tea and hot drop-scones from one of the waiters, while – keeping their distance – Katty Cooper, Mr Abbey and the rest, looked on . . . Katty Cooper grinding her teeth in jealousy.

"So what's the matter, my sweetheart?" Sir Matthew's rough, lumpish face was transported into concern, and he clasped his bear-paws round her small hands.

"I know Flint," she said. "Or rather, I knew him . . ."

"What? How could that be? He's a pirate!"

"But I know him." Selena looked at Sir Matthew, whom she liked and trusted, and she started to explain. She spoke of things that had been confined to the back of her mind for many months. And the more she spoke, the easier it got, until it all tumbled out: head over heels, disordered, stumbling and

214

repetitive ... but *all* of it. Right from the start: from the Delacroix Plantation to Charley Neal's grog shop to the *Walrus*, Flint's Island, his treasure, Danny Bentham and beyond. She told him every last thing. Even about the two men she'd shot dead in Charlestown. Even about Joe Flint, who was mad and who'd said he loved her, and even about John Silver, who certainly did.

And Sir Matthew listened, and said nothing, and held her hand, and the tea and drop-scones arrived and grew cold, and still she spoke and he listened.

Finally she sighed and stopped and looked at him, and he was pierced to the soul at the beauty of her lovely, vulnerable face appealing to him for judgement. In that instant he'd have stood between her and the world. He'd have jumped off a cliff for her, if it would have helped! And he'd have gone down joyful and content. But there was one point to discuss: a point such as couldn't be missed by so practical a man as Matt Blackstone.

"You're married, then? You're Mrs Silver?" he said.

"Yes," she said.

"But you left him?"

"Yes."

He stayed silent a long time. He gathered courage. He looked at her again.

"And would you go back to him now, if you could?"

There was an even longer silence.

"Wait!" he said, and shook his head. "Don't answer that, 'cos here's the way of it my girl: first of all, I don't care what you've done. After all, what choice did you have? And what care I if you did? Second, here's *myself* married, and *yourself* married, and church and state between us." He spread his hands and smiled sadly. "If I'd met you as a lad, I'd have said *no* to my pa and never married the old trout, and asked you instead!" He laughed. "But that were twenty year before you was born!"

She laughed too, and his heart leaped with joy to see it.

"Matt," she said, "you're a good man . . ."

"Aye, but an ugly, old one."

"No!"

"Yes! But here's what I'm offering: there can't be no marriage, and I ain't such a fool as to think you'd have me for love . . ."

"Matt!" she said, leaning forward to touch his rough cheek. He sighed and kissed her hand with utmost gentleness, but he shook his head.

"No. None o' that," he said, "for I'm a philosophical man. So! You're making good money on the stage right now, ain't you?" She nodded. "Then beware, my princess, for of all trades, that's the least certain and the least secure!"

"Is it?" she said, for she was in full flush of triumphant success.

"Oh yes!" he said. "You'll learn! The stage can turn you out tomorrow, whereas I offer this . . . I offer to settle regular monthly payments upon you, and a cash sum on my death, as'll make you a rich woman, secure in your own right with house and carriage and servants an' all." He wagged a finger. "And all signed and sealed by the lawyers. But –" he said, and looked her in the eye with the sharpness that had made him so formidable a man of business "– here's the bargain: *there shall be no other man than me* . . . and that too shall be written into the settlement." He nodded slowly. "For I may be old, and I do love you my little darling . . . but I'll not be made a fool of . . . and if I am . . . the money stops!"

"Matt," she said, "I'd never deceive so kind a man as you."

He laughed.

"Not you, my sweetness, not right now. But three years on, when you're bored and some pretty young fellow winks his eye at you . . ."

"No!" she said.

Sir Matthew smiled.

216

"Aye," he said, "whatever you say. But I'm serious in what *I've* said. Every word of it . . . Now! I'm off into Berkshire tomorrow, the which'll give you a few days to think. But when I come back, I'll want an answer."

She leaned across the table and kissed him.

And Katty Cooper sizzled in hatred.

Chapter 26

Noon, Monday, 26th November 1753
Tyburn
To the west of London

The javelin-men hit the Brownlough boys in a beating of iron hooves, a kicking of sharp-spurred boots, a snorting of yellow horse-teeth, and the massive impact of twenty-nine horses and men – twelve-hundred pounds weight per mount and rider – moving at thirty miles per hour and arriving knee-to-knee in a wall of muscle and bone.

And all the while Joe Flint kicked and twisted in his death agony.

It didn't matter that they weren't trained cavalry. It didn't matter that their spears were for show and not sharpened. It didn't matter that they had no military swords, only short-bladed hangers. They hit the mob as a sledgehammer hits a melon. The Brownlough boys didn't even have time to turn and run – though the sharpest of them tried, and were duly hit from behind.

Flint struggled and trembled. He throttled and fought for breath.

Men were thrown down with skulls smashed under horse-shoes and limbs broken and spines shattered and faces smashed into the ground and the dead and the dying piling up, and men smothering underneath, and others screaming, groaning and bleeding as the charge punched deep into the heaving, struggling, three-hundred-strong, gin-fired mass, with its cudgels and cobbles and knives . . . until the force of the charge was soaked up by sheer bulk of human flesh, and the horses began to trample and buck and kick, and the javelin-men bellowed and roared and stabbed with their blunt spears, and slashed with their short swords.

And Flint began to weaken.

Then one of the javelin-men got pulled from his saddle and was beaten with pitiless fury as the tide of the battle turned, for now not only the Brownlough boys fought back, but the mob itself was roused and it growled in the depth of its rage, instinctively taking the part of its fellows against the forces of law, and falling upon the javelin-men in thousands and tens of thousands, with clawing hands, swinging cudgels, a tremendous volley of stones, and limitless strength which pulled over not only the riders, but their shrieking mounts as well.

Flint's hands fell to his sides.

"Wait! Wait!" cried Silver. "No bugger goes without the word!"

"Arrrrrrgh!" they cried.

"Come on, John!" said King Jimmy, shaking with fighting fury.

"No! No! No!" said Flash Jack, and hopelessly sought a way out.

"*NOW!*" cried Silver, for he'd spotted a way through to the gallows. "Pistols now, boys! Mark your targets!"

"*Go*-on! *Go*-on!" cried King Jimmy, and thrashed the two horses; they leapt forward, taking the chaise and its body-guard of armed men darting into the gap Silver had spotted in the vast wall of flesh and blood that stood between them and the gallows.

Flint hung unmoving. He turned slowly on the rope.

219

There was a roaring, rolling volley of gunfire as the chaise met the mob, with Silver's and King Jimmy's men hanging on and shooting down any creature – man or beast – that stood in the way as the chaise drove through the hideous revenge being inflicted upon the wretched javelin-men.

Crack! Crack! Crack! went King Jimmy's whip and the chaise shot ahead at such a pace as to leave its bodyguard falling and dragging behind, and then they were up to the foot of the gallows and alongside of Flint's body with the executioner and his mates wide-eyed in terror, and in anger, too. And as King Jimmy pulled open a clasp knife, grabbed the hanging-rope from the height of the chaise, and commenced hacking and slashing . . . the hangman leapt up into the cart and struck an enormous blow with the lead-loaded club that he kept for moments like this, and caught King Jimmy on the brow with a crunch that stove in the bone and mashed the brains beneath.

"Bastard!" cried John Silver, and pulled out a pistol, jamming it into shirt and ribs, then a yellow flash and a roar of powder blew half a pound of catsmeat out of the hangman's body, and Flash Jack seized his beloved Flint by the waist, and strained to lift him to take the pressure off the rope, and Silver dropped the pistol, and drew a cutlass and sawed the rope . . .

And London trembled from east to west and north to south as such a cheer arose from Tyburn as had never been heard in all its five hundred years as a place of execution . . .

. . . as Flint dropped free of the gallows and fell into the chaise!

Silver heaved mightily to get the rope from his throat, and rubbed his chest and chafed his limbs and prayed for the life of the man he detested above all others, while Flash Jack kicked the dead from the chaise and whipped up the horses and drove speeding through the mob, which opened like the

Red Sea before Moses, except that Moses wasn't cheered, idolised, adored and urged onward as he passed.

Thus the chaise rocked and galloped away down Oxford Street, heading for London at dizzy speed, while Silver's and King Jimmy's men merged into the wildly milling crowd, and the newspaper writers ruptured themselves in the speed of their pencilling and loosing pigeons, and the few remaining javelin-men were beaten senseless, and the lightly wounded lay groaning, the heavily wounded lay dying, and the already dead lay stiffening, with the pickpockets feeling for their goods.

But the mob wasn't done. Not it! Not yet! It was more worked up than it had been for years. It had smelled blood. It had killed and had men killed. It boiled and seethed, and – fired up with wicked glee – it sought further entertainment.

First it robbed the pie-men and gin-sellers, then it wrecked and burned down the grandstands where the wealthy – now wisely departed – had sat. Next it conducted a diligent search of itself for Catholics, Jews, dissenters, foreigners and others whom it did not like, and sent them on their way with bloody noses and a boot up the arse. Then, swaggering, roaring and vastly steaming in the cold November air, it rolled down Oxford Street in the very tracks of the chaise that had rescued its hero, where it got to down to some serious work by over-turning carriages, smashing windows, looting shops and setting fire to any houses thought to be owned by persons hostile to the bold Captain Flint.

Meanwhile Flash Jack shook in horror in the galloping chaise, for the things he'd seen and the things he'd done, which were such as he'd never experienced in all his comfortable life. Then a voice yelled in his ear:

"Avast!" said Silver. "Back your topsail. Heave-to you swab!"

"Oh . . ." said Flash Jack, and hauled on the reins and brought the horses to a trembling walk, and they gasped and panted, as he did himself.

"Where are we?" said Silver, looking round the empty streets.

"Near Tottenham Court Road," said Flash Jack, born and bred in London.

"Poor bloody Jimmy!" said Silver. "Was he dead?"

"Yes . . . I think so."

"But you heaved him over anyway, poor bugger!" Silver shook his head. He pointed to the roadside. "Drop anchor over there."

With the chaise stopped, Silver knelt beside Flint, who was laid under the seat, unmoving. He put his head to Flint's chest. He took a silver dollar from his pocket, rubbed it on his sleeve and held it to Flint's lips.

"Pah!" he said in disgust.

"God, let him live!" said Flash Jack.

"Devil, more like!" said Silver . . . as Flint opened his eyes and looked at Silver, for he was indeed alive. He was alive but sunk in dread. He'd known what it was to die. He *had* died as far as he knew, and even the most tremendous of minds doesn't come clean away from *that*: not clean nor quick nor unharmed, and Flint shuddered and shook, as once again – in burning memory – he suffered the agonies of death by strangulation.

"John . . ." he said to the familiar face, and groaned and raised a hand to clutch for light and life, and escape from torment.

"Joe," said Silver, "you stay there. We can talk later." Then he threw a blanket over Flint so he'd not be seen, and sat up on the seat beside Flash Jack. "You're the fly cove! You're the bounding boy! So where are we going? We planned for Jimmy's warehouse, but all my dealings was with him. I can't trust his people without him."

"I've got a house," said Flash Jack, "off Cable Street."

"I knows of none better," said Silver. "Whip 'em up. But slow an' easy." He looked at the near-deserted streets. "There's no bugger, hardly, here to see us, what with 'em all gone to the hanging. But make it slow and easy."

Later, the chaise drove into Well Close Square, by the Danish church, and into a yard behind the house, where there was a small stable for the horses, and they got Flint to his feet and led him staggering inside, leaning on the two of them.

"Nice!" said Silver, when the door was shut and locked and Flint had been settled in a big Windsor chair in the parlour.

Nice was hardly the word. The room was exquisite: burnished, cleaned, polished, and neat beyond all reason. The whole house was the same, and fitted out with the most beautiful of furniture, ornaments and pictures: all in harmony, all elegant, all beautifully chosen.

Flash Jack smiled.

"It is my little quiet place," he said. "Where I bring friends."

"Do you now?" said Silver.

"Yes," said Flash Jack, for it was true, though the *friends* were always paid.

"Drink," said Flint, swaying and hanging on to the arms of the chair. "Drink, for the love of God." He was pawing at his throat, where a red weal had been burned into his skin by the rope. He was shuddering and shivering.

Flash Jack took over. He was an excellent host, an excellent cook, and kept a fine cellar. Soon he emerged from his kitchen with a couple of bottles of claret and a dish of buttered bread slices, cut into triangles, with sliced beef and pickles between.

"Very tasty," said Silver, munching one of the triangles.

"Johnny Montagu's own recipe," said Flash Jack, an incurable name-dropper. "He tells me they're to be named after himself: *sandwiches* – for he's the Earl of Sandwich, as you know."

But they weren't listening. Silver was looking at Flint, and Flint was looking at Silver. For them there was nobody else in the room. Far too much had passed between them for that.

Flint drained a glass, breathed deep, and spoke. His voice croaked and he was weak. He wasn't himself. Not nearly. Not by a hundred thousand miles.

"You got my offer, John?"

"The treasure for your life?"

"Yes."

"Aye. I got it, from him –" Silver nodded at Flash Jack. "Why else would I cut you down?"

Flint nodded. He shuddered, and in the extremity of his horror at meeting death, his mind was so altered that he was honest.

"The treasure?" he said, and drew a neat little silver cylinder from his pocket. About the size of a man's finger, it was a porte-crayon, designed to hold a pen or pencil . . . but this one didn't. Flint unscrewed a cap at one end, and shook out a tight roll of papers, covered in tiny handwriting . . . Flint's handwriting.

"The map," he said, "merely finds the island, where you can search for ever and not find the goods."

"I know!" said Silver.

"But these notes," said Flint, "give precision."

Flash Jack looked at the papers.

"Why so much detail?" he asked.

"To begin with," said Flint, "there are several burial sites, not one. They are in jungle clearings which even I couldn't find again without the bearings and measurements I took from such points as nature provided: great rocks and giant trees." Flint shook his head. "If once you go wrong, you'll never find the next bearing point. So it's all or nothing. Even half the papers would be useless."

Flint sank back, his voice weak from so much speech, and Flash Jack reached out to touch the cylinder.

"No!" gasped Flint. "Don't touch it, Mr Jackson. You can guess where I hide it, when searched."

"Ugh!" said Flash Jack, and recoiled as if from a spider, for he was intensely fastidious in all matters of hygiene.

"So," said Silver. "How's things, my cocker?"

Flint sighed.

"I never did admire that appellation, John. For it is crassly vulgar."

"Huh! So you ain't quite dead!"

"No," said Flint, straining to speak and fingering his neck. "But I'm not quite alive, neither, for the belly and bowels of me think that I'm dead!" And he shook violently as emotions heaved in the depths of his soul.

"Joe!" said Silver, half out of his chair, for the friendship had once been great, and Flint was suffering.

"No!" said Flint. "Be still." And he forced out words with great difficulty. "Here's a thing, John . . ."

"What?"

"When I was on the rope . . ."

"Leave it, Joe," he said. "Maybe later, when you're fit?"

"No. It must be said. When I was on the rope . . . and dying . . ."

"Don't, Joe!"

"I expected to see my father at the gates of Hell."

"What, to save you?"

"No! As my *punishment*." Flint looked at Silver. "Did you have a father?"

"Aye!"

"Was he a good man?"

"A rough bugger," said Silver. "Laid on hard with the belt."

"There are worse things," said Flint, and bowed his head and sat quiet a while. Then he looked up. "My father was not there," he said.

"No?" said Silver.

"But *you* were, John. I saw you."

Now Silver shuddered.

"What was I doing?"

"I don't know. But you were reaching out."

"Was I trying to save you?"

"I don't know."

"Why not?"

"Because *she* was beside you, and I was looking only at *her*."

Silence. Profound silence.

"And what was she doing?" said Silver, finally.

"Nothing. She wouldn't look at me."

Flint groaned, for the rejection was worse than death. It was damnation. He closed his eyes, ground his teeth, clenched his fists, and managed – just – to fight himself up out of the deep of despair . . . only to find a tempest of passions awaiting on the surface: unbearable relief, gratitude for life, guilt, remorse, and more. And under these tormenting forces, acting on irresistible impulse, he did a most tremendous thing . . .

He took up the papers which led to the treasure.

He folded them diagonally in half.

He pinched the fold tight with his fingernails.

And tore the papers in two.

"Here!" he said, handing half to Silver and keeping half himself: "Let us begin again."

Chapter 27

Mid-morning, Tuesday, 27th November 1753
The gates of Newgate Gaol
London

*T*he ram surged ahead, heaved by several dozen of the mob's finest. It thundered against iron-bound oak, and the locks and bars groaned, while all within the prison walls gulped and trembled. A few brave souls snatched up arms and fired on the mob through the windows . . . and received such a hail of brick-ends and cobble stones as sent them reeling back in their own smoke, battered and bloodied, and covered in the splintered remains of frames, putty, paint and glass.

"ANOTHER!" roared the seething mass at the gates, and the ram-bearers took a firmer grip, and staggered back, bowling over and trampling down all those who failed to get clear of their ponderous recoil . . . then . . .

"FORWARD!" they cried and the ram went in again.

Half an hour earlier it had been a respectable beech tree, growing peacefully in Warwick Square, doing no harm to any man. But then it had been hacked down, lopped off, and borne away in the mighty arms of chair-men, coal-heavers, butcher boys and all such others as were ready to raise a decent sweat in a good cause.

BOOOM! went the prison gates.

"ANOTHER!" roared the mob, now in its second day of fun, and dangerously swollen with all the trollops of the town, egging the men on and pouring drink down them, and charging sixpence for a stand-up against the wall.

The mob was tens of thousands strong. It was a pandemonium of wicked glee. It was an elemental force that carried all before it, invincible, unconquerable and unstoppable – except by the army. But the army was still in barracks, while the mob was fired up and bent on vengeance against the hated Newgate Gaol, where the hero Joe Flint had been incarcerated.

CRRRRRRRUNCH! said the gates to the gaol, and a mighty cheer arose as the timberwork gave up the fight and splintered and sundered and fell open, and the ram was dropped, bouncing, booming and recoiling and smashing feet and breaking limbs . . . and the mob was jamming, cramming and forcing itself into the narrow doorway and into the gaol, waving axes, hammers, knives, cudgels, and flaming torches.

At the back of the commotion Flash Jack watched and grinned. There were others like him who hung back from the action: sharp, slippery persons who trailed after the mob, grinning and winking, ever seeking safe opportunities for gain, but keeping well clear of the dangerous work of smashing gates and cracking heads.

Flash Jack smiled and looked around, and told himself how clever he was to go forth in the shabby clothes that he affected when he chose to. For he'd been a poor man once, and had had no choice, but when he *did* get money and put on fine raiment and became Flash Jack . . . why, he'd found that no man knew him if he took them off again, and put on his rags. They were, of course, very *clean* rags, but so long as he went discreetly and met no eyes . . . it was as if he were invisible.

This fascinating discovery had, for years, enabled Flash Jack to pass unknown through the streets of London, and was the reason why he'd gone with Silver and King Jimmy to rescue Joe Flint without the least fear of being recognised.

"And so!" he said to himself, and he let the mob and its followers leave him behind, and stood alone for a while before walking off through the deserted streets towards Covent Garden and Jackson's Coffee House. He had to walk, because it wasn't safe to be out with a carriage – not with the mob on the streets – and he entered Jackson's by a private back door with a private key, and so to his own room and hot water and soap, and his beautiful clothes and his splendid wigs and all else that made him Flash Jack once more: to be bowed to and grovelled to by his staff. So, straightening his back and fixing a smile, he opened the door to the big main room and went into the light and bright, and was pleased to see that, even today – with the mob not come to Covent Garden – there was good business and a body of patrons who saluted him, and nodded and smiled.

He smiled back. They'd let him out, had Flint and Silver, only because they wouldn't go themselves: or rather Flint *couldn't* go out: not yet, and Silver wouldn't be parted from him. Not now each had half the papers.

So Flash Jack was sent out to tell Silver's men their captain's location. But he was taking his time. He had things to consider: things like his present attitude towards Joe Flint, who was so obviously going to sail away in John Silver's ship and never look back! And there was plenty of time to think. Flash Jack shrugged. They wouldn't starve in his little quiet place. It was well stocked with food and drink. Pausing to bow to favoured clients, he beamed in their approval of himself, and passed on down the room, cane in hand, placing one elegant foot before the other.

He was so pleased to be his elegant self again that some of the pain of Flint's *personal* rejection was fading, for rejection it was. Flint had barely looked at him. Flash Jack sighed. It was ever thus! He was clever enough to recognise what a fool he was in matters of the loins, yet still foolish enough to make a fool of himself the next time . . . and the next . . . and the next. It was the same with the rough young men he entertained in his quiet place. None of *them* really cared for him either.

So Flash Jack's slippery mind turned to other matters. He needed to calculate where the balance of power lay between himself and these two fearfully dangerous men with their island and their papers and their eight hundred thousand pounds – of which he still hoped against hope for a share . . .

And then he stopped, surprised.

"Katty Cooper!" he said. "As I live and breathe!"

Three persons of consequence had just entered. They were theatricals like many of his best clients: theatricals at the very top of their profession: Mr Alan Croxley, manager of Croxley's Odeon Theatre, together with a small man Flash Jack didn't know, but who was intimate with Croxley. And – wonder of wonders, after all these years – there was dear little Katty Cooper: somewhat older, but pretty as ever, whom Flash Jack had known as an actress and later as a member of that profession celebrated by *Jackson's List*.

"Jack!" said Katty Cooper, and smiled wonderfully. She was *une chienne du premier ordre*, and he was a slimy sycophant, but they'd been friends once, or as close to that as was possible between such as them.

"Katty!"

"Jack!"

They stepped forward to embrace, and to kiss hands, and to stand back admiring one another at arm's length while the entire room looked on, and Mr Croxley and Mr Abbey smiled.

So great was the pleasure of this re-union that, after a brief exchange of pleasantries, all costs were waived to Mr Croxley's party, and Mr Croxley and Mr Abbey were left to order whatsoever they wished, while Mr Jackson led Mrs Cooper to a private corner where a congenial exchange was made of memories, histories and hopes, such that every topic imaginable was explored, until at last, the pretty smiles vanished as the beautiful Joe Flint and the beautiful Selena Henderson came under discussion by Jack and Katty, such that . . .

They perceived how much they'd been deceived.

They discovered artful plots against their precious selves.

They turned to spiteful revenge: sly, cunning and vicious.

Sunset, 1st December 1753
23 King Street
Off St James's Square
London

Selena laid her pistols on the dressing table, and sat in her chair looking at them. They were a pair by Ketland of Birmingham, box-locks for compact convenience with blued barrels and silver mounts. They weren't much longer than her own hands, but took balls weighing thirty to the pound, which were over half an inch in diameter . . . and knocked men down stone dead. She knew. She'd seen it. She'd done it.

She sighed as she looked at these constant companions which had come with her from *Walrus* and into *Venture's Fortune* and so to Polmouth, then to other cities, and now to London. Before that they'd been in Charlestown, South Carolina, where they'd done their killing.

She stared at them as they lay on the beautiful table, with its mirrors and furnishings, and the brushes and pots, and the cosmetics carefully chosen to suit her colour, so thorough were the arrangements of this expensive, beautiful house. She reached out and pushed the pistols away, and the maid standing behind her goggled and wondered. She'd never known a mistress who drew pistols from her pocket hoops.

"Are they yours, ma'am?" she said. She couldn't help it.

"Yes," said Selena, and smiled at the face in the mirror looking over her shoulder. It was a new thing, having servants. She'd had dressers for her performances, but they weren't servants: they were artistes like herself. Servants were different. They were astonishingly, unbelievably different for a black girl raised as a slave.

"A man gave them to me," said Selena finally.

"Oh," said the maid. "Shall I do your hair, ma'am?"

The maid knew the rules, even if the mistress didn't, for the maid had been as well chosen as everything else. The rules said, *Don't be nosy*. Not straight away. Mistresses didn't like that.

So there was no more conversation. Not proper conversation. Just the technical exchanges that enabled a maid to get her mistress out of her stays, hoops, petticoats and shift, and into nakedness in a silk dressing gown, and her hair undone and brushed out and laid over her shoulders.

"Will that be all, ma'am?" said the maid when the job was done.

"Yes, thank you," said Selena, and the maid curtseyed and made off with Selena's elaborate gown and its complex underpinnings, and took them to wherever it was that they'd be stored. Selena didn't know where that was. Not yet. She was new to this wonderful house, and its staff . . . all of which would soon be hers.

The maid went out. Selena got up. She looked at herself in the big, full-length mirror that stood beside the dressing table. She nodded, businesslike and assured. She knew that she was very lovely. She looked around the dressing room, taking in its elaborate fittings and elegant decoration, then shrugged and opened the door that led into the bedroom.

This was much bigger. It had long windows, now closed with shutters. It had hand-painted wallpaper of brilliant colours, displaying exotic tropical birds. It had upholstered furniture, a sideboard with wine and food of all kinds, it had a roaring fire in a red-and-green-veined marble fireplace . . . and it had a most elegant and enormous bed.

She looked at all this and thought of the Master's "special house" on the Delacroix Plantation, South Carolina. That, too, had been elaborately fitted out, though now she realised that it had been vulgar. It had been the coarse attempt of a provincial lecher to imitate his betters: his clumsy reaching for the elegant house she was now standing in . . . which nonetheless served precisely the same purpose.

Selena thought over the violent, ferocious events of her short life and the violent ferocious men she'd lived with. She thought of Flint. She thought of Silver . . . especially him, who she'd never see again in this life. She was sure of that now. He could never come to England. He was better as a pirate on the edges of the world, beyond law, beyond right, beyond civilisation. He could never change and she could never be with him . . . whatever she thought of him in her heart.

She sighed again. She was beyond all that. That life was gone, so the pistols could stay on the table, or in a box, or buried in the garden, or *anywhere!* She wouldn't need them again: ever.

And then, just as had occurred two and a half years ago when she'd been sent to the Master's *special house* where he ravished his slave girls, Selena found herself tired at the end of a long day and laid down on the bed to doze . . . and fell asleep. And just as had occurred two and a half years ago, she was awoken by a man, but this time not a drunken lout bent on rape but a gentle gentleman, who stroked her hand, and kissed her cheek and who looked down upon her with such an expression of limitless adoration as made his ugly face look homely and benign.

"Hallo, my little sweetheart," he said.

"Matthew," she said, and smiled.

"Selena," he said, and shook his head in utmost sincerity, "Devil take me to Hell if ever I make you unhappy. I may not be young, but –"

233

"No!" she said, and laid a hand on his lips. "You've said all that!" And she sat up and took his hand and led him to a sofa, and helped him off with his coat and boots and waistcoat, and sat him down and served him a glass of wine, which he drained, and he gazed and gazed at her in the inexpressible thrill of being alone with her and having her as his own, while Selena, for the first time in years, was at peace. Sir Matthew's offer would raise her high – soaring high – above anything she'd ever dreamed of. She would keep a salon; she would live in luxury; she would ride in a carriage . . . and she would be safe.

So she smiled at Matty Blackstone, and stood in front of him, and untied the neck of her gown and let the silk slide over her shoulders and fall hissing to the floor. He gasped and his eyes shone and he shook his head.

"God in Heaven," he said – he that loved beauty – for he was looking at luscious, sensual, glorious beauty: beauty such as sculptors forever attempt; as Blackstone well knew, being a patron of the renowned Gianlorenzo Bernini. But nothing achieved by that genius – nor even Michelangelo before him – could compare with Selena! For how can cold stone compare with satin skin, and the hot blood that races beneath it? Especially when the satin skin offers itself two feet in front of a man's nose, as he sits on a sofa at the end of a hard week's work, with a large glass of wine warming the inside of him!

"Ah!" said Blackstone, and he reached out and put his thick hands gently on her hips, and she smiled and raised her arms gracefully over her head – for she had the skills of a performer now, and sought to please this kind and loving man. Matty sighed and rubbed his face into the smooth belly and the gorgeous breasts, and slid his hands around her, and took hold and stood up, easily lifting her in his arms, and she laughed and caressed him, and kissed the top of his head, and the two together looked towards the bed: he with joy and she with full contentment . . .

. . . and a knocking sounded at the front door: *bang-bang-bang!*

"What the devil?" said Sir Matthew and frowned. He put Selena down, and growled in anger as scuffling and cries came from below, then rumbling feet charging up the stairs. He seized a heavy iron poker from the fireplace, pushed Selena towards the dressing room, and stood between her and danger. "Get in there, lass!" he cried. "Lock the door and . . ."

But the bedroom door burst open and two men charged in: Joe Flint and Billy Bones. Selena screamed. Sir Matthew swung at Flint's head with the poker, and was struck down by a cudgel-stroke he never even saw.

"Selena!" cried Flint. "Come! Quickly!" He was wide-eyed and staring, gaping at her nakedness while Billy Bones was dashing forward to seize her, but she was quicker and was into the dressing room for her pistols, and turning and cocking and aiming and firing . . . and Billy Bones flinching as the ball went through his hat, and herself aiming the second shot at Flint, and something flickering in the light, and an agonising pain exploding as Flint – facing death – instinctively hurled his cudgel end-over-end like a throwing knife to crack into Selena's brow, knocking her unconscious to the Turkish-carpeted floor.

"Oh no!" said Flint, cursing himself even as the blow struck.

"Bugger!" said John Silver, hopping and scrambling to catch up, and with Israel Hands behind him. "What have you done?"

"She had a pistol!" cried Flint.

"Aye!" said Billy Bones, and three men knelt by the small, fallen body, while Silver loomed over them on his crutch.

"It's all right!" said Israel Hands. "She's stunned, that's all!"

"Thank God!" they cried.

"Damn!" said Flint. "What could I do?"

"Dunno, Joe," said Silver, and reached out and pulled Flint to his feet.

"Billy," said Flint, "pick her up! Bring her!"

Billy Bones swept Selena up in his arms, Flint threw her dressing gown over her, and Silver stroked her face, groaning at the blood in her hair.

"What about him?" said Israel Hands, looking at Sir Matthew, who was stirring.

"Kill him!" said Flint, and pulled a knife from his sleeve.

"No!" said Silver. "He owns half Berkshire! It'd raise old Nick if we slit him!"

"So?" said Flint. "They can only . . ." He was going to say *hang us once,* but he couldn't. He couldn't get the words out. They revolted him to the very core of his self. He shuddered heavily, and felt his neck, and looked to Silver for guidance, but Silver was frowning and looking round the beautiful room.

"Wait a bit," said Silver. "Why's this been so easy? Where's the bully boys?"

"Aye!" said Israel Hands. "This is supposed to be a knocking shop."

"And no man's fought back, than him!" said Silver, pointing to Sir Matthew.

"It don't *look* like no knocking shop," said Israel Hands.

The four men fell silent. They could hear Sir Matthew's heavy gasping and the muttering of their fellows guarding the servants downstairs.

"Hark to that!" said Silver. "There's no bugger here but them –" He looked at Sir Matthew and Selena. "Them an' some maids and a cook." He shook his head. "This ain't right, shipmates!"

"Flash Jack said she was dragged here," said Israel Hands.

"Dammit," said Flint. "Are we nincompoops?"

"Best be gone, Cap'n," said Billy Bones, "whatever we be!"

So it was downstairs, and the servants locked in the cellar and the door closed nice and quiet, and Selena carried gently into a closed carriage with Flint and Silver inside, and Billy Bones and Israel Hands on the box, and the rest of Silver's men quietly making off on foot. A few faces appeared at windows, and curtains twitched in the houses alongside, but nothing else. They'd made little noise. That part – at least – of their plan had worked.

Within the hour, all hands were aboard *Walrus* and "Captain" Warrington was pacing his quarterdeck while "his" crew got up the anchors and made sail. Some of the remaining store of McLonarch's coin eased the suspicion of the Trinity House pilot, and that of other shore authorities, that *Walrus* was setting sail so abruptly. It was given out that she was bound for Newcastle to take on a load of coals for London, which would bring a good price with winter coming on. So, with a strong westerly, and the tide in their favour, *Walrus* cleared the pool of London and was off Canvey Island at the mouth of the Thames within twelve hours.

Meanwhile, Selena was made comfortable in a hammock slung in the great cabin, and Dr Cowdray bound up her head and said that her life was in the balance, and she must have utter quiet. Even Flint and Silver kept away from her after that, and it wasn't for many hours that Cowdray brought them in to see her, semi-conscious and murmuring to herself.

They stood looking at her and each other, awaiting Cowdray's words, in the gently rolling, lamp-lit cabin.

"She'll live," he said. "No bones are broken, and the scarring will be hidden by her hair . . . but what in God's name did you think you were at?" he demanded. "Both of you!"

"You heard Flash Jack," said Silver guiltily.

"He said she was sold by Katty Cooper," said Flint.

"Aye!" said Silver. "And you know *her*, Doctor!"

"And *you* said this was how she worked!" said Flint.

Now Cowdray blushed.

"Well," he said, looking at Selena, "that's how whores are made. A procuress like Miss Cooper sells the first use of them, which is taken by deceit or by force, and then – being debauched – the poor creature is held to the life by shame."

"And that's what Flash Jack said Katty Cooper was a-doing!" said Silver. "With that bugger of a brewer paying for it!"

"No," said Flint. He paused and looked at Selena, and forced himself to speak a truth that he didn't want to believe. "I think she was there by choice. Of her own free will."

Silver groaned and Flint unthinkingly put his hand on Silver's shoulder in sympathy. Cowdray gaped in wonderment, but the two men stood united by the very flaw that was Flash Jack's own. They'd believed him *because they'd wanted to*, not because it made sense. Each had wanted to come to the rescue. Each wanted Selena more than life, or reason, or sense.

"A-hem!" said Warrington, standing hat in hand in the cabin doorway. "Gentlemen, we've dropped the pilot and the ship's ours. So I was wondering what course to set? And begging-your-pardons, but it's coming on to blow."

Which it was. But the tempest was nothing compared with Selena's fury when she awoke.

238

Chapter 28

Three bells of the forenoon watch
3rd January 1754
Aboard Walrus
The Atlantic

"'**W**are the bugger!" cried a voice, lost in the violence of the storm, and a pair of strong arms hauled John Silver clear of certain death as his crutch slipped on the seething, heaving deck that was knee-deep in foaming water.

"Ah!" cried Long John as Billy Bones pulled him from the onrushing path of a loose gun: eight feet of barrel on a squat, rumbling carriage that trailed tackles, still fast-bound to the clunking, futile bolts that should have secured it to the ship's side: two tons of slick-wet, murderous oak and iron that groaned and scraped and slid from beam to beam as the ship heaved.

It was freezing winter. The blocks were jammed with ice. The sails were sheet iron. No man could feel fingers or toes, and it was devil's work to go aloft. An hour ago the gale had split the topsails, and without the steadying pressure of lofty sails, *Walrus* rolled horribly, causing one of the biggest guns – hanging by its tackles – to draw its bolts where hidden rot had spoiled their grip of the ship's timbers.

CRRRUNCH! The gun ground into the lee bulwark.

Already there was one man with a smashed leg, and the gun – having tasted blood – was clearly out for more. All hands were on deck with rolled hammocks, trying to get them under the gun's trucks to catch it and stop it. And all the while the gale was howling, the ship plunging, and themselves wrapped in hampering winter gear: fur hats, mittens and greatcoats with tarred waterproofs on top.

Flint was leading the hunt for the maddened gun. The crew looked to him for leadership in the matter, for *he* had two legs.

"Get below, Cap'n!" cried Billy Bones to Long John. "Ain't no place for a man what's lost a pin!" He wasn't mocking. He was concerned.

Silver marvelled at the change in Billy Bones, even as another thunderclap roared and lightning flashed, and hailstones came down like grapeshot that battered and bounced and made the decks yet more dangerous than already they were. Wedging his crutch under his arm, Silver clung on to a lifeline and looked at Billy Bones: alive and alert in this deadly danger, and roused from the solemn sadness that had been his when first he came aboard behind his master.

Meanwhile *Walrus* plunged her sharp prow deep into a wave, driven by the colossal pressure on her remaining sails, and green water rolled from bow to stern, just as Flint hurled himself in the path of the gun and got a sodden mass of hammock under the fat oaken wheels, and stopped the gun . . . only for the wave to sluice and lift and heave . . . and free the gun once more, and Flint staggered back, clear, by inches, as the gun charged forward like a bull.

He fell into the arms of Israel Hands and Mr Joe, who were hanging to lifelines, and he laughed and caught Silver's eye, for if Billy Bones was changed, Flint was changed marvellously. He laughed in the icy wet. It was fresh and clean. It was ruthless and simple. And there was a man's job to be done.

Flint leapt again, snatching a hammock from Israel Hands. Any other man would have gone to his death under the grinding wheels of the gun as the ship's motion set it off again. But not Flint. He was too quick. He caught it just as it boomed against the mainmast, smashing the stand of pikes that surrounded it, and he jammed the hammock under its wheels, and all hands fell on with lines to lash and secure the gun to the mast, and Flint stood back, gasping and panting . . . and happy.

"John! John!" he cried, clapping Silver on the shoulder, beaming a radiant smile.

And Silver cherished the warm belief that this was indeed a new dawn of old times. As for Billy Bones, he grinned from ear to ear, and was profoundly happy even on a bounding deck, soaking wet, and frozen to the marrow.

"Well done, Joe!" said Silver, with a full heart: not that any of this speech was heard, not with the heavens in fury and the wind roaring at the wild sea.

"Huh!" said Flint, in the comradeship of the moment, and saw so much that was good around him, and so little that was bad . . . Just two problems, of which the lesser was ignorance on their present position; Flint didn't know where he was within a hundred miles.

Later, in the master's cabin, Flint explained this to the ship's navigating officers: Warrington, Billy Bones and Mr Joe. Likewise Silver, who was no navigator nor ever would be but was captain . . . at least for the moment. The five men stood close together in the small cabin, peering down at a chart, under the light of swinging lanterns. The ship groaned and creaked around them, and the elements beat in anger on the planks above their heads, but at least they could hear one another's voices.

"So where are we, Joe?" said Silver. Flint frowned.

"Our course should have been south to the latitude of the Canaries or Cape Verde Islands, then westward to seek the trade winds to carry us across the Atlantic."

"Aye!" they said. They all knew that, even Silver. It was every mariner's route to the Americas.

"But . . ." said Flint ". . . first we were blown northwest for days, and now southeast – which is no bad thing in itself – but we're running before the wind, going two hundred miles a day or more – and even that's a guess, for the last time we hove the log, we lost it!"

They nodded. There'd been no measurement of the ship's speed for days, nor sight of the sun or stars.

"So," said Flint, pointing down at the chart, "we could be off Portugal, or Spain, or even North Africa!"

"But what's your guess, Joe?" said Silver, and reached up to pet the big green parrot that sat on his shoulder again, now that he was out of the storm. Flint looked at the bird that had once been his, such that he could stroke her without fear of losing fingers to the savage beak. But not any more. They'd parted badly. Which reminded him of the second problem: the greater one, the problem that bore equally on Flint and on Silver.

"I'm done with you both!" she'd said once she was awake: not angry or shouting, for she was more disgusted than anything else; disgusted that she'd been snatched away like a piece of property . . . *like a slave*. It hurt all the more for her steady, measured voice: "Matthew Blackstone was a kind man," she'd said. "Better than either of you, and I was making my own way, by my own choice! I was paid a fortune in Drury Lane to make people *happy!* What do I want with you bloody-handed *animals!*" The last word hurled with shrivelling contempt, right in their faces: an ugly thing for men to hear from the woman they've been dreaming about for month upon lonely month, she being the one above all others who stabs the heart with longing . . .

And when they'd explained there was no turning back – not with hangings awaiting in England, and the wind driving them on – then she really did lose her temper and every man aboard heard what she said.

It had been bad, very bad, for both men. And yet it united them.

"Joe?" said Silver. "Where are we?"

Flint said nothing, but Warrington and Billy Bones scratched their heads and screwed up their faces in concentration.

"I think we're in the latitude of the Canaries," said Warrington.

"Maybe nearer the Cape Verde Islands," said Billy Bones.

"I think the Cape Verde Islands," said Flint, and the matter was settled.

"So what do we do?" said Silver.

"Lie to!" said Flint. "It doesn't matter what's to loo'ard: whether it be Portugal, Spain or Africa. If we hold this course, we'll be driven ashore and drowned upon it just the same! So . . . we'll come about, as close to the wind as she'll bear, so she's making little or no headway, and so ride out the storm."

"Begging your pardon, Mr Flint," said Warrington, "not *too* close to the wind. I was in a ship once that made sternway laying to, and so lost her rudder!"

Flint smiled and smiled. He smiled right into Warrington's face at this statement of the blindingly obvious.

"Oh!" said Warrington, and gulped. "Not that you'd do that, Mr Flint. Not you."

"Not I," said Flint and they all laughed.

So *Walrus* came about, and met the wind fine on her bow, yards braced back as far as they'd go, and heeled over mightily, which eased her motion and stopped the hideous rolling, and enabled the topmen to strike the ruins of the topsails and bend fresh sails to the yards. It even allowed the cook to light his fire again for hot food – a great comfort to the topmen when they came off watch.

Moreover it allowed John Silver to call the council of all hands that he'd been wanting ever since the ship left England, and hadn't had the chance to do. So once *Walrus* was steady into the wind, and all made secure as could be, he brought the men together on the lower deck, leaving only the helmsmen and lookouts on deck, under Mr Joe as officer of the watch, and all those not present having appointed trusted messmates to vote for them.

Except that Mr Joe didn't stay on deck. Once he was sure that the ship was safe – for the while – he went below by the aftermost hatchway.

"Shipmates, brothers and gentleman o' fortune," said Silver, as nearly standing as a man of his height could do under the low deckhead. The men looked back at him, crammed tight together and taking it all in: the black flag draped over a barrelhead in front of Silver, and the Book of Articles placed upon it, with pen and ink standing by. The ship's officers sat on stools and chairs on either side of Silver, and the green bird perched on his shoulder.

"We're a mixed company aboard this ship," said Silver, looking round.

"Aye!" they said.

"There's some what's sailed with me."

"Aye!"

"There's some what's sailed with Joe Flint."

"Aye!"

"Some what came aboard in Upper Barbados, and some in London."

"Aye!"

"There's those among us who've fought one another as enemies!"

"Aye!

"And even some as received sentence of death from their brothers."

Few but Billy Bones knew what this meant, and he groaned at the thought of it.

It was the old Silver. All truth. Nothing hidden. He wasn't

the man he'd once been. Not any more, for he was changed. But there was much good left, including his instinctive oratory. It was measured, it was poetic, it was religious. Silver was binding them together, because they weren't the old band of *Walrus*es: not any more. Men had come and gone. There were twenty aboard that joined in London alone, having heard tales of buried treasure. They were all prime seamen. They were already a crew. But they weren't *brothers*. Not yet. That was a thing of the spirit.

Mr Joe crept down a companionway towards the stern cabin. The rumble and growl of voices from the council, sounding behind him, even over the creaking grumble of the ship's timbers working in the storm. It was hard to keep his footing. The deck was heavily sloped.

He reached the door. He rapped with his knuckles.

"Who is it?" she said.

"Me, ma'am . . . Mr Joe . . ." A brief pause, then the door opened, and Mr Joe gulped at the sight of her, for she was very lovely. Lovely but frowning.

"What do you want?"

"I want to ask you something."

She looked at him and saw that he meant no harm.

"Come in . . ." she said.

Silver reached the climax. He raised the book and read the articles aloud. The good old articles, re-drafted on fresh pages, with clean white paper beneath for signatures. He put down the book.

"So who will become a brother?" he said. "Who will be first to step forward and make his mark?" There was the briefest of silences, then Flint rose.

"I will!" he said and signed.

"I will!" said Israel Hands. "And I sign for Mr Joe besides!"

"And me!" said Billy Bones.

And so they signed, mostly with crosses or such little emblems – fish, daggers, serpents – as they chose, with Silver adding the man's name in these cases. Even Blind Pew signed, with Silver guiding the pen.

"So," said Silver when the signing was done, and all hands stood transformed by the mystic drama of the occasion, "we are brothers and jolly companions, and must now elect a captain. And for this matter, I stands aside, being compromised!" They laughed at that, and nudged and winked. "So I turns to Brother Hands," said Silver, "to make the proposals."

Israel Hands stood up. He stood forward and faced the men.

"Let it be Long John!" he said. "There ain't no bigger nor better man among us. Long John, say I! Long John for ever!"

Mr Joe sat down on the big bench under the stern windows. She'd lashed the chairs to the table – which was screwed to the deck – to stop them sliding in the crazily canted cabin. He looked around the cabin, then out the window at the evil grey sea heaving and wallowing just feet away. There was little light and much noise, for the sky was dark except when it was split with lightning.

"What do you want?" she said.

"I been reading, ma'am," he said.

"So?" She shrugged. "Why should that concern me?"

"You were a slave like me. You're black."

"And . . .?" said Selena, not pleased to be reminded of her origins, for she'd come a long way from the plantation. She'd played to thousands on the stage, and been courted by the richest man in England. Mr Joe guessed some of this, and tried again.

"Mr Hands, he's a good man. He taught me to read."

"Yes. I know."

"Did you know he got me a bible in London?"

"No."

"Well . . . I read about Adam and Eve."

"Yes?"

"They were the first, weren't they?"

Selena frowned. She was losing interest.

"What is your point?"

"Well, if they were the first, and we're all their children . . . we're all the same!"

"What do you mean?"

"Us blacks and the white folks. *We're all the same!*"

Flint saw Billy Bones was looking at him, as was Tom Allardyce, with his bandaged head, and some others who'd once followed Flint. But Flint looked at Long John and saw the old qualities of leadership that Silver had in such degree and he did not . . .

"I vote for Captain Silver!" he said in a firm voice, and all hands roared their approval.

Silver smiled, and the parrot squawked and flapped her wings.

"Cap'n Silver! Cap'n Silver! Cap'n Silver!" she cried.

"Well, Joe," said Silver, "I hope you'll be my quarter-master?"

"That I will," said Flint, and the rum was brought out.

"Here's to ourselves and hold your luff . . ." cried Silver.

"Plenty of prizes and plenty of duff!" cried all those who knew his favourite toast.

So Flint and Silver raised their mugs and toasted each other, and Billy Bones wept with joy.

"I got to go," said Mr Joe. He and Selena had been talking too long, and too intensely . . . about great things.

"What do you want?" said Selena. "In life?"

"Don't know," said Mr Joe. "I'd like to be first mate . . ."

"And a pirate?"

247

"Don't know. But I'll not be a slave again!"

"No."

"And what do *you* want?" he said, and Selena frowned.

"I want what I can't have."

"That Mr Blackstone and the big house?"

"Yes . . . no . . . I don't know. But if I could go there now . . . I would!"

"But you can't."

"No. Perhaps there will be another ship. I don't know."

"What about them two?" He looked astern. "Cap'n Silver and Mr Flint? They know where the treasure is. They'll be rich men when we lift it! They want you real bad. And Cap'n Silver . . . you're his wife. Don't you want *him*?"

She said nothing. Not *yes*, nor *no*, nor even *I don't know*.

"I got to go," he said. He went out.

Selena watched him go . . . and wondered.

Chapter 29

Seven bells of the morning watch
5th March 1754
Aboard Walrus
The Atlantic

The storm blew for seventy days of constant noise, constant wet, crushing misery and grinding labour. The ship was tired, the crew were tired and all aboard were driven to the limit of endurance, so it was no surprise when seventy-one days out of London, in the vast and empty ocean, a dreadful enemy crept aboard.

"It's scurvy, Captain!" said Cowdray, braced on the quarterdeck in his storm clothes. "There's two men in their hammocks with their gums swollen, and loose teeth, and bruises all over their bodies."

"Oh no!" said Silver, wiping the salt spray from his face. The storm raged unabated, the ship plunged under bare poles, and Flint and Billy Bones stood with Silver by the helmsmen. "But what can we expect?" he said. "We've been that long at sea!"

"Are you sure it's scurvy?" said Flint. "Not just idle lubbers that need the toe of Mr Bones's boot to help them turn out?" Billy Bones nodded.

"No," said Cowdray, "one has an old wound that's

breaking open afresh." He looked at Flint. "Believe me," he said, "I know scurvy when I see it!"

"Damnation!" said Flint. "I was with Anson on his circumnavigation. We lost half our people to scurvy!"

Silver sighed. "The men are weak enough already," he said. "If they gets the scurvy, we'll not be able to work the ship!"

"Aye," said Billy Bones, "them what it don't kill, gets drownded 'cos they can't stand to their duties . . . and the ship founders under 'em!"

"What can we do?" said Silver. "What can you give 'em, Doctor?"

"There is something . . ." said Cowdray. "But they'll not take it."

"Why not?" said Silver. "What is it?"

"Lemons," said Cowdray. "But the juice is sour and hurts their gums."

"Lemons?" said Silver. "What use is them?"

"I read a book, new published, when we were in London," said Cowdray, "by a Scots physician called Lind. He has cured men with lemon juice. Men with the scurvy."

"Bah!" said Silver. "Not that old tale! That's been tried before."

"Wait!" said Flint. "I was never affected when I was with Anson."

"No?" they said.

"No. I had my own supply of preventives against the scurvy: malt, sauerkraut, oil of vitriol . . . and lemons. I had a barrel of lemons."

"There!" said Cowdray. "It was the lemons that saved you. Dr Lind has proved it! And I have some barrels of lemons that I brought aboard . . . but the men won't take the juice."

"Huh!" said Silver. "Put it in their grog with a drop o' sugar. Then they'll take it!"

Two weeks later, and miraculously to the seamen, there was no scurvy in the ship, and the crew proclaimed united blessings upon Cap'n Silver . . . with unfortunate consequences . . .

"Why should *he* get the credit?" said Flint, privately, to Billy Bones. "It was Cowdray brought the lemons aboard."

Billy Bones felt his guts twist. He did so very much want to believe that his master was re-born but this could be the first turning from the light.

"Never mind that, *Cap'n*," he said, which honorific he applied to Flint, whatever his rating aboard ship. "It's yourself that all hands looks to, to bring us safe to port. There ain't none to match you at that!"

"Yes," said Flint, allowing himself to be flattered, while Billy Bones sighed with relief, and hoped he'd made all things right.

And it seemed that he had, when, a few days later, the storm eased and the ship's navigators took their first noon observation for weeks, and made their calculations, and met in the master's cabin.

"Youngest first, Mr Flint last," said Silver.

"Aye!" they said, for that way none would be tempted to copy Flint.

"Here," said Mr Joe, pencilling a cross on the chart.

"Here," said Billy Bones.

"Here," said Warrington.

"Huh!" said Silver. "What a precious art it is, this quadrant-walloping!"

For the crosses were vastly far apart. But even Silver knew this was nothing unusual after so long a period with only dead reckoning for guidance. Now everyone looked to Flint, who shook his head in surprise.

"Well done, Mr Joe," he said, and placed a cross almost exactly beside that of the nineteen-year-old, once an illiterate slave, and now – through talent and hard work – the best navigator in the ship . . . apart from himself of course! Flint smiled, "Like you, Mr Joe, I think we are almost exactly in thirty-seven degrees of latitude, and some hundreds of miles to the east of America, off the mouth of Chesapeake Bay and the Colony of Virginia." He opened a pair of dividers, set them to scale, and stepped them across several charts, to measure distance. "We should count ourselves lucky to be alive," he said. "But we are so far off course, and the ship and her people so enfeebled, that we must put into port soon, and I would suggest Alexandria, on the Potomac River. There are other possibilities, but it is a major port. More important, it is a place where we shall not be known."

"Aye!" they said, and the word went round the ship, and all aboard rejoiced at the coming end to their perils, with a run ashore, and fresh food and warm bread. The whole ship was merry and the weather stayed calm . . . with further unfortunate consequences.

Selena was deadly, utterly bored with being cooped up below by the storm. Moreover, she'd now put Flint and Silver in their place, and there was no creature aboard that did not know her view on being snatched away from London. That being done . . . it wasn't natural for a girl of her youth to sulk forever, especially a girl so ready to make best use of such opportunities as life presented. After all, it wasn't *that* much worse being an object of reverence aboard ship than being mistress to an ugly old man, however charming, and at least she didn't have to share his bed!

So: when the weather eased she dressed herself smart and went on deck, and all hands smiled to see her, and touched their brows, and she smiled in return, delighting in the fresh air, and talking to Dr Cowdray and Israel Hands. And as for Joe Flint and John Silver, she'd heard of their friendship, and the great change in Flint, and she saw their careful smiles at herself . . . and so . . . by stages . . . she began to smile back, as they tried to please her.

Thus Silver told silly stories . . .

"The Chinese, ma'am?" he said. "They eat everything from dog's pizzle to octopus-bollock soup, beggin' your pardon!"

And Flint courted her in French . . .

"*Bonjour, et comment vas tu, ma petite princesse?*"

And Billy Bones watched, and felt the first dreadful fear of the old rivalry, which, like the coast of America, was just under the horizon.

Two days later, *Walrus* came in sight of land and all aboard looked to see the black shoreline creep slowly upon them. The rain was drizzling under dull clouds, but the sea was kind, the wind fair for landfall, and the crew stood in their winter clothes, and smiled as best they could, and smelled the land: that indescribable scent that all seafarers know, after a long voyage.

Messmates stood together, Flint with Billy Bones, Long John with Israel Hands.

And Selena stood next to Silver, while Flint scowled, and Billy Bones looked on in agony.

As the hands pointed out the shore, and the masts of other ships hove up over the horizon, there was chattering and naming of prominent points, especially as *Walrus* came eastward into the mouth of the mighty Chesapeake bay.

Silver put his glass to north, and then to south, then offered it to Selena.

"Here, lass," he said, "take a look, for this is the beginnings of America! We're between the Virginia capes, which is Cape Charles to the north and Cape Henry to the south – named for the sons of King James a hundred and fifty year ago." He pointed to the distant shores. "The Capes is as far apart as England and France. And within . . . why, Chesapeake Bay is over two hundred and fifty miles long, and thirty miles wide at the widest!" He shook his head. "It's vast beyond belief, my girl, like all the Americas!"

Selena took the telescope, which was too big for her, and Silver drew it, and helped her take a sight through it, necessarily standing close, and brushing against her.

"That 'un there," he said, "that's Cape Henry, where the men of the Virginia Company landed in 1607, after a voyage of one hundred and forty-four days, aboard three ships, of which one was called *Godspeed*." He smiled. "Don't know the names o' the others. But there was a hundred souls aboard what founded Jamestown, the first English town of the Americas."

"A hundred and forty-four days," she said, looking at the green shore. "That's worse than ourselves, isn't it?"

"Aye. We been eighty-nine days at sea, by my reckoning," he said.

And she nodded, and handed back the glass, and smiled. Then she glanced at Flint, who bowed elaborately, sweeping off his hat and smiling.

"*Bonjour, madame*," he said.

"*Bonjour, monsieur*," she said, and laughed, and looked to Silver for the fun of playing them off, one against the other . . . a game that she knew was wildly dangerous, but it was exciting, and she was still punishing them.

Long John frowned and fretted and looked at his rival. He was a fine bugger, was Flint: fine face, fine figure, fine manners. He was everything that women liked. Even with two legs, Silver couldn't have matched him for looks. and never as a cripple!

So it wasn't only Flint who was turning from the light, but Silver too. In the storm, under urgent need for teamwork to save the ship, they'd stood together. Now, it was their tragedy that, left in peace with no overwhelming threat, they were pulled apart by rivalry for a woman: that ancient and corrosive acid, which was easily capable of dissolving their new friendship. For that had always had been shallow, depending as it did upon denial of acknowledged history.

Thus, day by day, the two men dug into their memories for the bad rather than the good, and once again they began to hate, until they were held together only by the two halves of the divided papers.

254

And all hands saw it, and muttered among themselves and worried: all except Billy Bones, who despaired.

Four days later, on 4th April, *Walrus* dropped anchor off Alexandria, on the western bank of the Potomac. It was new, raw and unfinished, with as many empty lots on its grid-pattern streets as there were finished houses. But it was a flourishing port, with tobacco going out and manufactured goods from England coming in, and many ships anchored, and wharves and warehouses besides. And of those houses that were completed, many were in brick and stone, built to best London standards, especially those of the major merchants, lined up along Fairfax Street, looking down upon the river.

Once again, and for discretion, Mr Warrington was made sober, made clean, and made captain . . . and charged with undertaking all dealings with shore authorities, while *Walrus* became *Sea Serpent*. There were days of busy traffic, of boats bringing fresh food, and other supplies, and storm damage made good, and the men allowed ashore, by watches, with their arms secured aboard ship, and under oath to behave.

Meanwhile, Selena was left wanting to go ashore yet afraid to do so. She spoke to Dr Cowdray.

"I'm wanted for murder in Charlestown," she said.

"That's another world," he said.

"But someone might know me."

"Selena," said Cowdray, "Charlestown is five hundred miles away. That's as far as England is from Spain! D'you think Flint would go ashore if he thought he'd be recognised? And he's wanted for murder *everywhere!*"

So Selena went ashore, where the first two taverns refused outright to receive her. They refused even though she was accompanied by two "servants" – Tom Allardyce, now fully fit, and Mr Joe – who carried her baggage and called her ma'am. The trouble was, that while entirely respectable, she was plainly of the negro race and therefore unacceptable as a guest within the house.

"I told you, ma'am," said Allardyce, "I said they wouldn't have you."

"Bah!" said Selena and stamped her foot. "What do they think I am: *a field nigger?*" Then, "Oh . . ." she said, looking at Mr Joe, "I mean . . . I mean . . . in London and Charlestown I was welcomed everywhere."

"That was *there*, ma'am," said Allardyce. "This is *here*."

In the end, it took the persuasion of Flint and Silver together, and a fat purse, to get Selena into Duvall's tavern – one of the best in the town, with private rooms for hire upstairs. But she had to take her meals in her room and come and go by the back stairs, which humiliation she accepted because *anything* was better than another day aboard ship! Even so simple a pleasure as a clean, dry bed, was close to Heaven, as was the ability to be alone to consider her future.

Meanwhile, being in Duvall's tavern, Flint and Silver found a seat by the fire, in a quiet room, with a few tables and some gentlemen smoking pipes. They sat down and stared, unsmiling at each other. They said nothing, for any conversation led to argument. So they had a silent dinner, and were steadfastly ignoring each other over a glass of rum punch when a loud argument broke out in the room next door.

"No! No! No!" cried a loud voice. "Be damned if I will!" And a chair crashed over, a door boomed like a cannon, heavy footsteps sounded, and a red-faced Virginian gentleman stamped into the room and sat himself down at the table next to Flint and Silver.

"Bah!" he said, and beat the table with his fist. "Bah!"

He was a very big man, well over six feet tall, with red hair and grey-blue eyes. His face was massive, he had huge hands and feet, and though he was quite young – only in his early twenties – he was a dominant, aggressive creature, full of confidence, used to having his own way, and capable of great rages when he didn't get it.

"Bah!" he said again, and glared round the room. But for once there were others present who were as dominant as he, and equally unused to giving way.

"Trouble, matey?" said Silver, staring steadily back.

"I do hope," said Flint, "that I, personally, have given no offence?"

"What?" said the big man, for he'd been paying attention to nobody but himself.

"Oh!" he said. "Your pardon, sirs." He frowned and sought to explain: "There is a *fellow* in that room –" he stabbed a huge finger "– who holds the king's commission, and tells me that the French and Indians must be met in the forest by platoon firing, with drums rolling and troops dressed in line!" He slammed the table with the flat of his hand. "Huh!" he cried. "D'you see the nonsensical ignorance of it?"

"Ahhh," said Flint and Silver, for they'd seen forest warfare. They'd seen how the slippery Indian outclassed the plodding musketeer. So they nodded, and made a friend.

"My dear sirs," he said, "I have exceeded the bounds of politeness. Would you do me the honour to share a bottle of wine, in apology for my behaviour?"

"With pleasure, sir," said Flint.

"Come aboard, shipmate," said Silver, indicating a chair at their table.

Which they soon regretted because he delivered a monologue on the war that was coming against France and Spain: an unremarkable prospect to Flint and Silver, who'd grown up among such wars, but the angry gentleman was fearfully anxious for the thirteen English American colonies:

"Consider," he said, "French Canada lies to our north – a despotic, military state – while the vast Spanish empire lies to our south!" He went on at length, especially about forest warfare and the Indian allies of the French. It was all very

257

tedious, but then Flint picked up a certain drift in his conversation.

"Tell me, sir," said Flint, "do these Indians use the musket or the bow? I mean the *bow as* in 'bow and arrow'." He repeated two of these words, slurring them together as if they were one: "*bow-as* . . ."

The big man said nothing, but his lips shaped the word: *Boaz* . . .

"I think you have *square*-ly hit the mark, sir," he said.

"I shake your hand on it, sir," said Flint, and held out his hand.

Silver frowned. Something was going on. Something secret. He watched as Flint and the other made a pantomime of holding their grip, and smiling little smiles. Then Silver saw the big man look at him, then raise his eyebrows at Flint, and Flint shake his head.

No, he was saying. Whatever it was the silly sods thought they were, he – John Silver – wasn't one! Secret bloody signs! Silver was fuming. It was just one more piece of shit from Flint!

"So," said the big man, "I welcome you to Alexandria, for I should *inevitably* have met you before, had you not been newly arrived."

Flint gave another little smile.

"I am Joseph Garland of the schooner *Sea Serpent*," said Flint, "And this is my friend, Mr . . . ah . . . Bristol. We are merchants and seafarers."

"Mr Bristol!" said the big man, shaking Silver's hand.

"And who are you, then?" said Silver, rudely.

"I am Washington. Colonel George Washington of the Virginia Regiment."

Chapter 30

Afternoon, 6th April 1754
Alexandria
Virginia

"So what the buggeration is sodding masonry?" said Silver, as he and Flint walked along the wharf to where their boat was moored.

"It's a piece of nonsense that some take seriously," Flint sneered. "The pope takes it so seriously as to forbid it."

"And what might that mean?" said Silver. "And what was you a-doin' of, with that Washington, with funny words and handshakes?"

"I'll show you," said Flint, and looked around. "Come over here –" He found a quiet spot among some bales and casks. The two men stopped and looked at one another.

"Huh!" said Silver, for they didn't do a lot of gazing into one another's eyes: not them, not John Silver and Joe Flint!

"Pah!" said Flint, as he looked up at Silver's big, plain face. "Give me your hand," he said, "Go on!"

Silver clasped his hand, and felt Flint's thumb pressing the first knuckle-joint of his first finger.

"That's *Boaz*," said Flint. "The grip of the *Entered Apprentice*."

"Hoss shite!" said Silver.

"Wait!" said Flint, and pressed his thumb into the space between Silver's first and second knuckles. "And that's *Shibboleth*, which is . . ."

"Which is bollocks!" said Silver, and pulled his hand away, and Flint's face darkened and the two fell to shouting at one another, and drew back, gasping and panting . . . well knowing why they must stick together.

"So what *is* it?" said Silver, fighting to be civil.

"It's a secret society," said Flint, "with exalted moral aims. And they recognise one another by special words and signs."

"And what do you know about it? Are you one of 'em?"

"Not I! But you know I was with Anson on his circum-navigation?"

"Aye. For you never cease to boast of it!"

"Huh! Well, I was master and commander aboard of *Spider*."

"So?"

Flint smiled. It was a nasty smile, and Silver's spine prickled, for he was looking at the old, mad Flint returned – plain as day – in all his wicked spitefulness.

"My first lieutenant was a man called Sam Higgins," said Flint. "He was a mason, like Anson and all his blasted clique, but he was the only one aboard *Spider* . . ." Flint's eyes half-closed as he remembered those times. He shook his head. "Poor Sammy! He never was fit for the sea life . . . So we played with him a little."

"Did you now!"

"Yes. Myself and the other officers. He was *different*, you see . . . delicate."

"Huh!"

"I suppose we made his life something of a misery."

"By thunder, I'll bet you did an' all!"

Flint laughed.

"Yes. We pressed him in various ways, for the secrets of . . . *The Craft*."

"Masonry?"

"Yes. And we got it all out of him in the end. All the rituals. All the secrets."

"But what *is* it? A religion?"

Flint frowned. He puzzled.

"I don't know. I could never make up my mind."

"So what do they do? Where did they come from?"

"Well," said Flint, "they meet in lodges. They hold ceremonies . . ." He shrugged. "The thing is about forty, years old, and started in London."

"And has it come out to the colonies?"

"Oh yes! Look at Colonel Washington."

"Ah!" said Silver. "He's cock o' the walk, that one, and no mistake!"

"He is indeed," said Flint. "It falls out of his conversation at every word. He is a senior officer of the Virginia Regiment, and is intimately connected in colonial society . . . and . . . therefore, through my knowledge of free-masonry I think that I . . . *we*," said Flint, seeing the look on Silver's face, "*we* . . . may become equally well connected."

"Meaning what?"

"I don't know," said Flint. "But we're here for a while, to rest and re-fit . . ."

"Aye," said Silver, "the crew's buggered. We're here for weeks."

"So . . . let's see what fortune brings. Fortune and Mr Washington."

"Aye," said Silver, and they set off again towards their boat. But just as they were settling in the stern, a thought came to Silver. "What happened to your Mr Higgins? Did he come safe home with Anson, or did the scurvy get him?"

Flint shook his head.

"No. Not little Sammy." He tried to stifle a laugh.

"Well?" said Silver.

"One night . . . he put on all his masonic regalia . . . and jumped over the side."

"You mean you pushed him," said Silver.

"No," said Flint, "there wasn't the least need for that."

In the next few days they met Colonel Washington again, several times. Him and others who were important men in the colony: planters, councillors, soldiers and others, of whom a surprising number were, like Washington, *in the Craft*. Silver soon left Flint to talk to these initiates, disgusted by the nods and winks and little signs that they kept flashing at one another, just as if it weren't clear for any man to see: any man who wasn't Blind Pew!

But even Silver saw that business ashore was thereby eased, and prices fell, and smiles were given and hats raised when Mr Garland and Mr Bristol walked through the town. In return, Colonel Washington and a few friends, some of the leading men of Alexandria, were welcomed aboard *Walrus* – which is to say *Sea Serpent* – and the ship and her people turned out for inspection, and the side piped and three cheers were given by all hands, as best they could in their current spent condition.

"Splendid!" said Washington, as he was introduced to the ship's officers. "If it weren't for an anxious mother," he said, "I'd have been a seaman myself and in His Majesty's navy!"

"Oh?" they said politely, as if the Royal Navy were their model and ideal.

"Indeed! For my brother had secured me a berth as a midshipman with a ship a-waiting to receive me." He smiled. "But my poor mother shed tears, and I was but a lad, and so I remain a landman still!"

Later, in the stern cabin, over a few glasses, Washington and his friends comprehensively bored Flint and Silver with an account of the colony's plans to expand inland, via the

Ohio valley and the great rivers that flowed in the vast interior.

"But war is coming!" said Washington. "And the French!"

"Aye," said his friends miserably.

"What about the French?" said Silver.

Washington shook his head in sorrow.

"They will use the great rivers to come down from Canada to encircle us."

"So chase them off!" said Silver.

Washington sighed and shook his head. "They are masters of forest warfare."

"Indeed they are," said his friends. "Which we are not!"

"And the rivers of the Ohio are their highways!" said Washington.

"Then the solution is plain," said Flint, smiling.

"Is it?" they said.

"Build a fleet," said Flint. "A fleet of the Ohio, to drive out the French!"

Everyone laughed at the joke, and soon after Washington left with his followers, which was all very jolly. But a few days later, he was back ... this time in his full uniform as Colonel of the Virginia Militia: red coat, gorget, scarlet sash and cocked hat.

He came at first light, in a boat pulled by men of his regiment. He wasn't smiling, and *Walrus*'s crew could see that he hadn't come to take wine in the stern cabin, for they looked ashore and saw a company of redcoats – who must have arrived in the night – standing by the quayside with their flag and drums, and a battery of field guns trained on *Walrus*.

An angry murmur ran through the ship, and all hands were mustered beside their officers as Washington came over the side.

"What's this, Colonel?" said Flint, and the big man stood alone, stood straight, and looked around at the surly mass of seamen without the least hint of fear.

"Perhaps we should talk privately?" said Washington.

"Bugger that!" said Silver. "We're one crew aboard this ship!"

"Aye!" cried *Walrus*'s people.

"Shall we run out the guns, Long John?" said Israel Hands.

"Any such move will draw instant fire from the shore!" said Washington.

There was a roar of anger and a rushing forward, and Washington was shoved against the rail, with only Silver, Flint, Israel Hands and Mr Joe standing between him and the crew's rage.

"Heave him over the side!"

"Hang him by the balls!"

"Kick his bastard head in!"

"Avast!" cried Silver, turning on them. "None o' that, for we ain't in no state, not to fight nor to run!"

Which was true, for *Walrus* was still unfit for sea. Some of her guns were dismounted, none were loaded, her yards were struck, and she was anchored in easy range of a battery with gunners ready and matches burning. Worse still, the hands weren't fit: not for a desperate fight against odds. So they grumbled and moaned, but fell back.

"Now then, Mr precious George Washington," said Silver, "what the buggery do you want aboard my ship?"

"Ah!" said Washington. "So it's *your* ship is it . . . *Captain Silver!*" The hands gasped. "And your companion is Joe Flint the mutineer!" said Washington. "A man whom England wishes to hang!"

"Colonel," said Flint, swiftly producing a pair of pistols, "please believe me that – should I be taken off this ship, *for that purpose* – then I faithfully, truly and most profoundly promise . . . that you will be already dead!"

"Aye!" cried some of the crew, but others gulped and looked at the battery ashore.

"Wait!" said Silver, and glared at Washington. "How'd you know who we are? And I asks you again: what do you want?"

Washington nodded calmly.

"I know Flint," he said, "by a letter just received from my friend Governor Glen of Charlestown, Carolina, which city Mr Flint visited two years ago. Mr Glen describes Flint's escape from hanging in London, which is news fresh landed and the cause of his letter. He also describes Flint's companion in Charlestown: a beautiful black girl named Selena . . ." Washington looked at Flint. "You are obviously him." He turned to Silver: "And with Flint goes Silver!"

"Maybe," said Silver. "But what, by thunder, do you want of me . . . and *him*?" He jabbed a thumb at Flint. Washington hesitated. He looked at the hands clustered all round, for there were sensitive matters to discuss.

"Never mind them," said Silver. "We're all jolly companions here, and gentlemen o' fortune besides!"

"Aye!" said the crew.

"So be it," said Washington. "In the first place, *England* may wish to hang Flint, but I am not England. Indeed, I am not even English but *Virginian*. So, listen well . . ." Washington pointed to the redcoats and the battery at the quayside. "I could sink this ship," he said, and there was a moan from the crew. "*But* . . . I have no intention of wasting assets so precious as a ship, and you two gentlemen." He looked at Flint and Silver. "Indeed not, for I have a task for each of you."

"Huh!" cried Flint. "I do no man's bidding than my own."

"Nor I!" cried Silver, but the crew stayed silent.

"Gentlemen," said Washington, sensing that he'd won, "you have my word that no harm will befall you . . . if you do as I bid." He smiled. "So what shall it be?"

Half an hour later, with the ship swarming with redcoats, Flint and Silver met by chance below decks. Billy Bones and Black Dog the carpenter were with Flint, bearing spare clothes, supplies, and arms and ammunition for all three. Flint and Silver snarled, and the others fell back in the shadows of the 'tween decks, keeping clear of the foul rage of their betters.

"You treacherous swab," said Flint. "Free with a ship and a crew!"

"And you with your shite-fire mouth and your *fleet of the bloody Ohio!*"

The break now was open and utter. They detested each other with poisonous hatred. They'd stayed together only because of the vast fortune on the island, and the two halves of the papers that led to it. Naturally, each had dreamed of killing the other to take his half. But that was no easy matter. It couldn't be done by stealth with the crew watching and ready to give justice under articles. And it couldn't be face-to-face . . . though neither knew quite why. Perhaps each feared the other? Perhaps *even now* they believed that they achieved more together than apart? The reasons – whatever they were – were deep and powerful.

So now, being forced apart by Washington, all that mattered was where and how the two men should meet again.

"Pah!" Flint crushed his anger. "Shall it be Savannah?"

"Aye," said Silver. "That's still open to the likes of us."

"Savannah, then!"

"*If* you can get free of bloody Washington!"

Flint laughed.

"Don't *ever* doubt it. Nor what I shall do to him first!"

"And shall the rendezvous be Charley Neal's place?"

"Ah . . ." said Flint. Charley Neal had been their agent, buying their plunder.

"What's wrong?" said Silver, spotting the look on Flint's face.

"Charley has . . . er . . . gone home to Dublin."

"You bloody bastard!" said Silver, guessing a nastier truth.

Flint shrugged. "His business is sold to a Mr Jimmy Chester."

266

"How d'you know that?"

"Charley told me just before . . . before he took ship."

"Then Chester's house it is!" Silver sneered. "And Charley's gone to Dublin, you say?"

"Yes," said Flint.

"You *fucking* liar!"

"Oh?" said Flint. "And do you always tell the truth, John Silver, as you used to?"

They glared at each other, and each promised himself that – this time – there *would* be a reckoning in Savannah, with a whole set of papers for just one man.

Chapter 31

Afternoon, 10th June 1754
Savannah
The Royal Colony of Georgia

S avannah had changed in the two years since *Walrus* was last there. It had grown considerably. But it was still a grid-pattern of greasy log houses, with a palisaded fort to one side, and it still knew how to greet gentlemen o' fortune.

Guns boomed from the fort in answer to *Walrus's* salutes, the townsfolk turned out all along the Savannah River's high banks – tall as a ship's topmasts – and gazed down at the fine schooner coming upriver under the Union Jack, wrapped in the smoke of her guns, her people in best shore-going clothes, and a prize following astern: *Inez de Cordoba*, a neat little brig of a hundred tons, flying British colours over Spanish, even though – just at the moment – there was peace between these powers.

Savannah was the youngest port of the youngest colony in British America: hacked out of virgin forest, and in constant fear of the Cherokee, the Cree and the Chickasaw. It was also the most southerly colony, just a hop and a spit from Spanish Florida, and in fear of that too: mortal fear, because the Spanish – if they came – would come not with mere hatchets and scalping knives, but with cannon and the

Inquisition. So Savannah was rough; King George's law ran only on Sundays, and today was a Thursday and there was business to be done.

The anchors went down with a rumble. Sail was taken in, topmasts struck, all made snug and proper, and *Walrus* was jolly from stem to stern. For one thing it was warm, and all hands remembered the freezing, murderous passage across the Atlantic, and staggering ashore like cripples, not fit to be called seamen. But now they were fattened up on Virginian beef, soothed by the tropics, and they had a lively cruise behind them, the tarts of Savannah in front of them, and a prize astern to prove their manhood.

"Three cheers for Long John!" cried Israel Hands. "Three cheers for our cap'n!"

And they bellowed and roared, and waved their hats, and the people up on the banks cheered too. It was a merry time . . . even for Selena, standing on the quarterdeck in her sea-going rig of breeches, boots and shirt, with pistols in her belt as natural as if they'd grown there.

"Well, ma'am," said Silver, and hopped forward with his parrot on his shoulder.

"*Well, ma'am!*" said the bird, and Selena and reached out and stroked it.

"Ah," said Silver, "there's few as can do *that* and count five fingers!"

"I know," she said, and smiled. She smiled straight into his eyes, and the sun shone bright for John Silver, and he sighed with pure happiness, and all the merrier since the past weeks hadn't been easy.

Washington had sent forth *Walrus* as a licensed privateer, to spy out what the Spaniards were doing at sea, with a war coming. In return, the Colony of Virginia would quietly ignore King George's law, and provide safe haven for *Walrus* and her people, and a legal share in any prizes taken: which delighted the crew. The crew, but not Silver. Left to himself, he might – just possibly – have taken the ship and Selena, and sailed over the horizon . . . Which he couldn't, not with a crew that wanted it all ways: any prizes they could take, *plus* the treasure, for they knew all about the divided papers and the rendezvous with Flint.

So, even on a ship at sea, Silver was trapped, and had no choice but to do what Washington wanted . . . at least in the matter of taking Spanish prizes: which – and for the moment – wasn't such a bad thing. Not at all. Not with her smiling at him.

"This is better, ain't it?" he said and dared, just as she had dared, by touching her cheek.

"If it really is legal," she said.

"I've told you. I've shown you the papers. Letters of marque from Washington!"

"Yes," she said. "If you say so." And she laughed again.

"And ain't I all sweet and kindness to them as we takes?"

"Yes," she said. For it was true. *Inez de Cordoba* had tried to run, been easily caught by the sharp-hulled *Walrus* and had surrendered at the first salvo, which had been fired to frighten not kill. Then Silver steered for the coast of Florida, and put the prisoners – who included two women – into the Spaniard's longboat, within easy pulling distance of land. And none were touched nor their possessions despoiled. All this she had seen, and she knew that it was done for her.

Only the Spanish captain – Ibanez – was still aboard. He'd tried to fight, and had been cut down by Mr Joe and sewn up by Dr Cowdray, but had been too weak to go into the longboat with his mates.

And so she smiled and went to the rail to wave at some children capering and dancing on the bank up above.

"That Washington," said Israel Hands softly, looking at Selena.

"Aye?" said Silver, likewise staring at the small, beloved figure.

"Are you really sure that Washington can write letters of marque?"

"It wasn't him. He got 'em from the governor of Virginia."

"Aye . . . but can *he*?"

"Clap a hitch, Mr Gunner," he said, and raised his voice, looking at the brig: "Pork and biscuit, wine and salt, fish and rice." He smiled. "And the ship herself, with all her tackles and gear!" Selena heard him and came back.

"Of which a good share goes to the governor," she said.

"Of course. That's what makes us legal!"

She laughed in his face at that, and Silver shrugged. What did he care? She was here with him and not off with Flint. That was enough. She'd come aboard when the ship left Alexandria, fed up with the back stairs and folk treating her as less than them. But to Silver it had been like those days when he was first courting her, aboard this very ship, and before she turned against him. She was still slinging a hammock alone, though, and wouldn't be his wife.

"Cap'n!" said a voice, and Silver jumped. "Cap'n!" It was Israel Hands again.

"Mr Gunner," said Silver.

"Boat's alongside for to go ashore, Cap'n!"

"Thank you, Mr Hands," said Silver, formally.

"And we've swayed the Dago aboard. Dr Cowdray says he's well enough."

"Well and good," said Silver, and moved over to the rail. He looked over the side, and saw the heavily bandaged Captain Ibanez, laid in the stern, made fast to a plank. He turned to Selena, "Will you not come?" he said.

"Like this?" she said, looking at her clothes. Silver shrugged.

"Put women's clothes on!"

"No," she said. "Not here. I was a slave here."

So it was Silver and Israel Hands who met the authorities of the port of Savannah, taking with them Mr Warrington, who, when sober, was convincing as ever in his role of honest

271

mariner. But aside from passing some dollars to officials who needed help to look away, and getting the Spanish captain a berth in the fort – where the militia had what passed for a hospital – there was little for Warrington to do.

And so to Jimmy Chester's grog shop that had once been Charley Neal's, and before all else inquiring after Joe Flint, who'd not yet arrived in Savannah. Then, leaving Mr Warrington in a happy corner with a bottle and a mulatto girl, the real business was done with Jimmy Chester, who proved to be very like Charley Neal, except he was thin where Charley had been plump. But he had the same skills with money. He could digest a ship and cargo, and make guineas appear in bank accounts far away. So *Inez de Cordova* was swiftly dealt with, right down to setting aside a share for the governor of Virginia. And beyond that, Chester was deep into politics.

"We used to be a Trustee Colony, and now we are a Royal Colony," he said.

"Oh?" said Silver, bored, sitting in Chester's private room with Israel Hands and a jug and some glasses.

"But we await our first governor from England, and so in the meantime govern ourselves," he said. "And we have an assembly, of which I am a member . . ." He smiled ". . . and its president."

"How cosy," said Silver, and Israel Hands yawned.

"So I correspond with other colonial officials . . . including George Washington."

"Oh?" said Silver, sitting up.

"And I know why he sent you to sea."

"Oh?"

"Oh yes! He's acting for all the colonies. We need to know what the Spanish are doing at sea. He's desperate to know. We *all* are, and so we use who we can to find out!"

"What about the navy?" said Silver. "Washington never mentioned them. Ain't they spyin' out the Dagoes?"

Chester shifted in his chair, understanding Washington's reluctance to mention so delicate a subject as the need for the colonies – *occasionally*, and *of course* in the Greater British interest – to act *independently* ... even *contrarywise* ... to the policies of the beloved mother country ...

"Hmmm," said Chester, "you, see, Captain Silver, the king's navy acts on orders from London ... which does not precisely share our interests." Chester dismissed this awkward matter with a shrug. "So," he said briskly, "what've you found out about the Spanish?"

Silver and Israel Hands looked at one another. They said nothing, and stared steadily back at Chester.

"As little as that?" said Chester, and laughed. "And you don't care, do you?"

Silver smiled a sly smile.

"You're smart, you are, Mr Chester, smart as paint. I knew it the first instant I saw you. But how does a poor matelot know who he can trust in these dangerous times?"

"Trust?" said Chester. "And you a pirate?"

"I'm a privateer!" said Silver. "With Letters of Marque."

"Is that what you think?"

"Bah!" said Silver.

"See here," said Chester, and leaned forward and lowered his voice.

"Well?"

"The cargo aboard *Inez de Cordoba*: pork, biscuit and the rest ..."

"What about it?"

"Didn't you wonder what it was for?"

"Why should I?"

"Because it's victuals! *Inez de Cordoba* was on her way to provision a fleet."

"How would you know that?" said Silver.

"Because there's a Spanish squadron in these waters."

"So?"

273

"So didn't you ask that Spanish captain where he was going?" Silver shook his head. "Didn't you ask him anything?"

Silver shrugged. "He wouldn't talk. He said I was a damned pirate and he wouldn't talk."

"And you didn't find means to persuade him?"

"No," said Silver, thinking of *her*. "For aboard my ship, it's all sweet kindness."

"Rubbish," said Chester. "You're being stupid."

"Watch your lip, mister! Don't be a clever bugger with me!"

Chester blinked, swallowed, and tried another approach.

"If you knew where he was going, you could lie in wait ... for others like him!"

"Ahhhh!" said Silver. That was much better! That was prizes and plum duff!

"And maybe find out what that Spanish squadron's doing ...?" said Chester.

"Wouldn't that be jolly, an' all?" said Silver with a sour smile.

"Yes," said Chester, knowing he'd got most of what he wanted. So he smiled, and they drank up, and they parted as friends ... almost. For just as Silver was leaving, Chester had a final, little word.

"Captain Silver," he said.

"Aye?"

"I knew Charley Neal very well."

"Did you?"

"Yes. And he mentioned that there was an island ..." Silver frowned "... where your friend Flint ... left some goods ..."

Thump! Thump! The crutch bumped over the floorboards and Silver stood dark and tall over Jimmy Chester. He stood so close that Chester could hear the hiss of his breath as Silver whispered in his face with quiet, deadly menace:

"Cock an ear, mister," said Silver, and Chester's knees

274

quivered and his hands shook. "Now there ain't no blasted island, nor there ain't no blasted goods. D'you hear me?"

"Yes."

"And we'll be jolly companions, you and I, if you never mention this again."

"Yes."

"Well and good!" said Silver. "And how do I get to see that Spanish captain?"

An hour later Silver and Israel Hands were at the town-side gates of Fort Savannah, a hundred-yard square of puncheon logs with a ditch all round and bastions at the four corners, mounting heavy guns. They clunked across the drawbridge and were challenged by redcoat sentries with muskets. There were great works in hand with pick, spade and wheelbarrow: deepening the ditch round the fort, and throwing up the spoil to strengthen the bastions, and a battery being emplaced to command the river. And all this for fear of the Spanish, and the work so urgent that not only slaves were sweating in the sun, but white men too, including most of the fort's militia, which numbered many hundreds of men.

Silver tipped his hat to the sentries, showed a paper signed by Mr President Chester, and was saluted and let in. The same paper, presented to a sergeant, then to a captain, got Silver and Israel Hands into the inner quadrangle of the fort, with a militiaman to lead them past its barrack block, bakehouse, officers' quarters and well, to a squat gaol, which doubled as a lazarette for persons with dangerous infections.

"Very tight," said Silver, looking at the massive log walls. "Very nice. And is the Spanish gentleman in there?" He pointed at the heavy door.

"Yessir," said the militiaman. "T'ain't locked, sir. But him being a Dago, we didn't know where else to put him. We done the best we can, sir, an' the 'pothecary'll be round later, to let him some blood."

"What a blessing that'll be," said Silver. "Should do him a power of good! And is there a grog shop in the fort?"

"Canteen, sir. Over there, sir."

"Then here's a dollar for you and my shipmate here, to take a drop on me."

"Thank you, sir. Proper gennelman, sir!" said the militiaman.

"You sure, John?" said Israel Hands, frowning. "Don't you want me to . . ."

"No," said Silver, "you take a drink, my old messmate."

Silver watched them walk off. He tried the door. It opened. He went into the cool, dark interior which reeked of piss and vomit. There were a few narrow wooden beds. The Spaniard lay on one. He was awake and alert, but too weak to get up.

Silver hopped across and stood beside the bed, with his long crutch and swirling coat-tails, looming huge and menacing over the helpless man, who looked up in great fear. And the parrot which had sat happily on his shoulder thus far, squawked and flew off and fluttered to the door. Silver watched her for a moment, scratching at the planks with her great talons, and cursing fluently in five different languages. Then he let her out, and closed the door behind her, and went back to the bedside.

"*Buenas tardes, Capitán Ibanez,*" he said.

"*Buenas tardes,*" said the hoarse, quiet voice.

"*Tengo unas preguntas,*" said Silver. "I've got some questions . . ."

Chapter 32

Evening, 23rd May 1754
The confluence of the Youghiogheny and Monongahela rivers
West of the Colony of Pennsylvania
In disputed land

The Indians roared with laughter in the flickering light of the campfires as Long-Hair jumped up and hopped from foot to foot with blood dripping from his cut hand. They yelled and stamped and whooped.

"Are you done?" said Flint. "So soon? Am I among men or boys!"

And the Indians howled and shrieked and playfully shoved Long–Hair from one to another, as he clutched his bloodied hand, but grinned and yelled with the best of them, to show that he saw the joke, and was indeed a man.

Flint smiled. He sat cross-legged before a flat rock and placed the knife down again, with the blade facing himself and the handle towards the Indians. It was his knife, a fine knife with an antler hilt and a razor-edged blade. It was a knife any man would covet.

"Sun Face! Sun Face!" cried the Indians, and whooped all the louder, for they loved Flint. They loved him for his lightning speed and the grim darkness of his humour, which tickled their savage souls.

"Why do they call him *Sun Face*?" said Washington, thirty feet off by the white men's campfire that was likewise surrounded by grinning faces.

"It's what *them others* called him, sir," said Billy Bones. "Them Indians on the island, sir. Someone must've told 'em," and his jaw dropped and he looked away. "Oh!" he said, knowing he'd done wrong.

"Ah!" said Washington. "This *Island* that Mr Flint does not discuss."

"Dunno, sir," said Billy Bones. "But *them* Indians, they called him Sun Face."

"Aye, sir!" said Black Dog. "That they did, an' all."

"Did they admire him as much as our Indians do?" said Washington.

"Yessir," said Billy Bones. "But then, we all did ... we all *do*, sir."

"Aye, sir!" said Black Dog. "There ain't none like him, sir!"

"Aye," said Billy Bones. "Not as a seaman, a leader, nor a man!"

Meanwhile the Indians had settled down, nudging and leering.

"So," said Flint, "I will remind you good fellows of the game ... *Flint's game* ... I shall put my hands in my pockets ... like this ... and I shall await any man to sit opposite me ... and pick up the knife by the handle, and take it as his own."

The Indians screeched and yelled and found a volunteer: one who'd managed to get some trade gin inside him, for all that Washington forbade it on the trail. This was Broken-Foot, a man in his forties, who should have known better.

He sat down, grinning stupidly. He looked at the knife. The entire camp fell silent. It would be so easy ... Sun Face would have to pull out his hands, and reach *over* the blade to get the handle, while he – Broken Foot – had only to pick it up!

He paused.

He tensed.

He pounced . . .

. . . and howled with pain as his hand closed on sharp steel, and Flint snatched it free by the handle, and jauntily tapped the blade against his own nose, leaving a tiny smudge of blood.

Flint grinned, Flint smiled . . . which the Indians and Washington saw. But they didn't see what went on inside of Flint's unique and remarkable mind. They didn't see him howl with laughter and hug himself with glee, and roll over with his legs kicking the air . . . at least in spirit . . . because Flint could see that all things were becoming right again, having been dreadfully wrong for weeks.

He chuckled and cleared his throat . . . *A-hem*. Then he looked at them all: especially Washington. Flint touched his hat as if respectfully, and saw the big man nod. He'd had Flint close-guarded, so he couldn't run, then taken along on this expedition into the primeval forest: this voyage up the bum-hole of nowhere – *leaving Selena behind with Silver!* Flint bowed his head. He was so tormented with jealousy that he could bear it only by slamming the truth behind locked doors, in the cellars of his mind, and never, *ever* going there . . . except by chance, like now . . .

He groaned. He shook his head. Better to think of other things: even other pains, such as the fact that – once in the forest – they'd not even had to guard him, for it was trackless wilderness, which only the Indians knew and only *they* could find the way back to the coast. So Flint was as much trapped as if he'd been in prison, especially as those same Indians had the uncanny ability to track any fugitive attempting to run.

Flint smiled, because all this made the Indians so wonderfully important, and so very much worth recruiting to the true cause . . . the cause of Joe Flint.

And so . . . Broken Foot was jumping round dripping blood

from his cut hand, and the Indians howling with laughter. But Washington frowned.

"Enough!" he said, and looked at Flint. "I want fit men, not cripples."

"Aye-aye, sir," said Flint. "I did but seek to make the men merry, sir."

Washington got up casually and stretched.

"A word, Mr Flint," he said, and walked off.

"Sir?" said Flint, following him into darkness.

"Mr Flint," said Washington quietly, "I would wish to think well of you."

"Oh?" said Flint, looking at the big face.

"Your subordinates stand in awe of you," said Washington, "the Indians worship you. Your conception of a fleet was inspired!" Washington paused. "And . . ." he said. "And . . . there is that . . . *other matter* . . . of such vital importance when war comes. Not only to Virginia, but indeed to the British interest generally!"

Looking up at him, Flint suffered pure torture as the old demon wriggled within him: the one demon he could never entirely control. For the earnest and honest Colonel Washington had dropped into a pit of his own digging, and Flint was bursting to laugh in his face.

Flint knew, now, that the tale of the island treasure followed him everywhere, and was the *real* reason he'd been brought on this expedition, since the earnest and honest Colonel Washington believed the universal myth that *Flint alone* knew the whereabouts of the treasure. And Washington wanted it! He wanted it as a war chest for his precious Virginia, even though it was the ill-got, bloodstained loot of murderous pirates. Hence the fun. For Washington couldn't bring himself to mention the subject except slantwise and tangentially, enabling Flint to pretend he didn't know what Washington was talking about.

"Thus I am confident, in the end, of your patriotism, Mr Flint," said Washington.

"*Ya-rrrrrumph!*" said Flint, striving heroically to hide a snigger behind a cough.

"Hmmm?" said Washington, frowning and wondering. For he was no fool.

"Your pardon, sir," said Flint in a strangled voice.

"Quite," said Washington. "But this game with the knife . . ."

"Oh?" said Flint. He scented chastisement. It killed his laughter stone dead.

"You must play it no more, Joseph."

Flint frowned.

"It is but a contest of skill, sir."

"No! It is contemptible cruelty, for none can match your speed."

Flint said nothing. "And so," said Washington, "I charge you by *that high Craft* which we both revere, that there shall be no more of this! Not it, nor anything like it, for it shames you and makes you less of a man."

Slowly Flint bowed his head and trembled. Washington kindly laid a hand on his shoulder.

"We shall speak of this no more," he said. "I am moved by your contrition." And he walked back to the firelight, more wrong than ever he'd been in his life, for Flint was blinded with anger, boiling with outrage, and his hands were trembling for the antler-hilt knife, which stayed in its sheath *only* because he knew that he couldn't run and find the coast. Not with Washington's Indians on his trail.

Thus the life of the camp proceeded smoothly and, before dawn, the Indians were sent scouting: looking especially for Hurons, their counterparts on the French side, while the white men stood on the edge of the forest, looking down on two great rivers which merged and flowed towards the Ohio: the route into the unknown interior, but also into French territory, now only a day's march to the north.

The weather was mild, and a camp table was set up with

surveying instruments and a supply of paper. Flint and Washington stood at the table with Billy Bones and Black Dog, and behind them stood Washington's men. All but Washington, who was in uniform, wore faded, practical trail clothes, with fringed shirts, slouch hats, and strong boots, with a musket, powder horn and bullet-bag slung across their shoulder.

"Now, Mr Flint," said Washington, "it is time for you to display your skills!"

"With pleasure, Colonel," said Flint, and smiled as best he could, for his bitterly regretted joke about a fleet controlling the great rivers had been taken seriously. Hence this expedition, and the supposed reason for his being with it: to give expert guidance on building the *fleet of the Ohio*.

"There is the Monongahela," said Washington, pointing to the gleaming waters. "It is navigable all the way to the Ohio, and the Ohio is navigable for hundreds of miles beyond. So, Mr Flint – can a fleet be built from these timbers?" He looked into the mighty forest. "A fleet to keep out the French."

Flint thought, and found grudging interest in the matter.

"Yes," he said, "the Monongahela could float a squadron of the line . . ."

"Ah!" said Washington, eagerly. "That was my belief. But I am no expert!"

"I said *could*," cautioned Flint. "There are problems."

"Name them, sir," said Washington. "That is why you are here."

Flint nodded.

"There is a need for stores and provisions of every kind," he said.

"We shall build a road to supply them!" said Washington.

"And a fortification must be built, to protect the shipyard," said Flint, looking at Washington's excellent chart of the rivers. "Here, where there is flat ground and deep water." Washington

282

nodded. Flint turned to Black Dog. "What is your opinion, Mr Carpenter?"

"Well, Cap'n," said Black Dog, "we could fell trees, and cut timber to suit. But *properly*, we should wait a year or two for the timber to season."

"No!" said Washington. "There is need for haste."

"Then, sirs," said Black Dog, "that means buildin' out of green wood, which hasn't good strength, and will warp and twist besides." He saluted, and puffed out his cheeks in relief at being done. "I take my Bible oath on it, sirs," he said.

"But will such vessels last a season or two?" said Washington.

Black Dog pondered mightily.

"Aye-aye, sir," he said. "But no more."

"Good!" said Washington. "And can you, Mr Flint, contrive vessels for the purpose?"

Flint nodded. "Some sort of flat-bottomed sloop or cutter would be needed. Not too big, so they can be worked with sweeps, should the wind fail or be contrary. Vessels of perhaps fifty tons, with a few big guns and a line of swivels." He smiled, pleased with his solution to this interesting problem . . . and instantly wished he'd kept his mouth shut.

"Well said, Mr Flint!" cried Washington. "The Ohio valley will need your skills for years to come!"

Years? thought Flint. *YEARS?*

But he had no time to boil and seethe, for in that moment the camp's Indians – gone not an hour ago – came running back through the woods, led by Black-Ear, their chief. A line of black-eyed, eagle-nosed, tattooed men ran with him, swift as birds and silent as smoke.

"What is it?" said Washington.

"Hurons!" said Black-Ear.

"Dammit!" said Washington. "What numbers?"

"Many dozens."

"Strike the camp!" said Washington, "We shall retire at once."

His followers were expert woodsmen, who broke camp, triced up their gear and moved off in loose single-files without another word, with the Indians scouting ahead and covering the rear. The whole formation moved through the woods like the veterans they were, using bird calls to signal to one another, while Billy Bones and Black Dog lumped along like trolls in the middle, to the obvious disapproval of the rest.

As he walked along, trying to be as silent as the Indians, Flint noted this disciplined, skilful behaviour, but noted something else, too. When the Indians came back into the camp, and when Washington wasn't looking, Black-Ear had looked at Flint, and bowed his head, and placed a hand to his heart.

Flint smiled. It seemed that his diligent cultivation of the Indian interest had finally reached the tipping point, such that it was time to bid farewell to Washington's expedition . . . but not before dealing with the colonel himself . . .

Chapter 33

*T*he sea was calm, the wind fair, and the warm sun rose
out of the east from the depths of the sea, eating the
darkness and lighting the limitless, rolling depths of the
American continent, and the limitless, glittering expanse of
the Atlantic, now in beauteous and peaceful mood. All the
world was fresh and clean and it smiled to itself as it awoke.
And with the beautiful sights came gentle sounds: ripples and
breeze and birds; the quiet, morning voices of men, and the
soft clunk and chatter of ship's gear.

It was such a moment as makes a seaman's heart tingle
and his soul to soar unto Heaven; such a moment as can only
be understood by those who have felt the pitiless cruelty of
the same ocean when its wrath breaks lofty masts and mighty
timbers as if they were twigs that an infant snaps with his
tiny hands.

All aboard shared the moment, and stood quietly to their
duties, proud of themselves and of their ship, and of their
trade, and eager to swell their wealth with another such prize
as *Inez de Cordoba*. Better still, they grinned with the happy

285

knowledge that their captain now knew exactly where to find another prize, since he knew exactly what the Spanish were up to!

"Look!" said Warrington, standing over a chart on a barrelhead by the tiller, with Mr Joe, John Silver and Israel Hands beside him. "The whole coastline here is ragged with rivers and creeks, and with islands close offshore. This one is St Helena Island."

Mr Joe leaned over the chart.

"Is this the best we've got?" he asked. "This chart's old and it's French!"

"Perhaps," said Warrington, "but it is drawn fair and clear, and it has soundings and sandbanks, and all such perils as mariners must fear." He was defensive, for the chart was his own.

"Well enough," said Silver, and laid a hand on Warrington's shoulder. "And the Frogs is fine seamen, an' all. So! Where's them other islands what Ibanez told us about?"

Warrington drew his telescope and swept the seas ahead.

"There!" he said pointing. "And there! We are in mid-channel, having passed into the mouth of the sound, clearing the sands off St Helena, and having two miles of water on either beam. The islands we seek are about three miles ahead."

"Which one is El Tercero?" said Silver.

Warrington blinked. "The French gave them no names . . ." he said.

"Aye, but the Dons did," said Silver. "See! Working *in* from the coast . . . down the north side of the sound . . . *El Primero, El Segundo, El Tercero* and *El Quarto*: First, Second, Third and Fourth." He raised his own glass and looked ahead. "And them supply ships, they anchors between Tercero and Quarto, and waits for the squadron. That's their orders."

"And there's three ships in the squadron?" said Israel Hands.

"Aye," said Silver. "Two ships of thirty guns and one of sixty."

286

"We don't want to be meetin' them!" said Mr Joe.

"No danger of that!" said Silver. "They ain't due for a week, and Captain Ibanez said they're usually late. Meanwhile, they's out charting this here coast of the Carolinas – this *arky-pel-argo* of islands – and seeing where big ships can anchor . . . for to land troops and guns."

"So there *is* going to be a war?" said Israel Hands. "With Spain?"

"Every bugger says so!" said Silver, and he straightened up, and raised his voice: "*Allllll* hands!" he roared.

"Aye-aye!" they cried.

"Can you hear me in the tops?"

"Aye-aye!"

"Can you hear me forrard an' aft an' all?"

"Aye-aye!"

"Then listen well!" he said. "Lookouts keep sharp! Guns run out and matches burning! Stand by, boarders! And a double share for him as first sights a prize!" They cheered. Silver grinned. "*Quiet*, I said!"

"Aye-aye!"

Slowly, carefully, *Walrus* ran up the sound, picking out El Primero, then El Segundo, and then things got difficult. The shoreline on the starboard bow was idyllically beautiful: first dunes and salt marshes alive with water-fowl, then sandy beaches with dark green forest behind them. That, and so many river mouths that it was hard to tell which was an island and which was not, and the old French map didn't quite show what was really there.

But no man complained. Not when a prize might be waiting just around the next corner. *Walrus* was king of all the world. There wasn't another ship in this glorious expanse of shimmering water, and no sight nor sound of any other man. This was pure, primeval wilderness, holding no power greater than *Walrus*'s guns and *Walrus*'s men.

"Ahoy, foretop!" cried Silver.

"Aye-aye!" cried the lookout.

"Don't look for topmasts! They'll be . . ."

He was about to warn that the supply ships would strike all above the lower masts, and hide themselves with leafy branches cut from the shore. That's what Captain Ibanez had said. But the lookout wasn't listening. Not now.

"Fair on the starboard bow!" he cried. "That's my double share!"

"Huzzah!" cried all hands, and they ran to the starboard rail in a thunder of boots and a roll of the ship. Even Selena was among them, and even she was smiling.

"Ah!" said Silver, and raised his telescope. It was just as Ibanez had said. Yards and topmasts struck, and the vessel green with boughs.

"Well done, John!" cried Israel Hands. "This is all your doing!" he beamed.

"Aye!" said Silver. "Ain't it just?"

Israel Hands came close. He spoke soft.

"How'd you do it?"

"What?"

"Get that Dago to talk. He wouldn't say nothing before."

But Silver merely peered down his nose at Israel Hands, and tickled the parrot's green feathers . . . and looked away.

"Ahoy, Selena!" he cried, and pointed at the carefully hidden ship. "There, my lass! All ours! All legal!" And so she smiled.

She smiled because she was young and the young don't stay miserable for ever. And the weather was glorious and the scenery magical. So – accepting she was where she was, and not where she might have wanted to be – she made use of her natural talent for making the best of things.

"Ah-ha!" she cried, and stamped her booted foot, slapped her thigh, and struck a heroic pose: legs apart, hands on hips, head back . . . just as she'd been taught by little Mr Abbey for pantomimes on the London stage, and the crew whooped and cheered every bit as loud as the audiences in Drury Lane. Like any artist, Selena responded to applause, and so she acted a little more. She mimed the act of drawing a telescope. She studied the bough-covered ship and turned to Silver with a mock-serious expression.

"How shall we take her, Cap'n?" she said, affecting a manly voice. "For it's a narrow creek! We'll not get the ship alongside of her!"

The crew roared with delight. Silver laughed, Israel Hands laughed, Mr Warrington cried, "*Brava! Brava!*" and clapped his hands.

"Quite the master mariner, madame!" said Silver. "But you're right. We'd not get the old ship up there without warping." He took a breath and lifted his voice and bellowed: "Boats away! Boarders away! Look lively!"

And so, the warm sun of the Carolinas shone, the little waters chuckled, the sky was blue and the gulls sang alongside the fowl of the salt marshes, and all was rum and plum duff . . . until suddenly it wasn't. Suddenly one lookout remembered his duty, and took a glance astern, which he'd not done for a while, being entirely concerned with looking for prizes. So he turned . . . and gaped . . . and gasped.

"Sail astern, Cap'n!" he cried. "Three of 'em!"

All hands looked astern. They let go the lines they were hauling to launch the boats. They left off checking the priming of pistols and the edges of blades. All who had telescopes raised them and looked at what was coming behind them.

Silver studied the three ships in the round eye of his telescope, which revealed their secrets for all that they were three miles away. They were in line abeam, and he didn't need the scarlet and gold of their banners to know their nationality, for they bore crosses on their topsails in the old way, proclaiming Christ, Salvation and Spain.

Two were frigates, and big ones, heavily built in the

289

Spanish style. They'd have eighteen-pounders at least in their main batteries. They'd be spacious, comfortable ships, with room for men to live who might be at sea for years. They'd be strong ships to withstand the battering of an enemy's guns, and the violence of the seas. Oh yes! The Dons knew how to build, for their empire stretched not only across the Atlantic, but the vast Pacific too, and circumnavigation was nothing to them, nor rounding the Horn in a gale.

Silver focused on the middle ship, and sighed again, for it was old and massive, with a high stern, a spritsail under the bow, and a steep tumble-home that told of a powerful battery on the gun deck. It was almost a ship of the line, and might have been considered one in its day, with a complete row of guns below and more in the high stern and in the bow. It rolled slow and ponderous, proclaiming its weight and its power . . . Twenty-four-pounders on the maindeck, thought Silver.

In open water, he'd have snapped his fingers at the three of them, for no ship can serve all purposes and these weren't built for speed, which *Walrus* was. He'd have sailed them hull under in an hour. But these weren't open waters . . .

He slammed shut his glass, and saw every man aboard gazing at him and the boarders frozen in the act of hoisting out the boats.

"Huh!" he said. "You can belay that, my jolly boys, for we won't be taking no prizes today!" He turned to Warrington and his French map. "Is there any way out than that way?" He pointed at the oncoming ships. Warrington swallowed and gulped and peered pitifully over the chart, trying to find that which didn't exist.

"No, Captain," he said finally. "Only rivers that would take us inland."

"Well then," said Hands, "looks like that Spanish squadron found us after all. Looks like they've come early."

"Aye!" said Silver. "Either that, or that Dago captain sold me a pup!"

"What we going to do, Cap'n?" said Hands.

Silver said nothing. He didn't know.

Chapter 34

Night, 27th May 1754
A forest, west of the Colony of Pennsylvania
On the borders of British territory

Flint shook Billy Bones awake, clasping a hand over his mouth so he should make no sound. Billy Bones nodded: he'd been well briefed. Black Dog was likewise woken, and the three men, with their packs and guns, silently got up and made their way out of the camp. They hadn't far to go. They'd laid themselves down close to the edge of the camp.

It was dark and the only sentries were Black-Ear and five others: Mingos like himself. They followed Flint. Thus three white men and six Indians vanished into the dense trees. Then there was a pause, while Black-Ear's men silently brought in the remaining Indians: four more Mingos, and four Iroquois, who were close followers of Colonel Washington. They came merrily and willingly, assured that Sun-Face had a new and secret game to play, in the darkness away from the other white men.

And indeed Sun-Face greeted them warmly: Mingos and Iroquois together, and he motioned for them to come close and to stand in his presence, which they did, while Sun-Face smiled and raised a finger to his lips for silence, and drew the antler-hilt knife, along his finger.

"Ah!" he said sharply, and waved his finger as if cut.

"Wuh!" they said and shuffled forward still further, with the Mingos quietly giving the Iroquois pride of place, closest to Sun-Face, and in front of themselves. Flint watched, and saw that all was good, and smiled ... and cut the throat of the nearest Iroquois in a single slash, while the Mingos fell on the remaining Iroquois with the skill of a lifetime of ambush: grappling, stabbing and slicing, with tight hands to crush their victim's mouths, and each Iroquois seized by at least two men, so he should make no noise as he fell, nor Flint's victim either, for Flint imitated the Mingos and threw his arms round his blood-gargling victim and hung on hard while he kicked and choked and slumped into death.

Not even a bird awoke as the Mingos laid out the dead, and Flint watched in uttermost fascination as they slid their scalping knives busily round the hairlines, put a knee into each man's chest, and wrenched off the blood-dripping scalps with single, sharp pulls.

RRRRRIP! said the flesh as it tore away from the bone. It was the loudest sound of the entire operation, and even *that* didn't disturb the forest ... But Billy Bones did. He retched and heaved at the sight.

"Shut up, you fool!" hissed Flint.

"Sorry, Cap'n ... I can't help it ..."

"Just shut up!"

"Aye-aye, Cap'n."

Billy Bones fell silent, but he groaned within.

"Sun-Face," said Black-Ear, "will you fetch Washington now?"

The Mingos were clustered around him, grinning, while those who held the scalps showed them off to the rest, for the night was going well ... but they'd been promised a far greater treat. They'd been promised the removal of one leader by another.

"Oh yes!" said Flint. "I'll fetch him. Just you good fellows wait here."

Minutes later, Flint moved through the white men's silent camp. He didn't creep, for that might have caused suspicion. Instead he went confidently but quietly, as a man might who'd gone to empty his bladder in the night, and didn't want to wake his mates. So nobody stirred: not even when Flint knelt down to shake Washington's shoulder, and whisper in his ear. For why should they be suspicious? Weren't the Indians alert for danger?

"Colonel?" said Flint.

"What is it?" said Washington.

"Sir, I have been thinking."

"Oh?"

"Your appeal to my patriotism, sir . . ."

"Ahhhh!"

"Could we talk, Colonel?"

"Of course . . ."

And so, in his wish to fund a war chest for his homeland, George Washington found himself alone and unarmed in a dark forest clearing, away from his men, following Joseph Flint, who turned to face him with a nasty, sly expression on his face that Washington didn't like. As yet, Washington was merely angry. He was not afraid, being a big man who cherished the belief that he could deal with Flint if he had to.

But then Black-Ear and his men silently appeared out of the trees, and stood behind Flint, as did Flint's own followers, though with considerably more noise.

"Flint! Black-Ear!" said Washington. "What is this?"

"Colonel," said Flint, "I have explained to these excellent fellows –" he waved a hand at the Mingos "– that your luck is broken and that they should follow *myself* instead of *yourself!*" And he laughed.

"What!" cried Washington.

"Shut up!" said Flint, and drew a sea-service pistol from his belt, and levelled it at Washington.

"You contemptible traitor!" said Washington.

Flint laughed again. "Whatever you say, Colonel. But don't cry out . . .or you're dead."

Click! said the pistol, as Flint cocked it.

"You pompous, uncultured, colonial oaf," said Flint. "You pretentious, ignorant, tin-soldier! By George, I'm going to enjoy this!"

"Pah!" said Washington, and pointed at the Mingos, "D'you think these men will follow you for shooting an unarmed man? Is that how you'd win their respect?"

"Oh no!" said Flint. "Not at all!" And he uncocked the pistol and threw it aside, and did the same with the other that he wore. Then he drew the antler-hilt knife and threw it to stick in the ground, between himself and Washington. "There!" he said. "Will you move first, or shall I?"

"Wuh!" cried the Mingos and rushed forward for a better look. What a fine night this was, and no mistake! They clustered round Flint and Washington, and stared like the front row at the Roman games.

"You bastard!" said Washington, and trembled, for he'd seen Flint's speed.

"Afraid?" said Flint merrily, and stepped back a pace. "There," he said. "Now I've given you every chance." And he grinned and waited in such confidence . . . that he nearly lost everything, for Washington leapt not at the knife – which Flint was expecting – *but straight at Flint himself*, with hands outstretched to strangle and mangle and crush.

"WUH!" cried the Mingos.

"Cap'n!" cried Billy Bones and Black Dog.

Only Flint's speed saved him. He was moving as Washington struck, diving to one side such that the huge, broad hands caught his coat-tails not his throat, but even that pulled him over, kicking and struggling, with Washington hammering a

295

fist into his back and the two rolling on the ground, and the Mingos yelling and Black Dog trying to find a clear shot for his own pistols, and Billy Bones pulling him off for fear of hitting Flint, and Flint jamming a heel into Washington's shoulder and Washington punching Flint in the belly and the two gasping and cursing and Flint knowing himself the weaker man, and Washington roaring and hauling himself hand over hand towards Flint's throat and Flint flailing out a hand *and chancing on one of the pistols!* And Washington thumping an elbow into Flint's chest and Flint aiming the pistol . . . which split the dark, with a bang and a flash, and the ball went nowhere, and Washington got a grip on Flint's neck and squeezed and squeezed . . . and:

Thump! Flint swung the heavy pistol by the muzzle and caught Washington on top of the head, the thick butt landing with the force of a hammer.

"Ugh . . ." said Washington.

Thump! said the pistol, again. Thump! once more.

And Flint was getting up, and swaying on his feet, and Washington lying still.

"Give me a knife!" screamed Flint, eyes white round the pupils, and froth on his lips. "*Give me a knife!*" he shrieked, and the Mingos sped forward, entranced with the entertainment, each seeking the honour of lending his knife to Sun Face, and Flint snatched a knife, and dropped to his knees and felt for Washington's hairline and put the sharp point to the warm flesh . . .

"No!" cried Billy Bones, and threw himself down and grabbed Flint's hand, such that the knife wavered and trembled and Billy Bones heaved to pull it clear of Washington's face, wrestling nose-to-nose with his wildly angry master.

"Don't do it!" gasped Billy Bones, in anguish. "Not that! We're seamen, not bloody savages. Ain't it good enough you beat the bugger fair an' square?"

"You blockhead! You deadeye! You swab!" cried Flint, and

wrenched free, and leapt up with the knife in his hand and death in his eyes. He would have fallen on Billy Bones, but Black-Ear pushed between them with wide eyes and arms raised.

"No, Sun-Face!" he cried. "The white men come! From the camp! We must be gone. Listen!"

And the Mingos, as one man, raised their long guns, and aimed at the shouting that even Flint could hear now. The white men's camp was roused, and looking for its leader, but Flint was still shaking with rage. He pushed past Black-Ear to get at Billy Bones . . . and stopped in his tracks, confounded, astounded and doubting the sight of his own eyes, for Billy Bones wasn't cringing as ever he'd done before in the face of his master's wrath. He was stood firm with a drawn pistol in his hand. It wasn't raised, but it was ready, and there was a surly determination on Mr Bones's face that Flint had never, ever seen before.

"Billy, Billy," said Flint, in a mad voice. "Don't *ever* tell me what to do." And in the unhinged fury of the moment he took a step forward and raised the knife, and positively gaped as – incredibly – Billy Bones *cocked and levelled, aiming straight at Flint's heart!* They stared at one another. Only God Almighty knew which was the more amazed by what was happening, and neither moved. But the Mingos did. They ran.

"Sun-Face!" cried Black-Ear, and "Sun-Face!" again, because Flint was ignoring him. "Come now! We must be gone!"

And there came the crashing of bodies charging through undergrowth, alongside the shouting of Washington's men.

"What?" said Flint, thick-headed with anger.

"Cap'n," said Billy Bones, "we got to go." He lowered the pistol.

"Go?" said Flint.

"*Now!*" said Black-Ear. "The whites are bad trackers, but

297

even *they* can follow when the light comes. We must go . . .
now!" And finally Flint moved, for it was his own deepest,
most profound wish to get out of this detestable wilderness
and make his way to the coast, and life, and everything that
was important.

"Huh!" he said, and threw the knife away, and stared at
Billy Bones until the other dropped his eyes. "Lead on!" he
said to Black-Ear.

"Come!" said Black-Ear and set off, and left George
Washington groaning on the ground where his men soon
found him, allowing him to enjoy other adventures: some, of
no little consequence, and all thanks to Billy Bones who was
soon suffering agonies of self-doubt for defying the man he'd
followed like a dog, and still admired beyond all reason.

But even that wasn't as bad as the pain of the pace Black-
Ear set through the woods, for it wasn't only the men of
Washington's expedition that might be after them. Black-Hair
feared far more the Hurons, whose territory this was and
who would pursue with skills far greater than mere white
men, and would punish those they caught with infinite cruelty.

The first days were the worst. Flint and Billy Bones strained
to keep up while Black Dog was near death, for he was older
than them and a stranger to exercise of any kind.

"Mr Black," said Flint as the wretched man begged for
rest when first they camped for the night, in a cold circle
without a fire, for that might have betrayed them. "I appreciate your predicament," said Flint, "and I have a solution."

"God bless you, Cap'n," said Black Dog, clutching Flint's
arm and shedding tears of relief. But Billy Bones saw the look
on Flint's face and shuddered. "See here," said Flint, pulling
out one of his small pocket-pistols. "It's primed and loaded."

"Loaded, Cap'n?" said Black Dog, with round eyes.

"Yes, my dear fellow," said Flint. "If you place it *so* . . ."
Flint opened his mouth, and inserted the pistol barrel, and
paused for the manoeuvre to be appreciated. Then he removed

the weapon and offered it to Black Dog with a smile. "If you aim upwards at the brain," said Flint, "why, a single shot will see you off without the least trouble."

Black Dog groaned. "But why?" he said with fresh tears, this time unhappy ones. "Why should I do that?"

"Because, Mr Black," said Flint, "if you cannot keep up, you shall be left behind, and if you are left behind you shall be discovered by the Hurons, in which case you will be grateful for so swift and painless a deliverance from their attentions."

Black Dog kept up after that. He staggered and scrambled and wept, but he kept up and was fortunate that he had to run no more when Black-Ear found what he'd been looking for: a hidden place where a small clan had a settlement, with lodges and canoes by a tributary of the Potomac. The clan was equally fortunate, for the men were away hunting, while the women and children fled into the woods at the barking of their dogs, and were saved.

So Black-Ear's men stole all the food in the settlement, and took two canoes, built of birch bark and willow, and caulked with pine-gum. They were neat little vessels: delightful for their lightness and buoyancy and the ease with which even one man alone could drive them forward with a paddle. So all hands went aboard, and they proceeded downstream – with a grateful Black Dog semi-conscious on his back – moving this time, not at a miserable dozen miles per day, but at five or six times that speed on the rushing, living highway that led to the Chesapeake and the Atlantic Ocean. And even when they faced rapids and waterfalls, so light were the canoes that they were easily carried overland to the lower waters, where the swift, easy journey continued.

Moving night and day, they soon came down into the white man's lands, and either avoided settlements or passed through them at night, until the river broadened mightily, and the little canoes had to hug the shallows of the shoreline, and finally – at night – the lights of a small fishing village were visible on the bank ahead. Black-Ear turned and ceased paddling and spoke to Flint.

"Sun Face! This is Morgansville. The place of which I spoke."

"Good! Will there be ships?"

"Yes. Sea-ships. For fishing and trade. But not many."

"No fort? No soldiers?"

"No. It is a small place."

"Then here we must part," said Flint.

Billy Bones watched as Flint's intuition drove him to ceremony. Even Billy Bones knew how formal Indians could be, but Flint had them all go ashore, and drag the canoes from the water, and make a fire and sit around it. There, Flint thanked Black-Ear and his men for their help, and gave each a gold piece.

Then Black-Ear spoke in praise of Flint, and drew a knife, and the two men stood, and Black-Ear slashed his palm, and Flint offered his own hand to be cut and clasped by Black-Ear to mix their blood, and the Mingos sighed and Billy Bones and Black Dog winced.

"My brother!" said Black-Ear.

"My brother!" said Flint.

And Billy Bones saw the unnatural perversity that a man who'd been a king's officer, at ease in the salons of London, and a matchless navigator, mathematician and seaman . . . was happiest among wicked savages.

But later Flint played the role of civilised man as he led Black Dog and Billy Bones into Morganstown, all three on their best behaviour, affecting mild harmlessness and good nature, and bowing and smiling and paying in gold, and there – by Flint's charm – they were so well received, and spent so handsomely in the one small tavern that next day Flint had a word with a Mr Davison – a shipmaster – such that Flint and his men went aboard Davison's ship, *The Merry Jane*: an ugly little blunt-bowed lugger, more used to the crab fisheries than the deep seas, which made a slow and lumbering passage out of Chesapeake Bay, and south down the coast of America, much delayed by foul weather.

Nonetheless, in early July she came up the Savannah River and dropped anchor by the town, with Flint mightily relieved to see that *Walrus* wasn't among the ships moored there, which gave him the chance to put certain proposals to Jimmy Chester . . . without John Silver being around to interfere.

Chapter 35

Morning, 13th July 1754
Aboard His Catholic Majesty's ship San Pedro de Arbués
St Helena Sound
The Carolinas
A week's sail north of Havana

*T*he flagship doubled to the task of launching the longboat. This complex task first required the removal of the
ship's other boats, which nestled one-inside-the-other, in the
longboat. Thus a great triple block was bent to the mainstay;
then a hundred men – chanting and hauling to the music of a
pipe – whisked each boat aloft, such that it could be swung
aside, by lines bent to the main yard, and set down out of the
way, enabling the great longboat itself to be drawn aloft.

Standing behind the gilded balustrade at the break of the
quarterdeck, in the blue coat, red waistcoat, and gold-laced
hat of his king's sea service, and with his officers respectfully
in his lee, Capitán de Navio Adolfo Peña-Castillo watched
in satisfaction as his men went about their duties. Many were
not even Spaniards, for the ship had been thirty years on
Caribbean duties, and there were as many Indians as white
men on the lower deck. But all his officers were Spanish, and
all hands were proud of their Havana-built ship, for she was
so stoutly made, of such massive Cuban mahogany, that she

was believed to be invulnerable, and in all her service no enemy shot had ever pierced her sides.

Peña-Castillo glanced at the two big frigates that made up his squadron: *Andrés de Pez* and *Lepanto*: splendid names both! The former celebrated an Andalusian admiral, and the latter the battle whereby the navies of Spain and her allies had smashed the Turk and saved Christendom. These fine ships were hove to with backed topsails at the mouth of St Helena Sound, for there was plenty enough depth to float the flagship, and Peña-Castillo was pleased *personally* to confront the English schooner that was trying so hard to avoid him, and which had sailed past the supply ship, concealed between Tercero and Quarto islands, and darted into another inlet further up the sound, like a rat into a rabbit hole.

In all this, there was a pleasing satisfaction to Peña-Castillo, who was a logical, intellectual man – talents profoundly unusual in a sea officer – since he was merely *sufficient* in seamanship, but came of excellent family, was ruthlessly hard-working, and was gifted with a powerful mind nourished by extensive reading. Behind his back, his men called him *el cerebro gordo* . . . the big fat brain.

And now *San Pedro de Arbués*, with all way taken off, was slowly rolling as the heavy longboat finally heaved aloft and went down into the water with a coxswain and a dozen men aboard, oars raised like standing soldiers, in as neat a piece of drill as a seaman's heart could desire.

"Señor Capitán," said a teniente, stepping forward and touching his hat.

"Ah," said Peña-Castillo, "Burillo!"

"Permission to disembark, Señor Capitán?"

"Permission granted!" said Peña-Castillo. "And remember my orders!"

"I shall search as you bid, Señor Capitán!"

Teniente Burillo was an aggressive, heavy young man,

ever ready to urge the men to their duties with a kick, but he was diligent and active, and in every way ideal for his allotted duty. He saluted again, and ran off beckoning to a dozen of marines standing ready with their muskets, and an equal number of seamen with pistols and cutlasses. These swarmed over the side and into the big boat, and took their places. Burillo nodded. It was well done. Finally – raising his hat to the image of San Pedro in its shrine under the quarterdeck – he went over the side himself, and took his place in the stern, with the sides of the great ship looming over him, and her masts, yards and sails shadowing out the sun.

"Give way!" he said, and the longboat pulled towards the English ship, which was less than a hundred yards off, anchored in the midstream of one of the sound's many rivers, where she affected to be harmless and at peace with all the world. Burillo smiled. She'd better be peaceful! He had nearly forty men in the longboat, and *San Pedro* was broadside on, with her main battery run out and bearing directly on the schooner . . . which of course placed the longboat in the line of fire . . . but Burillo shrugged. This was a risk that went with the sea life!

Clank-clunk! Clank-clunk! Clank-clunk! The longboat surged forward, the schooner drew close, and Burillo nodded in appreciation of her fine lines, broad spars and sharp prow. Everything about her said "speed". She was neat and ship-shape, well found and in all respects fit for action, being pierced for fourteen guns: a heavy battery for a ship of her size. Fortunately, in this present moment, the gun-ports were secured, no black muzzles were in sight, and no hostile move threatened. But . . .

"Oh yes," muttered Burillo, "she's a privateer, all right. A blind man could see it . . . a privateer or a pirate."

Meanwhile, there were men peering out from the schooner, and grinning and waving in the most friendly manner. And there was a tall man with a green bird on his shoulder. He was waving from the quarterdeck.

Bump! Boom! The longboat came alongside the schooner, and Burillo leapt for the main chains and hauled himself aboard, with his nimble seamen instantly following, and the marines with their encumbering muskets coming over the side seconds later. Burillo glanced around him. The schooner was in excellent order: neat and polished and lines coiled down. More than that, the men now standing looking at him had been busy with holystones, mops and buckets, scrubbing the decks . . . decks which were already white and gleaming.

There were only a dozen men on deck, and it seemed to Antonio Burillo that he was master of the schooner . . . but you never knew with the English. He saw the careful looks on his men's faces as they looked round with firelocks raised.

Good! he thought. But, bump . . . bump . . . bump! Here came the tall man.

"Good day to you, Señor Teniente!" he said in ready Spanish.

Burillo looked at him and saw that he was a cripple. His left leg was entirely gone, and he leaned on a long crutch that thumped the deck as he moved. He was a strange figure, for a huge green parrot sat on his shoulder, and he was indeed tall, towering over Burillo and smiling politely out of a pale, English face with yellow hair showing under the handkerchief that was bound round his head . . . his hat being already doffed and held respectfully in a big hand.

"Good day," said Burillo. "Who is captain here?"

The tall man bowed.

"I am," he said. "John Silver, at your service! John Silver of the good ship *Walrus*."

Burillo frowned. He was puzzled. The Englishman spoke good Spanish, but with a strong Portuguese accent.

"*Silva*?" said Burillo, mistaking the word. "*Da Silva*? Are you Portuguese?"

"English, señor, but born of a Portuguese father. Da Silva was his name."

"So," said Burillo, "what is your business here, Capitán Da Silva?"

The tall man smiled. He shrugged his shoulders. He reached up to the parrot, which gently nipped his fingers with a beak that looked capable of snapping a marlin spike.

"I am a dealer in skins, Señor Teniente. I am here to trade with the Indians."

"Ah," said Burillo. "And have you any aboard?"

"Indians, Señor Teniente?"

"No . . . *Skins*."

The tall man smiled regretfully. "I fear not, señor, for business has been bad."

"How unfortunate."

"Indeed, señor. And might I ask *your* business . . . here in British waters?"

Now Burillo shrugged. He shrugged and smiled.

"The ships of our squadron were damaged by foul weather. We seek shelter to make repairs and to rest our men."

"Ah," said Silver, looking at the immaculate perfection of the Spanish ships.

"There is also the matter of piracy, Capitán Da Silva," said Burillo.

"Piracy?" The tall man recoiled in horror.

"Indeed. Spanish ships have been lost off the Carolinas," said Burillo, "and my squadron serves the duty of all civilised mankind in seeking to extinguish piracy by capturing the pirates . . . and hanging them."

Silver forced another smile.

"Might I offer you a glass of wine in my cabin, Señor Teniente?" he said. "And perhaps I might present my officers?"

"Perhaps," said Burillo. "First, might I look at your beautiful ship? And in any case, it is my pleasure to offer *you* the hospitality of my commander, Capitán Peña-Castillo, aboard our flagship." He gestured towards the huge bulk of *San Pedro* which so utterly dominated the sound.

"Look at my ship? A pleasure, señor!" said Silver, and led the way, pointing out features of interest while Burillo stared at everything comprehensively, especially the decks and the gunports, and eventually made his way aft and found the lockers where the ship's flags were kept. There were rows of them, carpentered into the taffrail, neat as bookshelves, each deep, narrow recess closed by a square wooden flap that hinged upwards.

"Looking for anything, señor?" said Silver, his smile fading.

"Yes . . ." said Burillo, and glanced up to make sure that his men were close by.

Clap! Clap! went the wooden covers as Burillo's busy fingers raised and dropped them. Then . . .

"Ah!" said Burillo. "What's this?" and he hauled out a large black flag. Turning to Silver, he held it up. "Isn't this the skull and bones?" he said. "The flag of piracy?"

"Mother of God!" said Silver, and piously crossed himself. "How did that get there?"

Soon Capitán Da Silva was making his way up the ponderous sides of *San Pedro,* a feat he managed with surprising ease: his crutch swung from his shoulder by a lanyard, and the big green bird left aboard his own ship. Having clambered over the massive rail, he wedged his crutch under his arm, and looked up and down the decks of one of the most powerful ships in the Americas, for the broadside guns were indeed twenty-four-pounders, which were indeed run out and shotted, and matches burning beside them in tubs. Meanwhile the decks were thick with men – hundreds of them: far too many even for so big a ship as this, for as well as seamen and marines, there were Spanish infantrymen, in their French-looking white coats with coloured turnbacks, and all of them peering in patronising curiosity at the creature Teniente Burillo had brought aboard.

"Follow me," said Burillo, and led the way under the break of the quarterdeck, into the depths of the ship, and towards the stern. Nudged by the muskets of the Spanish marines, Silver hopped after him, pausing only to cross himself as he passed the shrine of San Pedro. Burillo stopped at the ornate, carved door that led to the great cabin. Two more marines were on duty. They saluted.

"Wait here," said Burillo, and knocked and went in.

Silver waited for a good, long wait, until Burillo emerged, and beckoned. Ducking his head, Long John went inside with his hat in his hand. The cabin was magnificent: carved, painted and gilded in the style of a generation earlier. The furnishings were rich with scarlet upholstery, religious paintings hung in rows, and behind the stern windows there was a massive balustraded balcony, for the captain's private use.

Thus Capitán Adolfo Peña-Castillo sat in the bosom of his power with a broad table before him and his stern gallery behind him, and he faced this Englishman, whose father was Portuguese. Peña-Castillo waved at Burillo, indicating that he should take a chair, and glanced to either side of himself where sat his first officer and his personal secretary and other officers. He turned again to the Englishman, whom he left standing . . . or rather leaning on his crutch.

"Capitán Da Silva," he said, "Teniente Burillo has explained that it is my duty to hang pirates?" The Englishman said nothing. He merely nodded and licked his lips. Peña-Castillo nodded in turn, and smiled cynically, "But," he said, "Teniente Burillo tells me that your ship cannot be a pirate because she mounts just eight guns . . . four on each beam."

"That she does, Señor Capitán," said the Englishman.

"Yet she is pierced for fourteen."

"Yes, Señor Capitán. That's how she was when I got her."

"So where are the other ten guns?"

"Sold, Señor Captain." The Englishman smiled. "I have no need for them."

"Because you are a trader in skins?"

"Yes, señor."

"And yet you have no skins in your ship?"

"No, señor."

"But you have the black flag aboard. The skull and bones."

"I swear on the blessed virgin that I know nothing of that flag!" said the Englishman promptly, and it was Peña-Castillo's turn to smile.

"Accepting for the moment your pretence of being in the true faith . . ."

"The which I am, by sweet Mary's blessed name!" cried Silver.

"No doubt," said Peña-Castillo with a small, sour smile, "but there is still the matter of the missing guns, for Teniente Burillo – who is a most observant officer – tells me that he saw the marks of their wheels on your decks, which decks you were swabbing and scraping in the attempt to hide them." Silver said nothing. Peña-Castillo continued: "Which suggests to me that, on seeing my squadron, you cast some of your guns over the side to hide the fact that you are a pirate."

"Never! Not on pain of my immortal soul! Not by –"

"Please!" said Peña-Castillo, waving a hand. "I am not a fool."

"Bah!" said the Englishman, and hopped forward and dragged a chair out from Peña-Castillo's table, and slumped down in it. He sighed heavily, drew out a handkerchief and wiped the sweat from his brow, and glared at the Spaniards. "Well then, Señor Capitán," he said, "since you've made up your mind to hang me, you won't mind if I take the weight off my legs, of which I've only got one . . . and put mine arse to an anchor!"

Burillo sprang to his feet. The rest gasped. But Peña-Castillo merely smiled. He was amused. He'd taken this posturing

Anglo-Portuguese pirate for no more than a clumsy villain, but looking at the man now as he stared straight back into Peña-Castillo's eyes . . . perhaps he was something more.

"And why should I not hang you, Capitán Da Silva?"

"*Silver*. Just Silver."

"By whatever name, why should I not hang you?"

"Because I'm a privateer, with a commission from the governor of Virginia."

"Ah! The governor of Virginia," said Peña-Castillo. "Another commission?"

"What?" said Silver.

Peña-Castillo smiled again. "Do you think you are the *only* pirate with such papers? The only one that I have captured?"

"Well, bugger me through me breeches!" said Silver, but he said it in English.

"What?" said Peña-Castillo.

"I said I'm a licensed privateer. All proper and legal."

"No, Capitán Silver. An English colonial governor may not issue letters of marque. Only your king can do that, and even his commission is valid only in time of war, and there is no war – at present – between England and Spain. That is the law, as you well know."

Peña-Castillo saw his words strike like a roundshot. He saw Silver bow his head in despair and grind his teeth. And Peña-Castillo noted how Silver thought deeply, searching for escape, and shaking his head as if struggling within himself, and looking this way and that as if to find guidance in the ship's dark timbers.

Finally Silver made his decision . . . and looked up . . . and cleared his throat . . . and met Peña-Castillo's eye. All this the Spanish captain watched with fierce concentration. He was a penetrating observer who spotted the little signs others would have missed. He felt a prickle of excitement. He was watching a man fighting for his life, and in Peña-Castillo's opinion, Capitán Silver had just searched his imagination for

310

a way out, and found it . . . but was not proud of it, because his conscience did not like it.

"Señor Capitán," said Silver.

"Señor Capitán," said Peña-Castillo graciously.

"I blame myself for the black flag!" said Silver.

"Do you?" said Peña-Castillo.

"Yes. I should've thought of it and got rid of it!"

"Ah!" said Peña-Castillo, as if sympathetically. "No man is perfect. We all make mistakes." He smiled a little smile, for he sensed there was more to come and wished to encourage Capitán Silver.

"Huh!" said Silver, and shifted in his chair. "So here I am, on a lee shore, dismasted and rolling gunwale-under."

"Indeed," said Peña-Castillo.

"Yes," said Silver. "For you could hang me . . . but you'd be a fool if you did."

"A fool?"

"A damned fool!" Silver beat the table with his fist and glared at Peña-Castillo. "For what are you doing here, Capitán, in British waters, with a ship full of soldiers . . ." Silver stared hard at the Spaniard ". . . And siege guns besides?"

Peña-Castillo spread his hands innocently, but he made no denial . . . and knew on the instant that he'd given something away. There were no siege guns on deck, but there was indeed an artillery train below. Silver was clever! More so than he'd thought.

"You're here to land men and guns," said Silver. "To take and capture British settlements! You're here to be best placed, so soon as that war starts – which all the world knows is coming." Silver leaned forward across the table, looking in his turn for the little signs on Peña-Castillo's face. "Or maybe even *before* it starts?"

Peña-Castillo never blinked, but the men on either side of him gaped in amazement, and their round mouths made Silver laugh at the accuracy of his guess.

311

"Well then, Señor Capitán," said Silver, "how about starting with Savannah? It's a fine big fort they're building to defend the town, with guns a-plenty and a garrison to man them. If you try to take that by siege you'll lose men by the thousand with maybe nothing to show for it!"

Peña-Castillo's clever heart began to beat faster. Capitán Silver was coming to the point at last.

"What's more," said Silver, "it ain't just the big fort! Them Savannians've placed guns at the mouth of the Savannah River itself. I saw the works last time I came past."

"We know," said Burillo, "we've seen –" and he shut up fast as Peña-Castillo glared at him.

"Been looking, have you, Teniente?" Silver sneered. "So you'll know that if this fine squadron sailed up Savannah River, then it'd come under heavy fire, and some of you might not get out again!"

"Perhaps," said Peña-Castillo, for there was no point in denying it.

"But what if I was to give you the fort and town of Savannah?" said Silver. "What if I was to give them to you *without a shot being fired*?"

"But you are an Englishman," said Burillo.

Peña-Castillo winced, despairing at his subordinate's interruption at this crucial moment. But Silver never wavered.

"Yes," said Silver, "I'm an Englishman: and I'm a *live* one, and one as wants to go on living!"

Chapter 36

Afternoon, 13th July 1754
Woods outside Savannah
The Royal Colony of Georgia

The thick, wriggling body – all muscle and writhing life – tumbled and shone, and the light flashed from the scales of its brown-mottled hide, and the black slits of eyes as it soared up above the campfire, where a dozen men sat cross-legged. It reached its apogee, and fell twisting and hissing ... and seeking flesh to bite.

"Whoooa!" cried the audience and leaned back out of the way.

Joe Flint had a new game and new friends: some of Savannah's half-breeds, who lived on the edge of the town, between the settlers and the local Indians, and were despised by both communities. Such men were found on the fringes of all the colonial towns, and it was Flint's genius to seek them out, befriend them, and use them.

"Huh!" cried Flint, catching the copperhead viper neatly behind the head, and holding it twisting and lashing and angry. He turned its triangular head towards himself. He smiled into the gaping mouth. He smiled at the needle fangs and the venom that dripped from them. He brought it to his lips and kissed its nose.

"Yeeee-hah!" cried the half-breeds, slapping their thighs, and leering and nudging one another in glee.

Then Flint leapt up –

"Boo!" he cried, dancing round the fire and thrusting the captive snake at first one man, then another, and chasing them as they staggered, falling and rolling, and laughing and laughing and swigging from jugs of the cheap, vile spirit that Flint had provided in such quantities.

"Flint! Flint!" they cried, gap-toothed, sweat-reeking and filthy. Some would pass for white men, though most had mixed blood, some wore feathers, and all had the deep-wrinkled, dirt-ingrained skin that comes from a lifetime of outdoor living and absolute innocence of soap. They bristled with knives and hatchets, and each one nursed a trade-musket in his arms.

Billy Bones stood watching. He stood well back from the fun. He didn't like snakes. They made his flesh creep. And he didn't like the company. They were worse than Indians. Indians smelled different 'cos they *were* different, but these buggers smelled *dirty!* They stank like a boghouse on a busy day.

So Billy watched as Flint juggled with the snake: throwing it up and catching it. And he watched as Flint dropped it to the ground and defied it to bite him: dangling a hand before the wicked fangs, and whisking it away before they struck. And finally, with Flint's own timing for the climax of a performance, and with Flint's own charm, and his audience held in his hand . . . he stood up, dangling the exhausted snake by the tail with the long body barely moving.

"Who shall have the head?" he said, and smiled his beautiful smile.

"Whoooo!" they said, and instinctively moved back.

"You, Lazy Joe?" said Flint to one of them. The man grinned and shook his head.

"Not me! I don't want the fucker!"

314

"No?" said Flint and viciously cracked the living body as if it were a whip, such that it snapped just behind the head, which flew tumbling and bleeding across the fire, to land neatly in Lazy Joe's lap, sending him jumping up, frantically brushing the hideous object from him, and bringing near-hysterical laughter from the rest.

Even Billy Bones grinned at that, and watched and listened as Flint brought these half-savages under his power, exactly as he'd done with the Indians: because the game was only the beginning. It was the hook to grab their attention. Flint would now apply the leverage of a carefully reasoned argument.

"So," said Flint, tossing away the limp body, "let's talk . . ."

And Billy Bones marvelled at the way he turned off their laughter, and brought them down, and gathered them in, ready to listen . . . and nod . . . and agree . . . and eventually to kiss his arse should he ask them.

". . . because, gentlemen," he confided, "a time will come when I shall need a fighting force of my own. I shall need you, and others like you. In that case, there *will* be danger, but there will be great rewards . . ."

Billy Bones nodded, as much affected as any man present, for Billy Bones was cursed by such irresistible worship of Flint that it arose forever from the ashes of despair and the teachings of bitter experience.

Later the same day, Flint alone attended another, very different meeting, in Mr Jimmy Chester's private room in his big house behind the grog shop. Six other men were present, representing between them the ruling class of Savannah, which class was exclusively composed of men on the make.

"Gentlemen," said Chester, "may I present Captain Joseph Flint, a master mariner of some repute."

"Ah!" said the company and smirked. They knew all about Flint . . . him and his treasure.

315

"Gentlemen," said Flint, and was introduced to each of them. Then he launched into the carefully prepared story that he had agreed with Jimmy Chester, giving just enough tantalising detail to win their support, and to keep them free of the wicked temptation of alliance with John Silver, should ever he return to the town. They nodded. They agreed. They shook Flint's hand warmly as they left: no surprise, considering the size of the shares they'd been promised . . . Not that Flint had any intention of allowing them to partake of such shares, but that was one of the things he *didn't* tell them.

Afterwards, he had a quiet drink with Jimmy Chester, who was much impressed.

"Well, Joe, you've got your consortium and your funding, I congratulate you!"

Flint smiled. "We must guard against all possibilities," he said. "Knowing Silver, he has probably won the support of *Walrus*'s crew. Thus *our* expedition . . ." he raised a glass to Chester.

"*Our* expedition!" said Chester, raising his glass.

". . . will need another ship!" said Flint.

"Yes!" said Chester, and smiled. "I must say, Joe, you're an easier man to deal with than Silver!"

"Am I now?" said Flint, and scowled at the thought of John Silver.

"Yes! I knew it the moment you walked in here, two weeks ago!"

"Hmm," said Flint, throwing off thoughts of death and maiming. "And have you arranged for me to meet the . . . ah . . . the last and most difficult person?"

"Yes," said Chester. "He'll see you tomorrow at the fort."

"Good!" said Flint. "It would be a pity if all parties were reconciled, except the one that deploys armed force!"

"Just one thing, Joe," said Chester, with a dreamy look on his face.

"Which is . . .?"

"Is it *really* that much?"

Flint smiled. "Oh yes! One hundred and ninety-six chests of gold and silver coin, plus four hundred and forty-six bars of silver. I counted them myself."

"God damn my eyes!"

Next morning Flint was strolling round the new battery that the Savannians had built to command the river approaches. With him was Colonel Bland, a professional soldier with a commission from King George. The colonel had command of Savannah's fort, together with its guns, its magazine, and every man who served the king in arms.

It was just like talking to Washington. Bland knew exactly what Flint was offering – Jimmy Chester had seen to that – and he was most certainly interested; Flint could see it in his eyes. But he wasn't about to touch upon the subject. Instead, he greeted Flint with careful formality, then showed him round the fort with a couple of young ensigns in tow, talking only of the coming war with the Spanish, who had ships in the region, and who might at any time fall upon Savannah.

"We have a garrison of four hundred," said Bland, as they walked past a troop of redcoats drilling on the fort's parade ground.

"Indeed?" said Flint politely.

"With another one hundred of woodsmen."

"*Woodsmen?*" said Flint.

"Light infantry," said Bland. "Civilians, equipped by the king, but skilled in woodcraft. Exceedingly useful men!"

"Are they now?" said Flint, thinking of his own small force of half-breeds.

"And as for artillery . . ." said Bland, and proceeded with his lecture.

It was only when he got Flint outside the fort, out from under the big Union Jack that floated above it, and got rid of the two ensigns, leaving himself and Flint standing by the new battery, looking down on the Savannah River and the ships at anchor off the town . . . only then, having looked – hilariously – in all directions . . . did Bland take Flint's arm and, dropping his voice, utter the words that gave Flint the pain of holding back laughter.

"Is it really as much as they say?" said Bland.

And in that moment Flint knew that he held the town of Savannah by the nose. He would never be better prepared to meet John Silver.

Chapter 37

*S*ilver stood beside the helmsman, raised his glass and looked at Savannah. The town, with its thousands of people, stood high above the deep-running river. It looked the same as the last time Silver had seen it, except that there were new works outside the fort where guns had been placed so as to bear down more easily upon any threat that might come upriver. There were ships anchored off the town, with boats swimming to and fro. Thus everything looked peaceful – and why should it not? Savannah didn't know *Walrus* and *La Concha* were coming upriver under British colours ... with five hundred Spanish soldiers below decks, to take the town. And all without war being declared.

Silver turned to look back at *La Concha*, the Spanish brig that had been hiding between Tercero and Quarto islands in St Helena Sound. Now she was under Spanish naval command, flying the Union Jack over Spanish colours, as if she were *Walrus*'s prize.

"Will they believe us, John?" said Israel Hands, who was nervous. Warrington and Mr Joe stood beside him, and Selena too, in the Spanish gown of taffeta that had been found for

319

her from among the store-chests of the Spanish squadron, so that she could appear aboard *Walrus* as a fine lady, to calm any suspicions.

"Why not?" said Silver impatiently. "Why shouldn't they believe us?"

"'Cos o' them!" said Israel Hands, and looked at the big longboat towing astern of *Walrus*, and another behind *La Concha*. "They ain't right. They ain't natural."

"Bah!" said Silver. "Who's going to notice? Who's going to care? Nobody! Not unless there's some bugger up there what don't trust his own mother's milk and sees suspicion everywhere." He sighed. "And how else do we get them Dago musket-mongers ashore fast enough to capture the riverside? It's got to be done quick! We can't go launching skiffs and jolly-boats. Not under the guns of the fort!" He nodded towards Teniente Burillo, strutting the quarterdeck in a great-coat and straw hat, and a couple of Spanish *aspirantes* – junior midshipmen – astern of him, dressed the same. "An' they ain't worried, are they?"

Burillo saw Silver's glance and raised a hand to his hat: living out the pretence that he was a mere passenger. Indeed, he was not worried in the least. He was grinning all over his face, full of excitement at his mission, and imagining himself already promoted.

"Señor Capitán!" he said, then added in Spanish: "How long till we man the boats?"

"Soon enough, Señor Teniente," said Silver. He pointed ahead: "There's the anchorage. We shall get as close to the stairs as we can."

"The stairs," said Burillo, nodding. He drew a glass and looked ahead. "I see," said he. "That is how our men shall scale these cliffs –" he pointed at the greasy, near-vertical river banks that loomed up to the height of the mainyard.

"Aye," said Silver, smiling, but speaking English which Burillo could not understand, "'cos they can't *fly* up, the

320

bastards, can they?" He turned to Israel Hands, and the smile vanished. "And you can take that soddin' look off your face. I've saved all hands by this, my cocker!"

"But ain't we going to do something?" said Israel Hands, and he looked at the hatchways, each of them guarded by Spanish soldiers in seamen's clothes. Below decks there were two hundred and fifty men, crammed in tight, with their arms and ammunition, waiting for the order to swarm into the longboat. They'd planned it, and they'd rehearsed it as a drill under Peña-Castillo's watchful eye. They'd grown quick and clever at doing it, and with such numbers of them aboard, *Walrus* was trapped in the Spanish fist, with just enough of her own people still free to work the ship.

"John," said Israel Hands, "we're giving up Savannah to the Spanish."

"Go fuck yourself, Israel," said Silver, exasperated. "Didn't I get all hands aboard? Didn't I argue with that Spaniard when he wanted to keep our shipmates as hostages aboard his ship? Didn't I say it was all or none?"

"Aye, but our shipmates are down below, in chains."

"D'you want 'em *hanging* in chains, and dipped in tar?" said Silver, then he nodded at Selena and Mr Joe: "You two ain't bothered, are you?" he said.

Selena shook her head. "I was a slave in Georgia," she said, "and a slave in South Carolina. And in Virginia I had to come and go by the back door! What do I care about these people? Let the Spanish have them!"

"Aye," said Mr Joe, "English or Spanish, they treat me just the same."

"I know," said Israel, and he placed a hand on Mr Joe's arm. "I know, my lad, and bad luck to every bugger what did you down. But that's the flag of England there," he said, pointing to the big red ensign at the stern. "John," he pleaded, "don't that mean nothing?"

But Silver wasn't listening. He'd focused his glass on the

row of onlookers that always crowded the landing at Savannah when a ship came in with a prize. Word would go round and the most powerful and important citizens would shove their way to the head of the stairs to see what business promised. *Walrus* was coming up to the anchorage now, with the hands aloft taking in sail, and the bosun's crew standing by to let go anchors . . . and Silver could see faces through his glass now: faces and figures among the well-fed, well-dressed men, with their sunshades held by slaves behind them, and their hats off fanning their faces in the humid heat. But one face – one smooth and smiling face – stood out from all others.

"Flint!" he said.

Flint laughed and chatted among his new friends: Mr President Chester and all those others who clung to Chester's coat-tails at moments like this. They were "leather-apron men" mostly: a locksmith, a baker and a printer. But among them was Colonel Bland.

Then Flint pointed downriver.

"See, gentlemen," he said. "He comes at last!"

"Ah!" said Chester.

"Ah!" said the rest.

And all these good friends looked at the sharp-nosed vessel coming upriver with her prize astern of her, most knowing enough of ships to recognise the schooner *Walrus*, under command of the one-legged John Silver with his green bird, and his half-share of a colossal secret.

"You're sure he'll have it, Mr Flint?" said Chester quietly.

"Oh yes!" said Flint. "He'll never be parted from it."

And now, there they stood: the consortium united, greedy for gold, surrounded by the innocent chattering folk of Savannah, and glancing from time to time towards the new battery at the very edge of the river bank, where five eighteen-pounders were comfortably seated behind timber-revetted earthworks on planked emplacements, complete with all tackles and crew, bearing directly down upon the anchorage opposite the landing stairs, where any incoming ship would want to anchor.

The battery had been built against the Spanish, but today it splendidly complemented the precautions taken to receive Captain Silver and his crew, who were believed to number some seventy men, all of them desperate villains and armed to the teeth. Against that peril, the garrison's men were mustered out of sight, in the fort, while a most formidable warrant of arrest, drawn up in the name of the Assembly of the Royal Colony of Georgia, was sitting in a leather satchel borne by a little slave boy who stood behind Mr President Chester.

Thus all things were perfect: the sun shone, the flies buzzed and the waters chuckled. And then a little tickle of doubt...

"Look!" said Chester, peering at the oncoming ships. "*Walrus* is towing a longboat. Why should she do that?"

"Give me that!" said Flint, snatching a big telescope from Chester's slave boy who carried that instrument, among other baggage. "Hmmm..." said Flint, and for the first time he caught sight of the big boat towed astern of *Walrus*. "Too big a boat for *Walrus* or the prize brig," he said. "And, hallo ... the brig's towing a longboat too!"

"Why should they do that?" said Chester.

"I don't know," said Flint. "More important: where did they get them? Those are such boats as belong to men o' war: ships too strong for *Walrus* to tackle!" Flint peered down the telescope and his quick mind sought an explanation, for he was indeed one who never trusted his own mother's milk – not *that* or anything else about her – and he did indeed see suspicion everywhere: he saw suspicion, betrayal, lies and deceit. For, like the Emperor Nero, Flint believed all others to be as base as himself.

"Perhaps they *found* the boats?" said Chester. Flint sneered, "Or perhaps..."

Flint ignored him.

323

"Colonel Bland!" he said.

"Mr Flint?"

"Are the guns of your battery loaded?"

"They are, sir!"

"With what shot?"

"Roundshot."

"Could I suggest that you immediately load grape over the roundshot and stand by with canister for close engagement?"

"But why?"

"Because one reason for towing longboats is to have them ready to embark a large force of men at utmost speed."

"For what purpose, Mr Flint?"

"To effect an armed landing, Colonel!"

"Ah!" said Bland. "And that's Silver down there? Capable of any foul trick?"

"The same, Colonel!"

Bland nodded and ran off towards the battery, clutching his hat to keep it on his head, and his sword to keep it from tripping him. He shouted as he ran. The gunners gaped, but then their sergeant started bellowing too, and the men reached for their rammers, and Flint nodded in satisfaction. Silver was coming for a reckoning just as much as Flint was, and in Silver's place, with ships and prize money to hand, Flint would have brought every man he could hire! So there might be a great need for grape and canister.

For a moment, Flint allowed himself a smile.

And then he groaned.

"No!" he said, "No! No! No!" For, staring hard through his telescope, he'd just seen the flash of taffeta on *Walrus*'s quarterdeck. He'd seen who it was that might receive the deadly fire of Colonel Bland's guns. He'd not thought of that, not *clever* Joe Flint, *jolly* Joe Flint, *vain* Joe Flint . . . the immeasurably cunning, resourceful and talented Joe Flint. He'd not thought of that at all.

*   *   *

"Señor Teniente," cried Silver, "I will not hoist Spanish colours until your men are in the boats and pulling for the shore!"

"No!" cried the red-faced teniente, with his men massed behind him: the dozen of them that were on deck in their seamen's clothes, all of them glaring angrily at Silver and his men. "I will go no further, except in my king's service, under my king's banner!" cried Burillo. "Were I to do otherwise, my men and I could be shot, under the laws of war!"

"Jesus, Moses and Mary!" cried Silver. "Will you look at that battery up there? And the guns of the fort? Them bastards'll open fire the instant they see Spanish colours! You'll have a chance if it's at the last moment, but otherwise they'll be sending shot aboard when you're most helpless, as you man the boats and take up oars!"

"No!" said Burillo. "The world is at peace – the fort's guns will not even be loaded! We will have plenty of time to act with honour and yet to get our men ashore! So hoist the colours now, or I will send my men to do it!"

"Oh no you won't, my bully boy!" said Silver in English, and he looked to his own men. "Walruses, to me!" he yelled. "And none o' them Dago swabs to touch the halliards or the flag lockers!"

"Aye!" roared Silver's men. There were nearly as many of them on deck as there were Spaniards, and they were gentlemen o' fortune besides, that had smashed heads and slit livers all their lives, while the Spaniards were mostly honest seamen. So there was a great growling and scowling, and some shuffling forward . . . but for all Teniente Burillo's orders, no man of his moved forward to hoist the banner of Spain.

"So," said Burillo, "I at least shall act with honour!" And he threw off the greatcoat that was covering his uniform, cast aside his straw hat, and took his laced hat and sword from a canvas bag that one of his aspirantes was carrying. They did the same, and the three of them stood proudly in the uniform of their service.

"And now," said Burillo, "enough! I shall bring my soldiers on deck, and by the persuasion of their bayonets, you – Capitán Silver – will hoist proper colours!" He turned to one of the aspirantes: "Alvarez!" he cried.

"Señor Teniente!"

"Summon the drummers! Sound the muster!"

"For God's sake, don't!" cried Silver, pointing up at the landing stairs and the fort and the battery, where crowds of people were now visible even without a telescope. "You'll bring down fire on the ship, and there's no better target than men mustered in ranks. You'll lose half of 'em before they even go over the side!" He lurched forward, pushed all others out of his way, and clutched at Burillo's laced sleeve. "I'm begging you, Teniente," he said. "As I'm a seaman and you're one too – and I believe a brave one and a good one – don't hazard our ship and all aboard of her!"

"Oh . . ." said Burillo, "ah . . ." He was much moved, for Silver's words were from the heart, man to man, and authentic good sense. "Well . . ." said Burillo, ". . . perhaps not."

But then Israel Hands cried out from the quarterdeck:

"John! John! Beware astern!" And everyone turned to look at *La Concha* and knew the debate aboard *Walrus* to be irrelevant, for *La Concha* had already struck British colours, and the scarlet and gold of Spain streamed out from foretop, maintop, and stern post.

"Oh no!" said Silver, and turned to look at the battery. There was a horrible pause:

. . . a pause of . . . great . . . long . . . plodding . . . seconds . . . then:

Orange flashes and eruptions of white smoke, and a reverberating *thud-boom-boom*, bouncing around the river banks . . . and the howling scream of approaching shot.

Chapter 38

*T*he first salvo missed, but the river heaved and churned around *Walrus* and a shower of foaming, muddy water came spattering down on her decks, drenching all hands.

"Bring up the men!" cried Burillo, in Spanish, and Aspirante Alvarez ran to the hatchways shouting and waving his arms. A stream of white-coated Spanish infantrymen poured out and on to the maindeck, led by their drummers who stood to attention and beat the muster with fierce concentration.

"God help us!" said Silver, and he turned to Israel Hands: "Might as well run up their blasted flag, shipmate. Can't do no harm now, and it might save our necks if we're took."

"Aye-aye, Cap'n!" said Israel Hands, and within seconds the big Spanish banners that Burillo had brought aboard were breaking from the halliards and catching the wind, to a huge cheer from the Spanish soldiers, and a great waving of hats and raising of muskets in delight.

"Bring the longboat alongside!" cried Burillo. "All hands, stand by for boat drill!"

"Bugger!" said Silver, studying the battery, which was ideally placed to hurl shot right through his decks, for the smoke of the first fire was blown clear and he could actually see the black muzzles running out into their embrasures, as the crews behind them heaved on their tackles.

"John!" said Selena, and tried to say something, clutching and hanging on to his arm. But he wasn't listening.

"Clap a hitch, my lovely!" he said, and looked down into the small, beloved face, and in that terrible instant he damned the fighting and bitching there'd been between them. He damned it from the bottom of his heart, and wept for the lies and broken promises he'd made. Then, in fear of imminent death, he cast his arms around her and kissed her and pushed her towards Mr Joe.

"Take her below, lad," he said. "Take my girl below, for I can't see no harm come to her! Not one hair nor one fingernail!

"Aye-aye, Cap'n!"

"Just get her out of reach of shot!"

Mr Joe vanished below decks, dragging Selena behind him, even as dozens more Spanish soldiers poured up from their hiding places, all cheering and waving along with the rest. Burillo and his officers were bellowing and calling, and shoving them into line, and a picked team of soldiers and Spanish seamen were hauling the longboat alongside, then discipline finally fell upon the whole seething mass of men, muskets, bayonets, cartouche boxes, and rank and file formed, with a regimental flag to the fore, and the drums sounding a long roll.

"*España!*" cried Burillo, skewering his hat on his sword and holding it high.

"*ESPAÑA!*" they roared.

But the deep bellow of pride, even from two hundred and fifty men, was drowned, flattened and overwhelmed by the thunder of eighteen-pounders as the battery fired again . . . and all aboard *Walrus* cringed to the hideous screech of hurtling iron. And this time, timber splintered, planking erupted, rigging parted, and the precious living flesh of men was smashed, ripped and pulped into rags of offal, into out-jutting fractured bone, and into such mutilation as blasted the eyes of those who lived to see it.

A full salvo of roundshot and grape had struck fair and square into the heart of Teniente Burillo's parade.

Flint was running with all his might; running with heart, soul, mind and strength: all of it, every last ounce. He ran through the wildly milling crowd, leaving Chester and his followers behind. He ran through the rolling powder smoke, along the edge of the precipice river bank, he ran around the earth-works protecting the battery, and in among the gunners, who with hats and coats thrown off, had re-loaded the five pieces and were running them out again.

"Heave-*ho*! Heave-*ho*!" cried the teams, hauling on their lines, and . . .

"Left-left-left!" cried the gun-captains, as men strained with handspikes and tackles to train the guns around to bear on the target – a moving target that slid under reefed topsails to attempt an anchorage below.

"Bland!" cried Flint, with the taste of blood rasping in his throat, and his chest heaving. "Bland! Not that ship! Not *Walrus*!" Flint staggered, exhausted into the arms of Colonel Bland, who was standing with the artillery captain in charge of the battery and a battery sergeant major.

"What?" spluttered the captain. "Who's this, Colonel?"

"It's Flint," said Bland.

"Ahhh!" said the captain and sergeant major, and they looked at one another with raised eyebrows, for Flint had a great reputation in Savannah.

"Don't fire on that ship, Colonel," gasped Flint. "You'll kill Silver and lose everything! *Everything*! D'you understand me?"

"Oh!" said Bland, understanding instantly. "Oh, my eyes and limbs!"

329

"Let them get into the boats," said Flint, "*then* fire! But not at the ship!"

Yet Bland hesitated.

"They're Spaniards, dammit! They ain't just pirates come for treasure. This is war!"

"Treasure?" said the other two, their eyes round; for in Savannah, certain secrets weren't as tight as they should have been.

"None o' your business, dammit!" said Bland.

"No!" said Flint.

Meanwhile, off to one side . . .

"*FIRE!*" cried the young lieutenant in charge of the guns.

B-BOOM-BOOM-BOOM! cried the battery with earth-shivering thunder, and the young lieutenant, whose name was Laurence, saw his shot strike home with dreadful effect as hurtling balls ripped through the clustered mass of white-coated troops, sending fragments of men tumbling into the air, to cascade in soggy splashes into the river.

"Bloody Dagoes!" he said, and turned in pride towards Colonel Bland and the rest, and was amazed to see the colonel, white-faced and angry, running towards him crying:

"No! No! No!"

"What?" said Laurence, for he'd very properly been concentrating on his target, he'd certainly paid no attention to the discussions of his superiors, and in any case he was half-deaf from the concussion of the first salvo.

But Flint was close behind Bland, and threw himself on Laurence with unhinged anger, such that Laurence survived *only* because Flint's ever-present knife – the one which lived up his sleeve – was no longer present, having been shaken out, dropped, and left behind by Flint's desperate running. Added to that, Flint was still so exhausted that Bland was able to pull him off when – abandoning the futile search of his sleeve – Flint tried to wring Laurence's neck.

"Uch! Uch!" said Laurence, staggering back.

330

"Flint! God bless my eyes and limbs!" said Bland. "What is it?"

"Tell him not to fire on *Walrus*!" said Flint, unhinged in his fury.

"Nor shall we!" said Bland, turning to Laurence. "Lieutenant! You shall concentrate your fire upon the second ship, until such time as the enemy may attempt a landing, then you shall fire on his boats! Is that understood?"

"Yes, sir!" croaked Laurence, gawping at Flint, and rubbing his neck.

"Go on then!" said Bland.

"Yes, sir!" said Laurence, and staggered off to his gunners.

"God bless my precious soul, what's the matter with you, Flint?" said Bland.

"Nothing," said Flint.

"Huh!" said Bland, and stepped back a pace as Flint, who'd been so reasonable a gentleman until now, stared into his eyes with such an expression as would befit some basilisk of mythology rather than a civilised man. Bland gulped and shuddered. To say that Flint was mad was to say that the sea was wet. The hairs stood up on the back of Bland's neck.

"Ah . . . hmm . . ." said Flint, seeing Bland's reaction and recovering himself such that the manic light went out of his eyes. "Just don't fire on *Walrus*!" he said. "Don't do that . . ."

Bland was bright enough to realise that – as far as Flint was concerned – there was far more aboard *Walrus* than some papers that led to treasure! Wealth and riches made a pretty pair, but a man didn't go galloping mad for them. No, there was something else that Flint valued more than life and soul. Bland wondered what it was.

Teniente Burillo looked up. He was overjoyed to see the Spanish colours that gleamed in brilliance against the blue sky. He smiled and tried to look around him, but he couldn't.

He could only look up. Nor could he stand or move, nor even hear very well, for all the vast bustle and commotion around him sounded strangely flat and quiet. Then Aspirante Alvarez's face filled his vision. It was pale and shouting and horrified.

"*Teniente! Teniente . . .*" said Alverez's mouth, but Burillo could no longer hear.

"*TENIENTE!*" screamed Alvarez, who was old for an aspirante, being an incompetent seaman who'd failed to distinguish himself at sea. He was pot-bellied, pop-eyed, the butt of his comrades' jokes, and now he knelt beside the smashed, limbless torso of his commanding officer, where it lay in a pool of its own entrails. "Ugh!" said Alvarez, shuddering as the life went out of Burillo's face and his eyes closed.

"Get your men in hand!" cried a voice at his elbow, and Alvarez looked up to see the English-Portuguese captain with his long crutch towering over him, his coat-tails swirling as he reached down to haul Alvarez to his feet. "Get up! On your feet," he commanded, "for there's no man left but you!"

Alvarez stood. He looked around him. It was blood and death on all sides. At least thirty men were dead or laid in pitiful ruin: moaning, slobbering, and broken – and that included all the officers, even the other aspirantes. Meanwhile men ran hither and thither, some trying to bring the longboat alongside, others – the seamen – trying to work the ship and make good her damage. They worked with a will, Spanish beside English, in the manner of their trade, but the soldiers were near despair, and if they'd been ashore they'd have run away.

Then the guns thundered again: the guns up in the English battery, and Alvarez shuddered as the shot flew overhead and screams, crashes and falling timbers sounded astern, from *La Concha*. Instinctively, Alvarez thanked God for the respite, and then was ashamed for wishing death on his comrades. But the English captain was shaking his shoulder and shouting again.

"I'll sail the ship," said Silver, over the din of gunfire, cries and screaming. "I'll con her to anchor, but you must take command of your men or we're lost. I can't sail her out, for the wind's against us, and we'd have to kedge or warp, which is too slow and they'd sink us! So the only hope is for your men to take the battery. It's that or the ship's lost – and all aboard of us! Can you do that? Can you do it, señor?"

"Yes," said Alvarez. But his face said "no".

"Huh!" said Silver, and grabbed hold of one of his own men, and gabbled at him in harsh, barking English, before turning back to Alvarez. "We're hit below the waterline, which I must attend to ... So, can you do it, señor? Take that battery?"

"Yes," said Alvarez in a tiny voice, and he shook as the guns fired again.

"Come on," said Silver, desperate to put heart into the little swab, desperate to save the ship and the woman he loved. "*Santiago!*" he said. "Go on, boy, shout it out!"

"Santiago!" said Alvarez, mouthing the war cry of Spanish Christendom.

"No," said Silver. "*SANTIAGO!*" And he yelled with all his might.

"Santiago!" echoed some of the Spanish soldiers, turning round.

"There! Go on, my son," said Silver.

"Santiago! Santiago! Santiago!" cried Alvarez, and the Spaniards cheered.

Better yet, a big *sargento* named Ortiz – a veteran with a fine moustache – got up from where he'd been sitting in misery with an arm off at the elbow, lashed a line around the stump, and came and stood beside Alvarez.

"Santiago!" cried Ortiz in a deep bellow.

"So!" cried Alvarez, and found his way to his duty. "Bring the longboat alongside." He said it weakly, anxiously looking for reassurance at Sargento Ortiz, who nodded firmly, such that Alvarez drew breath for a real shout: "All hands to boat drill! All hands fall in by the larboard rail!"

The men cheered again. One of them picked up the regimental colour that had gone down when the standard-bearer fell. He raised it, and waved it, and emotion filled them all, as they did their country proud, in the skill and efficiency with which they hauled in the longboat, dropped Spanish seamen into her to man the oars, then filled her with every last man she could hold, which was fifty soldiers and ten oarsmen, the boat being an exceptionally big one, which like *San Pedro de Arbués* that owned her, was built in the style of the last century.

Alvarez went over the side last of all, and all aboard cheered . . . and all aboard were lucky, for the plunging shot and howling grape that sizzled down from the battery was concentrating exclusively on *La Concha*, which now slewed crabwise with yards dangling, sails trailing, blood running from her scuppers, and a slaughterhouse of dead and mangled humanity cramming her decks among the shattered gear, shards and splinters.

And yet, even *La Concha* was manning her longboat. Smashed and bedraggled as the ship was, the men aboard hadn't given up, and their own shouts of "Santiago!" echoed across the water to sound beside those of Aspirante Alvarez and his men. Soon two boats were pulling for the landing and the stairs, crammed and manned to the gunwales, and enjoying a brief respite from the fire of the battery, as if the guns didn't know which target to choose, allowing the Spanish seamen to pull their hearts out . . .

Clunk-clank! Clunk-clank! Clunk-clank!

But then the black muzzles found their way, and roared together and shot flew through the air again.

"Where's this bastard shot-hole, then?" said the carpenter's mate as he dashed forward to find Silver, Israel Hands, Mr

Joe and all the rest who were free, waiting for him in the companionway outside the stern cabin.

"There ain't none," said Silver. "But them Dagoes is going to be gone in a brace o' shakes, and most of our lads is in irons below. So I've summoned all hands, for this is our chance to take back our ship!"

"Aye!" they said.

"Aye!" said Silver, and he thought long and hard, and listened to all the noise and fury around him. The soldiers were all on deck, yelling encouragement to their mates in the longboat, while below decks all was quiet.

"Have you got your tools, Mr Carpenter?"

"Aye-aye, Cap'n!"

"And you, Mr Gunner?"

"Aye-aye!" said Israel Hands.

"So let's strike the chains off our lads, and be a crew once more!"

"Aye!" they all said.

"And set sail!" said a voice.

"Aye!" they roared.

"No!" said Silver.

"What?"

"We'll take the ship, and break out the fire-arms and man the guns!"

"Aye!"

"But then . . .we must hold hard, and stay put."

"Why?"

"First, because we don't know who's going to win the fight up above, and whoever wins'll be master of that battery, the which we can't get away from, without the wind changes, for we'd be sunk before we could warp out!"

They nodded. It was true.

"But," said Silver, "there's more . . ."

"What?" they said.

"Have we come this far to walk away penniless, shipmates?"

335

said Silver. "Penniless, when we could be rich men riding in carriages? You all know I've only *half* the papers that lead to the treasure, while that bastard Flint has the rest."

"Aye!"

"So are we gentlemen o' fortune or bumboat men? Shall we let Flint keep us from what's ours?"

"No," said the old hands. But some of the youngsters were silent, for not all had sailed with Flint, and to them, his treasure was a fine tale but not reality.

"So what would you do, John?" said Israel Hands.

"What would I do? Why," said Silver, "I'd let the Spanish and the Savannians knock seven bells out of each other, and while they're at it – perhaps tonight – then a band of us shall go ashore, find Jimmy Chester – him as will lead us to Flint – and get them papers off the swab, and his silver case too, if we have to cut it out of him while we roast his arse on a fire!" Silver growled in venom and spite, he clenched his fist and stamped his crutch on the deck. "And by thunder, I'll do it an' all," he said.

There was another silence, then Israel Hands spoke again.

"Beggin' your pardon, Cap'n," he said, touching his hat formally, "but this is for all hands to decide, in council. For we're gentlemen o' fortune, like you said, and there's some what'd wish to take their chances with the battery, or sail upstream, past their reach, and wait for a better wind."

"Aye!" said the others, and Silver nodded, for he had no choice.

"So be it," he said. "Let the council be held!"

Chapter 39

Morning, 20th July 1754
The Savannah River

*T*he longboat bumped into mooring posts at the foot of the timber stairs. The men cheered. Alvarez shrieked in relief and joy. They'd made it! They'd come ashore! They'd got under the reach of the slaughtering, murdering battery. They couldn't be hit any more! And thump-bump-crunch, the second longboat – *La Concha*'s – was alongside and crammed with yelling mouths, glittering bayonets and black moustaches. The second boat had been badly hit by grape and there were dead and wounded rolling in her bilges, but she still disgorged a load of fighting men.

"Santiago!" cried Alvarez.

"SANTIAGO!" they all roared.

"Follow me!" cried Alvarez, swept away by the triumph of the moment, and he made ready to jump for the stairs with sword in hand.

"Aspirante," cried Sargento Ortiz, grabbing his arm, "shall we not send the boats back for more men?"

"*Oh! Ah!*" cried Alvarez. "Soldiers of Spain, follow me! Seamen, return for another load!" And then he was off, fired with fury, erupting with passion, and for once in his life leading from the front with his men following after, boots pounding, muskets clattering, swarming, tumbling out of the wallowing boats, with the seamen urging them on, and thundering up the wooden stairs that creaked and swayed under their load, and pouring out at the top, with Alvarez leaping with excitement and the civilian population of Savannah shrieking and screaming and running in all directions: men and women, children and adults, black, white, red and mulattos of every shade scattering. Some ran to their houses, some to the forest – but mostly they ran pell-mell towards the heavy grey timbers and the smooth, looming earthworks of Savannah's fort . . . and never a blow struck in defence of the town and never a glimpse of a red coat . . . except a hundred yards off to one side, where the troops in the now-silent battery stood in their smoke and peered through the embrasures at the Spaniards, now firmly in control of Savannah's stairs.

"Cease firing!" cried Lieutenant Laurence, hoarse with shouting, deafened by his guns, and eyes streaming from powder smoke. "They're under our fucking reach and it ain't no fucking good!"

And the men gulped and sweated, and stood by their hot black guns and trembled with the effort they'd put out in serving them. They'd hit one of the boats, and mauled it badly, but now they couldn't depress their guns any lower. They couldn't even see the boats.

Laurence sighed. Left to himself, he'd have stood back and waited for a target, but Flint was on him like the wrath of God, with Colonel Bland after him, at first for fear Flint had lost his temper again, and then understanding and yelling agreement wildly.

"Listen!" cried Flint, seizing hold of Laurence, "they'll come ashore up that blasted staircase! *I* shall drag out two guns to bear upon it! *You* will stand by your remaining guns, laid on your last sight of the boats, and stand by to fire as they

338

emerge to collect more men! You will ensure that fire is properly controlled such that each boat is pounded, and you will not – under any circumstances – fire upon *Walrus*!"

"Yes! Yes!" cried Bland, nodding his head off at Flint's words, and marvelling that ever he'd doubted the sanity of so superb an officer, so steady under fire, and so much a master of the hour.

But Flint wasn't done, for the swirling clouds of his personality always had contained – amongst all the rest – a very fine officer indeed. So he clapped his hands behind his back as a sea-officer should and turned on Colonel Bland and gave him his orders.

"Colonel!" he said.

"Sir!" said Bland instinctively.

"You will take command of all your forces and engage the enemy!" Flint nodded towards the Spanish troops that were driving Savannah's people before them, led by an officer who leaped and cavorted and waved a sword over his head.

"You will bring the garrison from the fort!"

"Sir!" said Bland.

"You will send out your woodsmen to fall upon the enemy's rear!"

"Sir!" said Bland, and saluted.

Without a word, without hesitation, Bland dashed off towards the fort where his men were waiting, while Flint took command of two gun crews and began hauling guns out of their emplacements and around the earthworks to face the river bank, the stairs and the Spaniards. It was heavy work and slow, because the guns' small wheels constantly bogged down in the soft earth. But with Flint leading, the gunners persevered.

"Heave-*ho*! Heave-*ho*!" cried the Spanish oarsmen, and they backed water to clear the stairs, then each helmsman steered for his ship, for *Walrus* and for *La Concha,* and without the weight of a cargo of men the big boats made better speed. From the two ships came cheers and cries to urge them on. Even the wounded in *La Concha*'s boat did their best to cheer, and gave up groaning.

"Heave-*ho*! Heave-*ho*!" The boats pulled for their ships, and came out from under the protective brow of Savannah's river bank . . . and once more into the sight of the eighteen-pounders, which opened up, at maximum depression, with a bound and a roar and a bank of smoke. But this time it was three guns, not five, with two firing at *La Concha*'s boat and only one at *Walrus*'s. More than that, the soldiers aboard *Walrus* had the sense to open fire with her two-pounder swivels, which, small as they were, had the advantage over her carriage guns in that their mountings allowed unlimited elevation, enabling an aim to be taken – by squint and by guesswork – at the battery up on the river bank.

Following the example of their comrades, those aboard *La Concha* likewise loaded the swivels mounted on her gunwale and aimed up at the battery and cracked and banged in company with *Walrus*'s fire, sending a steady stream of iron shot whistling up at the earthworks . . . where they did no harm at all to the eighteen-pounders or their solid defences, for most missed entirely or buried themselves in the earth-works, but one or two lucky shots howled over the heads of the gunners, reminding them of mortality and making them flinch.

More important, with eight or more swivels burning powder, a nice cloud of white smoke began to roll around the anchorage below Savannah's stairs, making it hard for the gunners in the battery to see what they were aiming at.

"Damnation!" cried Lieutenant Laurence. "Load grapeshot! No more solid ball!"

"Sir!" cried his gunners, for it was good sense. Grape might not sink a big longboat as a roundshot shot would, but it greatly increased the chances of a hit. And soon Laurence's men were cheering as water foamed in a deadly circle all around *Walrus*'s longboat, now re-filled with Spanish soldiers and pulling for the shore, and a good dozen one-pound iron balls crashed into the boat such that blood, bone and flesh leapt into the air and cascaded down and smeared the living survivors with the guts and slime of their mates, and fragments of teeth, skin and hair, and pieces of fingers and limbs.

But the boat didn't go down! It wasn't holed so bad that bailing couldn't save it, and most of the oarsmen survived and pulled on with desperate strength, and the dead and dying hanging over the sides between the heaving oars, and a greasy trail of blood and tissues trailing aft like the slime of a monstrous slug.

"Aspirante!" cried Sargento Ortiz. "The battery! We must silence the battery!" Ortiz was weakening. He'd lost much blood. The stump of his arm was pounding horribly, and seeping and dripping, and Ortiz was gasping from chasing Aspirante Alvarez and trying to get the little sod to take command of the men, who'd soon be breaking doors and looting if they weren't stopped.

"Oh!" said Alvarez, and looked around, and saw the empty streets and the few running figures, and his grinning, gasping men, and Sargento Ortiz's accusing face. And then . . . B-Boom! the battery fired again, and Alvarez remembered and rushed back to the river bank and looked down at the dead and dying and the wreckage floating in the Savannah River. Five hundred men had mustered in arms on the maindecks of *Walrus* and *La Concha*. Of these, as Alvarez could plainly see, a good hundred were already dead or ruined, and now the oarsmen were losing their stroke aboard one of the boats, and looking over their shoulders for the smoke and flash of the battery's guns, and the other boat was landing more men at the bottom of the stairs, and the river was filling up with smoke from the battery, and – Alvarez gaped in surprise – swivel guns were firing from the two ships.

"The battery, señor," said Ortiz, and staggered. His face was yellow-white around the black moustache. "We must storm the battery or we cannot take the town."

Alvarez blinked, and tiredness fell upon him from too much running and shouting. He was spent. He'd never been a very good officer, he'd got this far through hysterical excitement, and now that was gone. Seeing that, Sargento Ortiz swayed with sickness and groaned.

Colonel Bland found confusion at the fort. He yelled at the sentries, who let him through the drawbridge and gate. They saluted as he ran in, under the gateway bastion, and into the fort's main quadrangle. There indeed stood the garrison – paraded with bayonets fixed, cartridge pouches filled, and their drums, fifes and colours beside them. But . . .

"Ah!" thought Bland, "God bless my soul . . ." For he wasn't the only person who'd run into the fort from the town. There was a mob of civilians, in dread of Spain. There were weeping women, howling children and fathers with their arms around their families, in fear of rape, fire and the Inquisition, and loudly calling for the gates to be closed, the drawbridge raised and the guns of the fort manned. All this had shaken the militiamen, whose lines were wavering, and they were talking to one another and pointing towards the town in alarm.

"God bless my hopes of Heaven!" said Bland, then . . .

"Colonel!" cried a handful of wide-eyed officers, running up to him. "Thank God you're here! How many of them have landed? How many regiments?"

"Regiments?" said Bland. "I saw no more than a few boat-loads!"

"But it's two ships!" cried a voice. "Everyone says so!"

"God bless you, yes!" said Bland. "But *small* ships, and I saw no more than a few dozen Spaniards come ashore!"

"Ahhhh," they said, and their spirits soared and they straightened their backs and thrust out their manly jaws.

"Stand the fort to arms!" cried Bland. "Muster every man in the fort, and sound the march! I shall lead forth our men to drive these invaders into the river!"

"Huzzah!" they cried, and soon the drums were sounding a rattling beat, the fifers were blowing "Come Lasses and Lads" and the redcoats were marching boldly out over the fort's drawbridge with hysterical cheering from the civilians behind them. At their head strode Colonel Bland, transported into glory, with sword in hand and fire in his heart.

At the same time, and with much less fuss, a hundred woodsmen marched quietly behind the regulars, and took early opportunity to lope off, in loose formation, trailing their arms. Bland never gave them a thought, but they were trained to seek opportunity, and any means whatsoever to take their enemies by surprise; and they were as determined as any redcoat to fight for their homes and their families.

A Spanish army officer charged up the stairs with the latest boatload of men from *La Concha*. He was a commandante – a major – and with him came two capitáns. Alvarez saw them and nearly wet himself in relief. He stood to attention beside Ortiz and thanked the Virgin and all the saints.

"Señor Commandante!" said Alvarez, and received a curt nod, for the commandante believed that no drop of use whatsoever could be squeezed out of a sea-service aspirante on land, and in this case he was entirely correct. Instead he yelled at his juniors and the trumpeter he'd brought with him, and mustered his men – of whom he found he had nearly two hundred and fifty, and plenty more to come from the ships. He looked at the town, and saw no threat. He looked at the fort with its English flag and saw no threat. But he looked at the battery . . . and saw the teams of men hauling guns out to bear upon himself and his men.

"Mother of God!" he cried. "Grenadiers to the front! Follow me! The rest, stand fast!" He was a very brave man, if not a particularly inventive one. He saw the two heavy guns in the instant of being loaded. Men were ramming home, they were training and levelling, and the range was just over one hundred yards.

He turned to the body of fifty grenadiers – big men with bearskin trim on their caps, the swaggering bullies among the ranks, who thought themselves better men than all the rest. Now the English gunners were standing clear while the gun-captains swung their linstocks.

The commandante ran to the side of his men.

"Present muskets!" he cried. "Make ready . . ."

Cli-cli-cli-clack! said the locks.

"Fire!" and the muskets roared. "Santiago!" cried the commandante and charged.

"Santiago!" cried the grenadiers, and ran after him with bayonets levelled.

BOOOM! BOOOM! cried the pair of heavy guns, with monstrous voice.

At one hundred yards, not a single musket shot found a human target, while – firing from soft, churned-up earth – the eighteen-pounders on their sea carriages recoiled so heavily that their muzzles twisted wildly off target. But the load was so heavy – totalling over eleven hundred musket balls – that it screamed and sizzled and scoured like the Devil's broom, such that when the smoke cleared only fifteen grenadiers were left standing, and the rest, including their brave but unin-ventive leader, were dead, dying or wounded, and compre-hensively riddled with shot.

But the rest of the Spaniards charged the now-empty guns. There were two officers left, and nearly two hundred men, and every chance that they could over-run the battery before the gunners had time to reload. So thought the two Spanish capitáns, and they led their men in a rolling, ragged charge over the bodies of the grenadiers and the commandante. They ran with gleaming bayonets and bellowing roars, which swelled with delight at the sweetest sight a soldier ever sees in the field: the backs of their fleeing enemies. For the English gunners, seeing sense, were running away, without even taking the time to spike their guns.

But their triumph was brief. No sooner had the artillerymen run off towards the English fort than the sound of fife and drum signalled the advance of an English column: a giant red centipede with white legs and a rippling steel crest, emerging from the fort, and coming in strength.

Aspirante Alvarez gasped. Sargento Ortiz said nothing, for he was dead from loss of blood, but the two capitáns, reinforced by another boatload from *Walrus,* carefully drew up their men and marched towards the English column, with Spanish drums beating, and with profound satisfaction that this wretched business of being fired upon by batteries had come to an end, with a correct and proper battle about to begin, in the correct and proper way.

Alvarez watched as the two columns – the white and the red – advanced upon each other and deployed into line in the open ground between the fort and the town. He saw that there were more red than white, and he searched in his conscience and found that his duty was now at the *bottom* of the stairs, not the *top*, for there was more boat work to be done, and himself a sea officer.

At the bottom of the stairs, he found two shot-riddled boats, half-sunk, with the dead and wounded sprawled within them. And there he cringed as the first volleys rolled out in the fight for Savannah.

Chapter 40

Dusk, 20th July 1754
The Savannah River

"John!" said Selena, "It's nearly night. The battery can't see us. We can work the ship out of reach of it, before daylight!" She looked over the quarterdeck rail at the line of heavy timbers, driven into the Savannah river bed, each with a heavy ringbolt secured at its cap: the *dolphins* present in any civilised anchorage to enable ships to move against the wind. "Even I know how it's done," she said. "Secure a line to one of them, and all hands haul on the line, and pull her from one to the next!"

"Aye, lass," he said. "And a proper little sea-madame you are, an' all!" and he sighed and reached out to stroke her cheek. She still had on the taffeta dress, and he was pierced to the heart with the loveliness of her. The two of them were alone on the quarterdeck, with all the Spaniards gone and a mass of the ship's people in the waist, making ready for what the council had agreed.

"Then why must you go ashore?" she said, and looked up to where the town lay uneasy in the dark, with the red glow of fires and occasional gunshots in the streets. "We could be gone from all that!" she said.

But Silver shook his head.

"I got to go, lass," he said, "for Flint –"

"And his half of the papers?"

"Aye," he said. "I do want them, and no mistake . . . but I'm going mainly for *himself!*" He sighed. "See here, lass . . . if we sail away from here, we'd never be safe! We'd forever be waiting for him – and by God and the Devil he'd come, and nothing'd stop him! For the bugger ain't human and he ain't holy, and we'll have no peace till he's dead!"

She fell silent. It was true . . . And in any case, all hands had voted to follow John Silver's plan. For when it came to hard choices, most wanted a share of Flint's treasure, and the rest had been won round by Silver, Israel Hands and by Blind Pew, who as always was listened to with respect, and who wanted the gold as a pension for his sightless future, when at last he should be cast up on dry land.

So Silver went over the side into *Walrus*'s launch, with a dozen men who weren't the best in the ship by a long way, for there'd been suspicion among the hands as to what others might do, once they'd got their hands on *both* halves of Flint's papers! And suspicion became distrust, until Blind Pew proposed that those who went with Silver should be chosen by lot. Thus Silver sighed as he sat in the stern sheets, for he was facing Tom Morgan, who was stroke oar, and whose head was thick as teak, and beside him was Darby McGraw, an idle swab who was drunk more often than sober, and a precious pair they made for such a task!

But Mr Joe sat beside Silver, and was rated coxswain, and there were others who were near as good as him.

"Give way!" said Mr Joe, and the hands pulled muffled oars, sending the launch out into the dark: for all was deep shadow on the river with its up-rearing banks that left it deep in gloom.

Silver couldn't land at Savannah stairs, for the Spaniards might be there, but knowing the river as he did, he steered upstream, just past the town, to a muddy shoreline beneath the river banks. Here they landed and faced a near-vertical cliff of mud that would have left landmen helpless and dismayed. Landmen but not seamen. A grapnel was swung round on its line and heaved upward to take hold of the scrubby trees above. Then the nimblest man swarmed up the thin line carrying a block and a one-inch rope, and secured the block to a tree-trunk so those below could heave up the next man in a bowline, until enough were on the bank to haul directly on the line to lift their mates – by which means John Silver came last and rose like a soaring bird.

"Now then, lads," he said, "gather round, for there must be no noise."

"Aye!" they said: a ring of dark faces and pale eyes.

"We must march around the fort and enter the town from the land side."

"Aye!"

"It'll take some hours, for we must keep away from all that . . ."

They glanced towards the town, with its fires and gunshots, and nodded.

"We'll let them buggers fight, and we'll steer clear! For it ain't no matter of ours!"

"Aye!"

"Our course is to Jimmy Chester's house, the which I knows well."

"Will Flint be there, Cap'n?" said Mr Joe.

"Huh!" said Silver, and spat at the ground beneath his feet. "You bet your dick on it, my son! I've *seen* the swab, so I knows he's here! And he's seen *Walrus,* so he knows *I'm* here!" Silver nodded. "Oh, he's as sweet to see me as I am to see him . . . and the place agreed between us is Chester's house!"

They nodded, they growled in anticipation of the fight. They gripped their muskets, their pistols and blades.

"All hands together!" said Silver, and took a sight on the stars, and led them off into the night.

"So! What's afoot?" said Flint to Lazy Joe, with his fringed shirt and long gun, who'd crept into Jimmy Chester's grog shop with its shuttered windows and one candle burning. Lazy Joe was one of many who'd gathered, at Flint's orders, and who now sat together, stinking and sweating in a malodorous group, gulping and jumping at the gunfire outside, and feeling for their weapons.

Lazy Joe was given a chair at the table, with its solitary light, where Joe Flint sat with Billy Bones, Black Dog, and Jimmy Chester himself. A pewter mug of drink was shoved across the table and the wild man swallowed half and wiped his lips.

"They've fought 'emselves out, Cap'n," he said.

"What do you mean?" said Flint.

"Our'ns and the Spanish'ns. They fought to equal parts."

"Yes – go on."

"They fired volleys, with drums and flags an' all, and killed a lot of each other, and when they'd had enough, then our'ns fell back on the fort, and their'ns fell back on the town. But our woodsmen are out making trouble in the dark!"

"So that's the firing?"

"Aye!"

"But neither side has the advantage?"

"No."

"Good!" said Flint. "Here –" he held out a silver dollar.

"Thank you right kindly, Cap'n, sir!"

"Now, join your fellows!" said Flint, and Lazy Joe got up. As soon as he'd gone, Flint turned to Jimmy Chester. "This is excellent!" he said.

"Is it?" said Chester, plainly terrified.

"Aye," said Billy Bones.

"Aye," said Black Dog, but . . .

349

B-b-b-bang! went a whole volley of musketry outside.

"Uhhhhhh!" cried the malodorous ensemble, jumping to their feet.

"SIT DOWN!" roared Flint. "Or you'll bring them in among us!"

Silence. The room sat down.

"Good!" said Flint, and went back to his whispering: "Jimmy, we've done well! There's hundreds of them out there: redcoats and whitecoats, bogged down, each side afraid to advance in the dark – leaving room for us to manoeuvre. And meanwhile the dull and the slow of Savannah have run to the fort!"

"Where *I* should've gone," wept Chester, wringing his hands.

"And lose your share of eight hundred thousand?" said Flint.

"Mhhhh . . ." said Chester, whimpering like a child. He clutched at Flint's sleeve. "I can't do this," he whispered. "I'm a merchant, not a pirate!" And he groaned so loud that the room began to groan in company.

"Bah!" said Flint, losing patience. "Mr Bones!"

"Cap'n?"

"Take this swab and lock him in his cellar. And if he squeaks you may silence him by any means you please!"

"Ohhhhh . . ." said Chester as Billy Bones loomed over him in the candlelight and, seizing him by the collar, dragged him away. "Ohhhhh . . ."

Then *clump* went Billy's fist and all was peaceful except for a limp slithering, and Billy Bones's puffing and blowing, which faded as he left the room.

Flint stood up to speak.

"Now my roaring boys!" he said, turning on his tremendous charm. "Who's for a share of the greatest treasure – in gold, dollars and diamonds – that ever was brought together in one place?"

"Ah!" they said, and the mood in the room went up like a rocket that burst in joy, and Flint had them in his hands from that instant, and he gave them their orders and divided them into teams, each to separate duties. "There *will* be fighting," he said, "but such merry fellows as yourselves think nought of that!" And they grinned back at him, dazzled by Flint and dazzled by treasure, in their broken-nosed, foetid, animal squalor.

Huh! thought Flint. *You'll fight, my little weevils . . . sufficient for the purpose!*

And soon, led by Flint, the whole crowd of them left the grog shop and made their way towards the river . . .

"How long have they been gone?" said Selena.

"Over an hour, by the sandglass," said Cowdray.

The two peered out into the dark of dark of the river, with all those left aboard *Walrus*, mustered under Mr Warrington, to guard the ship while her captain was away. The only light in the ship came from a few dim lanterns placed so that men shouldn't go arse-over-tit; for down here on the river bed Blind Pew was as good as any other man, it being so dark what with the river's deep banks blocking out the moon and stars, that a blind man's sharp ears were better than eyes.

"Lis-ten!" he cried. "Something's com-ing!" And he cocked his head to one side, and stood with his green eye-shade and his corpse face, and a boat cloak wrapped round him, who always felt the cold of the night, such that men shuddered at the weird figure that he made. But he was right.

"Aye!" cried Warrington. "Stand by, all hands!"

"Aye-aye!" they cried.

"A boat," said Selena.

"Where is it, Mr Pew?" said Cowdray.

"There –" said Pew, thrusting out a bony finger.

Everyone looked.

"Fine on the larboard bow," said Warrington.

Clunk-*clank!* Clunk-*clank!* came the distant sound of oars against pins.

Then they gasped as a light shone: a lantern waving in the dark, dimly revealing the outline of a man standing in the bows of an oncoming boat.

"*Walrus* ahoy!" cried a voice, and the oar-beat sounded louder.

"I know that voice," said Selena.

"*Walrus* ahoy!"

"Boat ahoy!" cried Warrington. "Who comes?"

"It's Billy Bones!" said Selena. "That's his voice!"

"Is that you, Mr Bones?" cried Warrington.

"Aye-aye! 'Tis William Bones, Cap'n, sir, aksing to come aboard."

Selena seized Warrington's arm, and shook it. "Where's Flint?" she said. "Billy Bones went off together with Flint!"

"He's Flint's man to death and beyond," said Cowdray.

"Aye," said the crew.

"Make ready, lads," said Warrington. "Be wary!"

Click-click-click-click! said the firelocks.

"Who's aboard, Mr Bones?"

"Myself, Black Dog, and the boatmen."

Clunk-*clank!* Clunk-*clank!* Clunk-*clank!*

"Where's Flint? Is he aboard?"

"Cap'n Flint, God bless him . . . is dead!"

All aboard *Walrus* gasped and stared down at Billy Bones, now plainly visible in the light of his lantern as the boat backed oars and came to rest under *Walrus*'s larboard quarter. They leaned over the side and looked down into the boat – a small one – that did indeed contain only Black Dog and a pair of oarsmen, apart from Billy Bones, who stood looking up, holding the lantern, with a mournful look on his face.

"What happened to Flint?" cried Selena. "Billy! What happened?"

"It were them Indians, ma'am," said Billy Bones. "In the forest."

"What Indians? What forest?" said Selena.

"Well, Miss Selena, ma'am, it were dreadful hard. It were shocking bad."

"What do you mean?"

"Well . . . ah . . . it were dreadful, ma'am . . ."

Billy Bones blathered. He dithered. He spouted nonsense. He ran out of words.

Cowdray spotted it first.

"It's a trick!" he cried. "This man is Flint's dog! He worship's Flint's shadow! If Flint were dead he'd have every detail in the front of his mind!"

"All hands take aim at that boat!" cried Warrington, and there was a surging forward and a great levelling of pistols, muskets and carbines over the larboard rail and the light shook in Billy Bones's hand. "Tell me plainly now, Mr Bones," said Warrington, "where is Flint?"

Billy Bones gulped and swallowed . . . and said nothing.

"I shall count to three," said Warrington, "before I fire . . ."

"Don't do that!" said Billy Bones. "Not that!"

"One . . ." said Warrington, and dozens of firelocks trembled as their owners began to squeeze the triggers, and Billy Bones looked up at certain death. "Two . . ." said Warrington.

"No! Don't . . . please don't . . . please . . ." said Billy Bones in a tiny trembling voice, as his sins rose before him and the Devil's breath fell hot upon his neck and Hell reached out for his soul.

"Last time, Billy Bones," said Warrington. "Where's Flint?"

"*Here, Mr Warrington!*" said a voice behind him – a voice that struggled to contain its fathomless mirth, its vicious glee, and its overpowering desire to laugh. "Fire!" it added, and a thunder of gunfire lit the night and deafened the ears, delivered point-blank by the dark body of men who'd pulled alongside *Walrus* with muffled oars, but on the *starboard* side, and swarmed over her starboard rail, while her people were busy elsewhere.

A dozen of *Walrus*'s crew went down in that single volley, then the half-breeds were screaming forward, Indian style, with hatchets and knives, driving *Walrus*'s people before them like sheep . . . at first . . .

Two Spanish officers stood at the intersection of four wide, earthy streets in the small quarter of Savannah that was theirs to occupy and hold. Some of the houses were on fire and cast a dull light. Smoke was everywhere and the two men were strung high with nerves at this fighting among houses from which an ambush might fall at any second. They jumped as gunfire came, not from the town, but from the direction of the river.

"What's that?" said Capitán Herrera.

"Firing, Señor Capitán!" said Teniente Lopez-Ortega.

"Yes, but *from the ships*?" said Herrera.

"From the ships?" repeated Lopez-Ortega, and they looked at each other, for the battle with the English had not gone well. Their company had suffered heavy losses . . . and the ships were their way out if things got worse. Which they soon would, for Herrera and Lopez-Ortega were standing in front of a dozen men, paraded in arms in case of emergencies, while the rest of the company tried to sleep, wrapped in their ammunition blankets, around pyramids of stacked muskets with the many wounded groaning and rolling in the mud.

Crack! A musket flashed orange in the dark from the corner of a nearby house, and a ball whizzed audibly – tangibly – between Herrera and Lopez-Ortega and killed a man behind them, who coughed and stumbled, struck fair in the middle of his chest.

"Stand to arms!" cried the sargentos, and the whole company were up on their feet, seizing their muskets and looking for targets, of which there were none. The two officers ran among them, followed by the sargentos, and together regained control of their men, who were nervous, exhausted . . . and on the point of breaking.

It was the same all across Savannah. The battle of volleys might have been a draw, but the woodsmen were wearing down the Spanish will to fight.

"This place is unsafe," said Capitán Herrera. "We must move the men at once to a better position!"

Flint's boat pulled steadily downriver through the black night, with himself at the tiller steering by compass and lantern, and Billy Bones alongside him, Black Dog pulling an oar beside the half-dozen surviving half-breeds, and an item of cargo in a sack in the bottom of the boat.

"We lost the ship, Cap'n," said Billy Bones miserably.

"It doesn't matter," said Flint.

"Hard bastards, them *Walruses*. They came back striking left and right!"

"Yes," said Flint cynically. "It makes you proud, doesn't it?"

"And they killed all the rest."

"*They* don't matter," said Flint softly, then raised his voice: "All the bigger shares for those that survive!" And the oarsmen grinned.

"But Silver weren't there!"

"Did you expect him to be?"

"Yes!"

"Oh, Billy! He'll have seen me up on the river bank."

"Yes?"

"So? Did you think he'd sit and wait for me to come?"

"Oh . . ."

"No, Billy-my-chicken –" Flint peered around in the dark "– he'll be out there somewhere, trying to get to Chester's house, which is where we're going now, to meet him!"

"Will he do that?"

"Yes! Now be silent."

Billy Bones sat still until the boat nosed up against the pier of Jimmy Chester's private landing where lights shone for Flint to find it again . . . Flint who was hugging himself in glee for what he'd done. Flint who relished and rolled in the success of it, and in the completeness of his victory, and he chuckled in the joy of it, for his mind was running down channels that were different and new . . . even for him.

Something had changed. He knew it! He recognised it! It wasn't just the treasure any more. No! Flint had looked into the caverns of his self and seen that . . . yes, he'd have the treasure, if he could, and certainly he wouldn't let any other man have it. But *that* wasn't what he really wanted. That wasn't what he ached and longed for. That wasn't what brought the froth to his lips and the white around his eyes when he feared it was in danger. And it certainly wasn't what he'd gone after on this night's expedition.

Meanwhile Billy Bones reached down for the cargo, in its big sack, and heaved it up over his shoulder with a gasp and a grunt, like a load of coals.

"*Take care!*" shrieked Flint. "*Take care, you . . .*"

And Billy Bones gaped as a venomous eruption of filth poured forth from Flint, who never cussed and never swore, and never blasphemed, leaving Billy Bones standing with the sack over his shoulder and its contents wriggling, and himself trembling in the face of Flint's deranged wrath.

"Don't bump her!" said Flint. "Don't knock her! And don't ever, ever hurt her . . . *or I'll dig out your eyes and make you eat 'em raw!*"

Chapter 41

Night, 20th July 1754
The Savannah River

"Spaniards!" said Israel Hands.

"Bugger!" said Silver, and signalled for all hands to take cover and lie low. They were hiding in the old cattle pens: lines of wooden hurdles where Charley Neal had kept his beef, which had lain empty since his departure, for Jimmy Chester bought from the butcher.

"Bugger!" said Silver again, but under his breath. They were so close! One long side of Jimmy Chester's grog shop was right across the street, a big whitewashed wall with a line of windows, now tight-shuttered. And now here came a company of Spanish infantry stumbling along in the night, boots crunching, equipment clattering but only dimly seen. They were following the line of the wall, muskets aimed in all directions, nervous, staggering, struggling to keep their dressing in the dark, and a trail of wounded hobbling along in the rear. They twitched every time a musket fired somewhere in the unquiet night.

"Cap'n?" whispered Mr Joe.

"What?" said Silver.

"They're frit, Cap'n! Mortal feared!"

"Aye! Look at 'em!"

"They'd run if we give 'em a volley . . ."

"*No!* T'ain't our fight. Let 'em go by!"

Then a voice bawled out an order in Spanish, and the soldiers halted and stood gasping and panting. Then two more Spanish voices, different voices, arguing and protesting.

"What do they say, Cap'n?" whispered Mr Joe.

"One's saying they should go inside," said Silver, "for to take cover, 'cos it's a fine big house with thick walls. The other one says they'd be trapped in it . . ."

"If they go in there, we'll never find Flint," said Mr Joe. "What we gonna do?"

Silver groaned. Mr Joe was right. Chester's house was at the back end of the grog shop, built on to it . . .

Flint untied the lashings and pulled Selena to her feet, the sack now cast aside. Billy Bones looked on in dread as he saw the blood on the skin of her wrists.

"Bastard!" said Flint, thrusting the slim arms at Billy's face. "You tied that! I said to be *gentle!*" And he swung his hand, lightning fast, too fast even for the pugilist Billy Bones to duck, and caught him a full-blooded slap across the cheek. Billy staggered back, stinging and gulping. He'd taken oceans of abuse from his master over the years, but never . . . *ever* . . . before had Flint physically struck him, and Billy Bones was shocked to the marrow: more shocked by the act itself than by the pain.

And it wasn't only Billy Bones that gulped. So did Black Dog and the six Savannian half-breeds standing in Jimmy Chester's parlour with candles lit and Flint glaring at Billy Bones like a medusa, and an exceedingly beautiful woman hanging exhausted in Flint's arms, her mouth still bound with a gag, and herself half out of her taffeta gown. The half-breeds shivered at that. But they avoided Flint's eye, for none dared to be within it.

"I only did me best, Cap'n," said Billy Bones. "She was struggling!"

"Bah!" said Flint, and untied the gag. "Selena!" he said and forcibly, irresistibly kissed her full on the lips, a kiss of absolute, entire and abandoned passion, while she resisted to the limit of her strength, clawing and kicking and pulling away as he pawed at her, and slobbered and drooled.

Billy Bones shuddered and so did Black Dog, so – even – did the half-breeds. For this wasn't right. It was embarrassing. It was unmanly. It wasn't a thing that other men wanted to see. It was a man making the most complete fool of himself, because as well as forcing himself upon her, Flint was pleading, and groaning and sobbing with love, and begging her to love him in return.

"My love, my lovely, my darling, my own . . ."

"No," she cried, and spat full in his face.

"Cap'n," said Billy Bones, ashamed to the depths of his heart, "don't!"

But Flint didn't even hear. And neither did Billy Bones hear what was marching past the grog shop and the house. But the half-breeds did. They snuffed the lights, ran to a shuttered window and peeped through the cracks.

"Mr Bones!" said one of them. "Spaniards!"

"Oh!" said Billy Bones, finally registering the heavy tramp of feet.

"Come and see!" said one of the half-breeds.

Billy Bones stumbled forward in the dark, and peered out. The street was full of grey coats and twinkling bayonets, and behind him – when every sane man would have kept silent – Flint and Selena were pouring words into each other's faces.

"Oh Christ!" said Billy Bones, and fumbled his way back across the room.

Then a bit of moonlight shone out from the sky and into the dark room . . . and there was Flint, on his knees, hanging on to Selena's half-naked body, and him begging and pleading, now completely deranged.

"Cap'n!" said Billy Bones. "Clap a hitch!"

And then two tempers snapped entirely. She tore his hair and clawed at his eyes in desperate strength, and he sprang up, and caught her and threw her into Billy Bones's arms with final, abandoned and utter contempt. Confronted, in hideous, actual reality, with the hellish rejection he'd dreamed of while swinging on the rope, Flint was more wounded than he could bear.

"So!" he snarled. "So! It's come to this! Shall I tell you what I'm going to do to you? Shall I? SHALL I?" He glared at Billy Bones. "You hold her there, you useless piece of shit, you hold her there while I fetch some tools from Jimmy's kitchen, for I'm going to –"

And Billy Bones groaned at the horrors Flint's mind poured out. Such horrors of mutilation and debasement that shrivelled his spirit. Billy Bones felt the warmth of the girl, and remembered another girl, long ago, who'd felt like this, and an enormous rage arose inside of him, and he put her safe behind himself, and looked Flint full in the eye . . . And Billy Bones found his conscience and stood up straight, and turned on his beloved master.

"No!" he said firmly. "I shan't, and I won't!"

"What?" said Flint, blinking and trembling in his own rage. "Give her here!" he demanded.

"No!" cried Billy Bones, and raised his massive fists and leapt forward with all his strength, with all his might, and with all his will. He went for Flint with animal ferocity, to beat out his life and tear him apart.

And Selena screamed and screamed and screamed.

"What's that?" said Capitán Herrera, and broke off arguing with his Teniente.

"A woman screaming – in the house!" said Lopez-Ortega.

"Huh!" said Herrera, and waved aside whatever that might mean. He had more pressing worries. He looked at the trail of disordered men who followed him and now stood uneasily, fearing yet another shot out of the dark. "We shall go inside and take protection," he said. "That is my final word. Order the door to be broken in!"

"What's that?" said Silver, crouched in the cattle pen.

"Selena!" said Mr Joe, and jumped up.

"Get down!" cried Silver, hauling him back behind the hurdle.

"But it's her! She's screaming! In the big house! What's she doing there?"

"Flint!" said Silver. "It's him! He's got her! The swab's gone behind our backs!" He stood up, got his crutch under his arm, and cocked and levelled. "Come on, shipmates," he cried. "With me!" And he let rip with a flash and a roar into the white-clad mass feeling its way along the wall of the grog house.

"*Walrus*!" the crew cried, and fired off a thundering, rolling volley, for each man bore two pairs of pistols, and a blunderbuss too, for the ship's entire store of these latter and formidable weapons was present, and what with each one being loaded with a handful of balls, and the pistols firing besides, there was more flying lead in the air than an entire infantry company could have delivered, at less than thirty-foot range, splitting the night with fire, filling the street with smoke and falling upon the wretched Spaniards like the wrath of God – instantly followed by the wrath of the Devil, as Silver cleared the hurdle, and hopped forward.

"Come on, lads!" he cried, and he led his dozen men whooping, leaping, howling and bellowing, and laying on with sharp steel, such that the whole Spanish mass broke and sundered, convinced that a regiment at least had fallen upon them in the dark. And so they ran, knocking down and trampling over Capitán Herrera, Teniente Lopez-Ortega and all others who tried to stop them.

"With me!" cried Silver, scrambling over the dead, and

hurrying round to the front of the grog shop. "Here's the door!" he cried. "*Axes*, boys!" And he stood back as Tom Morgan and Darby McGraw, who'd been given this task for their muscles, ran up and smashed at the barred door, with the two biggest axes from *Walrus*'s carpenter's tool chest.

Crunch! Smash! In went the door and Silver was first into the black of the grog shop, with its lines of tables, and sanded floor.

"Dark lantern!" cried Silver, and the hot, smouldering tin-cylinder was handed forward for Silver to open the shutter and throw out a thin, yellow light. "All hands re-charge fire-locks, and then follow me!" he cried, and there was a great biting of cartridges and plying of rammers, then a *Huzzah!* as they followed John Silver blundering through the room towards the door at the back that led to the main house, and all hands falling over chairs in the dark and getting up again and bellowing and yelling and doors hacked down and corri-dors run, and the wrong way taken, and then made right, and charging into a pretty little moonlit courtyard with sweet flowers and soft scent, between the grog shop and the house proper, and another door smashed in . . . and into Jimmy Chester's parlour with the moonlight now strong through an opened window –

"Flint!" cried Silver.

"John!" cried Selena, and rushed towards him, to be swiftly embraced then pushed out of harm's way into his wake.

"Silver!" said Flint, standing over the bloodstained form of Billy Bones, who lay on his back with feebly moving hands and staring eyes . . . waiting for Flint to smash out his brains with a heavy candlestick.

"Avast!" cried Silver. "Don't move an eyelash, you poxy sod, or I'll shoot you dead!"

"Kill him!" said Flint, turning to the half-breeds, who raised their guns and fired. Darby McGraw fell, and then Flint's half-breeds went down under a tremendous hail of shot from

Silver's men, while Black Dog – who remembered who'd offered him a pistol instead of rest, and who'd heard what Flint planned to do with Selena – ran forward and knelt at Silver's feet and clutched the tail of his coat.

"I'm with you, Cap'n Silver!" he cried. "Don't shoot poor Black Dog!"

"Traitor!" gasped Flint, and stood with his chest heaving: sweat-soaked and exhausted from the fight against Billy Bones. But he recognised the still-twitching body that lay beside Black Dog. "And is that Mr McGraw there beside you, John? The celebrated drunkard?" He sneered and mocked. "Bring aft the rum, Darby McGraw!"

"Shut your trap," said Silver, glaring in venomous hatred, his pistol levelled square at Flint.

"Are you safe, lass?" he said over his shoulder.

"Yes!" she said, as Silver hopped close to Flint with the pistol outstretched.

"But did he touch you? Did he lay hands on you?"

"No." She stepped forward and pointed at Billy Bones. "He saved me – Mr Bones saved me."

"Did he, though?" said Silver, amazed. "More o' that later, my lass." And he fumbled in a pocket and reached out a small package tied up in oilskin. "Here's my half, Joe Flint," he said, and threw it on to a table. "So where's yours?" Flint blinked and gaped, and breathed deep.

"Well?" said Silver.

"Here," said Flint at last, and he took the silver porte-crayon from his pocket, and laid it beside Silver's little package.

Then Flint and Silver looked at one another . . . they who'd been the dearest of friends, then the foulest of enemies, and then friends for a while . . . and now this, and each looked at the woman that each, in such different ways, loved more than life or wealth, or the world entire.

"There's only one of us can walk away from this," said Silver.

"Yes," said Flint. "It's time the matter was settled."

"Aye," said Silver. For nothing stood between them now. Whatever it was that had always stopped them coming to blows . . . it was washed away, and swept away, and gone forever.

"Then shall you shoot me down, John? You that believes himself to be a gentleman o' fortune?"

The pistol quivered . . . and then came down. Silver put it and its partners on the table beside the package and the porte-crayon.

"No," said Silver. "We'll settle this, man to man!"

"No!" cried Selena.

"No!" cried Mr Joe.

"No . . ." said even Billy Bones in a slurred voice, battered and bloodied as he was. "Shoot him down, Cap'n Silver, shoot him like a dog!"

"Avast!" yelled Silver, and glared at them all. "Listen here, and listen good!" He looked at Flint. "He's mine, the evil sod! He's all mine, and don't none of you lift a finger to him!" There was uproar in the room, but Silver ignored it, as did Flint.

"Huh!" said Flint, and blinked, and wiped the sweat from his eyes. And then he stood tall, and bowed like a courtier and smiled Flint's smile. For he'd got a bit of his breath back, and saw only a one-legged man in front of him. "Shall it be swords or pistols then?"

"I'll see the liver of you, you bastard!" said Silver.

"Does that mean swords?"

"It does, God damn you," said Silver. "One o' you swabs give him a blade!" and he threw off his hat and baldrick and coat, and rolled up his sleeves, and drew his cutlass from its sheath and tried the blade on empty air, balancing neatly on his one leg and crutch. He was a fine, big man who towered over all present, and there were few that would choose to fight him. But still . . . he hopped on one leg while Flint danced nimbly on two, and all who cared for John Silver begged and implored him not to fight, and Selena hung on his arm shouting loudest of all.

But Flint, oblivious, breathed deep, calmed his thundering heart, and stood up in shirtsleeves, with Tom Morgan's cutlass in his hand, and bowed to Silver like a French fencing master, and saluted with the heavy blade.

"Bollocks to that, Joe Flint," said Silver, and "*Argh!*" he cried, and swung a blow at Flint that would have split him to the breastbone had it landed, which it didn't because Flint was elsewhere and slashing at Silver's one leg, which blow Silver blocked with a grinding of steel and a shower of sparks in the moonlit room, and Flint leapt back, surprised at his own slowness, for he was still tired from fighting Billy Bones.

Then clash-scrape-clang, the blades met in the air, to left and to right, and Silver laid on with incredible speed for a crippled man, and Flint slid back in the face of his attack, but tired as he was, still he met Silver's blade at every stroke. Then:

"*Ah!*" cried the room, as Silver swung the oaken length of his crutch and caught Flint a cracking blow on the knee that sent him hopping out of range with Silver following but slipping from going too fast. He nearly measured his length but, clang-bang, saved his throat from Flint's slash with a swift recovery in the uttermost split second before the death-stroke fell.

And then it was hammer and tongs, thunder and lightning, blood and sweat and a fight that leapt, barged and rolled around the room, more nearly equal than any man could have dreamed between two such opponents, except that Silver was losing the flush of his strength, while Flint, by hanging back just a little, and relying on the uncanny reactions that God – on a very bad day – had given him, was recovering. And the more John Silver faded, the more Flint rejoiced.

Because Flint knew that he must win.
And John Silver knew it too.
And so did every creature in the room.

Chapter 42

Night, 20th July 1754
Jimmy Chester's house
Savannah, Georgia

*S*ilver slipped and skidded. He was barely upright and the notched, dinted cutlass was heavy in his tired hand. He took a grip of his crutch. The sweat was blinding his eyes, and Flint was grinning. He was pointing his blade at Silver's face, poised and ready to strike.

"Where shall it be, John?" he said. "Shall we take off an ear or two? Or a piece of nose?" Then he laughed. "Or shall we put out your eyes?"

"Cap'n!" cried Mr Joe, leaping forward with his cane cutlass.

"No! No! *No!*" cried Silver, and he beat the floor with the oak of his crutch. "None but me, say I!"

"But he'll kill you, Cap'n!"

"Aye!" said the men at his side, bristling with arms.

"Stand back, by God!" said Silver. "*None but me!*" And he surged forward again, and Flint laughed, and stepped aside from Silver's charge, all slippery smooth and easy, and struck a blow that sent Silver's cutlass spinning and ringing from his fingers, and Flint laughed, and laughed and laughed ... and then blinked ... and his face froze into hatred, and Silver looked at death, and raised a feeble hand against it, and

Flint's eyes went white, and Flint took a grip of his blade, and drew back to strike . . .

Boom! A heavy pistol thundered loud in the room, spitting fire and smoke and glowing fragments of cartridge paper . . . *that* and a lead ball that smashed into Flint like a horse-kick, and sank him to his knees, and then full-length, face-down on the floor, with Tom Morgan's cutlass still firm in his hand, and such a look of hatred on his face as froze the souls of those who saw it.

Silver gasped. He turned to see who'd fired. Mr Joe turned. They all did. They saw Selena, in swirling powder smoke, with one of Silver's own pistols held out in two slim hands. Her arms trembled at the weight of it, and she let it fall, to clatter and bump on the floor.

Silver looked at her, and looked at Flint's body, and drew a great breath, and had the sense to be honest, and grateful, and not a hypocrite blinded by pride.

"God bless you, my lass," he said. "He'd have slit an' gutted me!"

"John," she said, and her limbs shook in the dread of what she'd done, and Silver took her in his arms, and closed his eyes, and gasped and trembled.

No one spoke but Billy Bones.

"Cap'n!" he moaned, and hauled himself up on to unsteady legs, his face disfigured and raw. And he stumbled across to Flint, and knelt beside him. "Cap'n," he said again, and he raised Flint's limp hand and kissed it, and the tears flowed in rivers down Billy Bones's dirty cheeks.

"We got to be gone from here," said Mr Joe. "Too much noise!"

"Aye!" said Silver, and he wiped the sweat from his eyes and looked at the package and the porte-crayon on the little table. "But I'll bring them!" And he picked them up.

"No," said Selena, pushing herself away from Silver.

"What?" he said.

"No! I'll have none of it. And neither shall you!"

"What?"

"John! D'you want it to be as it was . . . between us?"

"Aye!" he said, from a full heart.

"Then listen to me! There's much that's gone wrong. We've quarrelled. We've lost trust. You've lied!" Silver bowed his head. "And you brought me away from London . . ." she looked down at Flint ". . . you and him together, *for you're part of each other!*"

"Never!"

"You are!" she cried. "You stole me like sack of goods! Both of you!"

"Not I, by thunder!"

"Yes, *you!* For you're as bad as him!"

"Cap'n!" said Mr Joe. "There's men in the street!"

"So what do you want, girl?"

"No! What do *you* want? Because if you want me –"

"Which I do!"

"It's Spaniards, Cap'n," said Mr Joe. "White-coats – them what we drove off!"

"Then here's my offer, John Silver," she said. "I'll go with you wherever you go, and I'll be your wife, *if* –"

Gunshots sounded from outside. There were voices and shouting.

"Cap'n," said Mr Joe, "they're coming back – *driven* back! We'd best be gone!"

But Silver wasn't listening.

"– *if* you give up this trade . . . and Flint's treasure!"

There came a rumble of feet and shouting in Spanish.

"They're in the house!" said Mr Joe. "Spaniards, with redcoats after 'em!"

"Redcoats?" said Israel Hands. "But they're hiding in the fort!"

"Not now, they ain't!" said Mr Joe, and muskets roared and a drum rolled. "It's a battle! We got to go!"

Then some fool, carried away with excitement, fired from within the room, followed by a ringing volley from outside and bullets thumping into the ceiling through the window, and men running to get out of the room and away.

But all Silver could see was her face. As Flint had done, he looked into his heart and saw what was important and what was not.

"Come on!" cried Mr Joe, beckoning furiously. For, other than Silver and Selena, the rest had gone, save only himself, Tom Morgan, and Billy Bones – who remained bent over Flint's body.

"The treasure!" said Silver at last, and he drew the porte crayon and the package from his pocket.

"Cap'n! Cap'n!" said Mr Joe, pulling Silver by main force towards the door, while muskets roared from the grog shop, and Billy Bones grovelled on his knees, sobbing in his grief, gently turning Flint over and stroking his cheek, and laying his arms across his chest. Then as Tom Morgan ran for the door, Billy Bones reached out and grabbed him.

"Gerroff you swab!" cried Tom Morgan. But Billy Bones gripped like a gorilla.

"Have you got two coins, mate?" said Billy Bones. "For to close the cap'n's eyes?"

Morgan struggled to be free, but looked down and shuddered at the sight of Flint's open eyes glaring up at the ceiling.

"Here!" said Morgan, finding a pair of English pennies.

"Thank'ee, messmate!" said Billy Bones, and crouched over Flint's body, laying the coins on his eyes, before clutching his own massive fists together in prayer. Morgan gaped, then ran. And Silver shook off Mr Joe's arm, who cursed and ran after Morgan, and then, with his crew gone, and Billy Bones blinded with grief, and none to see but Selena . . . Silver made his decision.

"Bad luck to it, say I," said Silver, in cruel remembrance, "for I was an honest man once, that never told lies, nor shot young lads, nor mad Scotchmen neither, nor betrayed my own kind to the enemy!" And he threw the precious papers to the floor. "Be gone!" he said, and put an arm around Selena, and made best speed after Mr Joe, into a dark room where men milled around in ignorance, not knowing where to turn.

"This way!" said Silver. "I knows this house. It's *this* way, then out the window in Jimmy's counting house. There's few buildings on that side, and then it's the woods."

"Aye!" they all said.

And soon the house was empty, for Silver and his men vanished into the dark, and the battle went in favour of the Savannians, who fought the Spanish, butt and bayonet, and drove them out of the grog shop and chased them down the street . . . leaving Billy Bones alone inside.

He sat all night next to Flint. He said whatever prayers he remembered, which wasn't many. He wallowed in melancholy, thinking of the wretched life that he'd led. He thought of Livvy Rose. He shed more tears.

At dawn, he sniffed and got up, and stretched his cramped limbs, and blew his nose mightily on his handkerchief. Then, thinking at last of himself, he searched the house and found a considerable sum of money, which he took.

Finally he went back to say goodbye, and felt the crackle of paper in Flint's coat when he picked it up to cover the body. There was something sewn into the lining. He opened his clasp knife. He slit the silk. He found a map.

Huh! thought Billy Bones. *That bugger ain't no good. Not without . . .*

And then his heart began to pound. For there, right next to Flint's left foot, was the oilskin package and the portecrayon, nestled together like old pals. Billy Bones was amazed that he'd not noticed them before.

Chapter 43

Dawn, 21st July 1754
Aboard Walrus
The Savannah River

"Looks like the Savannians have won!" said Silver, studying the anchorage through his glass from *Walrus*'s quarterdeck.

"Yes," said Selena, "British colours flying from every vessel afloat, including *La Concha*, and redcoats on board of her, and no more fighting!" She had her own telescope. "The Savannians were lucky."

"We were lucky too!" said Silver, and he looked at the hands on the maindeck, still exhausted and raw from heaving the ship from one dolphin to the next all night. "We got clear o' that battery, and now the wind's come round in our favour and we can 'vast hauling and be gone!"

"But the crew is split," she said.

Silver shrugged. "Why should you worry?"

"Because you're lying to them, John!"

"What else can I do?" Silver sighed.

All hands knew that Flint's papers were lost and Flint's treasure with them. He told them it'd happened in the heat of the moment and shared out the remaining store of McLonarch's coin as compensation. With that small store of wealth, some of the hands found that they wanted no more fighting, and thought they'd try honest seafaring in Savannah, where no questions were asked. These stood ready to go over the side, with John Silver's blessing, and into the waiting launch. Others though, had laughed and said they could always beat up and down and find new prizes, especially with a fine new war coming on, and Long John for their captain! So he'd laughed along with them, and slapped their shoulders and promised to lead them to new riches.

Of those who were leaving, most were hands before the mast. But two were not. Dr Cowdray and Mr Joe were standing alongside in their best shore-going clothes, with their trugs packed – which in Dr Cowdray's case included a great bundle of books and several boxes of instruments.

"Are you set on this, Doctor?" said Silver.

"Yes, Captain," said Cowdray. "I had plenty of time to think, when I was secured below, in irons!" He sighed and hung his head. "And I am ashamed that I was struck down, a useless wretch, when Flint came to steal your lady." He looked at Selena with hopeless feelings that he knew could never be returned. Then he smiled a little. "You know, I found myself happy when we sailed under articles, even if they were false, because I wanted to believe in them, but . . ." he looked Silver in the eye ". . . Captain, I know that I was wrong to serve Flint, and I know I was a *better* man when I served you, but I can't live this life any more."

Silver sighed, and shook Cowdray's hand.

"Thank you for this!" he said, looking down at his lost limb.

"You are not a bad man, Captain," said Cowdray.

"Nor a good one, neither!" said Silver, and grinned.

"Good bye, Doctor," said Selena, and she kissed him. Cowdray blushed.

"A-ha!" said Silver, Israel Hands, and Mr Warrington, looking on.

"A-ha!" said the crew, and nudged each other.

"Goodbye, ma'am," said Cowdray.

Now Silver turned to Mr Joe: the clever, talented lad who'd come to them as an illiterate runaway with a violent temper and a cane-cutlass, and was now the ship's best navigating officer.

"And you, Mr Joe?" said Silver. "Shall you leave us, as well?"

"Aye, Cap'n," said Mr Joe. "An' the lady knows why!"

"Oh?" said Silver, and frowned. "Him, too?"

But Selena shook her head.

"It's not me, John." She looked at Mr Joe. "It's him. He doesn't like slavery."

"That I don't," said Mr Joe.

Silver shook his head. "It's a trade, my son!" he said. "A trade, just like any other!"

"Aye!" said Israel Hands and Mr Warrington.

"Aye!" said all the rest, even the blacks among them.

"No!" said Mr Joe. "We are all God's children. From Adam and Eve onward!"

"Hmm," said Silver. "So what're you going to do, Mr Joe?"

"Stop it. Fight it!"

"Shall you, though?"

"That I shall!"

Silver shrugged. "Then good luck to you, lad, for I wish you'd stay among us, I truly do!"

"Aye!" they all said.

"Thank you, Cap'n . . . And there's a thing I'd ask for to take with me."

"What's that?" said Silver warily.

"A name, Cap'n. Something better than 'Mr Joe'!"

"Is that all?" said Silver. "Why, take mine and be Joe Silver!"

"No," said Mr Joe solemnly. "I'm asking Mr Hands for *his* name. He who taught me my letters and my numbers, and raised me up." He turned to Israel Hands and took off his hat. "Mr Gunner . . . may I be Joe *Hands*?"

Israel Hands gulped and swallowed. He blinked and wiped his eyes. Then he threw his arms around the serious, earnest lad of whom he was more fond than he knew.

"My beautiful boy! My lovely lad!" he said. "Take my name and leave me proud! And if never again I see you on Earth, please God I should see you in Heaven."

So the boat was manned and pulled for the shore, and all those whose will it was to stay aboard stood silent and watched it go.

When it returned, with just two men pulling, they hoisted it aboard, made all shipshape, and set sail in the freshening wind. Within hours they were past the new batteries at the river mouth, which they saluted and were allowed to pass, for they sailed under British colours, and no man had reason to doubt them.

By nightfall, the mouth of the Savannah River was under the horizon, and *Walrus* was free and the whole world before her. Her people were happy, Mr Warrington was no more than decently drunk and well capable of setting course for Upper Barbados, where Captain Silver planned – so he said – to raise a new crew, new luck, and new riches.

"You're a skilful liar, John," said Selena as they stood together at the taffrail, with the ship heeling sweetly under sail. "Just don't ever lie to *me* again."

"I told you, my lass," he said, "once we drop anchor in Upper Barbados, then you and I can hop ship, and these lads can find themselves a new captain!"

"Why Upper Barbados?"

"Because that's where Charley Neal sent my earnings, in the old days."

"How much?" she said, and he winked and tickled her ribs so she laughed.

"Ah! You ain't so lily-white pure yourself, when it comes to money."

"But how much?"

"Enough to keep you and me cosy for life!"

"Doing what?"

"Running a business in England, the which I shall buy."

"An honest business?"

"Oh yes. No more gentleman o' fortune! Maybe a tavern? Maybe in Bristol? And how about 'The Spyglass' for a name?"

"Why that name?"

"So's we'll always be on the search . . . for opportunity!"

And John Silver put his arms around her, and kissed her, and for the moment was at peace, and the great green bird on his shoulder nibbled the ears of man and wife together, and chuckled in contentment.

Chapter 44

Morning, 21st July 1754
Chester's Grog Shop
Savannah
The Royal Colony of Georgia

"*T*his is Doctor Cowdray!" cried Jimmy Chester. "He's John Silver's surgeon, and was Flint's before, and has Latin and Greek and all the tools of his trade, and is qualified at all the universities of England!"

"No," said Cowdray, protesting, "I am self-taught . . . *Ex uno disce omnes* . . . I learn from each case. My teacher was practice, not scholarship."

But nobody listened, for cries and groans arose from the horrors of the grog shop, which being the biggest public building in the town, and lavishly furnished with tables . . . was now its hospital, where five whores, three washerwomen, a man-midwife and the fort's horse-doctor were trying to attend nearly three hundred wounded men, some already dead in their bandages, others bawling loudly, still others shivering in pain, and the stink, noise and squalor beyond all contemplation.

"Did you know, Flint locked me up!" said Chester to Cowdray.

"He did!" said the clump of Savannian assemblymen at their president's heel.

Cowdray looked at them, and the way they held their noses, and tried not to see the horrors all around, but glanced constantly at the door and the sweet outside.

"And we set him free!" they said, praying to be free themselves.

"And I was summoned when your boat arrived," said Chester.

"Thank God, you are here!" said the assemblymen.

"Doctor!" said a fat, sweating washerwoman in blood-drenched clothes.

"Our men won the fight, but at huge cost!" said the assemblymen.

"We brought them all here!" said Chester, waving a hand at the rows of wounded.

"There's a boy here won't be stopped from bleeding," said the washerwoman.

"Spanish and English together!" said Chester. "For we are Christians!"

"There's another one here," said the man-midwife.

"Should we heat irons, Doctor?" said the washerwoman. "Is that the best way?"

"Can we leave you now . . .?" said Chester, backing towards the door.

". . . to take command?" said the assemblymen, and fled.

"Doctor!" said a dozen voices, and horrific creatures advanced towards Cowdray: soiled, exhausted and slimy with blood. They looked like ghouls and monsters, but were those few noble, shining souls among thousands – and themselves some of the least in the city – who were doing their best, beyond duty, beyond praise, to save the hundreds of men slowly dying before their eyes.

But . . . *adveho hora, adveho vir . . .* come the hour, come the man, and Doctor Cowdray did what he'd done for twenty years. He sent for soap and hot water. He sent for braziers, charcoal and irons, which would indeed be needed. He cleared a table, laid out his instruments, went round the room . . . and divided the wounded into three groups: first, those who would surely die and who – in desperate extremity – must be set aside; second, those who would surely live, who were set aside for the present, and third, those whose lives could be saved only by treatment, and who were brought first to his table.

Thus it was many hours before Doctor Cowdray could rest, and he sank down trembling with exhaustion but deeply at peace within himself in the sure and certain knowledge that his skills had saved the lives of many men.

Barely had he sat down, when the fat washerwoman came up and bobbed him a curtsey, for all present now stood in awe of Doctor Cowdray.

"Doctor?" she said. "I sees you're done in, and done for . . . but we just found one poor sod – beggin' yer honour's pardon – what we was putting among the dead but what's still breathing."

"Oh . . ." sighed Cowdray, and tried to stand. He was sunk in weariness. He was so weak they had to help him to his feet.

"God bless you, Doctor!" they said, in their respect and admiration.

"Yes, yes," he said, "I'll come . . ."

"No need, your honour," said the washerwoman. "We brung him in a blanket."

Cowdray forced his legs to carry him to the table. He called for hot water and soap. He peered at this last patient: the one that wasn't dead after all. He couldn't see clearly. He was so tired he'd forgotten his spectacles. He found them. He put them on. But the lenses were smeared.

He rubbed them on a clean patch of shirt.

He placed aching hands on the patient's chest.

He gathered strength.

He blinked.

He looked at the face.

"*Auribus lupum teneo!*" he cried, and fell back in horror.

The Beginning

Morning, 11th October 1754
The Royal George Inn
Polmouth, England

*T*he usual collection of children, old wives and beggars was waiting to see the Bristol Lightning come in. But it was late. The church clock had already struck eleven, and no coach had yet come pounding up the road, which was therefore occupied only by plodding farm wagons, a drove of geese and a good number of respectable persons who gazed into the windows of the shops along Prince Rupert Street, which pronounced itself the most genteel emporium this side of London, and far superior to anything in Bristol – Polmouth's great rival for supremacy of the West.

"Ah!" said a lively beggar, nudging his mates, hitching up his "crippled" leg, and making ready to ply his trade. "Here it comes! Watch out, you little 'uns!" And all present cleared the way as a thunder of hoofs, a roaring of wheels, and the Crack! Crack! Crack! of the whip came from round the corner where Prince Rupert Street met the Bristol Road . . . and every eye turned . . . and the sound grew louder . . . then all cheered as the mighty vehicle burst in splendour into four-horse, four-wheeled, galloping sight, with the driver – high on his perch

– laying on furiously to make up time, and to ensure that the expensive passengers in their expensive seats got value for money by arriving – if not bang on time – at least in all the glitter and dash of a crack stage-coach only eight miles from the last change, and the beasts full of fury, and striking sparks off the cobbles with their iron shoes.

"Go-on!" cried the driver.

"Huzzah!" cried the street.

"Pity a poor soldier!" cried the beggar.

"An' his fambly!" cried the urchins.

"Ruined at Fontenoy in King-George-Gawblessim's-service!"

But all were ignored as the coach ground to a halt, its multi-layer paintwork half-covered in mud, the horses snorting and steaming in the cold air, the driver throwing off the blanket that covered his knees, shifting his feet in the box of straw that kept some warmth in, and turning back to the guard who sat behind him.

"Heave the mail, Jimmy, boy!"

"Right y'are, Davey!"

And the guard threw down the sealed canvas bag of letters, into the arms of Mr Kemp, proprietor of the Royal George, who'd stepped out the instant the coach arrived, backed by maids and ostlers of his staff. There was no official mail service, but the Polmouth and Western Staging Company, who owned the Lightning, carried letters to make an extra profit.

Then all parties set to. The ostlers took off the horses and put on a fresh team. The maids opened the coach doors, threw down the step, and bobbed and curtsied as five passengers got out, stumbling on cramped limbs. Most were desperate for the privy and ran straight into the house, to make haste before the coach was on the road again.

But one had arrived at his destination. He had no further to go. He stood waiting while his box was handed down. It was heavy, and he gave a hand so it didn't get dropped. It was a seaman's chest, much like any other, except that the initial "B" had been burned on the top of it with a hot iron, and the corners were somewhat smashed and broken as by long, rough usage.

"Handsomely, there!" he cried, in a voice accustomed to command. "Hand her down gentle!"

He was a tall, strong, heavy, nut-brown man with a tarry pigtail falling over the shoulders of his soiled blue coat. His hands were ragged and scarred, with black, broken nails; and the scar of an old sword-cut gleamed livid white on his cheek. He was a formidable man, but was melancholy and silent. He'd not spoken a word to anyone in all the ten, long hours from Bristol. He'd just dozed, and dreamed and muttered to himself, occasionally disturbing his fellow passengers by the foul oaths and dreadful things he said in his sleep. But none dared wake him or complain.

He was still standing outside the inn when the passengers scrambled aboard and the coach pulled out again. He ignored every one and every thing, except that, in an odd moment – perhaps thinking of better days – he astonished all the world as he turned to the beggar who clutched at his sleeve, whining and pleading . . . and gave him a silver dollar.

"Gedoutovit!" said the landlord of the Royal George, putting a swift boot up the beggar's breech. "You didn't oughter mind him, sir," he said. "Nearest *he* got to the Battle o' Fontenoy was a gin-shop of that name, down the road there!"

"What?" said the big man, whose mind was far away.

"Would you be lookin' for a room, sir? Clean sheets, good fire, good food?"

"D'you get much company?"

"God save you, sir, *yes!*" the landlord smiled. "Never been busier, sir!"

"Then it'll not do for me!"

382

"Oh."

"I wants somewhere quiet. Nearby and clean, but quiet. Here –"

"Oh!" said the landlord, and gazed at the incredible sight of a golden guinea.

Some hours later, the big man got down from the two-wheeled cart behind a miserable old horse that had brought him from Polmouth on the wind-blown cliff road that looked down over red, sandy beaches. Together, he and the carter heaved the chest into a handbarrow brought on purpose, since the final hundred yards wouldn't take wheeled traffic of any size.

And so, Billy Bones came plodding up to the door of the Admiral Benbow Inn, with his sea-chest following behind, and the inn's sign creaking over his head. It was so peaceful that his sombre mood lifted, and he gazed down at Black Hill Cove, which the inn overlooked, and he whistled and sang to himself . . .

Fifteen men on the dead man's chest,
Yo-ho-ho, and a bottle of rum!

He rapped at the worn old door, with a bit of stick like a handspike, that he was carrying. He rapped to announce himself, since it was already open, and inside he could see the public room, and a bit of company: harmless local folk, and a sickly, white-haired man in a long apron, serving them, with a lad beside him holding a jug. The kinship was plain in their faces.

"Good day to you, sir," said the white-haired man, touching his brow. "May I be of assistance? I'm Hawkins, proprietor of this establishment, and this here be my boy Jim."

Afterword

LONG JOHN SILVER: THE NEED FOR CHANGE

Readers of the two previous books in this series, *Flint and Silver* and *Pieces of Eight*, will have noticed the progressive change in Long John Silver's character in these books, and especially in this one.

This is because, as I wrote the books, I increasingly felt an obligation to deliver up Long John Silver, in the end, as the character that Stevenson created – which was not my original intention.

When first I set out to write this series, I was fed up with characters in popular culture who were anti-heroes, half-heroes, and non-heroes: Batman, for instance, depicted as more sinister than the villains he conquers.

So, I decided to present John Silver as a cross between Dan Dare and Douglas Bader – and if you've never heard of them, please look them up (try Google), because they shaped my values as a child and still exemplify the virtues that I admire today.

Fair enough, then: Silver could start out like that. But I realised that he couldn't be the same truthful, decent, gentleman o' fortune by the end of Book Three. And so I contrived that he was forced into lies, betrayal and murder.

Not that there's no good left inside him! Not at all. But – to the best of my ability – as my trilogy ends, he is now the equivocal, crafty bugger that Stevenson made him. And dangerous besides.

Also, there's plenty more of him still in my imagination ... such as the tale of what *really* happened to Jim Hawkins's expedition to Treasure Island ...

LONDON UN-POLICED: CATCHING CRIMINALS

In *Skull and Bones*, much of the action in London depends on the fact that in the 1750s there was no police force in the modern sense, only a medieval mixture of constables, marshal's men, beadles and watchmen.

In fact, there were quite a lot of them: about 3,000 for a city of 750,000 people,[1] which compares surprisingly well with modern figures. For instance, in June 2009, London's Metropolitan Police had c. 35,000 officers for a city of 7.5 million people.[2] Thus, both then and now, there were about four officers per thousand of the population.

But modern officers are trained, and fit, and in constant communication by modern media, whereas the 1750s equivalents were commonly too old, too slow, and too corrupt to keep the king's peace – and each one was utterly on his own.

The Bow Street Runners, founded in 1749, were a unique exception, being remarkably efficient and honest (by eighteenth-century standards). They worked both as detectives and servers of writs, going up and down the kingdom – and even overseas – on missions such as I describe for my fictional

1 Colqhoun, Patrick, *A Treatise on the Police of the Metropolis,* W. Fry, Finsbury Place, for C. Dilly, Poultry, Fourth Edition, 1797
2 Metropolitan Police Authority website, http://www.mpa.gov.uk

Philip Norton. They were the James Bonds of their time. But they were small in number (a few dozen officers), they had no uniform, and they did not patrol the streets to keep order: not them nor anybody else.

Another formidable obstacle to the apprehension of criminals was the fact that there was no way of showing a person's face to the public, other than by getting a talented artist to draw a likeness which would then be copied on to a copper plate – slowly, painfully, carefully – by equally talented engravers. Then prints could be made for wide distribution. This was a labour-intensive process, dependent on rare skills, and totally impractical for routine use, even if anybody had thought of using it to detect criminals, which they didn't! Thus recognition of criminals was strictly by eye, by people who already knew them.

Likewise there existed no means of mass communication, long-range communication, nor instant communication whereby the efforts of such officers as did exist could be united in the attempt to apprehend criminals.

Consequently, detection and apprehension of crime relied on direct, personal action, such as a householder catching a burglar, an employer detecting theft by an employee, or a traveller fighting back against a highwayman.

Thus, with Flint cut from the gallows, and the javelin-men beaten senseless, Silver and Flash Jack could spirit him away, because there was nobody whose duty it was to chase them. And once they were out of sight of those who could recognise them, then they were safe, because nobody knew who they were. Even Silver's crutch wouldn't necessarily give him away, for cripples were far more common then, than today.

LONDON UN-POLICED: THE MOB

As with crime, so with the London mob: that primordial force, deriving its name (as Dr Cowdray would have explained) from the Latin *mobile vulgus* meaning the moveable, or *fickle,* crowd for its dangerously volatile moods.

Once the mob was roused, there was nothing to stop it, as – famously – during the Gordon Riots of June 1780,[3] when Lord George Gordon, a Protestant fanatic, roused the mob against the government's plan to liberalise the laws proscribing Catholics from public service or commissions in the armed forces. Anti-Catholic prejudice was deep-rooted in English society and the mob turned out in vast and unknown numbers, rioting for a whole week, and doing some £30,000 pounds worth of damage (£30,000,000 in today's money), burning churches, prisons and houses, savagely beating any Catholics it could find, and lighting bonfires throughout the city.

My account of the Georgian mob at play, in Chapters 26 and 27, is an accurate and restrained – I stress, *restrained* – description of historic reality. Even if there had been a police force, the mob would have rolled over it, so vast and ferocious as it was. Then, as today, faced with civil disturbance on this scale, the only answer would be to call out the army. In 1780, it took a week to get the necessary numbers of troops together, and order was only restored with volleys of musketry fired into the mob, leaving hundreds killed and many more wounded.

Neither did I exaggerate in describing the use of paper-wrapped excrement as a missile, beloved of the mob. The eighteenth century even had a name for this little beauty: *a flying pasty.*[4]

THE MUDLARKS

As a further example of the lawlessness of eighteenth-century London, I point out that almost everything I wrote about these

3 A Web of English History, The Gordon Riots http://www.history-home.co.uk/c-eight/18reform/gordon.htm
4 Grose, Francis, *A Dictionary of the Vulgar Tongue*, London, First Edition 1785

river pirates is historically accurate: their strange name, their ferocious violence, their bribing the law to keep its nose out of their affairs, and their audacious thieving of anchor cables while a ship's crew slept. They were *diamond geezers* of eighteenth-century crime. I did, however, make up the title of 'King of the River' and there was no King Jimmy, as far as I know.

THE LEAP INTO HYPERSPACE: EIGHTEENTH-CENTURY STYLE

A common event in science fiction is the escape – say of *Millennium Falcon* – by leaping into hyperspace: that trans-dimensional realm where space is folded, time suspended and detection impossible. Well, an eighteenth-century sailing ship couldn't do that, but it did something very similar every time it went to sea, because once it had gone over the horizon, it was totally undetectable and totally unable to communicate with any person, place or ship that it couldn't see.

It is hard for us to appreciate the total isolation under which men sailed in those times, and their exclusive reliance on their own skills. For comparison, when Apollo 13 went wrong, the crew were the most isolated men-in-peril in all history. But they were in constant communication with base, where experts worked on a full-scale simulation of their vehicle to give advice.

And you didn't get that in the age of sail! You fixed it yourself or you died. You navigated skilfully or you died. You weathered the storm or you died. The sea made men out of boys, and heroes out of men . . . those it didn't kill.

There were a few and limited exceptions to the loneliness of sail. Warships routinely sailed in fleets, and in wartime merchantmen sailed in convoys. Also, ships – especially warships – could communicate by flag signals, but only when in sight of each other, only in daylight and only in good weather, and certainly *not* when you most needed it:

when the fog closed in, off a lee shore, in foul weather, at night.

So, think about *that* next time you use your mobile phone.

THE LEXICOGRAPHER: AN APOLOGY

As in previous books in this series, I have brought historical characters into the action. Thus George Washington survives Chapter 34 in such a way as should earn Billy Bones the Congressional Medal of Honor, at the very least.

More important (to me) Dr Samuel Johnson appears in Chapters 19 and 23. He was celebrated for writing a great dictionary of the English language, taking nine years to do it as sole scholar, by comparison with the French equivalent which took forty scholars of the Academie Française, forty years (so it is said).

The dictionary was published in 1755, not 1753 as I imply in this book – but then, I write fiction, don't I? On the other hand, Johnson was physically and intellectually exactly as I have described him, and since I admire him enormously I must apologise to him (where he sits among the righteous in Heaven) that I placed him in circumstances of embarrassment.

I therefore add that Johnson was not only a genius; he was not only wise, clever, and witty; he was an endearingly loving man, who adored his wife and was kind to his servants. In addition, he was so fond of his cat, Hodge, that he fed him oysters, which Johnson went out and bought personally, not sending his servants lest they should resent the cat and be unkind to it.

Good men are distinguished by small acts as well as great ones, and Johnson was a very good man indeed[5].

5 James Boswell, *Boswell's Life of Johnson,* Wordsworth Editions Ltd, 2008. Boswell was a pompous little sod, but I recommend his book. See also Wikipedia http://en.wikipedia.org/wiki/Samuel_Johnson

THE FIRST WORLD WAR: 1754–61

This is the war constantly referred to as "imminent" throughout this book, and I have not mixed it up with the dreadful war of 1914 to 1918. The 1750s version is better known as the Seven Years' War, because in Europe it lasted from 1756 to 1763. It was fought between combinations of Britain, Prussia, Hanover, Portugal (and others) against France, Austria, Russia (and others) – and a war doesn't get bigger than that.

It was a *world* war, because fighting took place at sea worldwide; and on land in Europe, the East Indies, the West Indies, and North America (where it started two years earlier in 1754 and is known today as the French and Indian War).

NOT JACKSON'S, BUT HARRIS'S LIST

In Chapter 17 I have shamelessly plagiarised *Harris's List*[6] a guide to the whores of Covent Garden published between 1757 and 1797, and written originally by one Samuel Derrick, who got his information from the chief waiter at the Shakespeare's Head Tavern, one Jack Harris, a man known as Pimp-General to all England.

The guide lists the descriptions, addresses, and services offered by the top tier of the London trade: girls who charged £1 a visit (£1,000 in modern money), or £2 for those few who permitted *entry by the back door*. The guide was published at Christmas, was eagerly awaited, and was packed with details, not only of the ladies themselves, but also of the liaisons in progress between these expensive professionals and the rich and famous men who were their clients: a directory of *Who's Having Whom*.

6 Rubenhold Hallie, *Harris's List of Covent Garden Whores*, The History Press Ltd, October 2005

It sold for a costly 2/6d, or £125 in modern money, since 2/6d (half a crown) was one *eighth* of their huge, one thousand pound "pounds" (do try to keep up). It was renowned as a Christmas treat for the gentlemen of the family, and doubtless their ladies too, for the Georgian female – unlike the Victorian – was not precious about such matters.

CURING SCURVY

In Chapter 29, Dr Cowdray saves *Walrus* and all aboard her by curing scurvy with lemon juice, a dramatic feat of medical intervention, since the mid-eighteenth century had no idea what caused scurvy (vitamin C deficiency), only that it came on after a long time at sea, and could wipe out whole crews. Flint refers to Anson's circumnavigation of 1739–44 during which over half Anson's crew – at least a thousand men – died of the condition.[7]

The book Dr Cowdray read while ashore was James Lind's *Treatise on the Scurvy*, just published, in which Lind recommended lemon juice, having experimented with using it to treat patients and proved that it worked.[8] Unfortunately, the world was full of quack cures for scurvy, the Admiralty was constantly pestered with them, and lemon juice had previously been tried and had failed – presumably through insufficient dosage, and perhaps because the men wouldn't drink it . . . until it was mixed with their grog, as Long John suggested in my fiction, and as was practised – eventually – by the Royal Navy, except that they used lime juice (another citrus fruit, rich in vitamin C).

7 Walter, Richard, *Anson's Voyage Round the World,* BiblioBazaar, LLC, June 2007

8 Tröhler U., "James Lind and scurvy: 1747 to 1795". The James Lind Library 2003 (www.jameslindlibrary.org)

Sadly, the issuing of lime juice in grog didn't happen until the 1790s. Who knows how many poor souls died of this easily preventable condition, before then?

(And no, I'm not going to explain why a certain American nickname for the English stems from this story. It's pointless because the nickname's obsolete – nobody's heard of it any more. Ask your granddad.)

AURIBUS LUPUM TENEO!

This phrase – spoken by Dr Cowdray – appears at the end of chapter 44. Literally, it means *I hold a wolf by the ears*, words which a Latin scholar might exclaim on suddenly discovering that he is right next to some horrible monster . . . or person.

GEORGE WASHINGTON: FINAL THOUGHTS

It is historic fact that George Washington was offered a berth as a midshipmen in the Royal Navy, with a ship waiting to receive him, and that his mother stopped him going aboard. So what if she hadn't? What if the great man had become a sea-service officer, serving afloat, far from colonial politics, and *remaining loyal to his king?*

Who then would have crossed the Delaware and founded the USA?

It is likewise historic fact that Washington was a freemason, as were many others of the Founding Fathers of the United States. This should be seen in the social context of the eighteenth century, when men's clubs of all kinds flourished and were an important means whereby men of all classes made friends and business or professional contacts. Some of these clubs were merely social, but others – especially in colonial America – were devoted to the self-improvement and moral advancement which was so vital to men struggling to establish European civilisation on a wilderness continent.

Consequently, given the high and noble aims of eighteenth-century American freemasonry, it is no surprise that it attracted men of great stature, including the first president.

And no, I'm not a mason. I'm just trying to reflect the truth.[9]

John Drake, Cheshire, England.

9 George Washington Papers at the Library of Congress, 1741–1799
http://memory.loc.gov/ammem/gwhtml/